The
Officer's
Bride

Merline Lovelace
Deborah Simmons
Julia Justiss

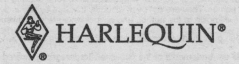

HARLEQUIN®

TORONTO • NEW YORK • LONDON
AMSTERDAM • PARIS • SYDNEY • HAMBURG
STOCKHOLM • ATHENS • TOKYO • MILAN • MADRID
PRAGUE • WARSAW • BUDAPEST • AUCKLAND

ISBN 0-373-83465-9

THE OFFICER'S BRIDE

Copyright © 2001 by Harlequin Books S.A.

The publisher acknowledges the copyright holders of the individual works as follows:

THE MAJOR'S WIFE
Copyright © 2001 by Merline Lovelace

THE COMPANION
Copyright © 2001 by Deborah Siegenthal

AN HONEST BARGAIN
Copyright © 2001 by Janet Justiss

All rights reserved. Except for use in any review, the reproduction or utilization of this work in whole or in part in any form by any electronic, mechanical or other means, now known or hereafter invented, including xerography, photocopying and recording, or in any information storage or retrieval system, is forbidden without the written permission of the publisher, Harlequin Enterprises Limited, 225 Duncan Mill Road, Don Mills, Ontario, Canada M3B 3K9.

All characters in this book have no existence outside the imagination of the author and have no relation whatsoever to anyone bearing the same name or names. They are not even distantly inspired by any individual known or unknown to the author, and all incidents are pure invention.

This edition published by arrangement with Harlequin Books S.A.

® and TM are trademarks of the publisher. Trademarks indicated with ® are registered in the United States Patent and Trademark Office, the Canadian Trade Marks Office and in other countries.

Visit us at www.eHarlequin.com

Printed in U.S.A.

MERLINE LOVELACE

After twenty-three years as an officer in the United States Air Force, Merline took up a second career as a romance novelist. She and her husband, Al, live in Oklahoma and enjoy traveling to all the historic sites she writes about in her novels.

Watch for *The Gunfighter*, a sweeping historical set in the American West. The second in Merline's WYOMING WINGS series for MIRA Books, *The Gunfighter* will hit the bookstores in January, 2002.

DEBORAH SIMMONS

is the author of eighteen historical romances and novellas. A former journalist, she turned to fiction after the birth of her first child when a long-time love of historical romance prompted her to write her first book, published in 1989. Simmons makes her home in rural Ohio with her husband, two children, two cats and a stray dog that stayed. Readers can write to her at P.O. Box 274, Ontario, OH 44862. For reply, an SASE is appreciated.

JULIA JUSTISS

wrote her first plot ideas for twenty-seven Nancy Drew stories in the back of her third-grade spiral, and has been writing ever since. After publishing poetry in college, she served stints as a business journalist for an insurance company and editor of the embassy newsletter in Tunis, Tunisia. After seven moves in twelve years, she and her naval officer husband finally settled their three children and three dogs in the Piney Woods of East Texas, where Julia teaches high school French. Her first novel, *The Wedding Gamble*, won the Romance Writers of America's Golden Heart Award for Regency and was a finalist in both the Golden Quill Award for Best Historical and *Romantic Times Magazine*'s Best First Historical in 1999. Readers can reach her at Rt. 2, Box 14BB, Daingerfield, TX.

Also by Jane Ashford

One

LORD SEBASTIAN GRESHAM PULLED UP AT THE TOP OF a steep ridge and leaned back in the saddle, giving Whitefoot a rest from the long climb. The view from this Herefordshire height was extensive. Before him, the land fell away in folds to a swift river at the base of the ridge. Green fields and pastures rolled out north and east, and mountains loomed to the west, the edge of the Welsh Marches. Straight ahead he could see his destination—Stane Castle, still a distant gray pile.

Thoroughly at home on horseback, Sebastian felt only pleasantly tired, even after the long cross-country ride. With a smile, he remembered a story his father the duke liked to tell, of how Sebastian's three-year-old self had clambered onto the largest hunter in the Langford stable and clung like a burr as he hurtled over a five-barred gate. It had taken two grooms to remove him, squirming and kicking and protesting that he *would* ride Thunderer, he *would*. Sebastian almost thought he remembered the incident. But perhaps it was just from hearing the tale.

He signaled Whitefoot with his knees, and they

started slowly down the path toward the river. Sebastian took in a deep breath of the soft summer air, so different from the reek of London. The scents were unlike those around his childhood home of Langford as well. Crisper, somehow, with hints of cold stone and evergreen. Georgina had said that her family's estate was at the "back of beyond." Certainly the country hereabouts seemed sparsely populated.

Sebastian fell into a daydream of his lively, golden-haired fiancée. Surely there would be many more opportunities for them to be alone out here. During the London season just past, they'd barely managed a few kisses, even though they were officially betrothed. Now, he had an extended leave from his military duties in town. A castle would have gardens, surely, perhaps even a maze to get lost in. With their wedding coming up in a few weeks, they ought to be allowed some freedom. Sebastian relished the possibilities this thought roused.

Whitefoot's hoof sent a shower of pebbles over the edge of a narrow slant of path, and Sebastian brought his attention back to the present. First of all, he had to meet Georgina's parents. Indeed, it was odd that he'd never encountered them, but apparently the marquess and his wife never came to London, or even Bath, which was nearer their home. That was why her grandmother had brought her out, Georgina had explained. She'd seemed uneasy, if not positively evasive, when she mentioned her parents' distaste for society. Still, Sebastian wasn't worried. The family that had produced a charming woman like Georgina must be all right. And, without false modesty, he knew himself to be a convivial fellow. He was confident the meeting would go well. If they didn't care for society, well, he'd be happy to let them be and spend more time alone with Georgina.

The zigzag path down the ridge came out at a ford. Sebastian guided Whitefoot across the river and found a lane that seemed to lead toward the castle, perched across the valley on a spur of hill. Another half hour, and he'd be there, he estimated. There was no sign of Sykes with the carriage and his luggage, but Sebastian wasn't the least surprised. Even though he'd lingered after Nathaniel's wedding and taken his time on the ride, it would probably be a day or two before his valet arrived. The roads in this part of the country were wretched. Sebastian would make do with the contents of the portmanteau lashed to the back of the saddle until then.

The road up to Stane Castle angled across the hill under a towering stone wall. As a military man, Sebastian appreciated the opportunities it provided to rain shots down on invaders. These days, tufts of wildflowers and weeds sprouted from between the great blocks. It had been years since Stane faced hordes of Welsh tribesmen boiling out of the hills to ravage the English countryside.

He rode through an open gate and into a tunnel of stone lined with arrow slits. On the other side of the wall was a cobbled courtyard, also enclosed. Sebastian dismounted as a competent-looking groom came out to take Whitefoot. "House that way?" Sebastian asked, nodding toward an arch in the inner wall as he relinquished the reins.

"Yes, sir. Through there and to your left," the lad answered.

Sebastian strode under the arch and out into an open space. Within the encircling bastion, the castle sprawled, a jumble of a building, obviously added to by generations of Stanes. An ancient moss-covered round tower anchored one end. Closer by was a more modern wing with tall windows and graceful stonework. The hoped-for gardens spread out like green skirts around the place.

Near the center of the edifice, Sebastian spotted a wide, studded oak door, up three steps from a stretch of lawn. Taking this for the front entry, he mounted the steps. There was no bell, only an iron knocker in the shape of a striking hawk. He raised it and let it fall. The thud was surprisingly loud, as if he'd struck a great drum.

The door opened at once. Primed to face a footman or maid, Sebastian blinked at the figure who confronted him instead. The slender, dark-skinned man wore a sort of long coat or tunic of figured brocade over narrow trousers. Straight black hair framed his aquiline features and brushed the raised collar of the garment. Intelligent dark eyes examined Sebastian. The man pressed his palms together and bowed. "You must be the young lord who is to marry my host's daughter," he said. "*Namaste.*"

His voice had a lilt that Sebastian recognized. He'd heard it from travelers native to India. "Er, yes," he replied, thrown a bit off his social stride.

The man moved back to let him enter. Sebastian stepped in, and paused to let his eyes adjust to the sudden gloom as the door shut behind him. He could make out a high-ceilinged, paneled hall in the light from small windows near the ceiling. Much of the far end of the chamber was taken up by a huge stone fireplace. A carved stair twisted upward at the back.

"I am Anat—" began the man, and stopped as a chorus of yapping arose in the distance. "Alas," he went on. "They come. They always answer the knock."

"They?" said Sebastian. The man's tone suggested calamity.

His companion merely gestured toward the stair. The yapping rose in volume, and then a positive sea of small dogs flowed down the steps and along the stone floor. They pooled around the Indian gentleman's slipper-clad feet, barking and sniffing and panting. The man crossed his arms over his chest with a pained look. "Can you command them?" he asked. "They will not hear me."

They were pugs, Sebastian saw. Fifteen or twenty of the tiny brown-and-white lapdogs favored by many older ladies in London. He'd never seen so many together. They milled about the other man, pawing at his legs, staring upward with bulging brown eyes, drooling on his feet, and all the while yapping like… Well, like pugs.

"Please," said the other man. He looked quite distressed.

Sebastian stepped further into the hall. "Here," he said, speaking as he would have to the well-trained dogs at Langford. "Come away from there."

Floppy ears pricked. Little heads came up. The dogs' prominent brown eyes shifted to him. After a moment's scrutiny, the pugs flowed over like a school of fish to surround him and began to scratch and slaver at his riding boots. One clamped its teeth on the end of his spur and tried to chew it off. The largest reared up, threw its front paws around his calf, and began moving against the leather in a highly inappropriate manner. "Stop that at once," Sebastian said.

"My thanks are yours," said the Indian man and slipped away through a doorway beside the steps.

"Wait," said Sebastian. "Where do these dogs belong?" But the fellow was gone. Another of the pugs flung himself on Sebastian's free leg. The two dogs pumped away in unison, huffing like little steam engines.

"Hello, Sebastian."

He looked up to find Georgina poised on the stair. A beam of sunlight from above gilded her hair and illuminated her oval face. She wore a pale-blue gown, and her hand rested on the wooden baluster, delicate as a flower. She looked like a masterwork in the portrait gallery at Langford.

The dogs panted and writhed on his legs.

Sebastian was not a man to blush, but he'd never found himself in a situation quite like this. Used to obedient dogs, he was torn between reaching down and pulling the two miscreants off him, which would draw more attention to their unsavory activities, and ignoring them, which was increasingly difficult. He lifted one foot off the floor and shook it a little, trying to dislodge the wretched animal unobtrusively.

"Don't kick them," Georgina said.

"Of course not." He was appalled at the idea of kicking a dog.

"People are tempted," she responded.

He couldn't tell if she was joking. Her voice sounded odd. She didn't smile either. Indeed, she looked somehow muted, constrained, quite unlike the elegantly composed young lady he knew from London.

"I can't call them off, I'm afraid. They only listen to my mother."

This was not the sort of reunion Sebastian had pictured. He wanted to step forward and greet her properly, perhaps even kiss her, but that was out of the question in his current plight.

"I'll get Mama," Georgina added, and hurried up the stairs and out of sight.

As soon as she was gone, Sebastian bent and grasped the offending dogs by the scruffs of their necks. He lifted them away from his legs and held them up so that he could stare at them sternly, one by one. "No," he said.

Two small tongues lolled below bright eyes, almost as if they were laughing at him. Small paws waved in the air.

He set them firmly aside. "Down. Sit."

Sebastian was used to command. Troops of cavalrymen jumped to obey his orders. Animals usually responded at once to the assurance in his voice. But this crew of canines stared at him as if he was speaking words they'd never heard before. The two primary offenders dashed forward, obviously ready to resume their assault on his riding boots. "No," said Sebastian again.

He took several steps back, nearly tripping as they flowed around his moving feet. It was a challenge not to tread on any of them. As he fended them off with gentle insistence—and an utter lack of success—he actually considered climbing onto a chair, out of their reach. Which was ridiculous. And to be found in such a position by his fiancée and her mother was unthinkable.

Georgina walked quickly along an upper hall and down another stair toward the room where her mother was most likely to be at this hour. She wanted to find her mother and get her dogs off Sebastian right away, and she also wanted to retreat to her bedchamber and hide from the scene that must result. Why had she imagined an auspicious beginning to Sebastian's visit? It had been a pretty picture—her family lined up in a smiling row, cordial greetings exchanged, offers of refreshment and easy conversation. But when had her parents had the time or interest for any of that?

She loved Mama and Papa—of course she did—but at this moment she couldn't help wishing that they were not quite so…individual. Back home after months in London among people who revered convention and cultivated elegant manners, she noticed it more than ever before. Sometimes it seemed that her parents positively dared strangers to misunderstand and mock them. If Sebastian didn't get on with her family, if he despised them… Georgina feared such a reaction, and resented the possibility for myriad reasons on both sides of the question. One thing was clear, however. She simply couldn't marry him if he did. The thought left her fiercely desolate.

Seeing him again had set her pulse pounding. All the sons of the Duke of Langford were tall, handsome, broad-shouldered men with auburn hair and penetrating blue eyes. When you added to that the muscular frame, dashing side-whiskers, and unconscious swagger of a cavalry major, the combination was potent indeed. From their first meeting, Georgina had been roused by Sebastian's bold, masculine presence.

She'd resisted, of course. Even her limited social experience had predicted that such a man would be insufferably arrogant. But Sebastian wasn't. He'd approached her with all sorts of inquiries about *her* thoughts and feelings. And then he'd listened to her answers. It was unprecedented.

Still, she'd been suspicious. There'd been something stilted about his conversation at first. But as the season went on, it became clear that his interest wasn't feigned. Their conversations grew deeper. He'd actually asked her help in understanding a cryptic conversation at a ball, and when she'd explained, he hadn't punished her afterward by drawing away or belittling her. As some men did. Many men, really. Why did they find it so insupportable, seemingly, to be schooled by a female? But not Sebastian. She'd heard him tell a mutual acquaintance later that she had "more brains in her little finger than I do in my whole head." Georgina smiled. She'd made up her mind to marry him in that moment.

And why hadn't she already done so? She could have married in London from her grandmother's house, Georgina thought as she entered her mother's workroom. This visit might have been postponed until after the knot was tied. He'd have had to take her family as he found them then. But no. She shook her head. That wasn't enough. She wouldn't avoid, still less disown, her family. It was out of the question. If only they could, sometimes, be just a bit more commonplace for an hour or two.

On the far side of the large room, her mother sat at a cluttered desk, pen in hand. Georgina watched her scribble on the page before her. It couldn't be denied that, as people often observed, Mama looked rather like her dogs, particularly when she was vexed, as she apparently was now, her lips turned down in her round face. A small, plump woman, with glossy brown hair and prominent eyes—though her eyes were blue, not brown—she had the same bustling curiosity. Sometimes, the similarity made Georgina smile. Today, it raised her protective instincts.

Mama's desk was the only conventional piece of furniture in the spacious chamber. Everything else catered to her dogs. There were rafts of colorful pillows where they could lounge, piles of sticks for them to chew, and scattered heaps of other toys. Hearths at each end kept the room warm in winter, and small, hinged flaps in two of the long windows gave the animals access to their own walled garden. There was a tiled area where they were fed and a large tub in the corner where they were bathed. The pugs were kept scrupulously clean, though their sheer numbers meant that the place still smelled just a bit of dog. "Sebastian has arrived, Mama," said Georgina. "You must come and say hello."

"In a moment," her mother replied without turning

in her chair. "I'm just writing Lady Fairford about the puppy I promised her. She has somehow gotten the notion that I will send Treva in a basket on the mail coach. Yet I made it perfectly clear when we settled on the arrangement that she needed to send a carriage and servant to fetch her."

Whatever the outer resemblance, Mama's voice was nothing like the pugs' yapping. It was deep and confident, surprising from such a small frame. Georgina often admired her parent's sublime self-assurance. *She* never worried about being thought odd. And why should she? a part of Georgina objected. "The dogs are bothering him," she added.

This got a reaction. Her mother straightened and turned. "Bothering? They don't like him?" Her tone was sharp with suspicion. Mama based her initial judgments of people on her dogs' reactions to them.

"They like him excessively," Georgina responded. "Aidan and Drustan are..." She never knew what word to use for the dogs' current activities, with which she was only too familiar. Every choice seemed vulgar. She settled on "applying themselves to his top boots."

"Rogues," said her mother indulgently. "I expect the boots are new. There's something about fresh leather that sets the boys off. I don't know why. It's curious, isn't it? Also, Nuala is soon to go on heat, you know."

Memories of the sights and sounds that would fill the house when she did rose in Georgina's mind. She stifled a sigh and said only, "Please come and get them."

"Very well." Her mother set the letter aside and rose. "Now that Lord Sebastian is here, we must make a push to plan your wedding, mustn't we?" She walked a twisting path among the cushions. "You know, Ninian could stand up with you. He is trained to rise on his hind feet."

Georgina couldn't decide whether to shudder or laugh. "I'm not sure Papa would like it." Her father had what could only be described as an uneven relationship with the pugs.

Her mother acknowledged this with a grimace. "Your father cannot wear that tabard at the ceremony," she replied. "Nor will there be any drinking horns at the wedding breakfast."

"No, Mama. I was thinking of something very simple. And modern."

"Very right. Although…" She stopped a few paces away and blinked as if struck by a sudden thought. "What about a sword dance? Like those astonishing Highlanders at the last church fete. Your Sebastian is a soldier, after all."

Georgina wasn't certain how the two things connected. "Oh, well, I don't know." Setting aside this dispute for another day, she took her mother's arm to urge her along the corridor.

Sebastian picked the two offending dogs off his legs once again. He held them up by their napes, glaring into first one, then another pair of bulging brown eyes. "You really must stop this," he said to them. "It won't do. These are not the manners of a nobleman's household." The pugs panted. They really did seem to be giving him mocking smiles. He was not imagining it. The larger dog looked positively glee-ful. And unrepentant. He was obviously only waiting to be loosed so that he could go right back to what he'd been doing. "My father's dogs would cringe with shame at the idea," Sebastian told him.

A stifled giggle told Sebastian that he was under observation. Two young faces peered at him through the wooden stair rails. "Hello," he said.

With this encouragement, two girls stood up and trotted down the steps. Golden-haired, in similar simple white dresses, they looked to be in their mid- to late teens. Their general resemblance to Georgina helped Sebastian recall that his fiancée had two sisters. There was a brother as well, he remem-bered, though he couldn't bring any of their names to mind just now. He realized he was still holding the dogs. He set them down as far from his boots as he could reach.

"Hello," said the taller, obviously elder girl. "I'm Emma."

"I'm Hilda," said the other. "It's a hideous Anglo-Saxon name."

With the intensity of obsession, the two dogs sought to return to his boots. The others continued to mill about Sebastian's feet, snuffling and yapping as he sidestepped to evade their leaders' attentions.

"Our mother breeds pugs," said the younger girl, with no trace of embarrassment over the creatures' behavior. "They're very popular. She sells them for *fabulous* sums."

"You're Lord Sebastian," said the other. "Here to marry Georgina."

"*Finally*," said Hilda.

Sebastian did not often find himself at a loss in social situations. Although never a wit like his brother Robert, he'd found that a warm smile and a compliment could get him through just about anything. But he was nearly at a standstill by this time, and mightily relieved to see Georgina coming down the stairs with a small, older woman in tow. As soon as the latter's foot touched the stone floor, all the dogs flowed over to surround her. They sat about her feet like a spreading skirt, as if the deity of their little world had arrived. Sebastian heaved a sigh of relief.

"Emma, Hilda, go and fetch Papa," Georgina said.

She still didn't sound quite like herself, Sebastian thought. It began to worry him.

"Can't you just ring?" asked Emma.

Georgina cut her off with a look. The two girls trailed out through a door in the back of the hall as she said, "Mama, this is Sebastian. Sebastian, my mother."

He made his best bow, sweeping off the hat that no one had taken as yet. "Very pleased to meet you, ma'am."

Charlotte, Marchioness of Pembridge, looked him up and down. "He's a handsome lad," she remarked in a surprisingly resonant voice. Not at all what one expected from such a little woman. "But then he comes of good stock. How is your mother?"

"Very well, thank you."

"I met her in Bath. It must be, oh, more than twenty years ago now. It was just before I accepted Alfred's offer. She had the whole raft of you lads with her. Quite a good breeder. A real run of boys, eh?"

Sebastian could think of no reply to this. He cast a glance at Georgina. She wasn't looking at him. He settled for the smile that usually had a good effect on females. Human females, that is.

"Perhaps I'll send her one of my puppies, now that we're all to be family."

It was obvious that she thought this a great favor. Sebastian knew better than to mention that the duchess disliked lapdogs—particularly pugs, he recalled.

"Are you fond of dogs?" Georgina's mother asked him.

This one was easy. "Yes, indeed. Of course."

"Here is Papa," said Georgina.

Her sisters were back with a big man, nearly as tall as Sebastian. The marquess was square jawed and deep chested, his blond hair in an odd bowl cut. Green eyes twinkled out at Sebastian from under thick brows. Long, drooping mustaches half hid a smile. He wore a hip-length white shirt with wide sleeves over buckskin breeches and top boots. His waist was cinched with a wide leather belt holding a sheathed dagger. Was it some sort of costume? Sebastian wondered.

Georgina's father held out a hand. Sebastian took it and found his fingers pressed in a firm grip. "Welcome to Stane Castle," said his host.

"Thank you, sir."

The marquess gestured. "This is the family. Except Edgar. He's off on a walking tour of Hadrian's Wall with some university friends. Met everyone, have you?"

"Yes, sir," said Sebastian.

"Good, good." The older man frowned. "He still

has his hat and gloves. What sort of hospitality is this? Where's Fergus?"

"You sent him and Dennis out to measure the Dyke at Knill," said Hilda.

Sebastian puzzled silently over this sentence. He thought perhaps there were dykes in Holland, but that didn't seem to apply.

"Ah, yes." The marquess nodded. "Well, where's Mrs. Trent, then? We must get our guest settled in properly."

"I sent her to Leominster to see about more meat," his wife replied. "For the dogs," she added when the others looked at her. She frowned as if this should be obvious.

It was a bit like gazing into the face of the largest pug, Sebastian realized. Without thinking, he glanced down to compare. Yes, his hostess looked rather like her dogs. He glanced quickly away. Not a thing to mention, obviously. Or be seen to notice.

"We'll take him to his room," Hilda piped up. "We know which one it is. Come on." She came over and tugged at Sebastian's sleeve.

He waited for objections to this unorthodox proposal. Why was Georgina so silent and distant? Had she seen him compare her mother and the dogs? Did she think him rude?

No one spoke, so he followed the two girls up the stairs into a paneled corridor. They led him to a bedchamber at the back of the modern wing of the castle. His portmanteau sat on an old-fashioned four-poster bed inside. The comfortable room also boasted a wardrobe, a dressing table, and two armchairs drawn up before the hearth. Hangings and a carpet of deep blue lent a bit of color.

Georgina's sisters came right in with him. Emma lingered by the door, but Hilda plumped down in one of the chairs. "You're going to marry Georgina soon, aren't you?" she said.

"Er, early September," replied Sebastian.

"That's weeks away!" the girl exclaimed.

He couldn't help but agree. He'd seen no reason to wait so long. At least, he hadn't before he arrived here. No, he still didn't. He was just a bit startled by the unusual family. He'd met Georgina in such a conventional household. He supposed he'd expected more of the same.

"Where will you live when you're married?" Hilda asked.

It occurred to Sebastian that she sounded like someone deciding whether to buy a horse. But that was ridiculous. What was wrong with him? "I have to be in town a good deal for my duties," he said. "We'll take a house there."

"London," sighed Emma. "I daresay Georgina will go to all sorts of parties and balls and…everything."

"As many as she likes," Sebastian assured her.

"And there are dressmakers and shops and… people," said Hilda. "All sorts of *people*."

"Do you like history?" asked Emma. She fixed him with a fierce stare.

"Me? No." In Sebastian's experience, history involved thick tomes and incomprehensible lists and other things that regularly defeated him.

"Good!"

In the silence that followed this emphatic approval, he eyed his two young companions. Both were golden-haired like Georgina, with the same pale skin and willowy frames, though that slenderness was still gawky on Hilda and just beginning to show a hint of Georgina's allure in Emma. Their faces bore the promise of similar piquant beauty, with large, expressive gray-green eyes and chiseled lips.

All three Stane daughters resembled their father in frame and coloring, but Sebastian could see something of their mother in the sharpness of their glances. The younger ones seemed as intelligent as his intended. He didn't know why that should seem unsettling. He admired Georgina's quickness very much. He wondered where she was right now, and why she hadn't given him just a hint of what was to come before this visit.

Her sisters stayed on, silently gazing at him as if he was a zoo animal. How could he politely be rid of them? "Shouldn't you go?" he asked finally. "It isn't really proper for you to be in my bedchamber?" It came out as a question, because Sebastian realized that he had no certain notion what this household might consider proper.

"You're our brother," replied Hilda. "Practically."

"Yes, but, ah, you need to give me time to unpack and…so on."

"You hardly have any luggage," observed Emma.

"My valet is on the road with the rest of it."

"Your valet," echoed Hilda, seeming to savor the word. "Is he very high-nosed and particular? Will he despise us dreadfully?" She appeared to hope so, for some reason.

"What?" Sebastian was feeling perfectly bewildered. It seemed to him that nothing had made sense since he set foot in this place.

"We'll go," said Emma.

"But…"

"Come on, Hilda. It's too soon. You know Georgina said so. And we promised."

"Oh, all right." The youngest Stane jumped up and moved toward the door. "We'll be seeing you all the time anyway," she said brightly as the two girls departed.

Sebastian stood in the middle of the room, gazing at the closed door. Too soon for what? What had they promised? And why should the idea fill him with foreboding? That made no sense, surely.

Alone in the front hall, Georgina silently berated herself. She should have had a better plan for Sebastian's arrival. But there'd been no way of predicting when he would come, or where the servants would be at any given moment. Her parents were always sending them off on strange errands. Which they often prolonged. Staff members at Stane enjoyed such expeditions, or they didn't stay on.

She wondered what Sebastian was thinking right now. She'd scarcely spoken to him. Had he thought her unwelcoming? She'd been terribly glad to see him—just so occupied with the way things were unfolding. Papa with his dagger… What had Sebastian made of that? She told herself she was being overly sensitive. Or was it cowardly? All families had their oddities. Hers might be a bit more eccentric than most, but she'd heard stories of worse.

Wasn't there some earl in Cornwall who kept a pig in the house?

An image of the Duke and Duchess of Langford rose in her mind. In the few times they'd met, she'd thought them perfect in every way. They were admired, even revered, leaders of society. Sebastian's oldest brother, Nathaniel, was a pattern card of virtue. His younger brother Robert was elegant and witty and charming, a model for young aspirants to fashion. She didn't know any of the others well, but she supposed they were equally worthy and decorous.

Georgina realized then that the Greshams had intimidated her. Somewhere deep down she'd formed the idea that Sebastian would expect a family like his own. And so she'd been afraid to try to prepare him for her unique, maddening, beloved Stanes. Yet this was where she came from; these were her people. If she and Sebastian were to marry, he had to accept them. And why had she thought *if*?

She turned toward the stairs. She had to see him, talk to him. He must be feeling… Well, she didn't know what he was feeling. And she needed to. Desperately.

Two

W HEN THE KNOCK CAME ON HIS DOOR A LITTLE WHILE later, Sebastian answered warily. He was delighted to find Georgina in the corridor outside. She'd tied a straw bonnet over her golden hair and carried a shawl over her arm. "I thought you might like to see the gardens," she said.

"Yes, absolutely." At last he would be able to talk to her.

She led him around a corner and down a stair he hadn't noticed. She didn't speak as they traversed a stone corridor that several times went up a few steps and then down again in the stitched-together building. Her silence worried him, and he tried to think of the best way to break it.

Before he could, she opened a small door and stepped outside. Following, Sebastian saw that they'd emerged near the ancient tower at the far end of the place. A path led under an archway twined with roses and into just the sort of secluded shrubbery he'd hoped for. A few steps into this sheltered walk and the castle was invisible. Georgina stopped and turned to him.

He scanned her face, partly shaded by the brim of her bonnet. Was she distressed? He couldn't bear that. "All well?" he asked.

"I hope so."

What was he to say to that? Unlike his brother Robert, Sebastian wasn't fond of oblique conversations. In fact, he detested them. It was all too easy to misunderstand when people began hinting and saying one thing when they meant another. As far as he was concerned, double entendres simply meant twice the chance of confusion. But then, words had always been one of the least trustworthy elements in his life.

Georgina looked up and held his gaze. Her eyes, that clear gray-green, were bright with intelligence. He could fall into them, trusting that all would soon be explained. Sebastian forgot whatever he might have been about to say.

She came closer, put a hand on his arm. "Is all well with you?"

Her beautiful lips parted a little. Sebastian couldn't resist. He bent his head. She didn't draw back but leaned a bit closer. He closed the tiny distance between them and kissed her.

In the whispering refuge of the shrubbery, Georgina slipped her arms around his neck and moved into the kiss. Sebastian pulled her close, the feel of her body against him a tender flame. It was all he'd anticipated on the ride up to the castle—the freedom they'd never had in London. He savored the sweet taste of her and let his hands roam a little, exulting when he made her breath catch with a daring caress.

All too soon, she pulled back. Sebastian was disappointed, but resigned. They couldn't continue like that for much longer without going beyond the line. He smiled down at her. They were both breathing more rapidly.

Georgina put her hands to her cheeks as if to press back the heat that bloomed there. "Oh," she murmured.

Sebastian was rather proud of the dreamy softness in her eyes. A delicious future reeled out before him.

"I-I wanted to talk to you," she said.

He was glad of it. He hadn't liked her silence during his arrival and introductions.

"About my family," she went on, her voice steadying. "We live so deep in the country here. There aren't many neighbors close by. I've thought that the isolation encourages people to…delve rather deeply into their particular…interests."

Sebastian nodded. That was a clever way of putting it. He'd have to remember the phrase when people asked about Great-Aunt Selina and her button collection.

"Mama has done so with her dogs. My father is very much taken up with local history."

Her sisters had mentioned history, though not very favorably, Sebastian thought. It was harder to gauge Georgina's attitude. Did she expect that he would join her father's studies? He hoped not.

Sebastian was well aware that his education was spotty. Indeed, that was a charitable word for it. He'd spent far more time on the school playing fields than at his books. Sport had been a joy, the classroom a torment. He simply couldn't master the skills required in those fusty, closed spaces, and he hadn't been able to make anyone understand why. By the time he was fifteen, he'd fully accepted that he was the stupidest of the Gresham brothers, at the opposite end from Alan, who was some kind of prodigy. And so he'd chosen a profession, and a manner, designed to conceal his flaws.

Brandishing a saber in cavalry training had suited him down to the ground. Riding was second nature. He fell easily into the bluff camaraderie of an elite regiment. But if Georgina expected him to learn a lot of cursed facts, he'd soon disappoint her. How he would hate that! She was so quick and intelligent. Would she change her mind about marrying him when she discovered how thick he really was? "I don't know much history," he confessed.

She waved this aside. "There's no need. Papa will be happy to tell you all about it."

That was all right then. He could listen and nod. He was quite good at that. Indeed, he learned better that way. As long as there weren't examinations afterward.

Georgina looked uneasy. "His…approach is a bit… unique."

Sebastian assumed an encouraging expression.

"He has invited an Indian gentleman to stay with us." Georgina hadn't known of Anat Mitra's existence until she arrived home last month. Nor was she aware of the more eccentric turn her father's studies had taken. Would she have invited Sebastian to visit if she had? No. Or, she'd so wanted to see him again, to learn more about him. That kiss had been…really splendid.

"Oh yes," said Sebastian. "He let me in when I arrived."

"Did he? And did you…talk to him?"

"I didn't have a chance. The dogs came running in, and Mr.—er, the Indian fellow took to his heels. He seemed quite afraid of them."

Georgina nodded, feeling reprieved. "Yes. Well, he and Papa are exploring…some…aspects of history." Georgina looked up at her tall, handsome fiancé. He smiled at her, and she yearned to throw her arms around his neck again and forget the rest. She simply couldn't go on. She'd said as much as she could manage for now. "So, not quite a usual house party," she finished lightly.

Sebastian shrugged. "I came for you," he said. He looked approvingly at the shrubbery. "I was hoping we'd have more chances to be alone. To, er, get better acquainted, I mean."

The warmth in his blue eyes seemed to suffuse Georgina. "I'm sorry about the dogs." His wry smile showed he was also remembering their uncouth attentions. Georgina's flush deepened. "I can't imagine such a thing happening at your home," she was compelled to add.

"Oh, I don't know," he replied. "My mother had a demented cat when I was small. Ruff would sneak into the room whenever she had guests—even though the servants went to great lengths to keep him out—and slink along until he found someone whose hand was hanging over a chair arm. Then he'd start suckling on one of their fingers."

Georgina burst out laughing.

Sebastian smiled and nodded, clearly enjoying her reaction, not the least bit embarrassed by this oddity.

"We boys soon learned to spot the victims. They'd look surprised first, of course, and then puzzled. They'd bend over to see what the deuce it was, and then, mostly, they'd be horrified. Ruff had a real knack for choosing people who hated cats."

"What did they do?" Georgina tried to imagine encountering such a situation in the duchess's parlor.

He grinned. "Well, it depended on the person, didn't it? A few jumped right out of their seats, yelling and shaking the, er, afflicted hand. Most just jerked their hands away and gave Ruff a scowl. The rest slipped the finger away from him, folded their hands in their laps, and pretended nothing had happened. Mama began to see it as a test of self-possession. Once she conceded that Ruff *would* find his way in, no matter what anyone did."

"But she didn't get rid of him? Have him sent off to a farm or something, I mean."

Sebastian shook his head. "He was a splendid cat in all other respects. And Mama thought his…quirk came from being taken from his mother too early. So she felt sorry for him, you see."

"Quirk," Georgina repeated. The unassuming word, and Sebastian's story, and the way he was taking his visit so far combined into a wave of relief.

"James tried to train him to single out certain irritating people, but Ruff never paid him any heed," Sebastian finished with another smile.

Georgina laughed a little more. It seemed that things were going to be all right. She put a hand on Sebastian's upper arm, feeling the hard muscle under the cloth of his coat. When she gazed up at him, he pulled her close, as she'd hoped he would. His lips captured hers; his arms encircled her. She lost herself in the storm of sensations his touch aroused.

The searing kiss was interrupted by distant yapping. Sebastian raised his head. "Are the dogs liable to join us?"

She didn't blame him for the lack of enthusiasm in his tone. She got on well enough with her mother's dogs, but they were often ill-mannered with strangers. She listened. "They're not out," she said. "They have their own garden. Mama doesn't let them run free. If they come to this part of the grounds, she's always with them. She's afraid a fox might get them—the young ones anyway. Drustan killed a fox once."

"Drustan?" Sebastian echoed.

"It's a Celtic name. Mama is…much taken with Celtic legends. Papa leans to the Anglo-Saxon."

"I…see."

"You get used to it. After a while," Georgina said. Except for this new start with Mr. Mitra. She hadn't gotten used to that. It truly seemed a step too far.

Sebastian resumed his exceedingly pleasant attentions. Georgina gave herself up to the delights of desire. Neither of them noticed a stir in the needles of a nearby evergreen. A branch was gently depressed, and two pairs of green eyes peered through the opening thus created. "He'll have to marry her if he keeps on like that," Emma whispered. "There'll be no crying off."

"Why would he?" murmured Hilda.

"The dogs, Papa's odd new start," said her sister. "But he won't."

The two girls watched for a while, fascinated, absorbing a thorough lesson in the art of kissing. Then a giggle escaped Emma. It was a small sound, but Sebastian raised his head at once. "Who's there?" he asked.

Georgina stiffened and stepped away from him.

"It's just us," said Hilda from the shelter of the shrubbery. "You don't have to stop on our account."

"You promised not to spy," declared Georgina. Her sisters knew every cranny of the castle and grounds, and used them. She'd known their curiosity and personal investment in her marriage were going to cause awkwardness, and she'd lectured them on the need for some privacy.

Emma and Hilda slipped from the screening foliage onto the gravel path. "We were out for a walk," replied Emma. "We didn't know you were here until we..."

"Sneaked through the bushes to find us?" finished Georgina.

"We weren't sneaking." Hilda paused, then added, "Not till right at the end."

Her youngest sister was honest, Georgina thought, if incorrigible.

"Anyway, when we come to live with you, I expect we'll see you kissing all the time," said Hilda. "So it doesn't matter. Indeed, we should become accustomed to it."

"Come to live with us?" Sebastian said.

He looked startled. Beyond that, Georgina couldn't tell. She resisted an impulse to march over and box Hilda's ears. She'd *told* them that nothing could be settled, or even discussed, until after the wedding.

Georgina sighed. She did feel sorry for her sisters. She certainly hadn't forgotten how lonely it was here at Stane, and how eager she'd been to get out into the world. It was also clear that her parents' peculiarities were growing more intense with age. They hadn't been so distracted when she was younger. She'd told Emma and Hilda that she would help them, and she would. But they'd taken this as a positive promise to add them to her household as soon as she had one, ignoring the fact that she couldn't do that without Mama and Papa's permission. And consulting Sebastian, of course. Principally that.

He was looking at her. Certainly she would never have brought this up on the first day of his visit. Heavens, he'd only been here a few hours, though it seemed longer. "Go on with your walk," she told her sisters. "Or…don't you still have lessons? Where is Joanna?"

"We only have to be in the schoolroom in the morning," said Hilda.

"She's gathering botanical specimens," said Emma at the same moment.

As if on cue, a female voice was heard, calling the sisters' names. "*She* is?" asked Georgina.

Hilda held up a rather wilted sprig of leaves. "We all are."

Emma, empty-handed, looked around, then quickly broke off a bit of evergreen.

Georgina gave them both a look. "Over here, Joanna!" she called. Unless she handed her sisters over to their governess, they'd tag along wherever she and Sebastian went.

A few moments later, the sturdy figure of Joanna

Byngham came striding down the path toward them, a basket full of plant specimens over her arm. Georgina greeted her with relief. Joanna's broad-shouldered, plain-featured presence had been a mainstay of the Stane household since she'd joined it fourteen years before. She could talk history with the marquess to his heart's content and help in his research. She shared a love of dogs with Georgina's mother. And she'd made the castle schoolroom a fascinating place, for Georgina at least. Joanna had a way of bringing subjects to life, throwing herself into each new course of study with the gusto of an explorer discovering new lands. They'd delved into them together, and Georgina knew that Joanna had been sad when she left her tutelage.

The newcomer came to a stop before them and looked out from under the edge of her broad-brimmed straw hat. "There you are," she said to Emma and Hilda. She appeared more resigned than surprised at their defection, which was probably common. Georgina was aware that her younger sisters showed little interest in their books. Perhaps they simply pretended not to care for education as a way to irritate Papa. They certainly weren't stupid. "Sebastian, this is Miss Byngham," she said. "Joanna, Lord Sebastian Gresham."

Her old governess showed no sign of objecting to this scrambling introduction. Her teaching had always concentrated on books and ideas. Joanna had never been one to give advice about how to make one's way in the world, and certainly not in matters of the heart. Indeed, she'd appeared to find the latter faintly ludicrous when the subject came up. Georgina looked from her to Sebastian and felt odd. She'd grown beyond her former preceptress in the social sphere. She only hoped she'd learned enough.

"How do you do?" Joanna said. She examined Sebastian with no more, and no less, interest than she might have shown in a new variety of plant.

He bowed. "Pleased to meet you, ma'am."

"He's going to marry Georgina," Hilda said.

"I know," replied the governess. "What have you got there?" She examined the limp leaves Hilda held.

"Um." Hilda gazed at the tired greenery. "Beech?"

"With those tripartite lobes?" Joanna shook her head. "You know better than that."

"Oak," said Emma impatiently.

"Correct. But you should let your sister answer." The older woman picked a sprig from her basket and held it up. "What about this one?"

As Hilda gave an exaggerated sigh, Georgina touched Sebastian's arm and led him down the path and away.

"Governess?" he said as they drew out of earshot.

"Yes."

"Good they've got one."

Georgina nodded and walked faster. She longed to resume their delightful explorations, but she didn't want to discuss her sisters' plans for their future. Not just yet. Cursing Hilda for speaking so soon, she hurried Sebastian back to his room and left him there.

❧

Surveying himself in a long mirror once he was dressed for dinner, Sebastian felt that he'd achieved a good effect even without his valet. The castle servants had pressed the wrinkles out of his evening wear. His hair and neckcloth were well done. The image that faced him in the glass looked polished and confident, not at all apprehensive about going downstairs. He nodded, a gesture of reflective reassurance.

"We'll be all right," he said aloud. "We've brushed through stickier situations than this one." He trusted his social address to get him through the meal, but he did wonder what further surprises might lie in wait in the dining room. There seemed to be a good deal going on that he hadn't expected, or didn't understand, and he didn't care for the feeling. "Forward, Major," he declared, standing straighter. "To the charge."

He reached the stairs at the same time as the Indian gentleman who'd greeted him on arrival. Still in his long brocade coat and narrow trousers rather than conventional evening dress, the other man looked darkly elegant. He gave Sebastian another of his bows with palms pressed together. Sebastian acknowledged it with his own, and they started downstairs together. "I am Anat Mitra, as I was about to say when you so kindly rescued me from milady's pets earlier."

"Not fond of dogs?" Sebastian asked.

"I revere all creatures of the earth," replied Mr. Mitra. "But these 'pugs' do not return my respect. They delight in… What do the English say? 'Dogging me,' isn't it?"

"They don't seem very well trained," Sebastian said, memories of the two dogs plastered to his legs still vivid.

Mitra waved a graceful hand. "Respectfully, I

would disagree, my lord Sebastian. I believe they are remarkably schooled for their purpose."

Sebastian made no attempt to reply to this cryptic remark. He never did when people chose to be obscure. Responding generally caused more trouble than silence, he'd found. Robert might delight in lobbing words back like invisible tennis balls, but he always seemed to find three meanings in every phrase rather than laboriously puzzling out one.

They reached the great hall and found the family gathered there. Going to stand beside Georgina, Sebastian was surprised to see her younger sisters and their governess nearby, also waiting to go in to dinner. Informality appeared to be a hallmark of the household.

He was seated on Georgina's mother's right at the table, and delighted to find Georgina opposite him, giving him a constant view of her lovely face. Emma and Hilda occupied the middle of the board, with Miss Byngham and Mitra on either side of the marquess at the other end.

A squat, powerful-looking man entered with a tray containing a huge, glistening roast. From his dress and demeanor, Sebastian concluded this must be the butler, Fergus. He was followed by two maids with other dishes. Perhaps the Stanes didn't employ footmen. He hadn't seen any. Sebastian was relaxed and more than ready for sustenance when he noticed movement near his feet. Two pugs had appeared in a surprise flanking movement, and he was pretty sure he recognized the larger one from his earlier skirmish. Fortunately, the dogs were ignoring him. They seemed utterly focused on Georgina's mother.

"You'll have a good, big slice from this boar, I'm sure," said the marquess.

Sebastian realized just in time that Georgina's father was addressing him. "Thank you, sir," he replied. He checked the position of the pugs. Still all right.

"A hunting party led by my gamekeeper took the beast in our west wood." Georgina's father smiled, his teeth square and white below his trailing mustache, as he wielded a large carving knife. "A real monster. I'll show you the tusks later on."

"Ah, splendid."

"Ever do any boar hunting?" the marquess asked.

"Never had an opportunity." Sebastian received a plate heaped with meat. One of the maids offered vegetables, the other a sauceboat.

"I've always wanted to try out my great-grandfather's boar spear," Georgina's father continued. He gestured with the knife, now dripping pink juices. "The spears have the crossbar, you know, because a boar will push right up the shaft to gore you, even as he's bloody and dying."

"Papa," said Georgina.

The marquess smiled at her as if she'd encouraged rather than admonished him. "Dreadful nuisances," he said. He returned to his work, producing flawless slices for the other diners. "A sounder of wild pigs can root up a planted field in no time at all."

"Not many to be found in my part of the country." Trying the meat, Sebastian found the taste strong but well flavored.

"That's a fine old word, eh? Sounder. A sounder

of swine. Even better. You're lucky. We're plagued by them hereabouts. But they make for good sport."

"Shooting partridges is sport," put in his wife. "Or stalking deer. Boar hunting is an occasional, perilous necessity. That old spear will remain on the wall, Alfred."

It sounded to Sebastian like an old argument. He kept his attention on his plate, with periodic glances at the hovering pugs.

"What would you be doing if you were in London now?" asked Hilda across the table.

No one objected to the change of subject, so Sebastian obliged with stories of the season just past. He pulled Georgina into the conversation with shared recollections, and together, they kept her sisters rapt for quite a time. In the pauses, he sometimes caught a strange phrase from the trio at the marquess's end of the table. Mitra declared that he "could not guarantee any particular era." Miss Byngham stated that "the theory is quite unproven." Georgina's father repeatedly mentioned someone, or something, called "Offa." Sebastian couldn't make any sense of it. He'd thought at first that his host said *offal*, which had startled him.

Through it all, Georgina's mother scarcely spoke. She smiled and nodded, obviously not in a bad humor, and occupied herself with a rather idiosyncratic way of eating. For each bite she took in the usual way, she also dropped a tidbit to the dogs at her feet, in a smooth, clearly practiced motion. The pugs did not beg for this largesse. On the contrary, they sat still, shifting only to catch the offerings with a neat precision that struck Sebastian as almost military. They also scrupulously alternated turns. There was no snapping, no jostling. They seemed different dogs from the mob he'd encountered earlier, and he didn't know whether he was impressed or unsettled by the alteration. What had Mitra said about them being schooled for their purpose?

"Kissing in the shrubbery," said Hilda.

Sebastian's attention snapped back to the table. He'd obviously missed a critical turn in the conversation.

"Do be quiet, Hilda," said Georgina.

The marquess was too engrossed to have heard, but Georgina's mother was gazing at Sebastian with an enigmatic smile. "Er," he said.

"A shrubbery is such a pleasant thing, is it not?" the older woman remarked.

She didn't seem to be angry. Sebastian couldn't tell what she was, only that with her head cocked to the side, eyes bright and alert, she again reminded him of her pets. What were they doing? He checked on the dogs; they sat at their mistress's feet, the picture of obedience.

"Are you finished eating, Mama?" asked Georgina.

The marchioness shifted her gaze to her daughter. After a moment she smiled and nodded.

Georgina rose, gathering the female portion of the group with a commanding glance. "Shall we leave the gentlemen to their wine?"

She'd gotten that tone from her grandmother in London, Sebastian thought admiringly. There was no arguing with it.

Miss Byngham looked as if she wanted to. Clearly

she would much rather have continued her conversation with Mitra. Emma and Hilda sighed audibly. No one objected, however. As the ladies left the dining room, Georgina glanced back over her shoulder, but if this was a signal, Sebastian didn't understand what it meant.

He moved down the table to sit nearer the gentlemen and accepted a glass of port. The contrast between his remaining companions struck him as he tried a sip. The Indian visitor was narrow and elegant as a blade, while Georgina's father was bluff and broad and blond, as English as a fellow could be. He wondered what they could have in common that would justify a lengthy visit.

His host leaned back in his chair, expansive. "So, Gresham, what do you think about reincarnation?" he asked.

Sebastian took another sip of the port, silently repeating the unfamiliar word. He was pretty sure he'd never heard it before. He tried to work the meaning out in his head. *Re-* was something happening again; that was clear enough. But the rest remained mysterious. There was a flower called a carnation, wasn't there? Could it signify putting something back into a flower? That couldn't be right. He'd just have to admit it. "Afraid I don't know the word, sir."

The marquess didn't seem surprised or disappointed. "I'll let Mitra explain it to you," he said. "He's the expert." With a nod and a gesture, he urged the other man to speak.

Mitra put the tips of his fingers together and looked resigned, then contemplative. "Reincarnation—which my people call *punarjanma*—is the process of birth, death, and rebirth."

Sebastian nodded as if this made sense to him, even though it didn't. He'd found, over the years, that people appreciated signs he was paying attention. It encouraged them to go on. And he often came to understand them eventually, if they kept talking. Of course, some took every nod as agreement or permission. That could be sticky.

Mr. Mitra's slight smile suggested that he understood Sebastian's confusion. "We believe that a person's…soul, the jiva or atman, goes through a cycle of births and deaths. The physical body dies, yes, in the common way, and then the jiva takes on another body, the form depending on the quality of its actions in life. There is no permanent heaven or hell for a Hindu. After services in the afterlife, the jiva returns as an animal, a human, or a divinity. This reincarnation, or re-bodying, you see, continues until moksha, the final release, is gained."

"Fascinating, eh?" said the marquess.

Sebastian sorted through the spate of words as quickly as he could. It felt as if it took too long. His mind lit on one point. "An animal?" he said.

Mitra nodded. "Those who remain mired in ignorance or overly attached to material desires may experience lives as nonhuman creatures, even a lowly worm." He smiled at Sebastian with what looked like gentle sympathy.

The thought of the dead returning as all sorts of different creatures expanded in Sebastian's brain until it felt too large for his skull. Sheep? Mosquitoes? He discovered he could almost accept the idea in the case of Mama's eccentric cat. There had been moments when Ruff looked uncannily calculating, like an irascible old man plotting revenge. But no. "This is in India," he said.

"Well, we believe it is the way of the world," replied Mitra. "But we do not insist that you agree."

"The thing is, Mitra has developed a process for revisiting your former lives," put in the marquess.

"A possible method," murmured the Indian. "An idea, a theory."

Georgina's father ignored his caveats. "I have no doubt that I was King Offa of Mercia," he continued. "Every inner impulse tells me so." He gazed brightly at Sebastian, awaiting a reply.

"From history," Sebastian said. He was pretty sure this was a safe bet. The marquess's nod confirmed it.

"Eighth century," the older man said. "Offa fought the Welsh all his life. He built Offa's Dyke to keep them out of this area. Ancient Mercia, you know."

The word sounded like *mercy*, but wasn't. Unfortunately.

"And now I can establish the relationship for certain," said Georgina's father.

"I have told you again and again that I cannot guarantee any particular—" Mitra began.

"I can almost feel the building of it," the other interrupted. He looked down at his large, square hands and flexed them. "As if it was in my bones."

"Offa's Dyke," echoed Sebastian, catching up. Dykes had been mentioned earlier. Not Holland, then, but this Offa fellow.

"We'll ride out tomorrow, and I'll show it to you,"

said the marquess. "Parts of it are still there after a thousand years. Can you imagine such an achievement?" Finally seeming to recognize confusion on Sebastian's face, he added, "It's a great earthen barrier that runs along the border between England and Wales. I've set Joanna Byngham delving through old records about it. Ha, delving, earthworks." He gave a bark of laughter. "Good, eh? Accident, I assure you."

Sebastian smiled and nodded.

"Too bad she's not here to tell you all about it."

Sebastian sent up a prayer of silent gratitude for her absence.

"The dyke's mentioned by some old monk in his biography of Alfred the Great." Georgina's father gave Sebastian a piercing look. "Another past life of mine, I believe. Same name, you see." He waited for Sebastian's nod before going on. "The fellow wrote something along the lines of: 'a great king called Offa had a dyke built between Wales and Mercia from sea to sea.' Not all of it's left, of course." He shook his head. "But that any should be, after a thousand years…" He gave a great happy sigh and spread his arms as if to embrace something. "Mitra's going to show me how to revisit Offa's court."

His Indian visitor's expression was wry, but he didn't speak.

Sebastian felt as if he'd wandered into some fantastic tale. He couldn't be drunk; he hadn't even finished his first glass of port, and he knew his capacity was well beyond that. Perhaps he'd wake up in a few minutes and find it had all been a dream.

"You're welcome to join in," said the marquess.

"You should! Damned exciting, ain't it? To think you might have lived anywhere along the way. Rome, Egypt. Maybe he was one of those pharaohs, eh, Mitra? Crocodiles and pyramids and palm fronds?"

"Everyone thinks to be a king," the man murmured.

Sebastian heard it, though he didn't think Georgina's father did. It occurred to him that rulers were very few compared to the mass of common people. What if your past life turned out to be the endless toil of a downtrodden peasant? Or the presumably dead bore of existence as a sheep? A worm crawling through the dirt? And…what was he thinking? He didn't actually believe in this idea of reincarnation. He shook his head.

"Why not?" asked the marquess, taking the gesture for a response to his suggestion. "Ah, but you've Norman blood, haven't you? One of the damned invaders." He glowered. "It was a dire day when we lost Harold at Hastings."

He spoke as if referring to someone they both knew, but as far as Sebastian could recall, he had never met anyone named Harold. "Ah, just so," he ventured.

"Well, it can't be helped," Georgina's father replied. "Difficult to find an English nobleman who doesn't, eh?"

Doesn't what? Sebastian gathered he was supposed to know. So he didn't ask. He smiled to conceal a growing sinking feeling. The challenges of this visit were racing so far ahead of anything he'd expected. He was becoming convinced that he should have waited until much nearer the wedding date to visit. Hindsight was always so acute, he thought. And foresight so dashed elusive.

In the drawing room, Georgina fidgeted as she waited for the gentlemen to join them. It was taking much longer than she'd hoped, and she was very conscious of having thrown Sebastian to the metaphorical lions when she left the dining room. He was bound to learn about her father's current enthusiasm at some point, however. There was no way around it. No doubt he would find it as surprising as she had when she'd returned home from London. Or was *disturbing* a better word? Georgina hadn't decided exactly how she felt about the idea that people lived a long succession of different lives.

Joanna took Georgina's sisters off to bed, and still there was no sign of the gentlemen. Georgina set aside the book she had been failing to read.

Her mother looked up from a letter. "I don't think you have cause for worry," she said.

Georgina turned to stare at her.

"Your young man is clearly enamored. I don't believe he'll be put off by your father's...foibles. Alfred always means well, after all."

Georgina was astonished that Mama had noticed her agitation. She seldom showed any awareness of emotional undercurrents. She was also gratified by her parent's opinion of Sebastian's feelings. Indeed, she would have liked to hear a good deal more on that subject. But she was hampered by a touch of shame over her wish that her father might be just a bit more conventional. Or at least rein in his...venturesome... spirit until after her wedding. It all added up to a complete inner muddle.

Her mother put down her pen and gazed at her. "Why did you choose Lord Sebastian? I understand you had a horde of suitors. As you were bound to, with the fortune Great-Uncle George left you." She sat back and folded her hands, her expression as complacent as Drustan's when he sat on the hem of one's gown. "It was my notion to name you after him, you know."

Georgina was too used to her mother's plain speaking to be surprised by any of this. And the answer was easy. "He listens to me," she replied. It suddenly occurred to her that he was one of the few people in the world who did.

Mama raised her eyebrows. "Does he indeed? That's a very good reason." She cocked her head, as if unexpectedly impressed. Drustan, sitting at her feet with his paws neatly crossed, mimicked the gesture perfectly. "You know, I didn't accompany you to London last season because I knew your grandmamma would do a much better job of bringing you out."

Georgina nodded. She'd heard this before.

"I also trusted your good sense."

"Thank you, Mama." That was gratifying.

"Which seems fully justified by young Sebastian." Before Georgina could pursue this interesting topic, her mother nodded as if concluding. "I just wanted you to understand that my absence was a decision, not neglect of my responsibilities."

She seemed about to return to her letter. But Georgina was eager to prolong this unusually open conversation. "You weren't sorry to miss a taste of society?" she asked. "You haven't been up to London for years."

"I never cared much for parties and balls," her mother replied. She laughed. "Emma and Hilda would make dreadful faces at such heresy, wouldn't they? I can't think where they get their longing for great crowds of people. Your father is just like me. Perhaps when they actually try to push their way through a stifling crush of chattering, staring strangers, they'll see their mistake. Do you think so?" She gazed at Georgina, seeming genuinely curious.

The vivid description gave Georgina a new and rather touching insight into her mother's character. "I don't know. I can imagine Hilda gathering a circle around her and chattering right back."

The marchioness's laugh altered the downward cast of her features. She looked much less like her pets and a good deal more like Edgar, Georgina realized. She hadn't seen her brother's resemblance to their mother before, because he was so different in other ways.

"Truly, you didn't find those great masses of people horrid?"

Georgina considered the matter. "No. A little oppressive sometimes, at the largest parties." She'd learned to carve out her own space, with friends, in such cases.

Her mother gave a decisive nod. "There, you see. It's in your blood. Your papa and I first formed a bond over our mutual dislike of society."

"But you…" Georgina felt daring and trepidation in equal measure. She'd wondered so often about her parents' marriage. She couldn't let this unprecedented opportunity pass. "You don't seem to have many interests in common."

Her mother's limpid blue eyes met hers. "We are both extremely *interested* in the freedom to pursue our own interests," she replied. "And if that sounds like a small thing, let me assure you it is not. What would I do with a husband who expected me to organize hunt balls and embroider slippers and pour tea for a pack of brainless gossips?"

Georgina couldn't imagine. And then she could. It wasn't a pretty picture.

"We share mutual respect," her mother continued. "Which is critical, my dear. Believe me. We also have you children. There's no connection stronger than that."

This didn't seem quite enough, though Georgina didn't say so.

"And of course there's physical attraction. That side of things is quite important, though it's never talked about. Which is silly, is it not? Such a very pleasant activity, too."

Georgina blinked. She felt a blush spread over her cheeks. She was getting more than she'd bargained for. She wasn't sorry, but the conversation was moving into…uncharted territory.

"I take it you enjoyed kissing in the shrubbery?" continued her mother. At Georgina's wince, she nodded. "Yes, Hilda needs to be kept busier. I shall mention it to Joanna." With a steady gaze, she waited for an answer.

Georgina swallowed. "Yes, Mama," she murmured.

"Good," was the robust reply. "He's quite a handsome

fellow, but pretty men can be as clumsy as ugly ones. More, I believe, as they don't have to try so hard to attract." She fixed Georgina with a steady gaze. "Make certain you keep on enjoying it, my dear. All of it. And if you aren't, say so, and urge him to correct the situation. Then you'll be fine." With a brisk nod to cap these startling pronouncements, she returned to her letter.

Georgina appreciated the respite, because she didn't know how to reply. She was glad her mother approved of Sebastian. Indeed, she hadn't known how important that blessing was until she had it. As for her advice, well, that was fascinating and astonishing and welcome and embarrassing all at once.

Her thoughts shifted back to the dining room. What was Sebastian thinking now that he had, no doubt, heard all about her father's latest start? She was used to Papa and loved him, and she'd found it exceedingly strange.

"He should enjoy it, too," her mother said. "But men generally do. So people say, anyway."

"I beg your pardon, Mama?" For a confused moment, Georgina imagined she was speaking of Papa.

"Your Sebastian. Ask him what he likes. It adds quite a delicious dimension."

Beyond the amazement at this new side of her mother, Georgina found her suggestion both daunting and enticing. It opened up a thrilling vista of pleasures beyond kisses. But would she dare ask?

"You should go and extricate him from Alfred's clutches," her mother added absently. "Ah." Apparently struck by a thought, she bent to scribble a sentence on her page.

Georgina realized that she'd been governed by the social strictures laid down by her grandmother in London. They were practically the only set of rules she possessed. But as her mother had made clear, such scruples hardly applied here. Neither of her parents were much constrained by convention. She rose. "I think I will."

"Yes, dear" was the vague reply.

With a mixture of regret and relief, Georgina saw that Mama had reverted to her customary manner. The sense of distance—of being only half heard—was more familiar, and thus more comfortable. But it was melancholy, too. Still, Georgina left her mother with a sense that she had a new resource at hand. Who knew what other unexpected gifts might emerge?

Three

In the dining room, Sebastian had lost the thread of the conversation some sentences back and was unlikely to ever pick it up again. Georgina's father and his Indian guest had dropped into a discussion peppered with foreign words and unfamiliar ideas. Sebastian longed to escape, but he didn't want to offend his newly met future father-in-law. So when the door opened to reveal Georgina, he'd never been gladder to see anyone.

"I haven't managed the full envisioning as yet," the marquess was saying as she approached the table. "Not as such."

"You must try harder to clear your mind during the meditation process," Mr. Mitra replied.

"Well, but I have a great many thoughts, you see," the other man replied with every sign of pride.

"Hello, Papa," said Georgina. "I'm going to take Sebastian away now."

Rising, Sebastian worried that the marquess would object, or protest this breach of convention, but his host merely waved them off with a casual "Very well, my dear."

Sebastian followed his fiancée's slender figure out into the corridor and along it to another. To his delight, he discovered they were headed not to the drawing room but into a small parlor at the end of the wing.

"I hope you don't mind being taken from your wine," Georgina said as she lit a branch of candles from the one she was carrying.

"Not in the least. Matter of fact, I was dashed happy for the rescue. My head was spinning from the…discussion."

"I hope Papa didn't bore you," she said without turning from her task.

Worried that he'd seemed to be criticizing her father, Sebastian said, "No, no. I mean, I didn't understand half of what he said. I'm too thick. But…" He forgot whatever he was going to add when she turned and looked up at him. In the soft light, her hair gleamed golden, and her eyes were hooded and mysterious. She was so lovely it took his breath away.

"You're not thick," she said.

Sebastian hesitated, then shrugged. It had been quite clear during their courtship that she was the clever one. She couldn't be expecting a sudden burst of intellect. "Well, I am. No sense denying it. I'm used to it."

"Used to what?"

He held up one hand with all five fingers extended, then waggled his other thumb. "Being the dimmest Gresham brother."

"Is that what you think?"

It wasn't a matter of thinking. It was a proven fact.

She must have noticed. He thought of telling her that she needn't worry about wounding his sensibilities by acknowledging the truth. And then Georgina sat down, her skirts spreading around her with a soft slither, and indicated that he should join her. The sofa in here was small; he had to sit very close. All remaining wisps of thought went out of his head as he breathed in the enticing scent she always wore.

Quiet surrounded them. There wasn't so much as the ticking of a clock in this little chamber, which didn't look much used. In fact, it was quite a secluded spot. A thrill went through Sebastian as he understood that Georgina must have known this when she brought him here. At this hour, most of the servants' work would be finished. It didn't seem likely they'd be interrupted. Still. "Sisters gone to bed?" he asked.

"Yes."

He gazed into her gray-green eyes and caught a hint of uncertainty. He wanted to crush her in his arms, but he needed some sign of her wishes. Had she brought him here—please God, no—to talk?

Georgina raised a hand. Slowly, tentatively, she reached over and touched his cheek with feather-light fingertips.

That was it. He kissed her.

It was their second real kiss. He didn't count the hurried brushes they'd managed in town. And it was tender and sweet. Her lips moved experimentally against his—not at all reluctant, but obviously inexperienced. As his veins filled with fire, Sebastian reveled in the idea that he had something to teach her. He was all right, more than all right, with matters that involved his hands rather than his head. There was no buzzing cloud of words to plague the life out of him. He was dashed good with his hands. And right now, they were like racehorses waiting for the gun. When he thought of all the pleasures they could offer her— in good time, of course, not here and now—it was almost more exciting than his own growing arousal.

In fact, he couldn't resist just a hint of what was to come for them. Deepening the kiss, he ventured a caress, running his fingers up the smooth cloth of her gown, letting them stray ever closer to the curve of her bodice. "Oh," Georgina breathed when they reached their goal. She arched closer, encouraging him to continue.

Sebastian gladly complied. He teased and tantalized, and when the sleeve of her gown slipped off her shoulder, he took advantage of the opportunity to touch her silken skin directly. Georgina moaned. In an effort to press closer, she slid a leg over his knee. When she tightened her arms around his neck, he drew her nearer automatically. And then somehow she was straddling him, her lithe body straining against his, her lips warm and eager. There was every indication she was about to open to him like a flower. One of his hands had already found its way beneath her dress and was sliding over the top of her silk stocking on its way to show her further delights.

Somewhere in the castle at their backs, a door shut with a thud.

Oh God.

With every fiber of him aching to rush on, Sebastian drew back. What was he doing? They could easily be discovered here. Her father had seen them go off together. He might be looking for them right now. Sebastian hadn't even been at Stane Castle one day. And while he yearned to carry Georgina off to his bedchamber and continue, he would never wish to embarrass or humiliate her.

He forced himself to abandon her lips, pleased to see disappointment on her face. Placing one hand on either side of her waist, he reluctantly lifted her and set her back beside him on the sofa. They were both breathing hard. Sebastian pulled at his ravaged neckcloth, trying to get more air. "Is there any reason to wait until September for the wedding?" he asked with a savage yank at the twisted linen. "Can't see one myself."

Georgina blinked as she emerged from a daze of desire. She was panting as if she'd been running. This must be what her mother had been talking about. Only, she'd had no need to tell Sebastian anything; he seemed to know just what she wanted, before she knew it herself. "None in the world," she said. But as her mind steadied, countering the demands of her body, she remembered. "Or…your family is set to come here then. Papa is so looking forward to it."

"Ah, right," said Sebastian. "I don't suppose we can change that. Mama plans their movements like a logistics officer. Always has sixty things to do."

He looked morose. Georgina almost felt she needed to apologize. "We Stanes have very few relations, you see. Only some distant cousins that I have never even met. And with living so out of the way as well, there's been very little opportunity for…family events.

Papa likes the idea of gathering everyone together." In fact, she was aware that this aspect of the occasion outweighed the actual wedding ceremony for him.

"Ha, it's just the opposite with us," replied Sebastian. "I feel like I'm kin to half the country sometimes. I could spend all my time at one do or another."

And it occurred to Georgina—only then, for some reason—that the Duke and Duchess of Langford would be making a significant stay with her parents. She'd been so focused on the perils of her betrothed's arrival that she hadn't thought ahead. Unbidden, unwelcome, a series of scenes began to unfold in her mind. Sebastian's oldest brother, Nathaniel, had recently celebrated his own wedding, to the extremely correct Lady Violet Devere.

Georgina imagined Lady Violet—no, she was the Viscountess Hightower now—being mobbed by the pugs. She always wore ruffles. Some of the younger dogs were driven into a frenzy by the fluttering of ruffles. Georgina closed her eyes on the image of several pugs hanging off the viscountess's gown by their teeth, like some sort of bizarre ornaments.

She opened her eyes again as she thought of how her sisters would positively *besiege* Sebastian's elegant brother Robert. They would pelt him with questions about the *haut ton* and the ways of society. As far as she could judge, he was a pleasant man, but could he stand up to such a campaign without giving them a withering setdown?

She saw the immaculate duke and duchess chatting with Mr. Mitra, perhaps being asked if they wanted to visit their past lives. Oh, they would be polite; they were always polite. But would they exchange amused, mocking glances when they thought no one saw? Which she would not be able to ignore? Georgina knew she'd be torn between wanting to impress Sebastian's family and sticking by Papa. There was the scientist brother, Alan, too. Would he view Papa's activities with contempt?

Georgina looked into Sebastian's blue eyes. The warmth she found there was reassuring, but not enough to counter all the worries popping up in her mind.

And then, just to cap it all, there came the sound of a dog scratching at the closed door of the room and whining to be let in. The scrape of claws on the wood was like an infernal confirmation of all her fears.

The noise stopped for a moment. There was a sharp bark, like a command. And then the scratching resumed with redoubled intensity. "Aidan doesn't like being shut out," Georgina said. "Of anywhere. He's always escaping the dogs' room and attacking closed doors." Feeling a confused mixture of reluctance and urgency, she stood. "Mama will come looking for him. And Papa hates finding marks on the doors. I'd better get him."

"You're going to bring him in here?"

"No!" She refused to even picture that. "I shall take him to Mama. Excuse me." She didn't look at Sebastian as she hurried out to gather up the dog. She was afraid of what she might see on his face.

Alone, Sebastian sat back on the sofa and tried to take comfort in the fact that he'd done the right thing. They would indeed have been discovered. He'd protected Georgina from that.

This effort failed. He wished for some of the port he'd passed up in the dining room earlier. Or something stronger, brandy by choice. But he didn't know where to look for it, and he didn't want to ring for it. So he took himself off to his bedchamber instead. It had been a very long day.

❦

Sebastian's valet arrived at Stane Castle two days later, his post chaise pulling up late in the afternoon behind a tired team. Sebastian was exceedingly pleased to see him, for William Sykes brought far more than clean shirts and expert care for his master's top boots. After a most unconventional beginning, Sykes had been with him for sixteen years and grown into a staunch ally over that time. His tall, gangling, immaculate figure would be a source of reassurance in this unpredictable household—unflappable, ingenious, discreet. Indeed, now and then, Sebastian suspected Sykes was omniscient.

Sebastian felt sorely in need of his valet's help. His visit was not going particularly well, at least from his point of view. There'd been no recurrence of the tantalizing encounter with Georgina in the small parlor. In fact, he hadn't managed to get her alone again at all. She wasn't avoiding him, which would have been disheartening. He could tell it wasn't that. It was simply everything else.

There was the pack of pugs roaming the house, for one. Sometimes they gave no yapping early warning, but simply flowed into his path, surrounding him, tumbling about his feet, drooling—or worse—on his trouser legs. Sykes would have a good deal to say about the scratches on Sebastian's boots. And one of the smaller beasts had developed the trick of hopping onto a sofa whenever Sebastian sat down, running along the back, and jumping onto his shoulder to slaver over his face.

Rather than reprimanding the dog, Georgina's mother watched indulgently, informing Sebastian that this was a mark of great affection. Since she clearly took Nuala's— that was the creature's name, Nuala—attentions as a favorable comment on his character, Sebastian couldn't complain. But he was feeling positively hunted. He'd taken to sitting in isolated straight chairs, and dashed uncomfortable they were. It was enough to make a fellow feel aggrieved, because he *liked* dogs.

When he did escape the pugs for a bit, there was still the problem of Georgina's sisters. They followed him about, founts of insatiable curiosity, able to track him down wherever he went. Hilda, in particular, seemed to have an almost preternatural instinct for the hunt. And she didn't scruple to knock on his bedchamber door if they couldn't find him elsewhere.

How was he supposed to know what a voucher for Almack's looked like? Or whether hoop skirts were still worn for a court presentation? He had managed to remember that Gunter's was the best place to purchase lemon ices in London. But then Emma pulled out some devilish book about the language of fans, and the two girls kept him captive in the drawing room for more than an hour trying to get him to say whether they were performing each gesture correctly.

If they snapped the fan open and shut at this rate, was that angry, or simply impatient? Did one flirt with this sort of twist and flutter? Was this peek over the top edge coy? Sebastian had no idea. Quite the opposite. He'd been horrified by the idea that girls had been trying to tell him things with their fans all this time. He'd thought they were just too warm.

He did know how to waltz. Well, of course he did. Dancing was a skill of the body that he'd easily mastered, and he rather prided himself on his ability. But he'd assured Georgina's sisters that he had two left feet and no memory for steps to avoid holding dancing classes in the schoolroom. Fortunately he'd had the support of their governess on that one. Miss Byngham found other subjects far more important.

Sebastian waited while Sykes saw that the luggage was carried upstairs. He allowed his valet sufficient time to be introduced to the resident staff and shown his own quarters. But when Sykes returned to begin unpacking the trunks, Sebastian could wait no longer. "I need to write Nathaniel," he told Sykes.

The valet nodded. He went to sit at the writing desk by the window and readied the pen and paper he found in its drawer.

"In the usual style, eh?" said Sebastian.

Sykes simply nodded. They didn't discuss the matter any further. In fact, they never had, not since the day Sykes had discovered his future master, a hulking lad of fifteen, bent over a blotted page, wrestling with a pen as if it was a writhing snake, and perilously near tears. Humiliated, Sebastian had turned away, crushing the page in one fist and throwing the treacherous writing instrument across the room.

And in that long-ago moment, he'd discovered that

William Sykes was a master at ignoring things that were better not mentioned.

They hadn't been acquainted then. Several years older than Sebastian, Sykes was the son of an upper servant's family at Eton. He was allowed to attend classes by some special arrangement. Sebastian didn't know the details. There was no reason he should. It had nothing to do with him.

Sebastian had been about to stomp out of the school library, using his best scowl to deflect questions, when young Sykes dropped into an armchair and said, "Would you do me a great favor?"

This was so unexpected that it stopped Sebastian in his tracks. They'd never even been introduced.

"I'm hoping to be a playwright," Sykes had continued, even more surprisingly. "For the London stage. My family thinks I'm an idiot, of course."

Sebastian had stared at the skinny, bright-eyed boy, with his wrists sticking out of his outgrown shirtsleeves.

"They think I should aspire no higher than schoolmaster or tutor. Can you imagine anything more dreary?"

Sebastian hadn't found a thing to say in response to this.

"But I'm absolutely determined to find a way. So, I wondered if you might allow me to write your letter for you. It would be such a useful exercise, you see. Developing a character, with his own particular voice. Very renaissance."

Sebastian had gaped at him, and an entire conversation had passed in one long gaze. Sebastian had understood that Sykes was an alarmingly bright and observant fellow and that, relegated to the sidelines by his ambiguous status at Eton, he'd noticed things Sebastian had labored hard to conceal. He offered no hint of threat; Sebastian would have thrashed him for that. Rather, he was silently suggesting an arrangement for their mutual benefit. Which need never be admitted, still less actually spoken aloud.

Even back then, Sebastian was a good judge of character. He'd trusted young Sykes, and he'd never been sorry. Without a word, the fellow had thought to mimic Sebastian's disgraceful handwriting as he penned the letter. Later on, Sebastian had seen Sykes's personal copperplate hand, a thing of beauty compared with that scrawl. He'd said nothing about that either. The whole exchange had been simply astonishing.

They'd gone on to formalize the connection when Sykes suggested that Sebastian take him on as valet once they'd left school. He'd made the scheme seem perfectly reasonable, nothing like an act of charity or a crutch. The position would give him many priceless opportunities to observe society, he'd said, and enrich the "texture" of his plays. Sebastian made certain that Sykes was paid very well and allowed ample time to go to the theater and write. To their mutual amusement, Sykes had thrown himself into the role, becoming such an exemplary valet, in public, that other young men routinely tried to lure him away.

Sebastian looked at the elegant figure seated at the desk, poised and alert, with pen in hand. He'd become a companion as much as a servant by this time.

"The usual greetings," began Sebastian. "Arrived safely at Stane Castle and all that."

Lately, since Sebastian's last promotion, they'd put it about that Sykes served as his secretary as well as valet. It sounded unexceptionable. Busy men had private secretaries to manage their affairs. His father the duke had two to handle his voluminous correspondence.

Sykes began to write. Sebastian knew he would transform his offhand remarks into the proper phrases. By now, Sykes was an expert at producing a missive in the style Sebastian's family was accustomed to from their second son. Or, to be more accurate, as Sykes put it, such letters were a genre Sykes had created from whole cloth.

Sebastian narrated some highlights of his visit so far. When he uttered the phrase, "a deuced sea of furry, yapping little rats," Sykes cleared his throat. It was his way of suggesting that perhaps another expression would be more apt.

"You haven't fought an engagement with the pugs yet," Sebastian explained. "I swear they planned that assault on Mitra. He's the Hindu fellow; the dogs make him nervous. Drustan—he's the ringleader, the beast who keeps going at my leg, evil little sod—got them all nipping at Mitra's ankles in turn. Diversionary actions, see? Then, at just the right moment, Drustan rushed in and tripped him. If you'd seen Mitra staggering about like a drunken sailor yesterday, trying not to step on the creatures, and then falling flat on the drawing room carpet, you'd grant that there's no other way to describe them."

Sykes conceded with a nod, and wrote.

Sebastian resumed dictation. "So I need something to repel dogs," he said. "Maybe some herb or ointment from an apothecary. If Nathaniel could discover a mixture that keeps them off me without disgusting people, particularly female people, and have it sent along posthaste, that would do the trick."

"Hmm," murmured Sykes.

"You know of something?" Sykes's brain was stuffed with facts of every description. "I should have thought to ask you."

"I believe dogs dislike the odor of vinegar, my lord."

"Well, so do I. So does anyone. I can't go about smelling of vinegar."

"No, my lord."

Sebastian examined him. Any other man, even a servant, might have been tempted to laugh at this point. He would have himself, if the shoe had been on some other poor fellow's foot. He wouldn't even have minded, very much. Sykes sat poised at the writing desk, resolutely in character. His idea of a proper valet was imperturbable. But if you looked carefully, you could see his brown eyes twinkling with amusement. Pugs would figure in his next dramatic opus, Sebastian suspected.

"I will look into the question further," Sykes said.

"Splendid." Sebastian remembered something. "Mitra seems to think that Georgina's mother has the dogs trained to… Well, I don't know. Do her bidding somehow. You might see about that as well."

"See?" Sykes cocked his head, brows raised.

"What she's up to."

"The marchioness?"

"That's it." Sebastian gathered his thoughts and went on. "I'm also desperately in need of amusements for two girls aged about fifteen and thirteen," he dictated. "Anything, doesn't matter how much it costs. But quickly. Underline that part," he told Sykes. "Make sure Nathaniel knows it's more important than the bit about the dogs."

"Yes, my lord."

"I don't suppose you have any ideas on that score?" It was hard to imagine. But you never knew with Sykes.

"I fear not, my lord."

Sebastian nodded, unsurprised. "I've got to find something to occupy them. You don't know what I've endured. They never stop talking, especially Hilda. I no sooner sit down than they appear and start in on me."

He didn't think that Emma and Hilda were trying to keep him away from Georgina. On the contrary, they were inordinately interested in when he would be kissing her in the shrubbery again. But their constant presence meant that he'd had no chance to speak to his intended about their…interlude in the back parlor. Georgina seemed calm enough when he saw her. But how else was she to appear before everyone?

As Sykes went off to dispatch the letter, Sebastian brooded among his open trunks. On the one hand, he was afraid he'd gone too fast and spooked his betrothed. He needed to make sure she was all right. Because, on the other hand, he wanted nothing more than to resume their exciting explorations, as soon and as thoroughly as she wished. Memories of the feel of her colored his days and haunted his nights. He'd never wanted any woman so much. This was splendid news for the future, he supposed. She would be his wife in a few weeks' time. But at present it was more of a penance—to be so close to her and yet always in public.

Four

THE MARQUESS'S EXPEDITION TO SHOW HIS GUEST Offa's Dyke had been put off by a period of heavy rain. But it was to happen at last early in August. Though she feared Sebastian would be bored by her father's historical orations, Georgina was glad for the chance to get out of the house and breathe freer air. She was certain Sebastian felt the same; he was a cavalryman, after all, accustomed to days on horseback.

Even if the size and composition of the group wouldn't allow for carefree gallops, it was splendid to be out of doors. And so as she guided her favorite mount over to join Papa, Fergus, Sebastian, and her sisters in the stable courtyard, Georgina smiled. It was barely ten. The sun was warm and the skies clear as they set off, clattering through the gate arch and out onto the path leading down from the castle.

Sebastian on horseback was a lovely sight, she thought. He rode as if born in the saddle, and his magnificent horse obviously loved him. The beast danced and curveted with delight at being out of the stable, and Sebastian laughed as he allowed him a bit of fun. He seemed as joyous as Whitefoot.

Watching her fiancé effortlessly control his spirited mount inspired all sorts of reactions. Georgina was full of admiration, hesitation, yearning. She couldn't take her eyes off him. Indeed, she'd thought of little else since their stolen embraces in the little parlor at the back of the castle. Recalling those moments set her aflame, and she did so all the time. Her knees had been stretched out on either side of those powerful thighs, now encased in snug buckskin breeches, she thought. Immediately, she felt as if she'd been dipped in steaming water. She flushed all over. She turned her horse so that the others wouldn't see the blush.

Her arms had been around Sebastian's neck. He'd kissed her so sweetly. Whenever she passed near the small parlor now, she longed to open the door and find him there and pick up where they'd left off. If his fingers had moved just a little further that evening, a few aching inches, what new realms of pleasure might have been revealed? Georgina's pulse thudded at the thought.

Sebastian glanced back at her and smiled. She could see no censure in his face, but she *could* hear her grandmother's scandalized voice, scolding her for going so far beyond the line. Her chief arbiter of proper social behavior—the preceptress who had guided her through a successful London season— would have been filled with horror at her behavior. It wouldn't matter a whit to her that they were engaged. She would declare Georgina's reputation in tatters.

Her mother's remarks had seemed to give her a

kind of permission, Georgina argued to herself. But she suspected—no, knew—that the advice had been meant for after the wedding. She didn't suppose Mama had pictured anything like what she'd done.

Georgina watched Sebastian ride along ahead of her. She wanted him to think well of her. Did he see her now as a wanton? Did he wonder where she'd learned such a trick? A huff of air escaped her. She rather wondered that herself. It had all seemed so natural, until he'd drawn away and set her aside like an unwanted doll. Then she'd been uneasy.

She didn't know how to talk about it with him. Should they ever have an opportunity for a private discussion. Emma and Hilda would not be persuaded to leave Sebastian alone. Georgina had unwisely voiced doubts about whether they could be added to her future household, and this uncertainty made them cling even harder.

Her father increased the pace as they reached the bottom of the ridge where the castle lay. He led them west onto a track that passed through forest and around crag. The country was green from the rain, scented with wildflowers and evergreen. The summer light would last well into evening. This expedition would be idyllic if she wasn't bursting with worry and impatience.

Georgina urged her horse into a lope to work off some of that excess energy. Sebastian started to follow, but he was stopped by a wave from her father, who called his attention to a scenic vista. For a family that approved her match, they were awfully quick to come between them, Georgina thought, fuming. She urged her mount onward, leaning forward and welcoming the wind on her face.

After half an hour's ride, Sebastian was more than ready to reach their destination. He'd had no chance to talk with Georgina. Her father seemed to think that he wished to know the history of each hill they passed, and in this long-disputed border district, each inch of ground appeared to have a tale. If the marquess didn't know it, he got Fergus to remind him. The fellow was more steward than butler, Sebastian decided, even though he served at table in the castle. He was more henchman than either.

At last, Georgina's father pulled up. "There it is," he said, gesturing at the ground before them as if presenting Sebastian with a special gift.

Sebastian surveyed the terrain. A hump of earth extended right and left ahead, matching the contours of the land as it stretched off into the distance. It looked a bit like a military earthwork, though worn and eroded in places. "Did they have a palisade on top?" he asked.

The marquess nodded approvingly. "No way to know, after a thousand years. But it makes sense, and I believe so. You're sharp to spot it straightaway."

Sebastian had been trained to think like a soldier. "It would take a good many men to defend this," he remarked.

"The army of Mercia," replied his host. "Though it was hardly what we think of as an army. Each land-holder was bound to provide a troop of armsmen. So you had a few competent swordsmen and archers leading a rabble of farmers with makeshift weapons."

"Against the Welsh," Sebastian said.

"Right. The Dyke marks a bloody border. The name of Offa's kingdom, Mercia, means *border people*. And it didn't end with him, by any means. Owen Tudor fought and died not far north of here." The marquess turned in the saddle and called to Emma. "You remember who Owen Tudor was, my dear?"

When Emma looked blank, Hilda replied for her. "The founder of the Tudor royal line, Papa. Ancestor of Henry VIII and Queen Elizabeth."

"Exactly. Have you forgotten your local history, Emma?"

Both his younger daughters smiled at him with fond impatience. "Yes, Papa," said Emma. "You know I don't care about fusty old facts."

"But you must feel something of the spirit of this place," their father said. "The echo of clashing spear points, the blood-soaked earth."

"Euww," said Emma.

"You know you decided that I have the sensitivity of a flint pebble," Hilda added, showing no regret over this assessment.

"Is it only Edgar then who shares my connection to the land?" came the plaintive reply.

"Well, he will inherit it," replied Hilda, ever practical. "But Georgina knows all that stuff, too."

Sebastian looked at his intended with interest. Here was another side to her. She didn't seem pleased to be singled out, however, so he searched for a remark to turn the subject. "It's certainly lonely country," he said. "It's miles since we passed a village." There was a sameness to the lines of ridges as well. "Must be easy to get lost out here."

Hilda looked oddly struck by this obvious fact.

"There's a story of a Stane losing himself in the border country," said the marquess with a nod.

"Geoffrey," Georgina said.

"Seems he fell in love with a Welsh lass," her father continued. "This was three hundred and fifty years ago, you understand, when Britain was in a right turmoil. Wars of the Roses. Border tensions very high."

Sebastian nodded to show that he was paying attention. He did wonder what kind of battle you could fight with roses.

"Nothing could stop young Geoffrey from crossing to visit his lady, however," said the marquess. "Not the wrath of her father or the threat of attack. And then one night as he was riding for home, a thick fog descended upon him."

"That's bad," commented Sebastian. Maneuvers in the fog were a bear.

His host nodded. "He would have been wise to stop and wait for it to clear," he went on. "But he was stubborn and eager to reach Stane again before he was missed. So he pushed on and soon wandered off the track. By the time he knew it, though, evening was coming."

"Dark and fog," Sebastian said. "Shouldn't have tried it."

Georgina's father nodded. "No one knows what happened to him," he added. "Geoffrey of Stane was never seen again. They searched, of course, but found no sign of him or his mount. Travelers do sometimes report the sound of hooves echoing on the trails, when there's a fog, with never any trace of a rider."

Emma shivered. Hilda looked around as if she'd very much like to see the specter of Geoffrey come clopping from behind one of the hills.

"His younger brother inherited," said Georgina in a prosaic tone. "I imagine he was a better landlord than Geoffrey would have been."

"Because Geoffrey risked everything for love, and lost?" Sebastian asked. As soon as he said it, he wished he hadn't, because there was an odd pause, as if everyone was listening for her answer.

"Because he didn't have the common sense to wait out a fog," she answered. Pulling on the reins, she turned her horse and rode off along the Dyke.

The group followed, ambling along the course of the earthwork for quite a time. It all seemed much the same, with no obvious features of interest beyond its mere existence. As the sun passed the zenith and began to descend, they turned back. Fergus distributed some dry sandwiches from his saddlebags, and they ate as they rode.

The two older men fell into conversation about the estate. Emma and Hilda began a racing game. And at last, Sebastian found a chance to ride beside Georgina. He seized it, but received only monosyllabic responses to his remarks about the day and the sights. "Is all well?" he asked.

"Yes," replied Georgina, although in truth she was struggling with the feelings roused by their embraces.

"The other day…" Sebastian began.

She waited. She was wild to hear what he had to say, but she wasn't going to finish the sentence for him.

"In the parlor," he added.

As if there was any other day he might mean, in the circumstances. Georgina had never minded before that Sebastian was a man of few words. It had been a pleasant contrast to London's incessant chatterers. Now, however, she wished he would get on with it.

"I don't know if an apology…?"

Georgina found that this wasn't at all what she wanted to hear. "Are you sorry?"

Sebastian offered her his charming smile. "Well, if you're angry, I'm sorry. Are you?"

She wasn't angry. Would a proper young lady be angry? Did he think she should be? "It's not sort of thing I do. You mustn't think that I have ever before acted so… In such a way."

"Of course."

Of course he knew that? Or of course he knew he mustn't think so? "If we weren't engaged, I would never have allowed such…liberties." There was a fine word, she thought. As if they had a choice to be free, instead of hemmed in by rules and expectations.

"Naturally," replied Sebastian. "I understand. I went too far."

"Good, then." He didn't look happy with this exchange. She certainly wasn't. But she had no idea how to tell him that she'd adored what they did, and wanted to do it again as soon as possible. Providing he understood that she wouldn't consider such wantonness with anyone but him. With him, she would consider… Well, she didn't even know, exactly. She was open to suggestion. Instruction. Seduction? One didn't say such things out loud.

"You know…" he began.

But she didn't get to hear what he thought she knew. With a thunder of hooves, Emma and Hilda came galloping up. They raced in a circle around them, rousing strong objections from Sebastian's mount and a snort from Georgina's. "Hilda!" said Georgina as her sisters slowed to join them. It was always Hilda who instigated the uproar.

"We saw a stag," replied the youngest Stane. "But Emma wouldn't ride after it."

"It would have left us behind in a minute," said Emma. "And I do not care to jump a hedged ditch."

"How many points?" asked Sebastian. He'd gone deer stalking at a friend's house in Scotland. It was good sport.

Emma shrugged, clearly uninterested in the beast. "What sort of riding habits do the fashionable ladies wear in Hyde Park?" She indicated her own buff costume with a contemptuous gesture. "They must be much smarter than this."

Sebastian certainly noticed a fine figure of a girl in close-fitting riding dress. The cut of a habit could be more revealing than a ball gown. Indeed, he'd been admiring Georgina's enticing outline in hers. But as to the habits themselves, he had nothing to say. They were different colors. Some had bits of decoration. His brother Robert would probably have a host of opinions on this subject. Sebastian had none. "I've seen epaulettes on some of them," he remembered. "And frogging." They'd seemed to be trying for the look of a military uniform, which was odd, now that he thought about it.

"Is that the latest thing?" asked Hilda.

"Why do you never ask me?" said Georgina. "You must know that I'm much more familiar with fashion than Sebastian."

"We want to know what the *gentlemen* like," replied her youngest sister.

"Hilda!"

"It's all very well for you," the other girl retorted. "You had Great-Uncle George's fortune, and so your future was settled like that." She snapped her fingers. "Emma and I will have a much harder time of it."

"When did you become so vulgar?" said Georgina, wondering what a son of the Duke of Langford could be thinking of this conversation.

"I've always been," Hilda replied cheerfully. "If that's what you call telling the truth. Mama says plain speaking is the only sensible course in life."

She did say that, Georgina admitted silently, and do it, too. As a child, Georgina had accepted this frankness as simply the way of things, but since she'd been to London and suffered the consequences of a few gaffes, she wasn't so sure. She did know that Sebastian had been trained to a high standard of civility. Anyone watching his mother navigate the shoals of society could only nod in admiration. And he certainly looked the soul of politeness now.

There was no sign that he found her sister's statements unacceptable. Indeed, he'd shown very little reaction to any of her family's behavior. But that didn't mean he wasn't having them. Georgina sighed. Life would be so much easier if one could read thoughts, or at least understand them clearly from facial expressions.

Sebastian *was* feeling uncomfortable. It wasn't the plain speaking in itself. He didn't mind bluntness. On the contrary, he often appreciated it. You knew where you were with people who said what they meant. It was the subject matter in this case—Georgina's fortune, and the undeniable fact that he'd begun his pursuit of her because of it. He'd been determined to snag a rich wife. Life as a duke's son was so much easier with a bit of money.

There was nothing wrong with that point of view, he told himself. All his brothers had the same concern. Well, except Nathaniel. He was the heir; all the ducal riches would be coming to him through the entail. It was the way of the world that the eldest son inherited. Sebastian understood that. You couldn't be chopping up an estate among the offspring in every generation. Very soon there would be nothing left of a grand heritage. And Nathaniel was a good egg, always ready to help out. The rest of them were left to provide for themselves, however, if they wished for more than their bare allowances and their oldest brother's charity.

James had a lump of prize money from his naval successes during the war. Sebastian didn't know the exact sum, but he understood it was enough to make his brother comfortable for life. Unfortunately, such largesse wasn't open to army officers. Their engagements yielded no conquered ships to tow back to friendly harbors and redeem. And Sebastian knew he was unlikely to rise further in rank. He would not be a colonel and command a regiment. His superiors liked him, but they'd taken the measure of his limits. Not that military pay was any great thing, no matter how high the level.

As for his other brothers, Alan had made money through some inventions that Sebastian didn't understand, and he'd settled on a relatively frugal existence in Oxford as well. Robert had been left a bit by his godfather, but he led quite an expensive life among the *haut ton*. Randolph had his living and expected to advance in the church, but he certainly wouldn't mind marrying money. It was no wonder, and no shame, that Sebastian had thanked his lucky stars when Georgina, with her fortune, accepted him.

As he came to know her better, though, he'd felt the urge to tell her that he valued the match for other reasons. More all the time, as a matter of fact. It was just deucedly difficult to begin such a conversation, and to go on without sounding like a coxcomb. It was the sort of thing a sneaking flatterer would say. And what if she asked whether he would've offered for her if she hadn't had money?

Although he couldn't now imagine marrying anyone else, he most likely wouldn't have. Well, he wouldn't have become well acquainted with her, would he? If not for the fortune waiting in the wings? She'd have been just another of the throng of debs vying for attention in a crowded season. He wouldn't have known to single her out.

Sebastian suffered a sudden shiver of apprehension. In that case, he'd never have discovered Georgina's sharp intelligence and quick kindness and delectable ardor. Which would have been a tragedy as great as any Sykes might want to portray in a theater. But then, he wouldn't have realized he'd missed them, Sebastian thought. He'd have passed her, unheeding, in crowded ballrooms and at stuffy evening parties. They both would have gone on to other lives with other people. The prospect was dire, but it wouldn't have been, because he would have been ignorant of her charms.

Feeling more than usually conscious of his dimness in this moment, his thoughts twisted into a damnable tangle, Sebastian gave up. He'd discovered long ago that it was better to remain silent than to flounder in a mire of words. Why demonstrate one's failings for all to see? He wouldn't get his point across, if he even knew what it was, and he'd be exposed as a dolt. He'd just have to find some other way to show Georgina that he valued her for herself, he decided. If only a bit of deft saber work or riding neck or nothing over rough country would convey the message, he'd be set.

"So is it?" said Hilda.

Realizing that she was addressing him, but with no idea of the topic, Sebastian summoned his very best smile. He'd found it a defense and a refuge when he'd lost track of a conversation or couldn't find the right words to contribute, particularly where females were concerned.

All three Stane sisters blinked as if dazzled by a sudden light.

A diversionary tactic gave you room to maneuver, Sebastian thought. But it had to be followed up with an effective offense. "What's that over there?" he asked.

"What?" Hilda and Georgina asked in the same moment. Emma turned to gaze in the direction he'd indicated.

It was nothing but more of Offa's long dyke, but Sebastian continued the ruse by spurring over and examining the earthwork as if he'd spotted some interesting feature. The others followed, and Hilda's question, whatever it had been, was lost. After that, Sebastian indulged Whitefoot in a good gallop that swept the cobwebs from both of their heads.

The next few days passed in the same sort of activities. When he wasn't concealing his limited grasp of the marquess's historical references or being pestered by Georgina's sisters or her mother's dogs, Sebastian grew a bit bored. He took Whitefoot out for a solid bout of exercise each day and walked in the gardens. The scraps of time he snatched with Georgina were tantalizing, and somewhat constrained. The latter worried him a good deal, but there never seemed to be an opportunity to find out the reason.

As he strolled into the shrubbery near the ancient tower on the tenth day of his visit, Sebastian heard footsteps ahead and sped up, hoping to see the lissome figure of his fiancée. Instead, he came upon Mr. Mitra, who started at Sebastian's sudden appearance. "Ah, the young lord," the other man said as they nodded a greeting. He made a rueful gesture. "Before this, I savored the rustle of leaves in the wind. Now, I jump like a rabbit at the sound, fearing it heralds a pack of small dogs. This is a melancholy change."

"I don't think they're allowed in this part of the garden," Sebastian said.

"Not alone. But our hostess brings them when she walks here. And if she sees me enter, she is often moved to walk. With *all* of her dogs."

"You think she doesn't like you?" Sebastian had gathered this much from some of the Indian gentleman's previous comments.

His companion shrugged. "As to that, I do not know. I believe she finds my visit...irritating. She does not appreciate her husband's new studies. I would depart, of course. But the marquess insists I stay. It is most awkward. Particularly when our host is occupied on the business of his lands, as today."

"What about we take a stroll together," Sebastian suggested. "If the pugs show up, I'll keep them off you. And if Georgina's sisters come hunting me, you'll distract them."

Mr. Mitra's chiseled features relaxed in a smile. "A splendid bargain. I accept."

The two men ambled along the sheltered path together. The day was overcast, with a sharp wind, and they were glad of the thick bushes on both sides. "How did you come to be acquainted with Stane in the first place?" Sebastian asked after a while.

"He read some of my writings," Mitra replied. "Or rather, Miss Byngham did, I think. A fellow at the University of Cambridge has translated three of my books into English. After that, his lordship wrote to me. We corresponded for some time. When he then invited me to visit, I could not resist the chance to see the home of the race that has so efficiently...insinuated themselves into our lands."

"Insinuated?"

"You are right," said his companion. "It is a paltry word for conquerors."

Here was another character with an oblique way of talking, Sebastian thought. There were far too many of them in the world. He didn't attempt a direct answer. "I suppose you're missing your home," he said instead.

This earned him a warm look. "You are the only one who has said this to me. The rest seem to assume that everything is better here than in Bengal, and so I must long to remain."

"Bengal?"

"You are not familiar with the lands your East India Company has... Perhaps I had better not say *overrun*?" Mitra raised dark brows.

"I was never much of a hand at geography," Sebastian answered. The other man's evaluating expression reminded him of schoolmasters, and a memory caught him. He and two brothers bent over a multicolored globe covered with tiny words; the letters seemed to swim before his eyes as if they were fish in the blue expanses of the pictured oceans. And just as slippery. "Part of India, isn't it?" he ventured.

Mr. Mitra cocked his head and gazed at him, then smiled slightly. "I miss my family a great deal," he said, as if the question of locales had never arisen. "And I am accustomed to a more...lively society than I have met here. However, I understand that some neighbors are invited to dine with us tomorrow night."

"Really?" Sebastian hadn't heard this, but he'd been out riding all morning.

"Indeed. It is the first such occasion since I arrived at this place. I am told that the long distance between estates in this province makes visiting difficult." He gave Sebastian a sidelong glance. "I *suspect* that our host's activities and opinions do not endear him to other members of his caste. Because he is clearly a very sociable person."

Sebastian thought he was right. Of course, Mr. Mitra was a visible, talkative demonstration of these eccentric views. A twinkle in the other man's dark eyes seemed to indicate that he was well aware of this.

"On this occasion, you are the attraction, I believe."

"Me?"

"A public introduction of the new member of their family?"

"Ah." He'd want to make a good impression, Sebastian thought. But he'd been to a hundred of his mother's country dinners. He'd do all right.

The sound of yapping reached their ears, and grew rapidly louder. Mitra sighed. "Alas. The hounds are loosed."

"Not hounds," Sebastian replied. The sound of the pugs was completely different. But perhaps as a foreigner, Mitra didn't know that. Sebastian looked around. They had come out of the shrubbery near the ancient stone tower that anchored one end of Stane Castle, and just a few steps away, a weathered wooden door pierced its walls. Sebastian went over and tried the handle. It groaned as it moved. The hinges were equally noisy, but the old door opened. Sebastian peered inside. A narrow stone staircase twisted upward. "In here," he commanded. "The two of us could hold off a regiment on these stairs." He gestured for Mr. Mitra to go first. The other man hesitated, but louder yapping sent him upward, with Sebastian on his heels.

They climbed past another wooden door on the first level, and then an arched opening further up. Mitra made as if to stop, leaning on the wall and puffing, but Sebastian urged him on until they came out on a dusty, dim landing. A narrower flight of stairs clung to the opposite wall, seemingly going nowhere. "A dead end," said the Indian gentleman.

Sebastian had spotted a trapdoor above their heads, however. He climbed the precipitous stair and pushed at the panel. It fell back, letting in a dazzling square of light. Blinking at the sudden illumination, Sebastian emerged onto a platform at the top of the tower, encircled by a chest-high parapet. Sweeping views of the countryside spread out in every direction, except where a small chamber with slitted windows sat at the southeast corner. "Come up," he urged. "You must see this."

With some grumbling and scraping, Mitra joined him. "Ah," he said. "Here is a panorama."

Sebastian kicked at one of the dry leaves scattered over the flagstones. "Here's a hiding place," he replied. "It doesn't look like anyone comes up here. And no dog can get through that trapdoor if you close it." He grinned at the other man. "I'll help you bring up a chair, if you like. You can sit here with your books." His fellow guest was always reading some hefty tome or other. "Outdoors, but safe from attack," he pointed out. "Under roof if it's wet." He indicated the small chamber at the edge.

All in all, it was a neat little refuge. It wouldn't do

in winter, of course, but this was August and likely to be tolerably warm. Sebastian had loved finding or creating this sort of secret nook when he was a boy. The landscape at Langford was dotted with refuges he and his brothers had carved out. He still rather liked it, he found.

"You are a most unusual young man, are you not?" said Mr. Mitra.

"Me?" Sebastian shrugged. "I'm a plain fellow, a soldier."

"To think of me in this way? And to offer your aid? I must disagree."

For several uncomfortable moments, Sebastian felt himself closely scrutinized. He'd always disliked such examinations, feeling that his many flaws would jump out to be recognized.

"No, indeed," said Mitra finally. "Not just a plain fellow. It is clear that you are much more than you realize at present."

What was clear about that? Sebastian turned away from his companion's piercing gaze. Feeling it still on his back, he walked over to the parapet and looked out over the garden. There was Georgina's mother, with a mob of dogs, striding through the shrubbery as if on a mission. Emma and Hilda came into sight around a corner of the castle, searching one path and then another. Here was a chance to find Georgina alone inside, Sebastian realized, if he could evade their pincer movement. He plotted a course through the greenery, then took the way down two steps at a time.

"Much more than you realize," murmured Mr. Mitra as he disappeared.

Sebastian hurried to the base of the tower and then carefully along his chosen route. It was easy to plot the position of the pugs; they were clearly audible. The younger Stanes were more elusive, and he had one close call, but he managed to make it inside without being detected. Safe behind walls, he headed for the castle's schoolroom. He'd observed that his intended often spent a few hours there in the mornings, with her sisters and Miss Byngham. It was a measure of her cleverness. She'd told him she never tired of learning.

He opened the door quietly and saw that his earlier reconnaissance had paid off. Georgina sat in a window seat at the back of the room, gazing pensively down at the garden. A shaft of sunlight penetrating the clouds illuminated her face and gilded her golden hair. In a simple gown of white muslin sprigged with tiny violet flowers, she looked delicately beautiful. She held a book, but she wasn't reading.

"Hullo," said Sebastian.

Georgina jumped. The book hit the floor with a thump.

"Sorry. Didn't mean to startle you."

She looked up at him, and up. His tall, masculine presence felt at once alien and…thrilling in this room where she'd spent much of her girlhood. He'd entered it as he'd entered her life, an unexpectedly exciting alteration. She'd been thinking of those broad shoulders and strong arms, of how it had felt when he lifted her off his knees. To be shifted as if she weighed less than a feather had been beguiling. But she'd been so bitterly disappointed that his hands had stopped their tantalizing progress into places that were responding now at the mere memory. Georgina flushed and stood up.

"Schoolrooms are all alike, aren't they?" said Sebastian. "The one at Langford is just the same."

She looked around. The long chamber was furnished with cast-off furniture, mismatched but comfortable and well able to bear rough treatment by boisterous children. A large table in the center served for study and projects. Shelves held a variety of volumes, from picture books to scientific guides, along with bits and pieces collected by Stane offspring over the years. The draperies were a bit faded. Nervous, she spun the great globe that sat on the floor beside her. For some reason, this made Sebastian flinch.

"Did you want something?" she asked, and flushed more deeply at the answering flare in his blue eyes. Something deep within her recognized it and leaped to fiery life.

"A few minutes of conversation with my betrothed," he replied.

"About what?"

"Doesn't matter. Just getting better acquainted, eh?"

He didn't look satisfied with this remark, and Georgina couldn't summon up an answer because the air seemed to have thickened around her. It couldn't have; that wasn't possible. But she was finding it hard to catch her breath. Silence fell over the room. Every detail of Sebastian's handsome figure called to her—his sharp cheekbones, his dashing side-whiskers bracketing sensuous lips, his thighs in tight buckskin riding breeches. She had sat just there, across them.

"Don't worry," he said. "I won't go beyond the line. Again."

Georgina hadn't known she could ache like this for a touch.

"What...what...were you...reading?"

He spoke as if he had to remember each word from a foreign language. Georgina followed his gaze to the book at her feet. She had no idea. And she didn't care. She wanted only one thing, and just at this moment, she couldn't think of one reason to resist her desires. She took a step, and another. Reaching Sebastian, she slipped her arms around him under his coat. She pressed against him—bodice, hips. She rested her head against his chest. The speed of his heartbeat under her ear reflected the pounding of hers.

He returned her embrace. For a long, delicious moment, he held her. Then one of his hands drifted up, brushing her cheek, gently raising her chin so that he could capture her mouth in a soft kiss. Soft, and then exploratory, and then searing. How could lips communicate so many nuances of emotion? How could their touch send bolts of sensation through her body?

She arched closer. One of Sebastian's knees slipped between hers as he pulled her tighter against him. Georgina felt as if she was melting. If he hadn't been supporting her, she couldn't have stood upright.

Her back came up against a hard surface. The door. They'd moved somehow. She leaned against it as Sebastian kissed her neck, her shoulder, and then took her mouth once more. She answered him, more practiced already. The kiss went on and on, incendiary. His knee pressed deliciously closer. Georgina shifted, willing it to reach the ache that consumed her. And then, as if they knew better than she how to manage the thing, her legs came up and laced around Sebastian in a second embrace.

He made a strangled sound. His hands gripped her bottom, holding her there. Buckskin rasped against sheer muslin. Georgina lost all sense of anything but the exquisite feel of that friction. It built as Sebastian pressed closer, rising unbearably until a great wave of release burst through her. "Oh," she cried. He caught the sound with his lips, kissed her as it shook her to the core. She clung to him, riding the delight from crest to ebb.

Supported by strong arms, slowly, Georgina relaxed. Her breath slowed. Limp, sated, she rested her head on Sebastian's shoulder.

He groaned. Then he carried her over to the old brown sofa and set her gently down there, skirts tumbled, face flushed.

Georgina leaned back. A country upbringing had shown her a bit about mating. She could see clear evidence of Sebastian's unsated arousal. "I should do something for you," she said. She had some ideas on that score. She reached up.

"Georgina?" called a voice from outside the room. Of course it was Hilda, with her genius for the inopportune moment.

The door handle rattled.

Rigid, Sebastian stepped away from her. She saw him grit his teeth as she straightened her dress. His face seemed full of longing.

"There you are," said Hilda as she stepped into

the schoolroom. "We've been looking everywhere." Emma followed her in. The two girls hesitated as if they sensed the tension weighting the atmosphere. "What's going on?" Hilda asked.

Georgina spoke quickly to save her fiancé from their curious stares. "We were just talking." Her gown was terribly crumpled, she realized. Her sisters were only too likely to notice.

"Must go," muttered Sebastian, his voice uncharacteristically thick.

"But we wanted to ask you…" began Emma.

"Not now," said Georgina as he stalked through the door.

"Did you do something to offend him?" asked Hilda. She shot Georgina a reproachful glance.

Georgina couldn't help herself. She burst out laughing.

Five

He would not go mad, Lord Sebastian Gresham thought as he joined the Stanes and their guests in the castle's great hall the following evening, awaiting the signal to go in to dinner. Even though he was closer to Georgina than he'd managed to get since their encounter in the schoolroom, even though her nearness affected him like a match to a powder keg. She was talking to one of the visiting neighbors, but Sebastian felt no envy of that. He didn't want to *talk* to her. Not at first, anyway.

He wanted to take up where they'd left off, but in the privacy of one of the castle's many bedchambers this time. Without the vast annoyance of clothing. He yearned to quench the desire that burned in him night and day. But though he could enjoy the fantasy of tossing her over his shoulder and carrying her up to bed, he couldn't actually do it. Such conduct was beyond the line for an honorable man. An army officer and a gentleman. He hadn't gone beyond the line. *She* had. Sebastian felt as if his blood was sizzling in his veins at the memory.

Georgina looked exquisite in an evening dress of pale-green gauze, a chaste flower in her hair. Had there ever been such a delectable combination of innocence and passion? She was a girl experiencing the realities of love for the first time. He knew that from the tentative nature of her kisses. But she had the enthusiastic instincts of…of a woman who would make him the luckiest man in the world. Soon. If he could just get the dashed knot tied and have her to himself.

The marquess, in conventional evening dress rather than his usual garb, brought an older man up to Sebastian. Time for introductions; time to do his duty. "My daughter's intended," said his host with customary informality. "This is Crowther. One of our neighbors, lives over near Hereford."

The white-haired, upright newcomer did not look pleased at this abbreviated presentation. His pale-blue eyes glinted, and his prominent jaw tightened. "Langford's son, eh?" he said.

Sebastian was used to this question. One day, he hoped to have a personal history that outweighed his status as the duke's son. But that day was not yet. "Yes, sir," he replied. "Very pleased to meet you." He offered a respectful bow and a smile to make up for the marquess's careless social style.

It had the desired effect. Crowther's expression eased. He summoned a plump raven-haired woman with a discreet gesture. "My wife, Baroness Crowther," he said, supplying information that Georgina's father had neglected. "That's my son Wyatt talking to our hostess, and his wife, Elaine."

The trio appeared to share an interest in dogs,

Sebastian noted. All three were bent over Drustan, who wriggled in delight at the attention.

"Here's Sir Robert Kenton," said the marquess, coming up behind them with a brown-haired, heavy-set man about his own age. "Has a place south of us. That's his son Charles hanging about Georgina. Too late, eh!" He laughed and clapped Sir Robert on the shoulder, an attention that was clearly not appreciated. "And his daughters Sarah and Eliza are over there conspiring with Emma."

"A pleasure to meet you," Sebastian said, with another bow and winning smile.

Hilda was not present. She was too young for an official party, and without doubt she was furious at the exclusion. Miss Byngham, also absent, had probably been delegated to ride herd on her. Sebastian wished her joy of that thankless task. He'd learned that Emma, on the other hand, was older than he'd realized—nearly seventeen, in fact—and champing at the bit to be officially out.

Anat Mitra entered, a picture of dark elegance in another of his long brocade tunics—this one glinting blue and silver—over narrow trousers. Conversation skipped a beat as he paused in the doorway. "My friend Mr. Mitra," the marquess boomed out. "A scholar from India."

In the subsequent chorus of acknowledgments, Sebastian eased over toward Georgina.

As if by mistake, Charles Kenton stepped in front of him, blocking his way. "Oh," the younger man said with an unconvincing start, "I didn't see you there. Georgie and I were just reminiscing." His laugh was too loud. "We are old acquaintances, you see. Practically cradle friends."

Sebastian examined him. Kenton had brown hair and eyes. He was shorter, narrower, and plainer than Sebastian, and clearly feeling every one of these things as a cruel quirk of nature. "Georgie," Sebastian said.

"A pet name," Kenton said.

"No, it wasn't," replied Georgina. "I was continually telling you that I didn't like it at all."

"Indeed, we were married once," Charles went on, as if he hadn't heard. He shifted from foot to foot, ready to lunge should Sebastian make a flanking move. "Under the arbor in the rose garden."

Sebastian might have been jealous, but it was obvious that Georgina didn't recall any such incident. Still, Charles Kenton was standing too close to her and clearly determined to keep Sebastian from approaching. Sebastian loomed a little. "Were you?"

"Solemnly." Charles stuck out his chest like a gamecock. "Edgar played the preacher. We were so very close in those days." He threw Georgina a languishing look.

"Oh, yes," she said. "I remember now. Fifteen years ago, wasn't it? I was attended by Drustan's grandparents. They, er, anointed the rosebushes during the ceremony."

Sebastian smiled at the picture, while vowing to ban the pugs from his wedding, if he possibly could.

"And perhaps one of your boots?" Georgina added.

"No!" said Kenton. "One of the little devils tried, but I…uh…I stepped away."

Sebastian met Georgina's green eyes, saw the

amusement in them, and released any lingering wisps of concern he might have felt.

"I've met your brother," the other man said, more belligerent now. "In London. During the season."

"Which brother was that?" asked Sebastian.

"Robert."

Robert was certainly easy to meet in town. He was invited everywhere.

"He's said to be a leader of fashion," the visitor told Georgina, as if she didn't know this very well from her own stay in the metropolis. "I couldn't really see it myself. Rather puffed up with his own consequence, though." He offered Georgina a conspiratorial glance. It was not returned.

This was going too far. Sebastian was a tolerant sort, and he sympathized with a man who admired Georgina. How could you not? But he didn't allow anyone to belittle his brothers in his hearing. He fixed Charles Kenton with a gaze his family jokingly called "the duke's doom." It was a look they'd all learned from observing their father in situations that required him to depress odious pretensions, wither malicious gossips, or ward off irritating toadies. Sebastian deployed the half-lowered eyelids, slightly raised brows, implacable set of lips, and stretching silence. As always, the expression did its job. Kenton coughed. "That is," he began, and stopped. He took a step backward.

Sebastian stood fast. The three of them formed a noiseless pool within a ring of chatter.

"Er, think my sister wants me," muttered Charles Kenton finally. He hurried across the room to join the young ladies.

"Your father's freezing stare," Georgina said.

Of course she'd made the connection. She was clever as they came. It would have been her most striking quality, if not for more...physical charms. Sebastian nearly reached for her as he matched her smile. "I'm not the best at it," he said. He and his brothers had staged staring contests. "Robert is. If he'd been here to hear that fellow..." Sebastian shook his head. "Nathaniel can beat him out if he really tries, but mostly he doesn't. Randolph tends to add flourishes, and he's more likely to be looking for the story behind the affront." However, Sebastian had seen him annihilate a fellow who'd been unkind to a little girl in prime style.

"What about James and Alan?" Georgina asked.

"I expect they remember it. Of course, I've hardly seen James since he joined the navy." Unable to resist, he took her hand. "Georgina, I'm..."

She gazed up at him with what looked like longing, but to Sebastian's intense frustration, Fergus appeared in the archway right then and nodded to Georgina's mother.

"Shall we go in to dinner?" the latter said, and led the way to the dining room. As she took no one's arm, the rest of the group merely followed her en masse. There was no further opportunity for talk.

Sebastian found himself seated between Sarah and Eliza Kenton at the table, while his wishful rival visibly gloated at being placed between Georgina and Emma on the other side.

With a blithe disregard for protocol, their hostess had seated the baron's son and his wife on her right and left. Clearly, she intended to continue their conversation and etiquette be damned. She had put the baroness and Lady Robert on either side of her husband, and then dropped the baron by Lady Kenton and Sir Robert by the baroness. The men looked disgruntled but resigned at this eccentric placement, slightly brightened by the presence of a young lady in the next chair.

As the baron engaged Sarah in conversation, Sebastian turned to Eliza and smiled. The girl—barely out of the schoolroom, he estimated—flushed crimson and looked down at her plate. Shy, Sebastian thought, and not accustomed to society. Suppressing a sigh, and a forlorn wish that Georgina was beside him, he set himself to draw Eliza out.

It was heavy going at first. Questions designed to discover Eliza's interests were met by monosyllables or mere head shakes. He managed to learn that Eliza and her sister were to make a joint come-out next season, but she made no effort to pick up on his conversational gambits. Clearly, he scared her, Sebastian thought. He knew only one answer to that.

He'd noticed that it was difficult to be frightened of someone who confessed to some foolishness. He turned the subject to London. "The first time I was in town, I was thrown from my horse right in the middle of Rotten Row," he told her. "Just when all the most fashionable people were out riding." He didn't mention that he'd been only ten years old at the time.

His dinner partner gave him a sidelong glance. "You were not."

"I assure you I was." And the fall *had* been quite

humiliating for an aspiring cavalryman. He'd gotten no sympathy from his parents. They'd warned him not to take a mount like Blaze into the throng of the park. "The town beaus had to pull up pretty sharp to keep from trampling me into the dust."

Eliza finally met his eyes. "I've started having wretched dreams about London," she confided. "I'm at a ball in a ragged old gown. Or I trip and fall on my face in front of the queen at my presentation. And everyone laughs and points at me."

"They dashed well pointed at me," he replied.

She giggled.

"And then they forgot all about it in a few days," he assured her. "Another bit of gossip always comes along." Sebastian happened to glance across the table. He encountered Georgina's laughing eyes, and his heart skipped a beat at the warmth he saw there. It was like suddenly stepping from shade into brilliant sunshine. At her side, Charles Kenton glowered at him.

Dinner proceeded. Eliza, now at ease, chattered on about her hopes and fears for the season. Sebastian simply had to listen. His efforts were further compensated by a very good dinner. Whatever he might think about the marchioness's manners, he couldn't fault her cook.

And so he enjoyed his food, and talked with Eliza's sister when the table turned, and watched the ladies file out of the room sometime later with regret. He would much rather have gone with them than stayed with the decidedly mixed male cohort.

The port was brought out. The gentlemen gathered at the marquess's end of the board—all but Mitra, who excused himself with a regal bow. Sebastian thought it a wise choice. The sort of talks Mitra and his host conducted after dinner would not go over well with tonight's guests.

"That fellow doesn't care for a good port?" asked Sir Robert when Mitra was gone.

"He didn't have any of the beef either," the baron added.

"He doesn't eat meat," replied Georgina's father.

"What?" Sir Robert looked aghast.

"Not any sort?" said the baron's son Wyatt. "Chicken? Pheasant?"

The marquess shook his head. "No. It's against his religion."

There was a stunned silence. Charles Kenton reached for the decanter and refilled his quickly emptied glass.

"Ain't he a Hindoo?" said the baron then.

Georgina's father nodded.

"Well, what about the nabobs coming back from Hindoo country with their curries? They've got meat in them. Fellow served me a dish once that nearly burned my tongue out of my head. I'm sure it had mutton in it."

The marquess shrugged. "There are different varieties of Hinduism, just like with us and our sects. Mitra's forbids meat. He drinks a bit of wine on occasion. Says all things in balance, you know."

It was clear that Sir Robert did not know. Looking incredulous, he finished off the last drops in his glass and grasped the decanter. His son followed his lead.

"What's he doing here in England anyway?" asked the baron.

"He's consulting with me on my studies," replied Georgina's father. "He's been very helpful."

It was a more circumspect answer than Sebastian would have expected. He hadn't thought the marquess capable of tact.

Talk turned to agricultural prices and the eternal complaints of those who drew their incomes from the land. The baron and his son were stark pessimists about the future. Sir Robert seemed determined to drink as much port as humanly possible, and Charles was not far behind him. All too soon, Charles was propping his chin in his hands, elbows sprawled on the table. "Duke's sons," he said with quiet vitriol. "Get whatever you want. Cut the rest of us out without trying. It's not fair."

Sebastian was weary of the company, and Charles most of all. "That's not true," he said.

"Georgina never would have looked at you if you weren't one," the other hissed.

Sebastian thought of the determined campaign he'd waged to win his fiancée, how hard it had been to stand out in the mass of her suitors. Several of them had had noble titles, far above a second son, duke or no. Many had been cleverer, without doubt. No, this he'd accomplished on his own, with the aid of Ariel's good advice, of course. It was a personal triumph, nothing to do with his heritage. And the opinion of this unpleasant sprig mattered not a whit.

The object of Sebastian's ruminations sat upstairs in the drawing room with the rest of the ladies, seething with impatience. The other pugs had been brought in to join Drustan, and they surrounded her mother and Elaine Kenton like spreading brown skirts. The two picked up and examined one dog after another, deep in discussion. It seemed that Elaine aspired to breed a similar kind of dog. But not *just* the same, so there was no danger of rivalry.

The baroness and Lady Robert sat nearby, chatting about the high cost of hiring houses in London and the wickedness of town-bred servants. The three girls looked over sheet music at the pianoforte, perhaps plotting entertainments for later, when the gentlemen at last arrived.

Georgina could think of nothing but Sebastian. She watched the doorway like a cat at a mousehole, waiting for him to appear. The mere sight of him had become incendiary. And after his kindness to young Eliza Kenton at dinner, she liked him more than ever. It was such a potent combination—admiration and physical passion.

"Do you not agree with me, Lady Georgina?" said the baroness.

Georgina turned to find the two older women looking expectantly at her. Should she admit she had no idea what they were asking? It was rude. "I'm not certain," she ventured.

"You've never had to manage a house full of servants," continued the baroness. "Wait until you do. You'll find that a season in London quite ruins good country workers."

"I haven't found that to be true," said Lady Robert. She spoke as if she'd been accused of some insensitivity.

"Well, perhaps with a much *smaller* staff…" began the other.

Lady Robert bridled, and it seemed as if a quarrel was in the offing when the gentlemen finally, finally came in. Georgina's pulse accelerated as Sebastian entered first. She scarcely noticed the baron, Wyatt, and her father behind him, talking, or Sir Robert and Charles straggling at the end of the group, clearly the worse for drink.

Emma, seated at the pianoforte in anticipation of this addition to their company, began playing at once.

Charles Kenton hurried over and took the seat beside Georgina, the one she'd been saving for Sebastian. He really was too irritating. It was true they had sometimes played together as children, but they'd hardly seen each other since. And as she recalled, he hadn't been particularly interested in her, or kind, in those long-ago days. Last season, in town, they'd danced together a few times, but she'd understood he was devoted to another young lady entirely. He leaned too close, and she was treated to a strong whiff of port. "How is Miss Winstanley?" she asked, sitting back in her chair.

Charles snorted indelicately. "Engaged to Torrington," he said. "She went for the title, as you ninnyhammers all do."

This was not only insulting, it was untrue, if it was aimed at her. She had not "gone for" a title. She very well could have. A belted earl had offered for her. But if she'd cared for that, she wouldn't have Sebastian now, which had become unthinkable.

Charles leaned closer and actually put a hand on

her arm. "Not too late to change your mind, you know." His wine-laden breath was hot on her cheek. His fingers moved on her skin. "I may not be a dashed duke's son, but I could show you…"

Suppressing a stinging retort, Georgina slipped free and stood. "Excuse me," she said. Furious, she walked over to the pianoforte and pretended to listen to her sister's performance.

Sebastian was at her side at once, a bulwark. "What's wrong?" he asked. Before she could answer, he said, "Kenton. Shall I haul him out by the scruff of his neck and thrash him?"

The picture made Georgina choke on a giggle. And with that, her mind cleared. Charles Kenton was nothing, an idiot who'd had too much wine and would be very sorry for his behavior in the morning. The man next to her was everything Charles was not. And he was hers. She longed with all her heart to touch him.

As if he could read her thoughts, Sebastian guided her by subtle degrees over to a window embrasure. He pointed as if showing her something outside and drew her into the shelter of the draperies. "That's some constellation or other," he said. "Has a story attached. Greek, I think. I forget the details."

Georgina laughed wholeheartedly this time. Then she turned and leaned against him. Sebastian slipped his arms around her and drew her tight. Heat raced through Georgina, head to toe, at the feel of his hands. She rested her cheek on his chest, listening to his heart pound. Her skin tingled; her breath quickened. This was the sort of feeling that made people throw scruples to the winds and do reckless things, she thought.

She checked over her shoulder. The curtains hid them, barely, from the rest of the party. She raised her head, laced her arms around his neck, and pulled him down to her. She wanted his kiss more than she'd ever wanted anything. Enflaming memories of the texture and tantalizing skill of his lips filled her.

"There you are." Charles Kenton swept the curtain back. He stood between them and the room, but it was obvious that the next moment would expose them. His glare was bloodshot and spiteful. "You must come play for us, Georgie." He stepped back as they moved apart. "We want Georgie to play, don't we?" he asked without looking at the others. His repetition of the rejected nickname was grating.

Georgina would cheerfully have hit him. Judging from Sebastian's expression, he was about to. "Emma is much more skilled than I am," she said. She moved out to stand between the two men.

"No, no, *you* must play." It seemed as if Kenton would grasp her arm, but an abrupt movement by Sebastian stopped him. He did not give up, however. "That ballad we loved so," he insisted.

"I don't know which you mean," replied Georgina coldly.

"'Forget Not Yet,'" said Charles through his teeth, naming a tune that had been wildly popular last season.

Everyone was looking at them with varying degrees of curiosity, disapproval, amusement. Eliza Kenton's mouth hung open. Suddenly, the whole scene seemed ridiculous to Georgina. A feeble, meaningless melodrama. She had to stifle a laugh. "I fear I have forgotten it."

"You have not…" Charles began.

"I know it," said Emma.

She started to play with great spirit, and Georgina decided she would never be annoyed with her sister again. She smiled up at Sebastian. The thunderous expression faded from his face. His blue eyes warmed. Their gaze held, saying all that needed to be said. And the recognition of their bond on Charles Kenton's face was all the revenge required.

Six

THE GAMES AND BOOKS SEBASTIAN HAD REQUESTED arrived, but they didn't have the desired effect. Emma and Hilda enjoyed the diversions, but they wanted the whole household to participate in their new pastimes. After an evening when they cajoled even Mr. Mitra into joining a raucous session of lottery tickets, Sebastian found himself much more in charity with them.

Flashes of resemblance to Georgina, in their looks and mannerisms, further endeared the two girls to him. Indeed, he thought he would like them very well if only they weren't around all the time. Their bright, inquisitive young faces continually came between him and his betrothed, and it seemed there was nothing to be done about it except wait for the wedding. If only he knew how to manage that without losing his wits.

And Nathaniel had sent nothing to keep off the dogs. His eldest brother had, in fact, been mildly sarcastic in his return letter, certain that his large, military brother could handle a few pugs. "He's thinking of one small, pampered creature lying in the lap of a dowager," Sebastian said to Sykes when he read this aloud. "He's never seen a moving carpet of the beasts. They egg each other on." His valet nodded; he'd had a few encounters with the resident canine mob by this time. Their affinity for leaping upon freshly ironed neckcloths irritated him intensely.

What was worse, the ringleader Drustan had developed a positive obsession with Sebastian. And as he was the dog most often let loose in the house, he was unavoidable. Sebastian wondered if this new persecution was due to Mr. Mitra's absence. The Stanes' Indian guest had followed Sebastian's advice and established a retreat at the top of the old stone tower, out of Drustan's reach. So if Georgina's mother *had* set the dog to persecute him, she was missing the mark.

On a sunny afternoon in August, as the pug followed him about the garden, Sebastian seriously considered dousing himself with vinegar after all. It might be worth offending the noses of his human companions if he could permanently repel Drustan. It wasn't as if he was getting close enough to Georgina for her to notice, he thought sullenly.

The dog's latest trick was to weave in and out under his feet, tripping him up and then yowling as if he'd been kicked each time Sebastian stumbled. His piteous cries had drawn Georgina's mother once already, and she hadn't seemed to find Sebastian's explanation persuasive.

Sebastian sat on a bench under the spreading branches of a great oak. Drustan rushed over to throw his front paws around Sebastian's boot and offer the leather his customary unwelcome attentions. "You are a thoroughly repellent dog," Sebastian said.

"He's spoiled," a feminine voice replied.

Sebastian looked up to find Emma standing on the pathway. Blushing, the girl kept her eyes well above ground level. "I brought you this," she said. "He hates it." She held out a tattered lump of fabric. "Mama told me you'd kicked Drustan, but I knew you never would have done so. And that he must be playing his tricks."

Sebastian gazed at the offered object. It was some sort of cloth animal, he decided. There were four stubby legs and an indeterminate head. It had clearly been chewed and battered over a long period of time.

Emma extended it further. "Show it to him," she urged.

Sebastian took the thing. It was a little bigger than his hand and meant to represent a rodent, he guessed. A rat? Feeling foolish, he pushed it toward Drustan's flat face. The intrusion broke the dog's obsessive concentration. Brown bulging eyes took in the gnawed snout, the hint of broken whiskers. Drustan gave a sharp yip. Then, whining, the dog backed off. Hardly daring to hope, Sebastian waved the stuffed animal at him. Drustan moved farther away, his pug face seeming anxious.

"Yah!" cried Sebastian, thrusting his newfound weapon forward. Drustan turned tail, literally, and fled. Sebastian gazed at the drooping toy in triumph. He'd feel like a fool carrying it about, but the cause was well worth the humiliation. He checked. Yes, it would just fit in his coat pocket.

"Drustan is a living example of the word *pugnacious*," Emma commented.

Sebastian turned to stare at her. "Pug…nacious," he repeated. "That's where it comes from." A link between a word and the world often came as a revelation to him. He noticed Drustan, crouched on his belly, peering out from a clump of long grass as if he hoped Sebastian had forgotten what he held. Sebastian shook the cloth rat at him. Whining again, Drustan actually took himself off. "Thank you for this," Sebastian said to Emma.

"I'm sorry I didn't think of it sooner. Mama keeps it shut away in a cupboard. It's been ages since any of us saw it."

"Why does he hate it so?" Sebastian turned the thing in his hands. It was ugly, but hardly frightening.

"No one knows," Emma told him. "He used to play with it all the time. Indeed, he would hardly let any of the other dogs touch it. And then one day he developed a horror of it. He's been that way ever since."

"Maybe he met a real rat and tried batting it about," Sebastian said. "A big one."

Emma looked surprised. "That could very well be it. How clever you are!"

It didn't seem clever to Sebastian. Merely common sense.

"Clever about what?" asked Hilda, slithering out of the bushes behind them.

Sebastian suppressed a start. Georgina's youngest sister was as stealthy as an army scout infiltrating enemy lines. She clearly had a network of unseen ways here in the garden. He hadn't been able to trace them, perhaps because of his larger size. But you could never be sure when she would suddenly appear.

Emma repeated the story of Drustan.

"It seems obvious when you say it," Hilda replied. "There's a family of water rats living down by the stream."

"There is?" replied her sister.

Hilda grinned at her. "Big ones!"

Emma looked around apprehensively.

"They don't come up the bank. Very often."

"How do you know?" asked Emma.

"I watch them sometimes." Hilda turned to Sebastian. "We should all go out riding," she said in a breezy non sequitur. "You haven't seen the waterfall west of here. It's very beautiful."

"It's more of a trickle at this season," answered Emma before Sebastian could respond. "I'm sure Sebastian has seen many finer sights."

"I doubt it," said Hilda. "And he likes to get out and roam."

She made him sound like a wild animal, Sebastian thought.

"It's going to be too warm today for a ride," objected Emma.

"Nonsense. And *Georgina* loves the waterfall."

The girls exchanged a combative look. Clearly, Hilda was hatching some conspiracy, and Emma didn't approve. But Sebastian didn't care. If Georgina was to be one of the riding party, he was all for it. Although her sisters were effective chaperones, it was still a chance to spend time with her, a thing that was confoundedly hard in this busy household. "Sounds like a fine idea to me."

"What if I refuse?" Emma said to her sister.

Sebastian didn't understand the defiance in her tone, and Hilda ignored it. "I'll go and tell Georgina," she said. She turned, then stopped short. "You should come with me," she said to Emma.

"Perhaps I want to stay here and talk to Sebastian."

"Perhaps Mama would like to know who misplaced her silver hairbrush," said Hilda.

Emma glared at her. For a moment they were like two cats contesting the same territory. Sebastian silently bet on Hilda to prevail, and he was proved right. After a bit, Emma slumped and walked away with her younger sister at her heels.

The marchioness proclaimed it too late in the day to begin an expedition, particularly since Georgina had promised to help her with some household chores. But the following morning Sebastian rode out with the three Stane sisters, his saddlebags laden with a rug and a picnic. Despite the sultriness of the summer day, everyone was in high spirits. Emma and Hilda seemed to have made up their quarrel, whatever it had been.

Hilda led them west, toward the Welsh hills, chattering about the features they passed, with a sprinkling of her father's historical knowledge. The other two Stane daughters chimed in now and then. Sebastian listened with one ear as he surveyed the country. It was a folded landscape. Narrow valleys filled with trees, often with the sound of water below, were punctuated by sharp ridges. It would be easy to hide a troop of men in those ravines, Sebastian thought, and dashed difficult to root them out. It was no wonder the Welsh Marches had been a contested border for so many centuries.

At last, they stopped near the top of a gentler rise. A faint trail up the side showed that others had come this way. "You should show Sebastian the view," Hilda said to Georgina. "You can see better from down there." She pointed at the crest before them.

Sebastian dismounted at once, eager for any chance of privacy. He stepped over to Georgina's horse, raising his hands to lift her down. When she met his gaze, heat washed over him, fiercer by far than the summer air.

"I'll hold the horses," Hilda said. "I've seen the waterfall a hundred times."

"I can show you—" began Emma.

"I need you to help me," Hilda commanded.

This was patently untrue, but to Sebastian's delight, no one said so. As Georgina slid from the saddle into his arms, he felt wholly in charity with young Hilda. Perhaps she'd finally understood the signals he constantly projected. Georgina smiled up at him, and he nearly kissed her then and there. Reluctantly, he let her go.

Looping the long skirts of her riding habit over one arm, Georgina led him over the top of the hill and down a little way, onto a stone lip projecting over a deep gully. Some yards away, at its head, a twisting fall of water cascaded over the edge into the green depths. "It's much larger in the spring," said Georgina. "But it's still pretty, I think."

"Beautiful," Sebastian replied, not looking at the water. With the sun glinting on her golden hair and the perfection of her form in the snug habit, she was the most beautiful creature he'd ever seen.

Georgina turned to him. When she raised her face to his, he saw all he desired in her eyes. He pulled her into the kiss he'd been longing for day and night.

The world receded. Sebastian was conscious only of hands and lips and the intoxicating scent of her. The more he knew Georgina, the more he wanted her. Her eager response made his pulse pound with exultation, and he lost himself in a dizzying whirl of desire.

He didn't notice the sound of horses' hooves until it had nearly died away. Absence more than presence alerted him. And then even the echo was gone.

Sebastian raised his head and listened to the silence. A breeze rustled the leaves; a bird called; the waterfall rushed in the background. All the signals he'd learned as a military man told him this was empty country. Puzzled, he released Georgina and strode back over the top of the ridge. Hilda, Emma, and all of their horses were gone.

"Where are they?" asked Georgina behind him.

"Perhaps Whitefoot bolted, and they rode off after him," said Sebastian doubtfully. "I don't see why he would though. He prefers my company, but he's well trained."

Georgina gazed at the empty ridges, the vacant path. "Damn Hilda!" She didn't care that her language made Sebastian stare. She couldn't believe her sister would have played such a trick. And at the same time she could. Hilda had been getting more and more impatient about the future. She wanted to leave Stane now, not in a few years when she had her London season. And she wanted promises from Georgina, assurances that she would be included in her elder sister's household. She seemed to think that Georgina could easily convince their parents to agree with this plan, if she would only try. Georgina had thought she was successfully fobbing her sister off, but it seemed she was wrong. Yet what did Hilda hope to accomplish by this piece of mischief?

"I suppose they'll come back in a bit," Sebastian said.

"I don't know." Georgina marched along the crest of the ridge to the path they'd ridden up. Riding boots were decidedly not made for walking, she thought as she peered down it. There was no trace of her sisters. "This is not funny," she muttered.

"What's this?" Sebastian said. He bent and picked up a cloth bag from the turf. Opening the drawstring, he looked inside. "Bread and cheese," he said. "And apples. Some kind of picnic?" He looked puzzled.

"You'll pay for this, Hilda," Georgina said as she tramped down the slope.

"Where are you going?" said Sebastian.

Too impatient to follow the long zigzags of the downhill trail, wanting something to fight, Georgina pushed through a thick line of bushes. Between one step and the next, the ground fell away beneath her, and she plummeted into an unseen crease in the earth. Twigs and brambles scraped her hands and arms as she flailed for purchase. The earth was damp and slippery, the slope nearly vertical.

She bounced and slid, cracked her head on a protruding stone, suffered a deep scratch on the back of one hand, and finally came to rest precariously with one foot wedged into a vee of branches above her head, the other dangling free, her shoulders barely supported by a tiny ledge. There was still vacant space below; she couldn't see how much. She reached up to try to free her leg, and slipped a little, pulled by the weight of her long skirts. If her perch gave way, she feared her trapped leg would crack. Searching for well-rooted plants, she gripped a bush in each hand and held tight.

"Georgina!" shouted Sebastian from above. Not for the first time.

"I'm all right," she called. "Or…not quite." *Stupid, stupid*, she thought. Why hadn't she looked where she was going? And where had this wretched ravine come from? She'd ridden by here a hundred times and never noticed it. Peering up in the dimness, she saw that it was completely overgrown. It was also only about six feet wide at her level. Impossible to see from the top. Her shoulders slipped again. A lance of pain shot through her leg. She couldn't help but cry out.

"Georgina!" shouted Sebastian again.

"I've hurt my leg," she told him. "And I'm wedged in. I can't move."

"Don't try," he replied. "I'll come for you."

He said it with utter conviction, as if it was the most natural thing in the world, unquestionable. And Georgina understood in that moment that he would always come for her if she was in trouble. Full bore. Without hesitation. She had to blink back tears. She hadn't known when she accepted him what a stalwart man he was. She hadn't understood her own good fortune.

A shaft of light lanced down as bushes were ripped away above. It widened, and then she could see Sebastian peering down at her. He looked intent and capable and perfectly confident. "I'll climb further up so I don't jostle you loose," he said, and disappeared.

A moment later, she heard branches creak and snap. A loud crack and protracted slide elicited a curse. "Are you all right?" she called.

"Perfectly," he replied, a little breathless.

There was a good deal more crashing, the noise of a large creature forcing his way through heavy undergrowth. Then Sebastian emerged from the gloom not far away. Fortunately, it seemed that the bottom of the gully was just a few feet below. His head was nearly even with hers when he squelched through the mud toward her.

He took in her position with one evaluating glance. Stepping close, he leaned against the earthen wall and set his shoulder under hers. It was like a bulwark. The sense that she might fall at any moment and break her leg disappeared. Georgina relaxed against that solid support. Their cheeks brushed. His breath warmed her skin. If she'd been less uncomfortable she would have turned her head and kissed him.

Sebastian reached for her trapped foot.

Georgina repressed a groan as he grasped her leg and tried to work it free from the crossed branches. It was tightly wedged by the weight of her body. Every movement hurt.

"I'm going to lift you a little," he said. He pushed one arm between her and the ravine wall and held her with it as he pushed upward with his shoulder.

Georgina couldn't hold back a groan as the movement pulled at her leg.

"Sorry," he said. "I'm afraid it's going to hurt a bit more now." With his free hand he shifted her trapped limb. "Can you bend your knee?"

Jaw clenched against the pain, she did so. He guided her leg out of the trap.

"There we are." He eased her down until he held her. "Sorry," he said again.

Georgina rested her head on his chest. "Don't be silly. You've saved me from the consequences of my own carelessness."

Despite the unfortunate situation, Sebastian enjoyed the way she nestled trustfully against him. He reveled in the feel of her body in his arms, the tumble of golden hair against his coat. Then she moved, and he saw the bloody scratch on her hand. He had to get her to safety. He surveyed the terrain—upward, from side to side. "I can't carry you up this wall," he said. The climb down had been more a series of slides and grabs. "I suppose we'll have to wait here until your sisters come back." He chafed at the inaction. Georgina's leg needed immediate care. "I still can't think what could have happened to them."

Minutes ticked by. Georgina rested in Sebastian's arms. Finally, though, she had to speak. "I'm not sure they'll be back anytime soon."

"What?" He gazed down at her.

"I believe Hilda is playing a prank."

Sebastian looked around at their constricted surroundings.

"She wouldn't have expected me to fall, of course,"

Georgina added. "I'm sure she didn't know about this gully either. But she may plan to leave us out overnight. The bag of food left here makes me think so." She noticed that he had the bag tied to his back by the strings.

"Why would she do such a thing?"

"Because she is incorrigible," exclaimed Georgina. "And to hurry things along."

"Things?"

"The wedding. She has this idea that all her problems will be solved once we are married."

Sebastian could sympathize with the idea, if not understand how it applied to Hilda. The feel of Georgina's body in his arms was rousing all sorts of inappropriate yearnings.

"It's outrageous."

That seemed to sum it up. More minutes dragged past. There was no sound of returning horses from above. Sebastian shouted anyway. To no avail.

"Do put me down," said Georgina. "You must be getting tired."

He was. And it was true that he couldn't hold her indefinitely. But he couldn't just set her down in the mud oozing around his feet.

"We'll try moving along and hope it opens up a bit," Sebastian said.

The gully was too narrow to walk straight down. He had to edge sideways, shoving through the tangled vegetation with the back of one shoulder, taking care not to bump Georgina's injured leg as he slithered onward. He didn't always succeed, and her stifled gasps of pain distressed him. How long could this crevice go on?

Quite a way, seemingly. The mud clung to his boots, weighing them down, making each step a greater effort. Twisted brambles caught at his coat and breeches. His arms began to burn. When no way out appeared, he tried to turn back. The declivity had grown so narrow that he barely managed to edge around. He pushed back the way they'd come, but the combination of snarled vegetation and an incline he hadn't noticed much going down defeated him. It was as if the brambles and twigs reached out and shoved him backward. There was no choice but to go on.

After another exhausting turn, he slogged forward. The tiny ravine twisted to the right, then left, the sides remaining nearly vertical. Sebastian pressed on, growing more and more tired as the minutes passed.

Just when he thought he'd have to take a rest, and had begun to search for a less muddy spot to set Georgina down, he broke through a heavy screen of branches into a more open spot. Here, the gully widened into a roughly circular area perhaps twenty feet across. The thick mud was interrupted by a pool of water, thickly edged by bracken. Staggering forward, Sebastian placed Georgina gently on a bed of moss near the wall. He put the bag of food beside her. Then he stood for a while panting, thoroughly winded.

"Can we get out from here?" asked Georgina. She gazed upward uneasily.

Sebastian shook his head. This slope was more difficult, not easier. It was undercut, as if some great hand had scooped inward at the bottom of the circle, forming a kind of dome in the rock. The shape made one think of raging flash floods. Thankfully, this was

not the season for heavy rain. They were not likely to
be swept away by a sudden rush of water.

The leaves were a bit thinner in the opening above,
lightening the green dimness. He stepped to the other
side of the space. Here, the ravine narrowed once
more, and the brambles closed in. He shoved a little
way onward. It seemed the same as what they'd already
traversed except for a towering pile of deadfall nearly
blocking the gully further on. This was probably the
cause of the circular space where Georgina rested.
Suppressing images of raging whirlpools, Sebastian
paused to scrape most of the heavy mud off his boots
with a split branch. Then he gathered a great armful of
dry wood and returned. It was chilly here deep below
ground level. He needed a fire to keep her warm. He
would have to explore further, but for now there was
no obvious escape.

He came back to face Georgina's anxious gaze. "So
far it looks the same ahead. I'll push on a ways in a bit.
We'll rest a while here first."

Quickly evaluating the small space, Sebastian found
a good place for his fire. He dropped the wood and
pulled some withered grass from under the stone over-
hang. Assembling a structure of tinder and twigs took
only a moment. He lit the grass with the flint and steel
he always kept in his pocket and made sure the wood
had begun to catch before lifting Georgina and placing
her between the flames and the wall. She would stay
dry here except in a torrential rain, and the arching
rock would reflect the heat of the fire. Nodding his
satisfaction at the arrangement, he looked up to find
her staring at him.

"How do you know just what to do?"

"Military training," he responded. "A soldier never knows when he might have to be self-sufficient." He'd added his own hands-on learning and experiences to the army's information. He enjoyed riding into wild country and using his own efforts to ensure survival.

"It's… You're amazing."

Though he was warmed by the admiration in her eyes, Sebastian had to shrug. It was all easy enough. Nothing like wading through a pile of books in a few days, as he had seen her do. "I should take a look at your leg," he replied.

Looking apprehensively down at her scuffed boot, Georgina nodded.

Self-consciousness descended as Sebastian pushed back the folds of her skirt and began to ease the boot off. "Sorry," he said when a groan escaped her.

"It's all right."

He had to tug, and he hated to hurt her. But if her foot and leg were swelling, it would only be worse later on. He took the last bit swiftly, to get it over, and there was her lovely leg revealed. Sebastian controlled his reactions. She was hurt. He was here to take care of her, to help her.

He didn't try to remove her silk stocking. To do that, he would have to venture into dangerous areas, and he could only stand so much. He took hold of her foot and gently probed the delicate bones. There was no break that he could discern. Same with her ankle. He let his hands move up the swell of her calf, his fingers careful and sure.

"Ow," said Georgina when he was midway to her knee.

He found swelling all around her leg there, but no break in the bones. Probably bad bruising and twisted muscles. "Just a strain, I think. Where those branches caught you. Hurts like the dev—a great deal, I imagine."

She nodded. "It feels better without the boot, though."

Sebastian continued his examination as far as her knee and found no more damage. His hands wanted to continue; he sternly forbade them.

Georgina nearly forgot the pain as she was flooded with memories of the way his fingers had gone further on a previous occasion. She was sorry when he let go.

Sebastian sat back. "Rest is the best thing for it. Anything else?"

There was a bump on her head, but it only hurt when she pressed it. "Just scratches." She held out her hand, exhibiting the deepest. Three lines of angry red ran from her wrist to her knuckles, ornamented by blotches of green from the vegetation. "It was the brambles, I think." It was nothing, really. But she couldn't resist being taken care of a bit more, since he took the task so seriously.

Sebastian took her hand and examined it. "Not deep. That's good." He pulled out his handkerchief and went over to kneel by the pool in the middle of the space.

When he didn't move for some moments, Georgina said, "What's wrong?"

"I want to see if there's a spring." After another interval, he nodded. "Yes, a tiny one." He wet the handkerchief. "That means the water runs through the rock. Which is good news as we'll have to drink it. At another season, it would be full of God knows what from upstream."

Returning to her side, he began to bathe the scratches with the wet cloth. The cool water was wonderfully soothing. Georgina watched his face—intent, assured, so handsome. It was clear he had no idea how incredible he was.

"There's a scratch on your forehead, too." He wiped the handkerchief gently across her face.

Alarmed, Georgina lifted her other hand to check.

"It's nothing," Sebastian assured her. "It'll heal up in a day or two."

Their eyes met from a distance of inches. Even in the dim light, his were so intensely blue. Firelight flickered orange on his skin. She would only have to lean a little forward, Georgina thought, and their lips would meet.

Tearing his gaze away, he drew back. He looked around as if seeking a change of subject. "There's some bracken," he said. "It makes a tolerable bed."

The last word seemed to hang in the air between them, like a signpost to uncharted realms. Georgina became acutely aware of her position, lying before him with her skirts hiked up, her leg bared, as if she was offering herself to him. Once in her head, the idea was riveting. They would certainly be here through the night.

Sebastian swallowed. "I'll fetch some," he added. Standing quickly, he shoved his wet handkerchief back in his pocket and moved away from her.

Georgina sat up. She ought to push her skirt down, she thought. Every tenet of her upbringing said so. Wasn't it interesting how all that training could go flying away in the presence of one certain man? She'd never felt such an urge around any other. But with Sebastian… She watched him bending, slicing through stems with his pocketknife, and straightening with an armload of bracken. Every movement of his tall figure was strong and sure. She wanted those exceedingly competent hands on her again. She wanted his kisses. She wanted what came after.

What would he think if she hiked her skirts a little higher, unfastened a button or two of the bodice that suddenly felt madly constricting? He turned toward her. Georgina caught her breath. Almost as much as she wanted those other things, she wanted him to think well of her. She pushed her skirts down.

Sebastian moved back and forth with piles of fronds, forming them into a pallet beside Georgina. He built up the fire and fetched more dry wood from the deadfall. They ate some bread and cheese. As darkness deepened, the circular space began to feel like a little room, illuminated by the flames reflecting off the stone walls.

Chores finished, Sebastian sat down on the other side of the fire. A fraught silence fell over them. Georgina was searching for something to say when she was distracted by rustling from the dark depths of the gully. It was pitch-black in that narrow crevice. Anything could creep up on them. "I don't suppose we need worry about bears or wolves," she said. "No, of course not. There aren't any large animals around here."

"And it would take an exceptional wolf to climb down those walls," replied Sebastian with a laugh.

"That is not funny," said Georgina, immediately imagining such a wolf.

"Sorry. You're right. There're no beasts like that in this part of the country. Foxes and badgers, perhaps. And I can certainly hold off a fox. Not so sure about a badger."

This time, she laughed.

"They're fierce creatures," Sebastian assured her. "My brother James tried to make friends with a badger kit once, and he was chased off by its mother and nearly mauled."

"This is not what I want to hear while sitting at the bottom of a crevice in the dark," Georgina informed him.

"Sorry. Of course it's not." He looked contrite. "Most animals are as reluctant to encounter you as you are them."

"What about the others?"

"What others?"

"You said 'most animals.' So the others…?"

"Oh, you mean the snakes and such?"

Georgina nearly jumped to her feet despite her injured leg. "Sebastian!"

"Only joking. It's too cold for snakes to be active."

Georgina crossed her arms over her chest. She'd never been able to overcome her strong dislike of snakes and spiders. "You might have said there weren't actually any snakes," she said with a shiver.

Sebastian pulled off his coat and held it out. "Here. You mustn't get chilled."

"I can't take your coat."

"Of course you can." He slid closer to put it around her.

Georgina leaned back into the circle of his arm as he settled the coat about her shoulders. His amazing competence and complete lack of fear were so comforting. She didn't want him to move back. She was filled with gratitude, as well as a spreading warmth, when he stayed. "I don't know what I'd do if you weren't here," she said.

"You'd manage. You're up to anything."

She could feel his voice rumbling in his chest where it rested against hers. She was touched by his confidence in her, no matter how misplaced. "No, if I'd been alone or with someone else…anyone else, I'd be so afraid now. With you, I'm not afraid at all."

Sebastian's heart swelled at the idea. He almost wished something would attack them, so that he could save her. Something not too dangerous and easily staved off, he amended quickly.

"You're like an ancient knight errant," said Georgina.

"A…what?" Sebastian looked down at her. It felt so natural to have her head resting on his shoulder. And at the same time so new and exciting. "Are you taking up your father's line now?"

"Maybe you were Lancelot in a past life," Georgina teased. "Or, no, not Lancelot. You're nothing like him. Gawain, perhaps. Brave and strong and noble and wise." Although a bit less nobility would be welcome, considering the way she felt right now. Anyway, these were fictional characters.

Sebastian frowned. "Wise? Me?"

"Terribly wise."

"You must be thinking of someone else. I'm a bit thick, really. It's you who…"

His self-deprecating puzzlement was so endearing that she kissed him.

For a startled instant, he was still. And then he was kissing her back in his thorough, intoxicating way. The one that seemed to melt her bones and set her on fire at the same time. Her body came alive, eagerly demanding more.

Georgina's hands slid up his shirtfront to twine around his neck and pull him closer. His free arm came round to hold her. Their kisses meandered from tender to blazing and back again until she ached with longing. His hand slipped along the line of her body, annoyingly blocked by the heavy cloth of her riding habit.

Georgina sank back onto the pile of bracken, pulling him down at her side. His leg slid between hers as if it had always belonged there. Twinges of pain from her injury were distant annoyances, overwhelmed by rising desire. She slipped her hands under his loosened shirttail and ran her fingers over the muscles shifting in his back.

Sebastian rose on one elbow, panting. He made as if to draw away. "Georgina. I can't hold back if we keep on like this."

She tugged him close again. "I don't want you to hold back."

The mixture of hope and caution on his face was almost funny. "Are you sure? Because…"

"Completely sure." As a mark of her certainty,

she began to unbutton the bodice of her riding habit. Clumsy with haste and the enticement of his smoldering gaze, she needed several agonizing moments to get free of it.

Sebastian simply pulled his shirt over his head, revealing his broad chest and arms sculpted by years of hard exercise.

Georgina unfastened the waist of her skirt and slithered out of it, kicking off her remaining boot in the process. Sebastian spread his discarded coat over the pile of bracken and pulled off his boots and breeches, pausing now and then to look at her as if checking for permission.

Georgina reached for him, reveling in the feel of skin to skin, pressing herself close. And then underthings were untangled and flung aside, leaving them totally exposed to each other in the flickering firelight. "How beautiful you are," she said.

"Me? You're the beautiful one," he replied. And then he moved with the grace of a tiger and the care of a man handling something infinitely precious, pulling her down onto the coat, skimming her sides with his fingertips. They lingered on her breast and teased as he kissed her even more urgently. Desire flashed along her nerves, utterly compelling.

Georgina tried to copy the sureness of his touches, but in the next instant, his fingers began a tantalizing progress up her inner thigh, caressing, pausing until she gave a murmur of protest, then slipping closer to the center of desire. When he at last reached it, in the midst of a melting kiss, she lost all sense of anything but his touch. She didn't know what she would have done if he'd stopped. But he didn't. He didn't tease any more. He answered the longing that carried her to the edge of taut endurance, and then broke like a cresting wave and swept her away.

Then he was above her, and inside her, and it hurt a little, but she was so loose and languorous that it wasn't much. The possessive delight she felt as she held him while he cried out in release was far greater. She'd never felt so close to anyone in her life as when he relaxed in her arms.

Together, their breath and pulses gradually slowed. Sebastian turned on his side, pulling her back close against his chest. He reached over to the jumble of discarded clothing and pulled the wide skirts of her riding habit over them like a coverlet.

Georgina felt incredibly cozy with the fire before her and Sebastian's warm body curled behind. Lost, outdoors, in a bramble-filled crevice, she was more content than she'd ever been in her life.

"Are you all right?" he asked.

"I am quite wonderful." He gave a little hum of approval, or perhaps pride. It made her smile. "And I'm absolutely going to love being married to you," she added.

"That's funny. I was thinking the same thing."

His breath stirred the curls near her ear. It tickled. "That I would love being married to you?" she asked.

"No," said Sebastian quickly. "The opposite."

"That I am *not* going to love being married to you?" Georgina teased.

"No! That I would, to you." He sounded frustrated.

"So, the same with shifting the pronouns, you mean?"

He didn't think he meant that, because he didn't understand it. But he was all too used to the slippery unreliability of words. "That I am the luckiest man in the world," he replied. He was on firm ground there.

"Oh, Sebastian," She turned in his embrace and kissed him with all her heart. And all else faded and was forgotten as they held each other close.

Seven

GEORGINA WOKE THE NEXT MORNING WITH A SENSATION of soft warmth at her back and cold, damp air on her face. She opened her eyes and saw the ashes of their fire, the small pool beyond, and the wall of the gully rising upward in dim green light. She was still lying under the skirt of her riding habit. For a young lady who had spent the night on the ground, naked and shelterless, she felt well. Better than well. She felt fine. Splendid, really.

Sebastian moved, and the welcome heat departed. She turned and found him gathering scattered clothing, preparing to dress. She watched him shamelessly as he put on yesterday's garments, rather the worse for a night on the damp earth.

"I'll make up the fire," he said without meeting her gaze. He sat and pulled on his boots. "Won't be a moment."

She watched him push through the vegetation at the far end of their refuge. When he'd disappeared into the undergrowth, she made discreet use of the space behind a bush that they'd designated for such purposes. She was back under the makeshift coverlet when he returned with a great armful of dry branches. He went about rekindling the fire with the same calm skill he'd shown the previous evening.

"There. You'll soon be warmer," he said when the flame caught.

Georgina examined the handsome lines of his face, admired his powerful forearms and the muscles moving under his rolled shirtsleeves. She felt no urge to leave her rustic bed. Indeed, she was wondering how to ask him to rejoin her in it when he spoke again.

"There's a great mass of deadfall just beyond the growth there," he said, pointing. "I'm pretty sure *I* could climb it."

The slight emphasis he put on the *I* told Georgina that the ascent wouldn't be easy. She flexed her injured leg. A lance of pain shot through it, making her gasp. She didn't think she could make a hard climb with this injury.

"I could go for help," he added. His tone was oddly diffident.

"We don't know where we are," Georgina objected. "And you don't know the country. It could take days for you to find someone on foot." She didn't want to wait that long alone in this desolate place. Its character would be entirely different without him.

"Or we could be close to a farm or cottage," he replied.

She couldn't dispute it.

"I thought of lighting a signal fire, but I'm worried about how this gully might funnel the smoke. It could swirl around in this opening and choke us."

"We won't do that then," Georgina said. It was a frightening prospect.

"No. I could climb to the top and see what's up there. Come back down if there's no sign of people."

It was a sensible plan, but she didn't like it at all. "Do we have to go right away?" As the words escaped her, Georgina realized that she didn't want their idyll to end just yet. Soon, yes. They couldn't live this way for any length of time. But she wanted him to herself for a little longer.

At last he looked into her eyes. Georgina thought she saw doubt there, and yearning. "The food we have won't last beyond this morning."

"I don't care," she replied. "Not yet." The last two words emerged as a plea more than an assurance. She held out her hand. He took it.

When she tugged him closer, green eyes warm with invitation, Sebastian released the scruples that had been plaguing him. He'd been afraid she might regret the step they'd taken. *He* didn't. But he wasn't a gently reared young lady who'd just spent her first night sleeping rough. That had been his second thought when he awoke—the first being to repeat the glorious lovemaking of the previous evening, with embellishments. Cursing second thoughts, he'd suppressed his arousal and seen to her comfort.

She pulled on his hand. "Come back to our… woodland bower."

He thrilled to see her in this wild place, where he knew what to do and was well able to do it. In a drawing room, with words flying about like showers of pebbles, he often had to hide how much he felt at a loss. Here, he was confident.

Her golden hair curled about her face, tousled. There must be hairpins scattered through the bracken, he thought. Her bare arm and shoulders emerged from the wrinkled folds of her riding habit like pale porcelain. Her fingers pressed his. Her lips parted.

He wouldn't have thought he could get riding boots off that quickly. He tore a button off his shirt. It followed the rest of his clothes into a heap as he joined her under the improvised cover once again.

"You hands are cold," Georgina said.

"Sorry." He started to draw them away.

She grasped his wrists and placed his hands between their bodies as she pressed close. "We'll soon warm them," she said, a laugh in her voice.

Indeed, the touch of her skin sent a flush of heat through him. He stared into her fathomless green eyes for the few seconds he could manage before he had to kiss her. Then their lips met, and rational thought departed.

She was right about his hands. The chill was gone in moments. He sent them wandering over her body, seeking the gasps and hums of pleasure that so gratified and enflamed him. He was sliding teasing fingertips along the soft skin of her inner thigh when she surprised him.

"Do you like to be touched there?" she murmured.

He groaned as she traced a delicious line up his member.

"Is that a yes?" She continued the caress. "Or a no?" She took her hand away.

"Yes!"

"Does it feel as good as when you touch me?"

"I expect so," he gasped.

He reciprocated her attentions, and they roamed together in the place beyond words, where Sebastian felt utterly at home. He knew the world of sighs and murmurs, bold intimacies, subtle caresses, sensation that crackled through your body like a lightning strike. His veins pulsed with exultation as well as release when she clutched him close and called his name as they reached the summit together.

They spent that day mainly in each other's arms, lazy and roused, passionate and sated, kept warm by the fire and their lovemaking. They drank water from the pool and felt no ill effects. They talked of childhood adventures in the country and thoughts for their future life. They closed their minds to demands from the outer world and the concerns of people there.

Sometime in the afternoon, it occurred to Sebastian that this was their honeymoon, much more than the journey planned for after the wedding. Here in this rustic nook, sharing their first solitude, they were more wholly together than they might ever be again. And how some of his brothers would laugh at him for thinking so. He could see Robert's satirical expression, Alan's amused disbelief. So he said nothing aloud, for fear Georgina might think the idea foolish, too.

At nightfall, they slept interlaced. But when light began to filter down from the ceiling of leaves on the second morning, Sebastian faced grim necessity. Their food supplies were gone; they had only the water from the spring. And Georgina's family must be frantic by this time. "I have to try to get out today," he said as they huddled close against the early chill.

"I know."

They gazed at each other across a few inches, silently acknowledging sadness at the end of their idyll and a readiness to be back in civilization.

Both emotions turned out to be premature. Sebastian didn't make it up the deadfall. When he attempted the climb, a log slipped under his weight, and the whole crisscrossed mass collapsed under him. If he hadn't been able to catch a protruding tree root as he fell, he might well have been killed. As it was, he sustained a stunning blow to his upper arm and only just managed to keep his grip as the mass of branches tumbled to the bottom of the gully. He scrabbled about with his feet until he found a bit of support in the wall, and then hung for a while gasping in pain. He'd never had a closer shave off a battlefield. His heart was pounding so hard he felt dizzy.

Georgina's anxious calls revived him. "I'm all right," he shouted back, willing it to be true. When he could move, he slid carefully down the earthen wall, leaning there a little longer after his boots touched the ground. Making his way back to their refuge, he collapsed by the fire.

"Are you all right?" Georgina asked, throwing her arms around him as if to verify his presence. "What happened? There was such a noise. I was terrified."

"The deadfall gave way," he answered. "Fell. I have to rest." He decided that lying down was a good idea.

"Where are you hurt?"

"Arm." He raised it an inch or so and let it drop.

Georgina gently pushed up his shirtsleeve and found a great bruise already forming on his bicep.

"It's not broken," Sebastian said. "I can move it." He flexed his arm. "Ow."

"Do not move it," she commanded.

"We're a pair," he said. "With your leg and my arm, I don't see how we'll ever get out of this hole."

"My leg is better. You will rest, and then we will try."

On the third morning, they did so. After the painful process of working Georgina's boot over her injured leg, Sebastian held her with his good arm and helped her navigate the treacherous, muddy floor of the ravine. The crash of the deadfall had left an opening just large enough to duck through, which they did with great care so as not to dislodge the pile any further.

Progress was agonizingly slow through the thick growth. After a while, Sebastian moved ahead to force an opening in the vines and branches. Georgina then limped through behind him. They had to spend a further night below ground level, very uncomfortable with no fire possible and no inclination to lie down in the mud.

It was afternoon when they at last came to a place where they could struggle out of the gully. Sebastian half carried, half supported Georgina up a lesser slope, stopping every few feet to untangle the brambles that caught at her skirts.

At last they emerged, exhausted, in a woods where huge trees blocked the light. There was much less undergrowth, and it was comparatively easy to walk away from the crevice that had imprisoned them for so long. "Do you recognize this place?" Sebastian asked.

Georgina shook her head. "It just looks like a forest." She sank down to sit on the ground. "We're covered with mud," she observed. She would *not* cry, she told herself fiercely. It was just that she was so sore and tired. And dirty. And thirsty. Very thirsty. And hungry. All joy had gone out of this venture during the last day of forcing herself through wet, prickly, unyielding vegetation. Her leg ached. So did her head. She saw that Sebastian was examining her anxiously, and tried to give him a smile. It was another challenge not to complain.

"I'll find the way," he said. He walked back toward the gully and checked the angle of the sunlight piercing the leaf canopy. Holding up his good arm, he sighted along it. "I think the gully runs northwest. There were some twists and turns, but that seems to be the general direction."

"I expect we're in Wales then. The waterfall is near the border."

He nodded. "Since there's no one about, I think the best thing is to walk back along it. We follow the ravine to where we went in, where they'll be searching for us. There may be people closer, but we can't know."

"Right." Georgina struggled back to her feet. She took a step and suppressed a wince. Her leg was better, but it still hurt when she put weight on it. Well, at least the pain distracted her from her grimy clothes, stinging scratches, and dry mouth.

"I'll carry you."

"No, you won't. It's much too far. I can walk."

"Georgina."

"I can walk if you help me," she amended.

And so they started out, with Sebastian's uninjured arm once more around her waist, taking most of her weight, keeping the declivity that marked the ravine on their right.

They couldn't go very fast. On top of their hurts, riding boots were not comfortable for long hikes. And it soon became hard to see just where the gully was. The ground leveled, and the undergrowth thickened until they could scarcely see beyond the next tree. When another evening began to close in, they were still surrounded by woods. And lost.

"It has to be Wales," Georgina said. "There's not so much forest anywhere else around Stane."

"We'll head east then, tomorrow." Sebastian had just returned from looking for the ravine, and had been unable to locate it in the failing light. It had veered away from them at some unknown point under cover of vegetation. "I'll make a fire."

"Can't you gather wild plants and snare a rabbit and make a savory hunter's stew?" Georgina asked, only half teasing. She was hungry enough to eat almost anything. They'd found a stream on their trek and gotten a drink, but the relief of water had merely sharpened her appetite.

"I was reared as a hunter, not a poacher," Sebastian responded with a short laugh. "I might be able to set a snare if I had some string or wire, but I've never caught any game that way. If we had a gun…"

"I shall take one whenever I ride out from now on," she declared.

Sebastian built a fire. He found a trickle of a spring that gave them another much-needed drink. They settled back against the trunk of a huge oak and watched the flames leap.

"My parents must be frantic," Georgina said. "They will have sent the whole household out to search for us." She wondered what Hilda had told them. Her sister would have had some wild story ready, but it wouldn't have held up this long.

"Sykes will be out looking, too," said Sebastian. "My valet," he explained when Georgina looked puzzled. "And up to anything." *As was Georgina*, he thought. How many women would have endured this slog across country without complaining or turning shrewish? She was a marvel. And she looked exhausted. He really had to get her home. He frowned. "I still don't see why we weren't found right away." They had wondered over this repeatedly. "It's all very odd."

"Yes." She looked at his profile in the firelight. What would she have done without him? "Though I'm not sorry it wasn't *right away*."

He turned to look at her. She saw the memories of their lovemaking in his blue eyes as he folded her hand tenderly in his. Too tired and battered to do more, they fell asleep side by side, sitting up, cradled by the trunk of the ancient tree.

The next day, they walked on eastward. In the afternoon, the forest finally began to thin as the ground rose.

"Is that Offa's Dyke?" Georgina asked a little while later.

"It's hard to tell one ridge from another," Sebastian replied.

"Don't let my father hear you say so. I think it is. Look, it goes on along that line." She pointed.

After a moment Sebastian saw what she meant. "I think you're right. If we only knew where we were along it, we could find our way straight back to the castle. But finding it is a step in the right direction."

"So to speak," Georgina joked.

He just glanced at her.

"The right direction… Never mind." Georgina had noticed that her betrothed wasn't quick with plays on words. This one had been silly anyway.

They struggled up the Dyke and over it to continue moving east. The light was starting to fade when Sebastian heard a sound in the distance and stopped. Georgina stumbled a little at the sudden halt. "Listen," he said. He strained his ears. He was nearly sure he heard something. "Over here!" he shouted at the top of his lungs, making Georgina jump. He waited. This time he was certain he heard a response.

They endured a tense time of inarticulate words flung back and forth, and then Sykes appeared in the gloaming, riding a dun horse and leading Whitefoot and Georgina's mount.

"By God, I knew you'd come looking," said Sebastian. "And a welcome sight you are, man."

"My lord," replied his valet, dismounting. "I must say the same. I'm very glad to find you. I knew you could not have eloped. I never believed it for a moment."

Eight

SEBASTIAN AND GEORGINA GAPED AT SYKES'S TALL, thin figure. Even in the midst of a wilderness search he looked impeccably groomed, his dark clothing without a speck of dust.

"Did you say *eloped*?" Sebastian asked. He couldn't have heard that right. Yet he was pretty certain he hadn't lost his wits, despite his dragging fatigue and gnawing hunger.

"The young lady said so, but I was convinced she had to be mistaken." Sykes might have been standing in Sebastian's bedchamber, discussing a choice of waistcoats. But their years of association allowed Sebastian to spot real concern in his valet's shrewd brown eyes.

"What young lady?" said Georgina. "No, never mind. Of course it was Hilda."

"Yes, my lady."

"I'll kill her."

Sebastian frowned, puzzled. "Perhaps Whitefoot did run off, and she thought…" But how Georgina's sister could have gotten from a runaway horse to an elopement defeated him. It simply made no sense.

Sykes gave a discreet cough. "I found Whitefoot and her ladyship's mount in a farmer's barn not too far from where you were last seen," he told them.

"Evans, I'll wager," said Georgina through a clenched jaw.

"That was the name," Sykes agreed.

"So the horses ran off to the nearest shelter," Sebastian guessed.

"Oh, I wager they were taken there," Georgina said. Beneath the dirt, her face looked grim.

"As to that, the farmer's son would not give me any information," the valet replied. "He claimed that he'd been, er, sworn to secrecy."

"You've gone too far this time, Hilda," said Georgina. She closed her hands into dirt-streaked fists. "I'll have her shut in the dungeons."

Sykes blinked. This interesting threat shook him a little out of his role as the perfect servitor. "Are there dungeons at the castle?"

"They're mostly bricked up. But I shall persuade Papa to reopen one." Her teeth flashed white in the growing gloom. It was more a snarl than a smile.

"But why would she say such a thing?" Sebastian wondered.

"*Why* is the least of it! How did she dare?"

Even in his current state, Sebastian could admire the crackle of her anger. He didn't envy young Hilda. Although, from what he'd seen, he expected she could hold her own.

"Shall we return to the castle?" Sykes suggested. "Your parents have been quite…concerned, my lady."

Georgina barked a laugh at this. "I'm surprised

we didn't hear the shouting from the bottom of the ravine. Yes, let us go. The sooner this is straightened out, the better."

She strode over to her horse like a trooper heading into battle. Despite, or perhaps because of, the streaks of dirt and verdure on her habit and the wild disarray of her hair, Sebastian thought she looked magnificent. He helped her into the saddle and mounted up himself. After days of trudging through mud and tramping around woodlands in unsuitable boots, the ride back to Stane seemed almost magically easy. Sebastian recounted their misadventure to Sykes as they went, omitting, of course, the intimacies he and his betrothed had shared.

They rode directly to the stables when they reached the castle. Sebastian had a feeble hope that he might get some food and a bath before facing the family. But word of their return spread like lightning through the place. They'd hardly made it to the front door when Georgina's parents were upon them.

"Where the devil have you been?" roared the marquess in fine, old patriarchal style.

"Your clothes, your hair," Georgina's mother exclaimed. "You look like you've been dragged through the spinney backwards."

Georgina put a hand to her snarled tresses. For the first time, she looked distressed.

Sebastian couldn't have that. He stepped forward to shield her. "We had an accident at the prospect overlooking the waterfall."

"You call eloping with my daughter an accident?" growled his host, red-faced and furious.

"There's been some mistake about that, sir. We had no thought of an elopement. Nothing of the sort. Wouldn't dream of such a thing. It was…"

"Then where have you been for *four days*?" the marquess interrupted. "Four days, you blackguard, God knows where, alone with my daughter. Do you tell me you're not married?"

"I fell into a ravine," Georgina shouted. Volume seemed to be the only way to get her father's attention. "Sebastian saved my life!"

This was an exaggeration, but Sebastian let it go. It made a good impression.

"Ravine?" echoed the marquess, turning on her. "What ravine?"

"There's a narrow crevice near the place we always go to view the waterfall, Papa. I didn't know it was there either, until I blundered into it. It's masked with bushes and brambles." She held out her hand to show her scratches. "I injured my leg rather badly in the fall. I must sit down, Papa."

Sebastian noted that she exaggerated her limp as she went over to a chair and sank into it.

"You must be taken up to your room," said her mother, stepping forward. "I'll send for the doctor."

"And something to eat, Mama." Georgina gave her parents a tragic face. "We've had no food in all this time. We're starving."

This combined appeal temporarily ended the interrogation. Orders flew about. The marquess carried Georgina upstairs, having fiercely rejected Sebastian's offer to do so.

Twenty minutes later, the errant couple was settled

on separate chairs in the drawing room in quickly changed clothing, faces and hands washed, with trays of sandwiches before them. Only the master and mistress of Stane Castle were in attendance. Everyone else had been dismissed. Hilda had done her best to linger, Sebastian observed. He suspected she was even now listening at the keyhole, but he was too busy devouring the most delicious bread, mustard, and roast beef he'd ever tasted to care. He let Georgina tell their tale; she knew her parents best.

"And so we walked east," she ended after a time. "And Sebastian's valet discovered us not far past the Dyke." She frowned at her parents. "He seemed to be the only one out searching."

"Hilda said you'd eloped," replied her father defensively. "Fergus and I led a party up the north road. When we found no trace, we thought you were long gone to Gretna Green."

"More than two hundred miles? On horseback?" Georgina asked incredulously.

Her mother gestured at the marquess. "Alfred supposed you'd made arrangements." The look she gave him had an I-told-you-so air.

"Why, Papa? Why would you imagine we'd eloped? Why should we? We're getting married in a few weeks!"

"Hilda seemed so certain," he muttered.

"Hilda!" Georgina stared at her parents until they dropped their eyes.

"This does not change the fact that you were gone for days," said her father. "Out there, alone." He gestured at the window. "Very compromising situation."

"We're getting married, Papa." One of Georgina's hands reached out, as if of its own accord, and took Sebastian's. He squeezed it reassuringly. "No one need know about this," she added. "We're far from the London gossips here."

"I fear it won't be quite so easy," answered her mother. Her tone was regretful and somehow smug at the same time.

"Why not?" asked Georgina. She looked from one parent to the other, frowning.

"Your papa told the duchess," answered her mother.

"What!" exclaimed Sebastian, dropping his fiancée's hand and sitting bolt upright. He grabbed for the tray as it nearly toppled off his knees.

"He wrote to her. Sent a fast courier."

Sebastian closed his eyes and gritted his teeth. He could all too easily picture this astonishing news running through his family—the letters flying back and forth, the disbelief and consternation. The surreptitious brotherly smirking. An image of his mother's astonished face made him wince.

"Some people think I don't care about convention," muttered the marquess. "Not true. And this was too much. An elopement!"

"Except that it wasn't, Papa," Georgina pointed out. "It was an unfortunate accident. I think you might have had more faith in my character."

Frowning at the floor, the older man said something too softly to be heard. Sebastian thought it might have been, "It wasn't *you* I was worried about."

"She's sending your brother," added the marchioness. She tried to speak blandly, but Sebastian got a clear sense of a woman getting the better of an argument at last.

The marquess glared at the group with a mixture of defiance and contrition.

"Which brother?" Sebastian asked.

"Randolph," supplied his hostess.

Sebastian groaned softly. If anything could have killed his appetite at this point, the news that a brother had been dispatched to sort him out would have done it. He supposed this was his mother's idea of just retribution for what she probably characterized as "antics." *She* would have known that he would never elope.

If she'd *had* to send a brother, she could've drafted Robert. He'd have made a joke of the whole matter and charmed everyone so thoroughly that they saw it the same way. Alan or James might have refused to be embroiled in such a tangle at all. Nathaniel was still on his honeymoon. Mama couldn't order him and Violet about quite so easily, anyway.

Randolph, though. Sebastian nearly groaned again. Randolph was usually glad for an excuse to take a few days' leave from his far-northern parish. And he positively delighted in helping. Sebastian supposed that was why he'd become a parson. Part of the reason. He'd also been asking "why" since he could speak. According to family legend, that had been the first word Randolph learned. Sebastian certainly remembered being followed about by a relentlessly inquisitive toddler.

Nathaniel, a responsible six-year-old, had become so tired of saying he didn't know that he'd taken to making things up. Sebastian still sometimes had to remind himself that discarded snakeskins were products of reptilian growth rather than intense surprise. Sebastian smiled. Randolph had spent several months trying to startle snakes out of their skin after that tale.

Then Sebastian's smile died, and he put down his last sandwich. Randolph would revel in Mr. Mitra and the marquess's lectures on reincarnation. There would be no end to his questions, or to the incomprehensible discussions after the ladies had left the dinner table. Sebastian only just resisted putting his head in his hands.

Georgina was looking at him, though, her expression anxious. He tried a reassuring smile. From her response, he judged that it was only marginally effective. He bolstered it, vowing to deal with Randolph. He would face anything to save her distress.

Georgina stood, holding her still half-full plate to her chest. "I believe I'll go to my room now," she said. "I'm quite tired."

Her father looked guilty, her mother approving. Sebastian wondered at the determination on her face. It seemed excessive for a walk up a few steps. Was her leg hurting? One look at her father told him he would not be allowed to assist her to a bed.

Night had deepened by the time Georgina managed to hunt down Hilda and corner her in a little-used reception room, where she'd apparently been holed up for a good while, judging from the cake crumbs. Georgina stationed herself between her youngest sister and the door and confronted her with hands on hips. "Have you lost your mind?" she demanded.

For a moment, it seemed that Hilda might deny everything, but then she slumped back on the sofa and let out a long sigh. "I only meant to leave you overnight, but everything went wrong from the very first. Whitefoot didn't like being led. He jerked the rein right out of my hand and ran away. I had to take your Sylph to the Evans farm before I could chase after him. It took hours before I got him there as well." She paused and looked indignant. "Emma abandoned me! She turned tail and rode home. And she's been practically hiding in her bedchamber ever since."

"Perhaps she feels a sense of remorse for having done something absolutely outrageous," Georgina suggested.

Hilda wrinkled her nose. "Well, we came back first thing the next morning to get you."

"That does not excuse…"

"And you were gone!" Hilda actually dared to look reproachful. "As if you'd vanished into thin air."

"Thick mud, more like," said Georgina.

"If you had just waited, or only walked a little way along the trail, we would have found you. And there wouldn't have been such a very great fuss. Why didn't you? How could you be so clumsy as to fall into a gully?" Hilda cocked her head. "I never even knew it was there."

"Don't even dream of blaming this on me!" Georgina gazed at her sister. They were alike in coloring and frame, but apparently their minds ran on entirely different paths. "What did you expect to accomplish by this…this idiotic prank?"

"I thought Papa would make you get married right away," came the prompt reply.

The gaze Hilda turned on Georgina was guileless. She truly didn't seem to see the many shortcomings of her plan. "Because you're impatient?" Georgina asked, though she knew the answer already.

"I simply cannot bear living in this place any longer," Hilda declared with a toss of her head and a wide gesture worthy of the London stage.

Georgina let the implications of that pass for now. She had larger questions. "But when you couldn't find us, why in the world did you tell everyone we'd eloped? You knew it was a lie. And a malicious one at that."

Hilda squirmed in her seat. "I couldn't figure out what had become of you! We searched, but Emma kept distracting me with her worrying, and then her blubbering. I didn't know what to do! And when we finally had to come home, I was afraid Emma would blurt out the whole before I had a chance to...to manage the story. I had to speak first. I was flustered. And...it just came out of my mouth."

"That I had eloped."

Hilda nodded. She did look contrite.

"And they all simply believed you." This was the part of the rigmarole that bothered Georgina the most, that her family should trust the word of Hilda—a known scamp—over her own history and reputation.

"They didn't at first," admitted her sister. "I had to say you'd left a note. And that I'd burned it because of the scandal."

"You...you what?" Georgina could only gape at her.

"Later, I set fire to a sheet of notepaper in my bedroom fireplace and then showed Mama the ashes." She seemed proud of her ingenuity.

"Ashes. Mama."

"Actually, Mama was the one person who kept on doubting," Hilda added. "Papa was much easier." Under Georgina's accusing gaze, she grew petulant. "Well, it seemed like something you *might* do."

"Elope?" Did her sister actually think her so lost to all sense of propriety?

"Go off and abandon us," Hilda replied. "Like you did for the season in London. Without caring a whit whether we went mad from boredom."

"Even you cannot think that makes any sense."

Her sister wilted under Georgina's glare. "It was a good story," she muttered, almost too softly to hear. "Like something out of a novel."

"It didn't occur to you to worry about us?" Georgina asked.

She received a blank look in return.

"When we couldn't be found?" she continued. "When there was no sign of us near the waterfall?"

"Well, I…" Clearly, Hilda hadn't reckoned with this aspect of the matter.

"I had a serious accident. I hurt my leg quite badly. Sebastian was injured trying to climb out of that ravine. We could even have been killed."

At long last, Hilda looked guilty. "I didn't think of that," she said in a small voice.

"You were too concerned about covering up what you'd done."

"I suppose so." Hilda hung her head.

"And you also didn't consider the fact that you would make me very angry."

Hilda's head came up like a hound catching an unfamiliar scent.

"So angry that I wouldn't wish to have you in my household." It was harsh, but Georgina felt she had to make Hilda understand the enormity of what she'd done. "If you care so little for me, why should I want you near me?"

Her sister looked stricken. "You wouldn't... I do care for you. Of course I do. You are my sister."

"Yet you didn't think of me at all as you plotted this. Only of yourself." Her sister started to speak, but Georgina forestalled her with a quick gesture. "You know the servants will have been gossiping. Some garbled tale will get out to our neighbors, and then on from there. Perhaps even to London next season. I will have to endure all sorts of whispers. And how am I to face Sebastian's brother when he arrives?" Not to mention recover the good opinions of his family, Georgina thought with real trepidation.

"But it's settled we are to go with you!" Hilda exclaimed.

"This is your only response to what I have said?"

"I'm counting on you!"

"I know you are," replied Georgina gravely. "But why should I wish to help you after this?" The flare of apprehension in her younger sister's eyes made her feel like a beast. Extreme measures seemed required to get Hilda to listen, however.

"I'm sorry!" her sister cried. "I'll make it up to you, I promise. I'll talk to Lord Randolph. He won't blame you."

"There's no need for that." Afraid she'd gone too far, and not wanting to imagine such a conversation, Georgina added, "Please just be more patient and...conventional."

"I'm not very good at being patient," said Hilda.

As if that had not been noisily evident since her sister was two years old, Georgina thought.

"Or conventional, I think."

"Hilda just…don't do *anything*."

"But I'm sure I could explain to Randolph why I had to…"

"No!"

Hilda pouted. Her inclination to hatch plots seemed to have overcome her remorse in record time. Georgina left her sister sitting chin in hand, pondering. She had the uneasy sensation that she hadn't improved the situation, only expanded its scope.

What was she going to do after she was married? Georgina wondered as she walked along the corridor toward her room. Because she had no doubt that Hilda would simply show up on her doorstep if no other arrangements were made. She would run away from Stane to get there, thinking herself up to whatever obstacles she might encounter. Anything could happen to her.

Georgina sighed. It wasn't that she objected to inviting her sisters to stay in her new household. It was just that she'd rather wait a while—six months or so, say. She wanted time for her new life to settle a bit, to anchor herself solidly as Sebastian's wife.

A thrill ran through her at the silent phrase. With it came vivid memories of their intimacies on the bed of bracken Sebastian had made for her. She was so eager to be Sebastian's wife, so happy in her choice.

Hilda would see six months as an eternity, however. She would take it as a refusal. Georgina shuddered to imagine what her sister might do then. She'd mentioned this problem to her mother, but she didn't think Mama had really taken it in. Perhaps after this latest prank she would listen.

Georgina reached her bedchamber, shut the door on this dilemma, and fell backward onto her bed. She hadn't realized how worn down she was until they were safely home. When she could let go of the fear and determination that had kept her walking, she'd discovered layers of exhaustion beneath it. Her eyelids drooped. She forced herself upright. It seemed too much effort even to ring for the maid she'd put off earlier. She struggled out of her gown, barely managing to undress and crawl under the covers before she was sound asleep.

The following afternoon, Sebastian caught Georgina as she was coming out of her mother's workroom. He'd been lying in wait for more than an hour, watching for her and evading her father. He felt the marquess's eyes on him wherever he went now, full of suspicion despite their explanations and Hilda's admissions of guilt. Somehow, Georgina's father continued to blame him, which bothered Sebastian almost as much as the large purple bruise on his upper arm. "Come into the garden," he urged.

"Mama sent me for a fresh supply of notepaper," his fiancée objected.

"She'll forget about it when one of the dogs calls for attention."

Georgina looked back over her shoulder, then shrugged. "Probably."

Sebastian offered his arm and was inexpressibly

relieved when she took it. After all they'd shared in the last few days, he hated being away from her. It seemed an age since they'd touched. They went out the back way and hurried straight into the shrubbery where they couldn't be seen from the castle. "Are you all right?" he asked her then. "Have you recovered?"

"I have great blisters on my heels," she replied. "That is a lesson I have thoroughly learned—never go walking in riding boots."

He nodded. His own feet suffered similar complaints. "And…otherwise?" He looked down. She looked up. Their eyes held. God, how he wanted her! Their time together in the wild had fired his desire rather than assuaging it.

"I am very well," she said. "My only problem…"

"What?" he interrupted. Did she regret what they'd done after all?

She leaned closer. "I am so impatient to be married," she murmured in his ear.

Her tone, her nearness, brought their lovemaking back even more strongly. "By God, yes!" He couldn't help himself. He kissed her.

She melted against him, meeting his longing with her own, and for a few minutes they lost all consciousness of their surroundings. Then the sound of pugs yapping and the marchioness calling broke them apart.

"I can't stay," said Georgina. "Mama is keeping me close. I think she suspects that we…indulged. And she doesn't know quite what to do about it."

"Well, your father is treating me as if I *pushed* you

into that gully," Sebastian replied, reluctantly letting her go.

"They'll get over it with a bit of time," she said. "But, oh, Sebastian, *your* family. What must they think? What will your brother say to me?"

"You needn't worry about that."

"Worry? They believe I consented to an elopement! The idea of your mother…and the duke believing that. It makes me shudder." She wrapped her arms around her chest and grasped her elbows as if to contain her reaction.

He should have gotten a letter off right away, Sebastian realized. It was just such a chore to produce one. But it had to be done. He should have known that. "I'll tell them different," he said. "Randolph will understand."

"You don't sound as if you believe that." She gazed up at him anxiously.

"Of course I do," declared Sebastian. "All will be well once I explain." That would be heavy work, he feared, what with his distressing tendency to flail about in a muddle of words. Randolph was just the opposite; words were his joy and his playground. He could get so lost in a book that they had to shout to get his attention.

"He's a clergyman." Georgina held her elbows tighter. "And I've never even met him. He'll think I'm a dreadful person."

"He will not!" The mere suggestion made Sebastian want to hit something. He put an arm around her. "He's not a priggish parson, far from it. You mustn't worry." Indeed, Robert had told him that Randolph had been relegated to his rustic parish because of "inappropriate levity" at a doctrinal conference. Sebastian thought of repeating this tidbit to Georgina, but he didn't know what it meant precisely, and he didn't want to give her the wrong impression of his brother.

Georgina was turning into his arms once more, where she belonged, when a slight figure burst out of the shrubbery and ran up to them. For once, it wasn't Hilda.

"I'm so sorry," panted Emma, clearly breathless from running. A sprig of evergreen was caught in her golden hair. "I was upstairs, and I saw you come out, and I wanted to tell you both. Together. I've never been sorrier about anything in my whole life." Tears began to leak from her eyes and run down her cheeks. "I'll never listen to Hilda again," she said. "Ever. I knew it was wrong to leave you out there. But I had no idea she was going to say that, about eloping. I swear I didn't! Please forgive me." She was weeping hard now.

Sebastian would have blurted out reassurances; he hated to see a girl cry. Or anyone, really, though fellows hardly ever did. But Georgina spoke before he could. "You should have told the truth at once," she said. "We were in some danger, you know."

"If I had realized…" began Emma.

"You knew we were lost," Georgina interrupted. "You knew something had gone badly wrong. And you knew we had *not* eloped."

Emma looked at the ground, snuffling.

"So it isn't just a matter of not listening to Hilda.

You must learn to judge for yourself what is right to do. And then do it, no matter how difficult it may seem. You see?"

As Emma nodded forlornly, Sebastian looked at his fiancée in admiration. She really was one of the wisest people he'd ever met.

"Georgina?" The marchioness's voice carried across the gardens. "Where are you?"

Emma started and took a step back. "I don't want to meet Mama," she said. "She's still angry with me. And I'm supposed to be in my room." Wiping her cheeks with the backs of her hands, she faded into the shrubbery.

"I must go," said Georgina. She took Sebastian's hand and squeezed it before walking quickly away.

Trying not to feel morose, Sebastian went off to find Sykes and prepare a letter to his mother.

"What a tale," exclaimed his valet an hour later, when Sebastian's dictation came to an end. Still holding the pen, Sykes sat back and gazed out over the writing desk into endless distance.

Sebastian watched as Sykes's free hand rose and sketched an indefinable shape in the air, rather like a painter at an invisible easel. Now and then, he was allowed a glimpse of another person behind the smooth facade of his gentleman's gentleman. This hidden Sykes never said "my lord" or made deferential bows. Those things fell away as if they'd never existed, and Sebastian wasn't sure Sykes even knew it. As now, this fellow's brown eyes were vague and dreamy rather than alert for services to perform. His spare frame arranged itself quite differently, with…somehow more carelessness and more weight at the same time. One could almost see dramatic vistas forming in his mind.

Despite the years of their association, Sebastian didn't feel well acquainted with this man. Nor encouraged to be. It was deuced odd. They hadn't much in common, of course, although Sebastian admired Sykes's artistic abilities.

"I declare it is *better* than I could imagine," Sykes said, clearly speaking to himself. "The wild tangles of vegetation, the heroic pair lost to all aid."

"You may have the ravine," said Sebastian. "With all its delightful mud and slippery walls and thorns as long as my thumb, but you mustn't portray Lady Georgina."

"I do not incorporate real people into my plays," was the absent reply. "I gather traits and quirks from a variety of individuals and…amalgamate them into a fresh character." Sykes's hands drew together as if scooping up eels, or something equally slippery.

This was all very well, but Sebastian had found certain figures quite recognizable on the rare occasions when Sykes read bits of his plays aloud. And he knew he wasn't the most discerning of auditors. He'd even mentioned it, but Sykes insisted he was mistaken. Sebastian didn't mind a large, nobly born cavalry officer turning up in Sykes's dramas. Not even the one who'd turned out to be a black villain. But… "Not Lady Georgina," he repeated.

Sykes nodded to show he'd heard—like a preoccupied artiste, not a servant.

Sebastian supposed he might feel differently about

the villainous colonel—a promotion, too—if the play was ever staged. Sykes had not yet achieved this goal. Sebastian had once offered to ask his father or Nathaniel for funds to mount a production, but his uniquely unusual valet had refused, insisting that his work must succeed on its own merits.

"This place is a veritable gold mine of material," Sykes murmured. "I've never seen such richness and variety of character."

That was one way of describing the Stanes, and Mitra, and the dogs, Sebastian thought. Actually, he rather liked the phrase. Perhaps he would repeat it to Georgina, should the chance arise.

"I must make notes." Sykes half rose, then hesitated. Sebastian watched him become fully conscious of his surroundings again. One day the man would move on, he thought. Indeed, Sebastian had asked him more than once if he wouldn't prefer some other living arrangement. Sykes had denied any such desire, claiming that the world of a duke's son was a source of endless inspiration, as well as a decent living. "I don't know what else I'd do to earn my bread, to tell you the truth," he'd said.

"You might be a great actor," Sebastian had mused. Sykes demonstrated his acting skills every day as the perfect valet.

But Sykes had responded to his offhand suggestion with all the hauteur of a prince being asked to keep pigs. "I wouldn't stoop," he'd replied.

Frankly, it had been a relief. Sebastian didn't know what he'd do without him.

Sykes straightened and somehow shook himself

without moving. With that, he was back in his valet role. "I'll get this off right away, my lord," he said, folding the page and sealing it.

"Thank you, Sykes."

Silently acknowledging the wealth of implication in his tone, the other man went out.

Nine

THE ATMOSPHERE AT STANE CASTLE REMAINED STIFF over the next two days. The only matter that everyone agreed on was the placement of a warning sign at the ravine. The marquess had ridden out to examine the site for himself. Or perhaps to verify their story—Sebastian wasn't sure. Afterward, with some grumbling that no one had ever fallen in before, he ordered a wooden alert to be prepared and erected. In his presence, Sebastian kept feeling he should apologize and then realizing that he had nothing to apologize for.

Georgina's mother kept her busy with household tasks or wedding plans or something. Her excuses differed. Sebastian found no more opportunities for private conversation. Had he not been inured to the often-inexplicable mandates of the army, he might have railed at the unfairness of it all.

Thus, it was actually a relief when Randolph arrived, prompt and eager, as always. Despite Sebastian's reservations, a brother joining him at Stane felt like reinforcements. When introductions had been made and a few pleasantries exchanged, Sebastian was happy to agree with Randolph's suggestion that he accompany Sebastian to his assigned bedchamber. There were a few points he wanted to make before Randolph went blundering among Georgina's family.

"Well, now, what can I do for you?" Randolph asked as soon as they were alone. He sat in an armchair beside the hearth, leaning forward, smiling, hands laced on his knees. "I am ready for anything, you know."

That was the trouble. Randolph's enthusiasm for helping out could take him far beyond what was wanted. At this moment, he looked ready to leap up and wrestle dragons. Sebastian sat down opposite him and struggled to summon a coherent, convincing narrative. Though Sebastian was two years older, he hadn't won an argument with Randolph since... well, ever. But this wasn't an argument. He only had to explain.

"You've contracted a very good match, I must say," Randolph went on before Sebastian managed to begin. "Lady Georgina seems a lovely girl... I expect we shall soon put things right." He offered Sebastian a reassuring nod.

"There's no need for you to—"

"What I don't understand is why you eloped," said his brother with one raised brow.

"We did not elope!" Sebastian felt like tearing his hair at the repetition of this word. "I wrote Mama the whole story. None of this was my fault."

"I've been on the road. I haven't received any letters. Tell me all." Randolph spread his arms as if to embrace the thought of a good tale.

And so Sebastian had to repeat the rigmarole,

interrupted by questions and reservations until he thought he would explode. It was all he could do to prevent the details from becoming incomprehensible.

"Hmmm," said Randolph when Sebastian had finished. He wasn't smiling, but he rather *sounded* as though he was. "This Hilda seems to be quite an… inventive young lady… Still, couldn't you simply have waited for her return the next morning?"

Sebastian liked the *simply*. Nothing about the mishap had felt simple. And he'd already explained this. Or thought he had. He gritted his teeth at the difficulty of translating what was in his mind into words. It was worse than beating his way through the thicket in the ravine.

"I couldn't keep Georgina standing all night in cold mud, with an injured leg. There *was* no place to wait, where she fell." He did not add that had he tried, he would have missed two of the most glorious days of his life. That secret was his and Georgina's, a memory to be kept close, and relished, for the rest of their lives.

"Ah." Randolph nodded. "Yes, I see. Well, it is certainly quite an upheaval."

"Only because Hilda was back here spouting a pack of nonsense!" replied Sebastian. "Or…mostly."

"What's become of her?" his brother asked.

Randolph certainly was far from a conventional parson, Sebastian thought. There was a smile somehow hovering behind his expression. "She's been confined to quarters except under escort of her governess. And she considers living at Stane a punishment in itself." Sebastian frowned at the hearthrug. "Some days, can't say I blame her," he muttered.

Randolph examined him. "But you do wish to salvage the situation?"

"There's nothing to salvage. I'll get married as planned, and all this will be forgotten."

"That was not the impression I got from the marquess."

It was true that Georgina's father seemed to be brooding on the subject of their unwitting adventure. As if he was sure Sebastian could have handled it far better. If only he could fly, Sebastian thought morosely, all would have been well.

"But I shall talk him 'round," added his brother. "Have no fear."

Sebastian could easily imagine Randolph talking their host's ear off. But the discussion would more than likely meander into the far reaches of philosophy and end up having nothing to do with him or Georgina. "Robert would have been much better at charming people," he complained. He was sorry as soon as the sentence escaped him because Randolph looked hurt.

"Robert has gone to a house party, as he always does at this season." Randolph sounded a bit wistful. "And what with James haring off on some quest…"

"A what?"

Randolph waved a hand. "Robert called it that. His exact phrase was *a quixotic quest*. Rather good, eh? A neat alliteration…" Under Sebastian's uncomprehending gaze, he added, "There's a girl involved."

Wasn't there always? Sebastian thought. "That's quick work. James has only been home a few weeks."

"She apparently followed him here from an island in the antipodes. Tried to shoot him at a garden party of Alan's." Sebastian stared. His brother grinned at him, not above enjoying his astonishment. "She missed. It seems she thought he'd stolen something from her home."

"Stolen?"

"All a misunderstanding, I believe."

"And they're at me about a few days away," Sebastian muttered.

"Only to help." Randolph leaned back as if signaling the end of the conversation, then dropped a bombshell. "Mama thought of coming up here herself, you know. She and Papa, that is."

Sebastian froze in place at the idea. He could almost hear his father's kindly, ironic comments on his conduct, feel his mother's lovingly questioning gaze. He wanted everything perfectly arranged before they arrived at Stane, so all that occurred was a wedding as smooth as Nathaniel's. Without the wolf skin, he noted to himself. How could he ensure that his brothers had no scope for pranks?

"But then they discovered that Nathaniel is driving in some mad carriage race. They went to Brighton to see about that instead."

"A race? Nathaniel?" This didn't sound like his eldest brother. Their father's heir was levelheaded and decorous and a model for them all.

"Odd, isn't it? They don't seem to think he's run mad, however." Randolph shook his head dubiously. "Even though I told them that he wrote to ask if bishops are distinguished by their markings, like waterfowl. All I did was *mention* that he'd found me quite the wrong sort of bishop."

"What?" Sebastian gaped at him. "Did you say waterfowl?"

"That *is* ridiculous, isn't it?"

"What sort of bishop did you want? What for?" It occurred to Sebastian that a clergyman might have some arcane use for a bishop. Now and then, he forgot—for a moment—that Randolph was a man of the cloth. He'd been just a brother for so much longer.

"Never mind," said Randolph. "Perhaps it's the effect of marriage. Nathaniel seems to have been altered. Having been altared." He smiled, enjoying the sound of his own words. "Do you think tying the knot makes you quite a different person?"

"No." Sebastian expected his wedding to solve all his current problems. He didn't foresee new ones.

His brother shrugged. "At any rate, my point is that you might want to be grateful it's me who came." He smiled.

It was a warm, affectionate smile. It reminded Sebastian of countless summer afternoon expeditions at Langford. Of Randolph helping him as he struggled to memorize Latin tags. Of their mingled tears at the death of an aged dog who had joined the household when they were five and three. He was suddenly filled with fondness for his brother, even his overenthusiastic bits.

Then Randolph diverted him by adding, "And I understand religion is involved."

"No, it isn't," said Sebastian, certain he was on firm ground there.

"I thought there was a Hindu gentleman in residence."

"There is, but…"

"A very interesting twist," Randolph said.

"It isn't a twist. He's just another guest here. Nothing to do with my affairs."

"An interesting opportunity, then. I haven't had the chance to learn anything of Hindu theology."

Sebastian sighed. There was no doubt that the after-dinner conversations at Stane were destined to become longer and more confusing. At least the marquess would be pleased. Georgina's father preferred an attentive audience.

Randolph stood and went over to open his case, exposing neatly packed clothes. "I haven't brought a servant. Perhaps Sykes could help me out now and then?"

"Of course." Sebastian rose as well. "You should tell him about the bishops." The curious linking of churchmen and waterfowl was just the sort of oddity Sykes relished. He'd probably even understand it.

"Tell your valet?"

"Never mind." He sometimes slipped and forgot that no one else knew about Sykes's true nature.

Randolph clapped him on the shoulder as he headed for the door. "It's good to see you, Sebastian. We scarcely had time to talk at Nathaniel's wedding. Have no fear, we'll soon set everything straight."

Sebastian wanted to believe him. But so far, *everything* had shown a distressing propensity to go wrong.

The Stane family and their guests gathered in the great hall before dinner that evening, as was their invariable custom. "Randolph's even handsomer than Sebastian," Emma whispered to Georgina as the brothers descended the stairs together.

Georgina had to admit that Emma was right. All the sons of the Duke of Langford were attractive men, but in Randolph all the elements that characterized them—tall athletic frame, auburn hair, classic features—had combined with particular harmony. Standing beside his brother, he looked a bit like a finished portrait next to a preliminary study.

Immediately, Georgina was indignant at her own thought. Sebastian was nothing of the kind. He was perfect and complete in himself.

Sebastian met her eyes, and a bolt of desire rushed through her. Her comparison sizzled into nothing. Sebastian was so alive, so compelling, while Randolph inspired no more emotion than she might have felt looking at an actual painting. Or, no, that wasn't true. His arrival had roused apprehension and defiance, an uneasy mixture.

Seeming to feel her attention, Randolph strolled over. "Good evening, Lady Georgina, Lady Emma."

Emma giggled. "No one calls us that here. Mama says titles are a waste of words, except to impress odious, encroaching mushrooms."

"Emma!"

"Does she indeed?" Randolph gazed at their mother, who was bent over Drustan, explaining to the dog that it was time for him to move off the train of her evening dress. He lay sprawled on the cloth, tongue lolling in what looked very much like a laugh.

"You must call me Emma, and I shall call you Randolph because you are practically my brother already," added her feckless younger sister. Emma was so relieved at having been released from her bedchamber exile, and thus in her mind forgiven for recent transgressions, that she was chattering like a magpie.

Georgina wondered if Randolph was a high stickler. He rather looked like one, with his conservative attire. She'd had no opportunity to become acquainted with him; he lived on his parish in the far north. Perhaps just knowing he was a clergyman was enough to answer the question.

"How funny to go from just one brother to having seven," Emma trilled.

Georgina had thought it a blessing that Hilda was still in disgrace, doomed to take meals in her room. But Emma seemed bent on making up for their unpredictable youngest sister's absence.

"You may find it a few too many," Randolph replied. "I know we sometimes did. When it was a matter of taking turns, for example."

"Oh no, why would I?" said Emma. "You will all have to dance with me when I go up to London for the season. I shall have a host of ready-made partners."

Randolph smiled down at her, and Georgina felt a measure of relief. "I hadn't thought of that," he said. "Although I must tell you I am hardly ever in London."

"Why not?" said Emma. "You're grown up and can go where you like."

"I have duties in my parish in Northumberland."

"Oh. I almost forgot you're a vicar." Emma cocked her head at him. "You don't seem like one. You're not all frumpy and pious."

Georgina nearly groaned, but Randolph merely thanked her.

"Can't you get somebody else to manage all that? A curate or something?"

"I could."

He looked thoughtful. Georgina was impressed by the attention he gave a young girl's careless query.

"But I don't wish to," Randolph went on. "I get a good deal of satisfaction from my pastoral work. Helping people, you know. I would like a post nearer town. And someday, I shall have one."

He said it with such conviction that Georgina had no doubt he would. Feeling under observation, she turned her head and found Sebastian staring at her. He raised his brows and mouthed something. She thought it was "All right?" She nodded and smiled. The smile she got in return sent a wave of heat from her toes to her suddenly flushed cheeks.

Movement caught in the corner of her eye. Georgina turned and found that Drustan had left her mother's skirts. He was trotting toward her group, his bulging brown gaze fixed on Randolph. Her heart sank. It would be just like the wretched dog to apply himself to Randolph's leg before everyone. She sometimes imagined, in her most fanciful moments, that Drustan viewed his vulgar attentions as a rite of passage for newcomers to the castle. Could she intercept him?

Before Georgina could try to intervene, Sebastian stepped into the pug's path and touched the pocket of his coat. Georgina glimpsed a bit of cloth peeking out. She couldn't tell what it was. It looked rather dirty.

To her astonishment, Drustan cringed. He stopped and pressed his plump little belly to the floor, head down. Sebastian was still, staring at him. Drustan edged away, crawling. When he was a few feet off, the dog rose and slunk back to her mother. Georgina watched him go, amazed. He hid behind his mistress.

"Drustan has developed a considerable respect for Sebastian," said her mother. She smiled as if this development was her doing, or her plan.

Sebastian didn't acknowledge the dumbfounded looks this triumph earned him, though Georgina could tell he noticed them. Mr. Mitra offered one of his characteristic obeisances, palms pressed together. Randolph looked bewildered.

Fergus came in to announce dinner. Randolph offered Georgina his arm before noticing the household's lack of ceremony. As they walked into the dining room behind the jostling crowd, she wondered if he would think this unconventional environment made her prone to other lapses, like elopement. "I assume Sebastian told you the story of our…mishap," she said, keeping her tone light.

"He did."

"My sister has far too vivid an imagination."

"Indeed, I look forward to meeting her," Randolph replied.

Unsure exactly what this meant, Georgina said nothing. Hilda was indefensible anyway.

Randolph saw her to her seat and then went to his own place at her mother's right. Mama had placed Sebastian on her other side, perhaps to allow the brothers to converse. Reflecting the incident just past, Mama beamed at her betrothed while Drustan placed himself on the opposite side of her chair.

Her father was flanked by Mr. Mitra and Joanna

Byngham, as usual when there were no prominent female guests. That left Emma and Georgina facing each other in the middle of the table. With no necessity to talk to a dinner partner, Georgina was free to eavesdrop. The party was small enough that she could hear what was said at either end of the table.

"This is a delicious ragout," said Randolph.

"Thank you," said her mother.

"'Good words are worth much, and cost little,'" he replied, his tone indicating it was a quote.

"That's Shakespeare, isn't it?" Sebastian asked. "My brother is very fond of poetry, ma'am. He has a deal of it by heart."

"Not Shakespeare in this case," Randolph said. "Though the bard very often has just the phrase you want. No, that was George Herbert, a favorite of mine. And a poet with far finer sensibilities, I believe."

"You don't often hear people say something like that," Georgina's mother responded. "Shakespeare is usually held up as a writer without peer."

"Such people need to delve deeper into our English literary traditions," said Randolph.

Georgina noticed that Sebastian was looking anxious. She wasn't sure why.

"A delver, are you?" replied her mother.

Randolph noticed the sarcasm. Anybody would, Georgina thought. Fortunately he seemed more surprised than angry. She caught Sebastian's eye and smiled at him reassuringly, trying to remind him that Mama spoke that way to everyone. She got quite enough "informative discourse" from Papa. Silent communications passed between them. They gazed

at one another until Georgina was startled by her
father's offer of a slice of beef.

"I have found some interesting references in an
unpublished memoir," said Joanna Byngham. "An
Irish gentleman who lived in India for twenty years
during the last century."

Georgina wondered if the governess had locked
Hilda in her room. Probably not. Joanna wasn't
stupid enough to tempt her charge that way. She cal-
culated the likelihood that Hilda was listening outside
the door right now. And put it very high.

"Have you any interest in Hindu practices?" her
father asked Randolph, speaking down the length
of the table with a serene disregard for convention.
"Being a man of the cloth yourself?"

Randolph nodded. "I appreciate learning about all
sorts of philosophies."

Georgina couldn't tell if he was being polite, or was
genuinely intrigued. She checked Sebastian's expression. He looked hunted.

"We'll have quite a lot to tell you then," said her
father with satisfaction. He turned to Mr. Mitra and
resumed their discussion more quietly.

The remainder of the meal passed in the clink
of forks and exchange of pleasantries. Georgina had
begun to relax by the time her mother signaled and
the ladies rose to leave the dining room. Randolph
was not an ogre after all, she concluded. He seemed
amiable and unthreatening. He was also clearly fond
of word play, in contrast to Sebastian, who had shown
over his visit that he had no inclination in that direction at all.

"This is the stupidest custom," said Joanna Byngham when Georgina came up to her in the doorway. Not for the first time, or the twentieth. Joanna always longed to remain in the dining room for the ongoing discussion. "I do not understand why your father keeps it up."

Because he wishes to, Georgina wanted to tell her. After her experience of other household arrangements in London, she'd lately realized that her father was a kind of artist of convention. He embraced the rules that aided his ends and discarded those that thwarted him with a very fine discrimination, until he had just the social landscape he preferred here in his castle.

People who thought he simply threw propriety to the winds were quite mistaken. Which made it easy for strangers to put a foot wrong with him. She wondered if her mother was aware of this selection process and concluded that of course she was. Didn't she do the same herself? It was another thing her parents had in common, indeed a kind of conspiratorial collaboration. It went along with the fact that where their daughters were concerned, they made no concessions at all.

Georgina sighed as the dining room door closed behind them. Like Joanna, she would have liked to flout convention, but in quite another direction. She didn't want to stay. She wanted to take Sebastian with her, and not to any stuffy drawing room, either. Her bedchamber would be her first choice, she thought, a little shocked at the blatancy of her longings. How delicious it would be if they could repeat all they'd done on a pile of bracken in her comfortable bed. And more. She knew there was more Sebastian could show her. Why, oh why, couldn't it be now instead of days and days away?

"Georgina?"

She started, and became aware that she'd stopped in the middle of the hall. The others were well ahead. Tingling all over from the fantasy she'd conjured, she hurried after her mother.

"So you're saying people come back after death?" Randolph asked as he filled his glass from the decanter of port.

Mr. Mitra nodded as he passed the bottle along without taking any wine.

"But it isn't like Judgment Day, when all souls are said to arise at the last trump?"

"Not like that, no. We believe a being has to live many lives and have many experiences before becoming perfect and uniting with the Divine."

"God."

Sebastian watched Randolph sip his wine. So far, the discussion was comprehensible. He didn't expect this to last.

"So everyone…ascends, as it were?" Randolph asked.

"Some manage it, some don't," replied the Indian gentleman with a shrug.

"Those who lead holy lives?" Randolph said.

"It is rather a process than a…straight line."

"And those who don't, what happens to them? Are they damned?"

"No." Mitra's smile was kind and understanding.

And somehow a little sly as well, Sebastian thought. "They return to the source through the great destruction that occurs at the end of each cycle."

"Cycle?" Randolph asked. He leaned forward. Sebastian recognized the fascination beginning to gleam in his brother's blue eyes. If Randolph had his way, they would be here for the rest of the evening. Longer.

"Time begins to end and ends to begin," said Mitra.

"That is a striking phrase," Randolph interjected.

Mitra nodded acknowledgment. "Death is but a gateway to the next cycle, to birth. This is also true of the universe itself. Rather like the rhythms of nature, you might say."

Randolph considered. "So you think the entire universe...er, reincarnates?"

"Ha, I like that," put in Georgina's father. "Very neat."

"It is a bit more complicated than that," said Mitra.

"Ain't it always?" said the marquess. "He says that about every point we try to make, eh, Sebastian?"

It was a polite effort to include him in the conversation. Sebastian acknowledged that. And perhaps a sign that Georgina's father was minded to forgive him at last. He would much rather have been left out of it, however. What with his brother gazing expectantly at him from across the table, and the marquess's beady eye fixing him from the side, he felt like a bug about to be squashed. He decided on a simple nod. After all, things mostly were more complicated than he wished. Nearly always, in fact.

Randolph acknowledged Mitra's remark with a gesture. "I'm sure there's a great deal more to it. But you know, I think the central core of religion is rather simple—whatsoever ye would that men should do to you, do ye so to them."

"The Golden Rule," said the marquess.

Mr. Mitra smiled. "Indeed, the Mahabharata teaches, 'This is the sum of duty; do naught unto others what you would not have them do unto you.'"

"Mahabharata," Randolph repeated, clearly savoring the sounds. "That is your holy book?"

"It is one of our sacred writings."

"So our philosophies have that idea in common." Sebastian's brother looked pleased at the thought.

"And with many others in the world," Mitra replied. "The Buddhists say, 'Hurt not others in ways that you yourself would find hurtful.' And in China the Confucians teach, 'Do not do to others what you would not like yourself. Then there will be no resentment against you, either in the family or in the state.'"

Randolph's face positively glowed with interest, as well as a healthy dose of intellectual competition, Sebastian thought.

"The Jewish Talmud says, 'What is hateful to you, do not do to your fellow man. This is the entire Law; all the rest is commentary.'" Randolph sat back as if he had scored a point.

"And the followers of Mohammed that 'No one of you is a believer until he desires for his brother that which he desires for himself,'" replied Mitra mildly.

Randolph grinned. "You are clearly a very learned man, Mr. Mitra. I am delighted to have the chance to exchange opinions with you."

"Our traditions are very ancient," Mitra replied.

"And not all talk," exclaimed the marquess. He was

practically squirming at being left out of the conversation. "We'll show you. Won't we, Mitra?"

"I'm not sure it is a good idea…"

"Of course it is. A capital one! Been meaning to get to it for days. We were only delayed by the 'accident.'" Georgina's father surveyed Sebastian. "We'll set things up for tomorrow. Then we'll see what you're made of, my boy."

The relish in his green eyes filled Sebastian with deep foreboding.

Ten

GEORGINA LOOKED AROUND THE CHAMBER HER FATHER had been using for his esoteric explorations, at the far end of the castle's older east wing. She hadn't been here since her father had taken up these studies; it wasn't a particularly comfortable part of the building. The walls and floors were stone, the fireplaces large and drafty.

Georgina wondered whether Mr. Mitra or her father had arranged the furnishings. The windows were heavily draped, the only light coming from a great candelabrum on a low table in the center of a thick Turkey carpet, brought from another room, she thought. The candles threw dancing shadows over a circle of eight mismatched armchairs. She recognized some of them from other places. Otherwise, the room was bare.

She was curious about whatever Papa had planned. She was also worried that he seemed to see it as some sort of test for Sebastian. Despite everything, Papa continued to eye her betrothed with suspicion.

Her mother had flatly refused to participate. Emma and Hilda had not been invited, to Hilda's vocal chagrin. And so their party consisted of herself and Joanna

Byngham, Sebastian, his brother, and Papa. Also Mr. Mitra, of course, who hadn't yet made an appearance.

Georgina looked at Sebastian, standing tall next to his brother on the other side of the circle. He gave her a warm smile, meant to be reassuring, she was certain. And she was reassured. She had begun to feel that when she was with Sebastian, she was safe, shielded from disaster. It was silly. No one had that power. Yet the feeling persisted.

Joanna was clearly excited. Tonight was a culmination of all her hours of study, Georgina supposed. Papa bustled about like the host of an evening party. He looked so happy. Georgina was touched to see it, even as she wanted to laugh. Who else had such a father? He was unique. She hoped the coming hours lived up to his expectations. As long as none of it distressed Sebastian, she was prepared to be amazed.

Mr. Mitra entered. He wore his customary narrow trousers and long tunic-like shirt, but tonight these garments were white. He carried a small cloth bag over one shoulder. Pausing beside the low table, he put his palms together and bowed to the group.

Joanna mimicked him. The rest of them, caught by surprise, managed more conventional acknowledgments.

In one smooth movement, Mitra settled cross-legged on the carpet. It looked entirely natural to him and, at the same time, made him seem alien. He'd been politely pretending to be just like his hosts since he arrived, Georgina realized, but he wasn't. He was the product of an entirely different society. Candlelight illuminated his hawk-like features.

"Everyone take a seat," urged Papa cheerfully.

He and Joanna chose chairs. Georgina sat in the one nearest her, and was glad when Sebastian strode over to sit beside her. Randolph was on her other side. "This is a ritual of your religion?" he asked Mr. Mitra.

"No. It is a… Call it a meditation of my own invention."

"Your own? Fascinating."

Mr. Mitra opened his bag and drew out a small drum, placing it on the floor before him. He reached in again and pulled out a small openwork brass elephant. Extracting a cone of incense from inside, he lit it from one of the candles and replaced it, setting the elephant on the table. The scent wafted upward, heady and aromatic. It was like what one smelled in church—and not like, Georgina thought.

Mitra began to tap out a rhythm on the drum. "I invite you to concentrate on the candles," he murmured. "Fire is a messenger, and a vehicle. Clear your minds of everything except the flame."

Georgina watched his face at first. Mitra's eyes were closed. He looked serene. It occurred to her that he had depths that none of them had been allowed to plumb. He'd hidden much of himself with cordiality and smooth courtesy. Still, over the weeks of his visit, she'd come to like him and had discovered no reason not to trust him. She fixed her gaze on the dancing flames.

Mitra began to chant, repeating one phrase over and over. "*Om Gum Ganapatayei Namaha.*"

"What's that?" asked Randolph.

Mitra paused, opening his eyes. "I am appealing

to Ganesha, the remover of obstacles. I speak to him in Sanskrit."

"Sanskrit. Yes, I've heard of it. It's said to be one of the oldest human languages, isn't it? I've often wanted to study…"

"Do be quiet, Gresham," said Georgina's father. "We'll get nowhere if you keep interrupting." Joanna made a sound of agreement. Randolph subsided, and Mr. Mitra took up his drumming and chanting once again.

Georgina watched the flames and listened to the rhythmic sound. The rich scent of the incense surrounded her. She began to feel a floating sensation—not at all unpleasant—as if the edges of the room had faded, or expanded somehow.

"Let go of time," murmured Mr. Mitra. "Time is an illusion of the senses. If you release it, you can be free. To move among ages, to see another lifetime." He took up the chanting once more.

Enveloped by the sound, the scent, the bright dancing images, Georgina experienced an odd dislocation. On the one hand, she felt as if she was drifting, like a leaf floating on the wind in autumn. Space opened around her; she could go anywhere. At the same time, she knew she was seated in an armchair in her home; she could feel the cloth of her gown beneath her fingertips. She could smell incense and hear small movements from the others in the room. The unusual double sensation went on, and on.

Next to her, Sebastian muttered incomprehensible words.

And then Georgina was looking down at a pair of

gnarled, work-worn hands, which somehow were, and were not, at the ends of her own arms. One held a mass of raw wool, while the other teased out strands and twisted them into thread, aided by a whirling drop spindle made of polished stone.

One part of her mind wondered how she'd identified that unfamiliar object. Others lost themselves in the pull, twist, stretch of the task. It was lulling, like the chant, which she still heard, as if from far away. She'd just begun to get a sense of a different, much shabbier room surrounding those aged hands when Joanna gave a triumphant squeak. The governess threw up her arms and snapped her fingertips against her palms in a quick, sharp tempo.

Papa grunted as if he'd taken a blow.

Randolph sprang to his feet so suddenly that his chair tipped over backward and bounced on the carpet. "Incredible!" he cried. "I must set down a complete record of this at once." Nearly stumbling over the downed armchair, he hurried out of the room.

Mr. Mitra fell silent. Georgina's father cursed even as Joanna Byngham gave a forlorn moan. Georgina blinked at the candle flames. She felt as if she was returning from a great distance, and yet had never moved from her seat in this room.

Only Mr. Mitra seemed undisturbed. Calmly, he put the drum back in his bag and extinguished the incense. He moved from the carpet to one of the chairs. When he sat down, it was as if the stranger Georgina had glimpsed in him had disappeared once more. Or retreated from public view, she thought. Papa's pleas had lured him out, but the…exposure had been temporary.

"We must each recount our experiences at once," said Georgina's father. "If we do not, they will fade and be forgotten, like dreams."

Joanna didn't wait for a further invitation. Leaning forward in her chair, eyes burning with a wild enthusiasm Georgina had never seen there before, she spoke. "I was the high priestess of a temple built from great blocks of buff-colored stone. It was hot. I could see palm trees through the archway. I had long, black curls and a band of gold around my forehead. I wore red skirts that swung out wide as I danced before a painted idol. There were bells on my hands." She clapped her fingers against her palms again, looking…exalted. That was the word for it, Georgina thought. And here was an unexpected side of her former governess. Meeting Sebastian's startled gaze, she decided it was a good thing Randolph had gone.

The others gazed at Joanna in silence. She ignored them, staring at the ceiling as if she could see right through it. Mr. Mitra was frowning. He seemed about to speak, then didn't.

"I was in a battle," said Georgina's father after a while. "I had a sword—not a saber, an old-fashioned long sword—and I wore a sort of chain-mail shirt." He took a deep breath and grinned at Mitra. "I think we did it, my friend. I returned to the age of Offa! Inhabited my former self. King of Mercia." He shook his head. "It was astonishing. Quite immediate. I took a heavy blow to my ribs in the fight." He put a hand to his side, then turned to glower at Sebastian. "If your brother hadn't disrupted the process, I daresay I would have found out a great deal more."

"Sorry," muttered Sebastian, wondering why everything was always his fault. Georgina's father might have expected that a churchman wouldn't care for…whatever that had been. He rubbed his forearms, hair still prickling with unease. It had been surprisingly unsettling.

The marquess turned to Georgina. "What about you, my dear?"

Georgina blinked and let out a long breath. "It was strange, Papa."

"In what way?" He leaned forward as if to draw the details out of her. "Just tell us anything your remember."

She gazed at the wall opposite. "I was spinning. I have never done so, but I'm sure, somehow, that's what it was."

"In a dance of some sort?" asked Joanna. "Was there a sacred enclosure?"

"No, spinning thread, I mean," Georgina replied. "From wool." She held up her hands and examined them. "My fingers were gnarled and wrinkled, as if I was quite old and had worked very hard for many years. And then just before Randolph left, I seemed to see a stone hearth and a battered wooden table, perhaps some bunches of herbs hanging from the beam above." She looked up, cocking her head. "It was rather like those cottages over near our northern borders, Papa. The ones you said needed rebuilding because they're so old-fashioned and run down."

The marquess frowned at her. "That can't be right," he said.

"It sounds like a peasant dwelling," commented Joanna. "Spinning has been a constant activity in such places for thousands of…"

"It can't have been real," their host interrupted.

Sebastian wondered what the marquess's definition of *real* might be in this case. He'd noticed that Mr. Mitra looked more interested in Georgina's story than the others.

"The Stanes have no peasant blood," declared the marquess. "None whatsoever. Georgina is simply too inexperienced to have done the thing right."

"I have said many times that this has nothing to do with family inheritance," Mitra said. He sounded weary.

Georgina's father ignored him. Turning to Sebastian, he barked, "What about you?"

Sebastian would have preferred to skip his turn, particularly now that the older man was clearly irritated. He knew he'd have even more trouble than usual putting this odd experience into words. But there was no avoiding it. Everybody was looking at him, waiting.

He held out his arms, clothed in his familiar blue coat. Of course they were. What else would they be? "I thought I saw…designs painted on my arms," he began. "Bare arms, I mean. All over them, wrist to shoulder. They were like the things sailors get. What are they called? Tattoos? Only these weren't pictures, just lines that rather…swirled."

That sounded daft, but he'd gotten the distinct sense that they moved as he watched. It had threatened to make him queasy. He'd had to look away. "Felt like there was a heavy bit of metal around my neck. Couldn't see that. And I had on really awful trousers. Some kind of hideous red-and-blue check." He looked at Georgina. "Not the sort of thing I'd ever wear," he assured them both.

Georgina's father, whose frown had been deepening, leaped to his feet, fists clenched. "A damned Welshman, by God! The kind of savage Offa fought off all his life."

Sebastian gazed up at him with no idea in the world what to say.

"I might have known! Dragging my daughter off into the wilderness."

"He did not drag me, Papa. I have told you and told you…"

"I had my suspicions, and now we see… Well, your engagement is at an end. I forbid it! We can't have a barbarian in the family. Out of the question."

"What?" Georgina jumped up to face him. "Don't be ridiculous, Papa."

"I forbid it, I say!" The marquess's face was red with anger.

"But…but if my story was wrong, why not Sebastian's as well?" Georgina replied.

"Because it fits, doesn't it?" He glowered at Sebastian.

Sebastian struggled to formulate arguments against this ridiculous accusation.

"No," said Georgina. "It does not. Sebastian is a fine—"

"Deceiver," her father interrupted.

"Papa!" Georgina looked as if she'd like to box his ears. Sebastian watched her struggle for control. "You said I was inexperienced," she went on finally. "Well, so is Sebastian. Even more. I've been listening to you talk about reincarnation for weeks. This was simply…a sort of dream, as you suggested."

"If I could—" began Mr. Mitra.

Georgina's father spoke right over him. "How would he know that the ancient tribesmen tattooed themselves or wore checkered clothing, eh? Answer me that. He's not exactly a scholar."

This familiar criticism stung, not least because it was so true. Sebastian couldn't think what to say to change his host's mind. If he could grab him and shake him, perhaps...but he couldn't. And it would probably just make things worse. No, certainly it would. Demonstrate his barbarian tendencies or some such nonsense.

"Listen to me!" Mitra exclaimed. His vehemence was so uncharacteristic that they all turned to stare. "You *cannot* directly associate these...possibilities we unearthed in the meditation with what is happening today." Mr. Mitra glanced at Joanna Byngham and then away. "There is no absolute succession."

Georgina's father glared at him. "You've also said that the lives a person experiences are determined by character and deeds."

"Yes, but..."

"Ha! And none of the rest of us turned up as uncivilized Welshmen, did we?"

"Papa," cried Georgina.

The marquess paid no attention. "Pack your things and be on your way," he said to Sebastian. "Today. You and your brother. He didn't even dare tell us what he saw, did he? Eh? What's he hiding?"

"Papa," said Georgina again.

Sebastian rose. He had the sense that he stood alone against a crowd. Georgina started toward him, but her father held her back. "Go on," he said. "Get out."

The man was his host, and the father of the woman Sebastian still firmly intended to marry. He couldn't fight him. And he couldn't think how to change his mind. If Georgina couldn't sway him, how could Sebastian hope to? He would only make things worse. Angry, bewildered, he walked out.

He strode through the castle corridors, his brain trying to make sense of what had just happened. It couldn't be that his future happiness was to be destroyed because of…an attack of imagination. That just wasn't possible. It was cruelly unfair. He didn't even have much of an imagination. But Georgina's father had seemed perfectly serious. Sebastian couldn't summon a shred of hope that he'd been joking. What were they going to do?

Sebastian stopped in the middle of a hallway, parade-ground rigid. One thing he wouldn't do. He wasn't leaving. If the marquess threw him out of Stane, he'd park himself nearby until he got Georgina back. He'd pitch a tent below the walls, if necessary.

As a last straw, Sebastian found Randolph lying in wait for him in his bedchamber. His brother sprang up as soon as Sebastian opened the door. "I hope I didn't offend our host," he said, moving from foot to foot as if anxious.

"Not nearly as much as I did," replied Sebastian dryly.

It didn't appear that Randolph heard him. "That was simply an…overwhelming experience. I could think of nothing but writing it all down. Astonishing. And then when I finished, I suddenly began to wonder what the council of bishops would say." He walked over to the window and back, looking at the floor rather than Sebastian. "They do not always find me... entirely congenial, you know."

"I don't think they're likely to hear of it," replied Sebastian. "Considering what happened after you were gone."

Deep in his own thoughts, Randolph didn't even ask what his brother meant. "Do you think they would consider it some sort of...spell?" he said.

Under any other circumstances, Sebastian might have speculated and probably teased his brother a bit. Now, his own problems weighed too heavily. "How would I know what a bunch of bishops would think?" he replied. "I like Mitra. But I wish to God he hadn't done...whatever that was."

Randolph looked regretful. "I suppose I shouldn't participate in any more..."

"You won't have the opportunity," Sebastian interrupted. "We've been ordered out of Stane Castle."

This penetrated Randolph's preoccupation. "What?"

Under his brother's increasingly astonished gaze, Sebastian related the scene that had just taken place.

"Your engagement is ended over imaginary tattoos and checkered trousers?" Randolph asked when his brother had finished. "Are you certain you understood him correctly?"

"He left no room for doubt," Sebastian assured him.

"Then perhaps he mistook your meaning," said Randolph. He hesitated. "Now and then you...garble a story...just a bit."

Sebastian's jaw tightened. But he had to acknowledge

the truth of it. Words were not his friends. "Not this time," he answered.

"Well then, Stane must be mad. Perhaps you *should* reconsider an alliance with his family."

"No." All of Sebastian's resolution rang in that single syllable.

Randolph eyed him. "No. Well, I'm happy to talk to him. Though I must say he seems an extremely intransigent fellow."

"No," Sebastian said again.

Randolph surveyed him. He nodded. "What do you mean to do?"

"Stay on," Sebastian vowed. "I'll find lodgings nearby, put up a tent if necessary, and remain until this idiotic mess is straightened out. And I am married, as planned." He caught his reflection in the mirror above the mantel. His expression was fierce, as well it might be. He wasn't going to lose, not for anyone or anything.

"Are you sure…?"

"Everyone's blowing this out of all proportion." Now that he was cooler, Sebastian felt this had to be right. "It was more like a party game than anything else. Stane will see that he's being ridiculous."

Randolph nodded as if this made sense. "I shall stay with you, of course," he said.

Of course he would. That was the thing about his brothers, Sebastian thought. When it came to the point of nonplus, they never let him down.

Eleven

DISTRAUGHT SHE MIGHT BE, BUT GEORGINA WAS NO fool. As soon as her father released her, she went to find her mother. It was a measure of the unusual nature of the evening that Mama was not in the drawing room but sitting in her workroom surrounded by her dogs. Of her sisters, there was no sign. "Oh, Mama!" Georgina cried.

The marchioness was self-absorbed, but not oblivious to an offspring's real distress. "What is it, my dear?"

The story came pouring out on a rising tide of emotion. The pugs responded to the latter with a swelling chorus of yapping. "And so Papa has declared my engagement at an end," Georgina finished.

"What?" Her mother sat bolt upright and stared at her.

"For no reason at all," she added. The unfairness of it overwhelmed her once again. "Mr. Mitra says that these…experiments—whatever you call them— have nothing to do with who one is today. Not in the least."

"Experiments," repeated her mother. She rose from her chair. "I'll show Alfred experiments."

She hadn't even noticed that she'd dislodged Drustan from the folds of her skirt, tipping him head over heels. Georgina saw a ray of hope. She trailed behind her mother like one of the dogs, rushing back the way she'd come.

Papa still sat in the circle of armchairs around the candelabrum. Of the rest of the group, only Joanna remained. She stood before him, making sweeping gestures with her arms as she slowly turned.

Georgina marched in behind her mother, who practically skidded to a stop, putting her hands on her hips. "Oh, lud," she said. "Alfred, what do you think you're doing?"

Joanna didn't seem to notice their arrival. She continued her eccentric movements.

Papa looked glad of the interruption. He rose and edged around the governess to join them. "Charlotte, our meditation had the most amazing results. You should have joined us."

"It appears so indeed. I could have prevented you from acting the fool with Georgina's future husband."

His face went stubborn. "That is at an end. My daughter will not marry a…"

"*My* daughter as well," interrupted Mama. "She told me the whole story. I've never heard anything so ridiculous."

"Gresham was condemned by his own words! He bore all the marks of a Welsh barbarian."

"Alfred, can you not hear how silly that sounds?"

He seemed to swell with anger. "Silly? This from a

woman addicted to tales of princes turned into swans and queens eating their children."

"That was a lie perpetrated by Rhiannon's enemies! As you know very well. And yes, I prefer a poetic, magical story to your roaring tales of hairy bullies blustering and chopping at each other. And this is their heaven!"

"Offa was a Christian king!" Georgina's father retorted. "And a proper man. Not some whining oath breaker like Drustan, Tristan, whatever his name was."

"He was *fated* to..."

"Mama," said Georgina.

Her mother turned to look at her. It took a moment. "Yes," she said then. "This is beside the point." She faced Georgina's father again. "Lord Sebastian, *my* daughter's affianced husband, is a welcome guest in my home. He will stay until the wedding, which will take place as planned."

"There will be no wedding! I told you, I have forbidden it. Gresham is to go."

"No."

Georgina's parents stood toe to toe. Though her mother was much the smaller figure, she was no less formidable. "I will not have this, Alfred," she said quietly. "I said nothing when you paid five hundred guineas for a supposed Anglo-Saxon crown—which turned out to be nothing of the sort—or when you nearly cut off Fergus's fingers with that 'war ax.' But I draw the line here."

"You will allow a savage's blood into our family?"

"Mr. Mitra *told* you that isn't true," Georgina couldn't help but interject.

Her mother held up a hand to restrain her. "If you persist, I shall have to order the servants to ignore your commands. That would be quite uncomfortable for me, but I will do it. I hired nearly all of them, you know."

"Fergus will stand by me," Papa growled.

"I suppose he will. Do you wish to see me standing before Sebastian's chamber door repelling an advance by the two of you?"

Papa shuffled and muttered and glowered. He seemed to be searching for further arguments, and finding none. Finally, he threw up his hands and stamped out, slamming the door with a resounding crash.

"He should take counsel from the ancestors," Joanna said.

Georgina had forgotten she was there. Clearly her mother had, too, because she jumped at the sound and whirled.

"They are founts of wisdom," Joanna added.

"Don't tell me you've been taken in by this nonsense," said Georgina's mother.

"I have been transformed!"

The two women gazed at each other. Georgina could almost see an unbridgeable chasm opening between them. She thought her mother saw it, too, because after a moment she sighed and said, "Well, it is time to go off to bed, whoever you have become."

Georgina went to tell Sebastian that he was not to be ejected from Stane Castle, but she remained uncertain and unhappy. For one thing, she didn't want to be at odds with Papa. She wanted his blessing on her marriage. And for another, she was concerned about what he might do to prevent it.

These considerations sent her to the top of the old stone tower the following afternoon. Mr. Mitra's airy refuge was well known by this time, and she did indeed find him there.

"Lady Georgina," he said, rising as she appeared at the top of the stair. He gave her one of his characteristic bows. "I have thought of offering you my apologies, but I didn't wish to intrude."

Or be dragged into her parents' disputes, Georgina thought. She didn't blame him for hiding. "I have come to ask if you can do something to change Papa's mind," she said. "He listens to you."

"Alas, that is only partly true," responded the Indian gentleman. "And less so lately. Your father certainly enjoys our conversations. He forms his own interpretations of what I say, however. And then holds to them very…firmly."

"But you are the scholar, the expert. He respects you very much."

Mr. Mitra bowed again. "I greatly value your good opinion. But I fear it is exaggerated where your father's…engrained views are concerned."

Sebastian's head appeared at the top of the stair. "Ah, we had the same idea," he said to Georgina as he climbed up. "You've got to do something, Mitra."

Mr. Mitra sighed. "As I was just telling Lady Georgina, I fear there is nothing I can do."

Sebastian came over to stand beside Georgina. "Couldn't you stage another of your…sessions? One where I turn out to be that Offa fellow's loyal retainer or something?"

Georgina couldn't tell if Mr. Mitra was offended

by this suggestion or simply weary of being misunderstood. Perhaps he was both at once.

"I do not *stage* them, Lord Sebastian. You must not imagine I don't believe in the principles I impart. Even though I take the liberty of doubting the…enthusiasms of some people."

Georgina had noticed Mr. Mitra's distaste for Joanna's declarations.

"Well, but—"

"I would help if I could," Mitra interrupted. "I simply do not see how it is possible."

"I *am* going to marry Georgina," declared Sebastian.

Georgina gave him a tremulous smile as he took her hand. It was an enormous comfort to hear him say that so definitely. She remembered how expertly he'd managed during their recent misadventure. He'd taken care of everything so confidently and capably. Taken care of her. Her spirits rose.

"I think you should do so," replied Mitra. "You seem admirably suited."

"That's all well and good to say," responded Sebastian. "But you've pretty nearly wrecked our engagement."

"I do not agree that I did so," was the polite but adamant reply.

"If you hadn't been there, drumming and warbling and putting us to sleep…"

Georgina broke into what was obviously going to be a futile argument. "You *will* help us if we can think of a…suitable way?" she asked the older man.

"Most happily."

Georgina tugged at Sebastian's arm and led him back down the stone stair.

"I think it *was* just a dream," he said as they went. "That room was very stuffy. We all nodded off. Or I did, at any rate." He frowned as they reached the first level of the tower. "It's how I would have known to dream of checkered trousers that stumps me," he added.

Georgina stopped him as he headed for the last rank of steps. "Over here," she said. She pulled him into a recess blocked off by an ancient wooden screen. No one else was likely to come into the tower, but if someone did, they wouldn't be seen. "We have to think what to do," she said. Sebastian looked down at her, tall and broad shouldered and strong. Despite their difficulties, when she was alone with him, she felt that all would be well. "We need a plan."

"Right." He looked at her hopefully.

She waited, silently willing him to take charge. "You must have made all sorts of plans as a soldier."

"Well." He frowned. "The first step in a military campaign is to list troop strength."

"Troop?"

"How many you can muster in the battle line." Sebastian ticked off one finger. "We've got Mitra. He promised to help."

"If we can find him a task he accepts," Georgina amended.

Sebastian nodded. "Same goes for Randolph. He'll do anything I ask. Though I don't want to get him in trouble with a bishop."

"What bishop?"

"Any bishop. He wants to be one himself, you know. Archbishop, even." Sebastian shook his head.

"It's odd enough to see your little brother rigged up as a cleric. Can't really picture him in the miter and robes."

It was a startling picture, if beside the current point. "No."

"At any rate, Randolph will stand by me. We can count on him."

"Mama is on our side," Georgina pointed out. "But she isn't tactful or…subtle. She's most likely to march right in and demand whatever she wants."

"A blunt instrument," said Sebastian, nodding. "We'll put her down as infantry, the division you throw straight into the thick of the battle."

Georgina had to laugh at the comparison. "A division likely to be distracted by a barking pug at a critical moment."

"The dogs," Sebastian mused. "They are distracting. To put it mildly. Perfect for diversionary tactics. Providing you can get them where you want them to go, of course."

"Diversion from what?" Georgina asked.

"I don't know. We're in the early stages of this campaign. There's Sykes; he's up to anything. He once stole a whole crate of oranges from a French cook tent. It was heavily guarded, too."

Georgina wondered how a valet could do this. She'd ask some other time. She hesitated, then said, "Hilda."

They looked at each other. "I expect…no, I know that she's not very good at following orders," Sebastian replied. "She'd be the sort of trooper who goes haring off on his own and gets a lot of people killed. Well, not killed, in this case, but…you know what I mean."

Georgina acknowledged the truth of this with a

nod. "She's daring, though. And highly motivated. She wants to us to be married, and she wants to make up for the prank she played." Georgina weighed this against her memories of Hilda's scrapes. "She does tend to improvise in the middle of things. You never know what she'd come up with."

"We'll hold her in reserve, as a last resort."

"That's probably best."

"Anyone else?"

"Not that I can think of," said Georgina. "I don't think we can ask Emma. She's too upset by the last misadventure to be involved."

Sebastian nodded. "Not a group I'd choose, necessarily. More like what my brother James would call a *motley crew*. Perhaps some of the castle servants?"

"They're trying very hard not to be caught in the middle of this. They naturally look to Mama for household orders, but they don't want to anger Papa."

"Neither do I," protested Sebastian.

"Too late." Georgina gave him a sympathetic smile.

"None of it was my fault!"

"It was not." She took his hand.

He looked down at her lovely face, shadowed in the tower's dimness, and saw everything he wanted in the depths of her eyes. "We *are* going to be married. Even if we have to elope after all."

After a moment, Georgina nodded. It was a mournful thing to contemplate, but if the choice was forced on her, she wouldn't be parted from Sebastian. "I'd rather not."

"Of course. I'd never ask you. Unless there was no other way for us to be together."

Something in that word, or in their locked gaze, ignited the atmosphere. Memories and hopes and pent-up desire drew them into each other's arms. The kiss was heady and tender, familiar and new. They stole another, and another.

Georgina pressed close, reveling in the feel of his hands on her. She wanted to wrap herself around him and never let go.

A sound drifted down from above, as of a chair scraping on flagstones. Sebastian raised his head. "Mitra might come down."

"Who cares about him?" Georgina muttered. But reality had come plodding back. "Papa will be looking for me," she admitted. "He's begun asking where I am every few minutes."

With mutual reluctance, they moved apart.

"All will be well soon," she said.

"We haven't actually made a plan," Sebastian pointed out.

"You'll come up with something, I know."

"Me?" He frowned. "You're the clever one."

"Not about…action campaigns." She smiled fondly up at him. "You're the master there. Look at the way you saved us when we were lost. I've no doubt you'll do so again."

"But…" This wasn't a matter of building a fire or cutting some bracken. This was a war of words. The admiration in his betrothed's gaze filled Sebastian with pride, and apprehension. She had no notion how stupid he could be when it came to intangible conflicts.

A distant call came from the garden outside. "Georgina?"

"That's Emma," she said. "Probably warning me that I'm wanted. I must go."

With a final squeeze of his hand, she slipped away. Sebastian remained in the recess, savoring the lingering scent of her perfume and memory of her touch, giving her time to get well away. He wanted nothing more than to impress her by saving the day. She'd compared him to a knight, he remembered. Those were the fellows who rode in like a one-man cavalry regiment and rescued the maiden in distress. If only it was a matter of riding… But it wasn't. Or saber work or navigating a forest path. He had no idea how to unpick the current tangle. It seemed all too likely that he'd fail.

In the dimness of the tower, Sebastian winced. He didn't think he could bear to see the impatience and disappointment in her eyes that he'd endured from schoolmasters and tutors throughout his youth. He'd thought he'd come to terms with his limitations, but now a whole new level of jeopardy opened before him.

"Sykes," he said aloud. Ideas were the man's meat and potatoes. Words were like the air he breathed. He'd think of something.

When he rang, Sykes appeared promptly in Sebastian's bedchamber, even though it wasn't a time of day when he customarily had duties. "You know the mess we're in," Sebastian said when the door had closed behind him. Outraged at the marquess's unfairness, Sebastian had recounted the story as he was undressing the previous evening.

"Yes, my lord." Sykes shook his head, and the playwright peeped out from behind the ideal servitor. "I never thought to hear myself say so, but it's beyond anything I could have invented. An Eastern magician. Visions of barbarians. A marriage in peril." He started to rub his hands together gleefully, then recalled himself.

"I wouldn't call Mitra a magician," Sebastian objected. "*He* certainly doesn't."

"Quite a modest fellow, as far as I have observed," Sykes said.

He appeared to think he was agreeing with Sebastian, when in fact this was quite off the main track. "Lady Georgina thinks I can make it all right," Sebastian told him. "But I've no idea how."

"A conundrum," Sykes replied. "They say in the servants' hall that his lordship never wavers once he fixes on a notion."

This was bad news. Worse, Sykes didn't sound as helpful as usual. Which worried Sebastian, even as he acknowledged that the problem was knottier than composing a proper letter or deciphering some wit's puzzling remarks. "Even nonsensical notions?" he asked.

"Particularly those," the valet responded with obvious relish.

Sebastian resisted the impulse to kick a nearby footstool. "I don't want to be at odds with my father-in-law. But I *will not* be bullied in this matter."

Sykes straightened like a trooper who'd been caught slouching on the parade ground. "No, my lord."

Sebastian turned to the window, looking out over the castle gardens. Even after so many years, he disliked asking outright for help. An inner judge always insisted that a man shouldn't need it. But *he* did. And for some reason, Sykes was making him say it, rather than anticipating his request. He had no choice but to speak. "You're always full of ideas. I thought you might have a suggestion."

"I can't say that I do, my lord."

Sebastian turned to him, surprised. Sykes never ran short of schemes. "Well, could you, er, think about it?"

"Very well, my lord. But you know, you may very well discover a solution."

Sebastian stared. If he'd had to describe Sykes's expression, which was never an easy task, he'd have said that he looked like a man who'd glimpsed a promising opportunity. Which was bewildering and quite at odds with what Sykes had said. Sebastian very nearly groaned aloud. If Sykes was at a standstill, then he really was lost.

Twelve

Sebastian had thought that things were bad enough with Georgina's father, but dinner that evening proved he'd underestimated the man's determination to express his displeasure. Every word he spoke seemed designed to show them all that he was not a man to be thwarted. He dominated the conversation at table, forcing everyone to listen to his discussion with Mitra and Joanna Byngham.

They went on and on about cycles of time and creation and destruction, using words Sebastian had never heard. He would have been content to let them, and never to learn the meaning of words such as *kalpa* and *yuga*. But every few minutes the marquess shot a question in Sebastian's direction, like a sudden volley from an entrenched position. The older man's expression, as he watched Sebastian struggle to reply, was evilly smug.

Georgina attempted to intervene at one point, saying, "Sebastian has not studied these topics for years as you have, Papa."

Sebastian was grateful, but also embarrassed that she should have to excuse his ineptitude.

And it earned her only a scowl and an irritable reprimand. "He might have benefited from more study and less running around in the woods," her father finished. "Like a savage."

He'd managed to work that particular word into the most unrelated topics tonight, Sebastian noticed.

Randolph took exception to this characterization of his brother. But he was hampered by his good manners, and the fact that he had fled the room before the pertinent exchange last evening.

Thus, his brother was like a man facing a cannon with a revolver as he challenged the marquess, Sebastian thought. Their host would always venture closer to outright offensiveness than Randolph ever could. Sebastian had to smile as he watched his brother struggle to get off a shot without ammunition. Randolph was the most punctilious of the duke's sons. He outdid even society's darling Robert, who sometimes put wit over courtesy. Which was just as well. Whatever Georgina's father might do, Sebastian didn't want to make things worse from his side.

When the marchioness finally objected, saying that her husband was boring half the table silly, their host launched into a long speech about the dearth of intelligent conversation in polite society. The ladies did not stay in the dining room long after that.

The situation grew both worse and better when they were gone. There were fewer witnesses to Sebastian's fumbling. He no longer had to endure Georgina's sympathetic gaze and wonder whether she secretly despised his ignorance. But the discussion grew so abstruse that he couldn't even pretend to follow. He was forced to confine his answer to "I couldn't say, sir" when yet another inquiry was thrown at him. His host took to repeating the phrase in a mocking tone that tried Sebastian's temper to its limits. Even Randolph sat tight-lipped and silent in the end.

When they rose to join the ladies in the drawing room, Sebastian's relief was immense, and premature. They strolled in to find Georgina, Emma, and their mother seated around the hearth while Miss Byngham bent over a thick volume in the corner. The marquess immediately said, "You all look very dull. We must find you some amusement. I know. Sebastian shall read aloud from that tale you like so much, Emma. *Waverly*, is it?"

Sebastian froze in the doorway. How had he betrayed himself? He was always so careful. He searched his host's mocking eyes. They were defiant and maliciously pleased. But he saw no evidence of deeper knowledge. No, Georgina's father was simply continuing in the same vein, mocking Sebastian's dislike of books. This was another subtle needle, not a bullet to the heart. "I'm not much good at it," he replied as casually as he could manage. "Randolph, now, he's a wonder. He can do different voices, like a play, bring you right to the edge of your seat."

Randolph stepped forward eagerly. "I'd be delighted to—" he began.

"I'm sure he's very competent," the marquess interrupted. "But as *you* are the one hoping to join our family, I think you should be the one to entertain us."

He made it sound like a forlorn hope.

"Reading is a pastime we enjoy very much," the older man added. "Don't we, girls?"

"I thought you despised *Waverley*," said Emma. "You said it was trifling."

"It would be much more pleasant if Emma would play and sing," said Georgina, giving her sister a significant glance.

Emma missed it. Randolph did not. "Some music would be most welcome," he said.

"Perhaps later," said the marquess. "After Sebastian has done his bit." He walked over to the shelves beside the fireplace and scanned them, picking a book from the center. "Here it is."

Georgina couldn't remember when she'd been so angry. Anyone could see that Sebastian didn't wish to read. And that Papa, thwarted in his effort to send him away, was determined to force her betrothed to do *something* he disliked. It was insupportable. "I don't believe anyone wishes to hear *Waverley*."

"I wouldn't mind," said Emma. This time, she caught Georgina's glare and blinked.

"Such a fuss over a simple request," said her father.

"You are the one fussing," put in her mother.

He was enjoying this, Georgina thought. It was like one of his learned disputes, only in the flesh. And Sebastian was too kind to squash him. Well, if Papa wanted a battle of wills, he could have one. "I'll read," she said, striding over to take the book.

Unfortunately, Randolph had had the same notion at the same instant. He approached her father from the other side and laid a hand on the volume just as she did, saying, "I take great pleasure in reading aloud."

For a moment, it was as if they were engaged in a tug-of-war over the book.

Georgina's mother, who had been distracted by Drustan's fit of wheezing, looked up and said, "Whatever are you doing?"

Georgina and Randolph went still, like children caught fighting over a box of sweets. Then Randolph smiled and stepped back with a bow. "I beg your pardon," he said.

"Let Randolph read," said Georgina's mother, ignoring her husband's incipient protest. "He has quite a melodious voice."

"Thank you, ma'am," replied Randolph with a smile and a small bow.

Georgina held out the volume. Sebastian's brother took it. "Where did you leave off?" he inquired courteously.

"Nowhere," answered Georgina, holding her father's gaze. "Papa refused to let us begin."

Her father made a little gesture, like a fencer conceding a hit, and smiled. But it wasn't amusing. This wasn't a game; it wasn't one of his philosophical disputes, where opponents scored points on one another with their cleverness. He was toying with her future. She couldn't allow him to continue this.

Randolph read from the beginning of the rousing tale of the Jacobite rebellion. As usual, he did a splendid job, holding his audience rapt. It was the sort of story that Sebastian might have enjoyed, had he not endured the preceding scene. As it was, he sat in an armchair in the corner and brooded, not even trying to place himself beside Georgina, as he would have any other evening.

He couldn't decide which was more embarrassing—
his inability to fulfill his host's request, or the intensity
of the rescue efforts. Georgina and Randolph had
sprung into action like mother bears defending their
cubs. With his brother, it was understandable. The
sons of the Duke of Langford naturally rallied to assist
each other, no matter how trivial the cause. And
Randolph had had years to notice his…limitations,
though he had never said anything. Now Sebastian
had to wonder whether Georgina had begun to see
through him as well. Why had she thrown herself so
fiercely into the fray? It was humiliating; he should be
taking care of her.

As Randolph reached a particularly gripping section of the tale, Sebastian studied her face from the
side. She didn't notice his gaze, as she often did, and
turn to meet it. Like the rest, she was transfixed by his
brother's voice. He couldn't tell how she felt.

Perhaps he shouldn't have come to Stane Castle
so soon, Sebastian thought. He'd given Georgina too
much time to observe him. He should have swooped
in, married her, and carried her off before she could
discover what a dunce he was.

And in that moment, it occurred to Sebastian that
this might not be fair. Was it deceitful, even dishon-
orable, to hide his failings? Was he obliged to tell
Georgina before the wedding? But would she still wish
to marry him if all was revealed? He couldn't bear the
idea that she might not.

Sebastian fought an urge to leap up and rush out
of this stuffy room, although he desperately *needed* to
move. His thoughts were always clearer when he was

on his feet, in action, and he needed to think. But leaving would be rude and draw yet more unwanted attention. He had to stay put.

And so he sat, frustrated, and wrestled with a question he'd never considered before in his life. Was it his duty to confess all his secrets to Georgina? With his family, this had never been an issue. They'd always been there. They were…simply the ground of his existence. They'd had ample time to conclude whatever they wished about him, and they took him as they found him. His friends did the same, for different reasons. Sebastian knew he was valued as a loyal comrade and convivial companion, admired for his sporting and military prowess. What lay beneath the surface was nothing to his cronies.

But Georgina was a different matter. For now, she fell somewhere between the two categories. Sebastian grappled with the distinction. He'd charmed her as he did his friends. But she was to become part of his family. Actually, it felt as if she already was. She'd promised herself to him for life. As he'd seen with his parents, this was a commitment that demanded more than surfaces.

Sebastian shifted uneasily in his chair, Randolph's voice becoming a drone in the background. Along with the physical delights they'd already sampled, he and Georgina would face challenges and sorrows together. There would be problems to solve. No one escaped difficulties. Didn't she deserve to know what sort of man she'd have at her side? He'd told her outright that she was cleverer, but that wasn't the whole of it. If…when…a day came and he failed her, would she blame him? An even bleaker thought followed this one. Perhaps what she really deserved was a quicker, wiser man to be her partner.

This last thought was like a blow, and it roused immediate rebellion. He didn't care. He wouldn't give her up. If that was selfish…well, then it was. In any case, it was too late for scruples; they'd already consummated their bond by the pool in the ravine. Sebastian felt a touch of shame at this conclusion, and an answering glimmer of exultation. Georgina was his. He'd simply have to find a way to be worthy of her.

He wondered if other people found impending marriage so complicated. He'd have sworn that Nathaniel felt no such conflicts as he stood beside him at the altar. But then, his eldest brother had been marrying for the dukedom, not for his own gratification. Fleetingly, he hoped that his brother had found a bit of happiness in the match as well. What had Randolph said about a carriage race?

Sebastian was startled by a round of applause. Randolph had finished his reading. Long familiar with his brother's skills, he easily joined the chorus of praise.

"You should go on the stage," said Emma, her eyes bright with admiration.

"He's a clergyman," chided Georgina.

Randolph smiled, setting the book aside. "I admit I've enjoyed taking part in a few amateur theatricals."

"I'm sure you were wonderful," declared Emma, throwing Georgina a triumphant glance.

"Indeed, I wonder now if it may be some vestige…"

His voice trailed off. Sebastian frowned at him.

Randolph had been in an odd mood since Mitra's "meditation."

"Some what?" asked Emma.

"Nothing." Randolph smiled again and turned away.

The group was shifting. The marquess would go to his study now, Sebastian knew. Though it was not strictly polite, he could slip away. Georgina looked surprised that he didn't come to her. Randolph approached as if to join him. But Sebastian just couldn't stay.

He headed for the place that had been his refuge since he was small, the stables. The long summer twilight would last a while longer, and frankly he didn't care if it didn't. "I'll see to Whitefoot when I return," he told the startled groom as his mount was saddled. "You needn't worry about us."

Once in the saddle, Sebastian immediately felt better. He let Whitefoot amble slowly down the road from the castle and out into the countryside. He'd ridden this way often enough that he could guide the horse back in the moonlight.

It was a profound relief to have space around him instead of walls. He felt as if his spirit expanded, like a deep breath or unfurled wings. The evening air was soft on his cheek. The birds were making their farewells to the dying light. He caught the rush of a bat above his head. Dewfall had intensified the scents of leaf and water. He would have known, even if he hadn't noticed on an earlier ride, that there was a tiny stream off to the left. From the set of the stars, he could see that he was riding west. Every element in his surroundings spoke to him so clearly. Out here, he felt more alive, more powerful. What was that phrase of Robert's? "Monarch of all he surveyed."

After half an hour or so, Sebastian pulled up at the edge of a stretch of forest. He dismounted, throwing a blanket he'd brought over Whitefoot's back. Gathering bits of dry grass and dead wood, he made a small fire and sat down beside it. For him, this kind of retreat never got old. Snug in a circle of firelight, back against a massive tree trunk, he felt like the master of his fate.

And ironically, on the heels of that thought, a host of painful memories rushed at him, like an enemy patrol bursting from ambush. Though he tried to dismiss them, it seemed he was doomed to review his long struggle with words on a page, even though he was so familiar with that sad history he needed no reminders.

It had taken Sebastian a long time to understand that others didn't see a line of type as he did. That letters marched in good order for his brothers, for example, and told them things he would never know. And then one day Nathaniel had been sitting beside him in the schoolroom at Langford. They'd been about eight and six, Sebastian supposed. His brother had been sounding out a difficult stretch of text, running his finger beneath the letters and speaking aloud. Watching and throwing in a question or two, Sebastian realized that he and his brother saw quite different things when they looked at the page. Nathaniel perceived separate segments, words, not a single clump of letters mashed together in a mocking jumble.

He'd tried to explore this mystery, but Nathaniel had been puzzled and then impatient to complete his assignment and go outside. His brother couldn't imagine a problem with what he saw so plainly. And who was to blame him? It was bizarre.

Sebastian had tried twice more, with a tutor and then with a teacher he'd thought sympathetic at school, but he hadn't been able to make them understand either. Partly, he'd made a hash of explaining, and partly the men were too accustomed to boys trying to shirk their lessons. It was obvious that neither had heard of anything like what he struggled to describe.

After that, Sebastian had accepted the fact that there was something wrong with him. His brain was flawed. He couldn't master a skill that everyone else found simple. He turned his attention to ways of concealing his stupidity and working around it, with varying degrees of success, while at school. There were times when he simply couldn't avoid public humiliation. He'd weathered such occasions through jokes and poses, playing the good-natured, thickheaded athlete, or the high-nosed, uncaring nobleman. He didn't think anyone realized how very much he'd hated his "education." His sporting success had masked a great deal. And after he escaped the classroom, evasion became vastly easier.

Until right now. Sebastian leaned his head against the rough bark of the oak at his back and faced the question again. Must he tell Georgina? The prospect made him more afraid than he'd ever been on a battle line. How would he even make her understand, if he did try? No one ever had. Even Sykes… Well, he didn't know what Sykes believed as he helped Sebastian beat his way through the thickets of language. Or what he would advise about Georgina. A man couldn't discuss his wife with his valet. Not even one who really wasn't, like Sykes. And his not-quite wife. He couldn't, at any rate.

The fire guttered. He'd need to add more wood if he was staying. Sebastian sighed. He would have liked to. It would be so pleasant to curl up here at the foot of the oak and spend the night. But it wouldn't do. He'd learned long ago that running away solved nothing.

Regretfully, he rose and extinguished the remaining flames. At least the household would be in bed by the time he returned. There'd be no need to face his brother or his fiancée and see the reflection of the evening's events in their eyes. Ought he to thank them? He didn't think he'd be able to manage that. Pulling the blanket from Whitefoot's back, he mounted and started slowly back the way he'd come.

At Stane Castle, Georgina had dismissed her maid and climbed into bed when she heard "Psst." She looked around, startled, in time to see her youngest sister emerging from behind the closed draperies.

"I thought Mary would never go," Hilda said.

"Aren't you still confined to your room?" Georgina asked. Not that unpalatable orders would ever stop her youngest sister.

"I put a bolster in my bed to make it look as if I'm asleep," she replied. "Mama thinks I'm sulking."

"Aren't you?"

"Not anymore." Hilda plopped down on the feather-bed beside her. "I heard what happened."

The whole household had no doubt heard by now, Georgina thought. Joanna was good friends with the housekeeper. Papa complained to Fergus sometimes. Servants overheard all sorts of things in the course of their work.

"Do you ever think that Papa is demented?" Hilda asked.

The thought had flitted through Georgina's mind now and then, but she decided it was best not to tell Hilda. And of course he was not.

"We have to do something!" Her youngest sister bounced on the bed. "You're going to have to elope after all. So you see, I will have been right. It wasn't a lie, but a…prediction."

"You will have been right?" The phrase struck Georgina as thoroughly characteristic of Hilda.

There was a soft knock on her bedchamber door. Emma looked around the edge. "There you are, Hilda. I looked for you in your room."

"I can't mope about there when we are in the midst of a crisis!"

"You'll get in trouble," Emma warned.

"How could I be in any more trouble?"

The two older Stane sisters had to acknowledge the truth of this. Emma came in and sat on the other side of the bed.

"And I have to apologize to Georgina," Hilda added solemnly.

"You did that," said Emma.

"Not properly." Hilda put one hand over her heart and assumed a deeply sincere expression. "I've thought a great deal about what you said. About not wanting me in your new household after what I have done, I mean. But what you don't understand, Georgina, is that I will be a…a pattern card of virtue once I am in London. And not so very bored."

"You've never been such a thing in your life," said Emma.

"Well, I've always been stuck in this…backwater. I think it must be the most tedious place on Earth."

"You seemed quite happy here when you were small," Georgina said. She remembered tiny Hilda tearing around the castle and the gardens, face alight, declaring that she was the captain of a pirate ship or queen of imaginary empires.

Hilda looked disgusted. "When I was a child."

She was still so much one, Georgina thought. And yet she was growing up very fast, too, and capable of more complicated mischief. She'd always been the most curious and quick of them. It was too bad Joanna was distracted by their father's studies. The governess might have kept Hilda interested in her studies otherwise.

"I won't elope," Georgina said. She'd been thinking, too, and discovered she had strong feelings on this subject. "I don't want my wedding to be some hurried, furtive affair, far from everyone I know. I want to be married in my home, with my family and Sebastian's around us, and everyone celebrating our happiness."

Emma blinked back tears.

"Well, I hope you can be," replied Hilda. "But just now I cannot place Papa in that affecting picture."

"Sebastian is going to make a plan." Georgina thought of the evening just past. She was still angry at her father, but as time passed she also wondered why Sebastian had balked over such a trivial thing. She'd responded instinctively to the emotion she'd seen in his face. He'd looked…really distressed. Even now, a fierce protective instinct rose in her. Papa had behaved abominably. But had this particular tussle really been necessary? Couldn't Sebastian have given in? She was also a little worried about the way he'd rushed off without a word.

"Sebastian is very handsome," said Hilda carefully. "And kind and charming, but he's…he's not a…deep thinker, is he?"

Georgina stiffened against her pillows. "He's a trained military man, a cavalry major." She started to tell them how splendidly he'd cared for her in the ravine, then decided not to. That conversation might lead to details she wasn't prepared to share with her younger sisters.

"Well, if we want to run Papa through with a saber, that might be helpful," her youngest sister replied.

"Hilda!" Emma exclaimed. Georgina choked back a horrified laugh.

"I only mean…" Hilda seemed to grope for words. "Papa is thinking all the time, isn't he? All sorts of… complicated thoughts. We need a sly, devious plan to get 'round him. I don't think Sebastian is very devious."

Georgina agreed with that. He was delightfully straightforward.

"I am much more devious than any of you," Hilda added.

"Even Papa?" Georgina had to ask, a bit amused.

"Yes." Hilda nodded as if to emphasize the word.

"Because he is head of the household and can give whatever orders he likes. I can't. So I have to find more indirect ways to…to accomplish my goals. I'm forced to be devious, you see."

Georgina stared at her. So did Emma, with rather more apprehension. Hilda gazed blandly back. Her youngest sister was well on her way to becoming a force to be reckoned with, Georgina thought. Did Mama have any notion? And was she really going to invite her to London? It was becoming clearer and clearer that looking after Hilda wasn't a task to be undertaken lightly.

"So, I was thinking, what if we fed Papa a drug?" Hilda continued. "When the kitchen maid had the toothache, they gave her a draught to help her sleep. It made her so muddled she hardly knew where she was. Or who she was. There's some left."

"How would you know that?" Georgina wondered.

"I make it my business to know things," was the worrying reply. "I know where the bottle is kept, too. We could dose Papa and then hold the wedding before he regained his senses."

"No, we couldn't." Georgina didn't know whether to laugh or shudder.

"Why not?"

Georgina couldn't help but envision her father stumbling about in a drugged haze before the entire Gresham family. She did shudder. "It wouldn't be… We just can't, Hilda."

Hilda heaved a great sigh, like a workman delayed by petty objections. "Well, that would be easiest. Because the dose is right here, you know. But…all right. My other plan is to send Randolph to town for a special license. You get them from bishops, don't you? He's a clergyman; he must be acquainted with any number of bishops. He could bring it back and then just perform the ceremony himself before anyone caught on."

"But Georgina wants to marry with all her family around her," Emma said. "She just said so. And I think she's very right." She gave Georgina a sentimental glance.

Hilda grimaced. "We are facing an emergency here, Emma. It may be necessary to cut corners. Mama could be present. And you and I."

Emma tossed her head, refusing to be overborne by her stronger-minded sister this time. "That's not what Georgina wants. Anyway, don't those license things cost a great deal of money?"

"Georgina is an heiress," Hilda replied. "She has heaps of money."

"Not in my pockets," Georgina replied. As it happened, oddly, she knew quite a bit about special licenses. During the London season just past, she'd become acquainted with a young lady who'd fallen in love with a man her parents found unsuitable. Selina had looked into every alternative for marrying and poured out her findings, along with her woes, to Georgina.

"Well, duke's sons must have some money," added Hilda. "Randolph could pay."

"It's not so easy," Georgina replied. "I am not twenty-one until December. So to get a special license, Randolph would have to swear, before the Archbishop of Canterbury at Doctors' Commons, that he had our parents' consent. He would not wish to offer a false oath. Especially in those circumstances." Indeed, she was certain he'd refuse. "As is only right," she added dutifully.

"Both parents?" Hilda asked. "Or would just Mama do?"

"I…don't know." Georgina's legal knowledge didn't stretch that far.

"I wager Mama would be enough. I could get her to write a letter."

"You could not," said Emma.

"Of course I could." Hilda was scornful.

Georgina decided not to ask how she could be so certain. "I don't think Randolph will be swayed by…technicalities. He knows very well that Papa does not consent."

"Oh, pooh. He mustn't let a little thing like that stand in his way. I'll explain it to him," Hilda said.

"Please do not! Promise me you won't."

Hilda sulked. "Somebody has to do something!" she declared after a while. "We can't just droop about like simpering ninnies and let all our hopes…collapse. While we die of boredom."

"I told you, Sebastian is making a plan." Georgina wondered again where he'd gone in such a hurry after the reading. "And I would hardly call these last few days boring."

"That's true." Hilda smiled. There was a gleam in her eye that Georgina didn't care for at all. "I shall offer Sebastian my help. If I explain it to him very carefully, I wager he can convince his brother to adopt my scheme."

Georgina thought that extremely unlikely. "You are not to plague Sebastian," she ordered.

"I'm not going to *plague* him," Hilda began. "I daresay he will be very glad of a...little boost."

"No," replied Georgina. "You should both go to bed. It's late."

Hilda hopped down with suspicious docility. "You must check the corridors as we go, Emma. To make certain no one sees me."

Emma stood up, but crossed her arms over her chest. "I am not helping you any more. Not ever."

"I am only going back to my room," Hilda wheedled. "Where I am supposed to be."

"Yes, but..."

"So you would be helping me *obey* Mama and Papa, in this case."

Watching Emma puzzle over this distinction, Georgina didn't hold out much hope for her future entanglements in Hilda's pranks. She would have to keep a close eye on her youngest sister. And warn Sebastian. And speak to Mama. And rein in Papa. And what else?

Her life had been so serene, so settled. And now in the course of one weird evening, it had been turned upside down. For a perfectly ridiculous cause. It would have been funny, if it did not include the threat of losing Sebastian. Georgina set her jaw. That would not, could not happen.

Thirteen

By a fortunate coincidence, Georgina encountered Sebastian as she was accompanying her mother to her workroom the following morning. "Come along," she said, taking his arm.

He hesitated, not offering his usual warm smile. Nor did he meet her eyes. "Is something wrong?" She immediately judged it a silly question. A great deal was wrong, obviously.

"No," he said. But he still hung back.

Georgina put his reluctance down to the dogs milling around their feet. "It might help if we both talk to Mama," she explained.

He walked with her then, clearly not in his customary good spirits. Her mother had gone ahead, and they found her sitting at her desk, sifting through a sheaf of papers. "Mama," said Georgina. She had to repeat it before she captured her mother's attention. "Our wedding is in less than two weeks' time," she said then. She refused to admit any doubt into her declaration.

"Yes, dear. Do you think you would like knots of

pink ribbon on your gown? There's still time to send to Hereford."

Georgina sighed, wondering if her mother could be doing this on purpose. It seemed perverse to express an interest in dress trimmings—a subject that notoriously bored her—when they had much more serious problems. But Mama was not so sly. "What are we to do about Papa?" Georgina said. "I want him to walk me down the aisle. I want us all to be happy together."

"Oh, Alfred will get over it," her mother replied with a wave of her hand. "You know he has these fancies. He throws himself into a subject, and then he abandons it for some new thing."

It was true. Yet his current obsession had lasted for months and showed no signs of fading. "None of the others involved forbidding my engagement," Georgina pointed out.

"I set him straight on that," her mother answered, as if she thought that Papa had listened to her. Then she stood suddenly, seeming to remember something truly important. She strode over to a pile of cushions and picked up one of the pugs lolling there. "Sebastian, what do you think?" she asked, displaying a small female. "I have gone into the matter very carefully, and I believe Fiona here might do for your mother."

Sebastian started as if he'd been pinched. "What?"

"As a gift, of course. No question of payment." The marchioness looked fondly down into the small dog's face. "Even though I could ask quite a sum for you, couldn't I, my lovely?"

Fiona yipped and licked her mistress's face.

"Oh, er, well."

Sebastian's polished manners seemed to have deserted him. Georgina examined her betrothed. He looked tired and not quite as…capable as usual.

"I'm not sure," he tried.

With a fleeting sense of what it must feel like to be the captain of a sinking ship, Georgina intervened. "You must ask the duchess first if she wants a lapdog, Mama. Not everyone cares to have one."

"Oh, but Fiona is a special…"

"And as she *doesn't* have one," Georgina interrupted, "she probably doesn't want one." You had to be blunt with Mama. She didn't bother with subtleties. And she preferred it.

Nor did plain talk offend her. The marchioness shrugged and set Fiona down, turning back to the documents on her desk.

"What are you going to do about Papa?" Georgina asked again. "It is all very well to talk of ribbons, but I want him to be part of my wedding. Gladly." Her voice quavered on the last word, which was annoying. But it caught both her companions' attention.

"I've told him he's being a fool," responded her mother. "I'll tell him again."

Which would do no good at all, Georgina thought. Her father thrived on opposition. A current of resentment ran through her. What should have been a happy time in her life was now tense and anxious. And Sebastian was giving her no help at all, standing stiffly at her side as if on parade. Though she supposed she couldn't expect him to argue with her parents. She certainly wouldn't have with his. She needed to talk to him alone.

She took his arm and urged him from the room. The corridor outside was fortunately empty, and she stepped quickly into a vacant parlor further along, shutting the door behind them. "Shouting at Papa will only make him more obstinate. Mama can never seem to realize that. We must think of something else." She looked up at her fiancé and waited.

Sebastian was feeling quite unlike himself. He hadn't slept well, and he always slept well. Despite performing his usual morning ablutions, he couldn't shake the idea that he looked rumpled and untidy. But most of all, he was burdened by the notion that not only was he not being honest with Georgina, he didn't wish to be. It was a dilemma he'd never faced before in his unexamined, openhearted life. And he didn't want to think about it—or think so much at all, for that matter. He was tired of thinking. Couldn't people see that he was no good at it? He wanted everything back as it had been, before these unwelcome scruples had risen to plague him.

Georgina was waiting for him to speak, gazing at him with such hope and trust. He stared at her lips, full and warm and his for the taking. He wanted her so much. Desire and concern squared off inside him like two armies on the battlefield. It wanted only the crash of cannon to complete his misery.

She smiled and put a hand on his arm, raising her chin, obviously inviting a kiss. He desperately wanted to kiss her. "When I'm with you, I know all will be well," she said.

It was how she should feel, how he wanted her to feel, Sebastian thought. He longed to take care of her. But he hadn't the first idea how to mend matters. Last night's scene in the drawing room came rushing back. If her father had pushed harder and he'd been exposed, would she be so confident now? Unlikely. Achingly close to her, dizzied by the sweet scent of her perfume, he was struck by a dreadful realization. There would be no way to sustain his deception once they were living together. He had a sudden vision of her bringing him a letter or a document—his wife come to consult him on a matter of importance to them both. Was he to fob her off? Summon Sykes? Unthinkable! Sebastian was washed by a flood of shame. Why hadn't this occurred to him before?

He felt his cheeks reddening. He couldn't face her. He groped for an escape and managed only the inane. "I should go and, er, check on Whitefoot," he said.

Georgina looked astonished. "What? Why?"

"I went out riding last night." Naturally, he'd groomed his horse and put him away properly, but he was stuck with this damnably silly excuse now.

"In the dark?"

Sebastian nodded miserably.

She gripped his arm more tightly. "Sebastian, what's wrong?"

"Nothing. Just…won't take but a few minutes." Like a coward funking it before a battle, he stepped away and fled.

Georgina stood quite still, feeling very much alone. She didn't think Sebastian had ever lied to her before. In fact, she was practically certain he hadn't. He had a certain…transparent quality. It was one of the traits that had drawn her to him. But just now, he had. She'd seen it in his face. Something was wrong, seriously wrong, and he didn't wish to tell her what it was.

Aware of a painful hollowness in the region of her heart, she sank down on a nearby sofa and took a deep breath. Had her family's eccentricities finally put him off? He hadn't seemed to mind them at all. But Papa had risen to new heights of…of nonsense with his railing about Welsh savages. Perhaps, also, Randolph's arrival and opinions had influenced her betrothed? Georgina nearly leaped up when she remembered that Hilda was all too likely to nag Randolph about a special license. Then she recalled that Randolph had planned to go and see their local church this morning. He was safe for the moment.

She leaned back and was assailed by anxiety once more. Was Sebastian sorry he'd become engaged to her? Did he wish he could draw back? And if so, was she obliged, in honor, to offer him an escape? She clasped her hands to keep them from trembling. The idea roused a wave of regret so intense it nearly over-whelmed her. It was answered by an equally strong impulse of denial. Georgina set her jaw. She was not going to do any such thing. She was going to marry Sebastian as planned. Nothing on Earth was going to stop her.

With this resolve burning in her, Georgina real-ized that she loved her noble cavalry major with all her heart. The feeling had taken root in London and grown rapidly in the months since, until it was twined through every part of her like an exquisitely blossoming vine. The progress had been so constant, so pleasant, that she hadn't fully taken it in till now. She loved him. Oh, how she loved him! Papa must be *made* to see.

Georgina rose and strode out of the parlor. She felt as if determination must be hissing off her like steam from a boiling kettle. She had no qualms, no doubts. This contest was life or death to her, and she meant to win.

But she couldn't find her father. He wasn't in his study or the library or the stables. She climbed the tower to see if he might have discovered Mr. Mitra's retreat, but he wasn't there either. And their Indian guest disavowed all knowledge of his whereabouts. Finally, Georgina tried the schoolroom, thinking he might be conferring with Joanna over some bit of research. He was not. Joanna was there alone, bent over a long table littered with bits of gilt paper, scissors, and a pot of glue. "I'm trying to reproduce the headdress I wore as a temple priestess," she said when Georgina looked in. She spoke as if they were continuing a commonplace conversation.

"The materials are far inferior, of course." She gestured at the gilt paper. "Even laughable. But I believe I may be able to catch the *spirit* of the regalia."

With no idea how to answer this, Georgina said, "Where's Hilda?" Teaching her sister was, after all, Joanna's job. Not that anyone seemed to care about that, despite Hilda's dire need of supervision.

"Still serving out her sentence" was the rather blithe reply.

Georgina didn't think her sister's punishment was meant to excuse her from lessons, but she couldn't think about that now. She hurried downstairs to check her father's study again. Still empty. She was about to burst with impatience when she heard male voices in the great hall. She practically ran toward the sound.

"It's a fine example of a Saxon font," her father was saying. "Supposedly blessed by Saint Ethelbert himself."

He'd gone with Randolph to show off the church, Georgina realized. It was just like him. She reached the landing as the two men came to the foot of the stairs. "Papa!"

They looked up at her, startled. "What's wrong?" asked her father.

"I need to speak to you."

"Well, there's no need to shout. Great gods, I thought the house must be on fire."

The front door opened just then, and Sebastian entered, blinking at the sudden shift from sunlight to dimness. He'd taken two steps before he noticed the scene before him. Stiffening, he started to retreat. It was like a tableau representing the current lamentable state of her life, Georgina thought. "I must speak to you now, Papa!" she snapped.

All three men flinched at her tone. If she hadn't been so focused on her mission, she might have enjoyed their expressions. They looked like small boys called to account for some piece of mischief.

"I'm entertaining our guest," her father replied. "Can't it wait?"

"No." Georgina marched down the stairs and practically dragged her father into the library, ignoring curious glances from the Gresham brothers.

"What the deuce is the matter with you?" he said when the door had clicked shut behind them.

Georgina stood quite close to him, her hands on her hips, her eyes fixed on his. What was she to say to persuade him? Words came in response to the thought. "So, Papa, it seems that my happiness means nothing to you."

"What? What are you talking about? Of course it does."

"And yet you are bent on ruining my wedding."

"Is that what this is…? My dear, you simply don't understand the ramifications of…"

"Stop it!" She hadn't meant to shout. It had just come out that way.

Her father stared at her, astonished.

"Stay right here," Georgina commanded. "Don't move. I mean it." Putting every ounce of will she could muster into her gaze, she waited until he gave her a sulky nod. Then she rushed out, scarcely pausing to notice that Sebastian and Randolph were gone, and hurried down corridors and up stairs. At the top of the stone tower, thoroughly out of breath, she collected Mr. Mitra by the simple expedient of grasping his forearm and hauling him to his feet. Ignoring his questions and protests, she hustled him back to the library. She was quite relieved to find her father still there. He'd moved over to the shelves and was examining a book.

"Sit there," she commanded, directing Mr. Mitra to a chair at a large table in the center of the room. He dropped into it with patent relief.

"Georgina," said her father.

She gave him a burning look. He fell silent. "You can sit there, Papa." She pointed to a chair opposite Mitra. After a moment's hesitation, he obeyed.

"What in blazes is wrong with you?" he asked. "This sort of behavior is—"

"Just what I learned from observing my parents," she finished for him.

Her father blinked, his mouth hanging a little open.

Georgina stood at the head of the table and gazed at the two men, her elders and superiors in intellect and knowledge. And she didn't care about that. Not a whit. "I'm out of patience," she said. "You are always talking, Papa, but this time you're going to listen to me."

"You are still quite a young woman," her father began. "You must defer to wiser heads in serious matters such as these."

"*Wiser* I will not concede," she replied fiercely. "How many times have I heard you say that years of study may not yield wisdom?"

"Yes, but I didn't mean… I wasn't talking about myself," he sputtered.

She wasn't enjoying this, Georgina thought. She didn't wish to argue with her father, only to redeem her future. She turned to their silent companion. "Mr. Mitra, I have heard you say, on more than one occasion, that the exploration of one's past lives is a delicate and complex endeavor. And that it is difficult to draw absolute conclusions."

"Very true," their guest replied.

Georgina knew that Mr. Mitra was pained by Joanna's recent excesses, particularly the "ancient sayings" the governess had begun to offer. Their supremely polite guest had even suggested that one or two made no sense. When Joanna had loftily informed him that they were far beyond any current level of understanding, Mr. Mitra had actually scowled at her. Georgina wondered in passing if Joanna would appear in her regalia tonight. And was she thinking of these irrelevancies to avoid the conflict in front of her?

She made herself continue. "You have also said that a being's growth and change determines the progress of their lives over the, er, centuries." As she spoke, Georgina realized that she'd picked up quite a bit from the interminable dinner table discussions. "If, for example, someone had actually lived a previous life as a Welsh…"

"Savage!" interrupted her father. He was recovering from her initial rush and was by no means cowed.

She looked at him. "Tribesman," she said. "Chieftain, perhaps. Prince, even."

"Grand labels make no difference," he replied. "They were all savages."

"And yet you have always told us, Papa, that we should not judge people by their external trappings, but rather by evidence of their inner nature."

"There are exceptions," he growled. But he looked away.

Georgina waited a moment, then turned to Mitra again. "Had that…history occurred. If we believed it wholeheartedly." She paused for Mitra's nod. "What are we to think if we find that this individual is…is now a fine, young English nobleman?"

"Not so fine, perhaps," muttered her father, like an unruly schoolboy rebelling against the teacher.

"From a highly respected family," said Georgina, louder. "With a sterling personal reputation."

"But who knows what we might not have heard?"

"Papa!"

He sat back in his chair at the snap in her tone.

"Would we not be forced to conclude that this… person has made great progress in his…" She groped for the right words. "His moral character."

"That would indeed be a plausible argument," Mitra replied. He smiled up at her.

"That he had improved? Grown, uh, more admirable?" Mitra nodded.

Georgina's father made a skeptical sound. "Once a savage, always a savage is what I say."

Georgina hit the table with her fist, astonishing them all. "Are you listening at all, Papa? I am asking the opinion of your honored guest, the expert you invited here to teach you about these matters. Perhaps you could explain it again, Mr. Mitra?"

"As I have *often* said," replied Mitra obligingly, "it is most unwise to draw conclusions from one or two fleeting experiences. We are dealing here with a vast accumulation of circumstances."

Georgina's father frowned. "You mean if he'd really been a benighted savage, he'd have been reborn as a beetle or something?" he asked.

Mitra winced. Georgina held his dark gaze, willing him to help her. She watched him struggle with his scholarly need for precision, or perhaps his deeply held beliefs. "Something like that," he said finally.

"So you're saying Gresham's redeemed himself?"

"I don't care for that way of putting it," Mr. Mitra

began. Georgina frowned. She didn't want to bully him, but he *had* promised to help them. The Indian gentleman sighed, bowing his head. "I…grant you could see it in that light. In a way." He gazed at the tabletop. His lips moved soundlessly. Georgina couldn't tell what words they formed, or even if they were English. A complaint? A caveat? A prayer?

"Hmmm." Her father tapped his chin with his fingertips. "Well. I suppose…it's possible Gresham's all right then."

Georgina needed more than that. "I think there can be no doubt," she said.

"Perhaps." Her father never liked letting go of a point of dispute.

"Absolutely. And so everything is back as it was. My wedding will go on as planned. Yes, Papa?"

He gestured airily. "Yes, all right. There's no need to breathe fire over me, my dear. What a great fuss you've made over nothing."

As she could not box her father's ears, Georgina spoke through clenched teeth. "You will *happily* escort me to the altar."

He straightened as if she'd insulted him. "Of course I will. Who else but me?"

"And join in all the celebrations," she added. "Without any grumbling."

"Naturally."

He said it as if the whole disaster had been of her making. Georgina had to stifle something very like a growl.

Her father's square chin came up, and a new thought lit his green eyes. "We'll have to organize some proper shooting for Langford's visit." He rubbed his hands together gleefully, as if the uproar over the wedding had never occurred. "Do you care for it, Mitra?"

"Shooting what?" the other man asked.

"Birds, at this season. Pheasant, partridge."

Mitra shook his head.

"Ah, right. You don't eat 'em. I imagine you don't shoot 'em either."

"You are correct."

Nearly unable to contain her exasperation and bemusement and relief, Georgina left them to it. Outside the library door, she nearly tripped over Hilda, who'd obviously been listening at the keyhole. "How did you even know we were in there?" But it was a silly question. Somehow, even in the confines of her bedchamber, Hilda learned such things.

"You were amazing!" exclaimed her youngest sister. "Heroic. Or…heroine-ic. Is that a word? I want to be just like you when I'm older."

"*Heroic* seems a bit strong." Georgina realized that she was trembling. She'd been all right in the heat of the argument. Now she was ready to sink.

"No, it doesn't. The way you laid matters out for Papa? I wish Mama had been here. She might have learned something."

"Don't be silly."

"I'm not," Hilda replied. "She shouts at him, but she never bothers to give him proper reasons."

Embarrassed and curiously flattered, Georgina turned away. She wanted to give Sebastian the good news. And to throw herself into his arms, she thought, if she possibly could. She needed the safety and comfort of that newfound haven.

Fourteen

THE GRESHAM BROTHERS HAD TAKEN REFUGE IN A reception room on the other side of the entry hall, leaving the door ajar. As the sounds from the library mounted, Sebastian wondered if he ought to charge in on a support mission for Georgina. He hadn't been any help with her mother. When it was a matter of fencing with words rather than sabers, he was hardly of the first rank.

He could stand at her side, however. A fellow officer had once told him that he'd tipped the scales of a confrontation simply by looming, large and menacing. Of course, it wouldn't do to threaten his future father-in-law. Unless he tried to bully Georgina. In which case... As Sebastian hesitated, indecisive, they saw Hilda slip down the stairs and across the hall, crouch by the library door, and apply her ear to the keyhole.

"That girl is extraordinarily...enterprising," remarked Randolph.

Sebastian nodded. He was more reluctant to move now that he had to pass a gatekeeper.

From their vantage point, the brothers could hear

nothing but noise from the library. Sebastian tried to judge how it was going from the changes in Hilda's expression. She seemed mainly amazed.

Not long after this, the door opened. Sebastian stepped forward as Hilda sprang back. Georgina came out, spoke to Hilda, and then saw him waiting. She rushed over and into the reception room, coming to an abrupt stop before the empty hearth. "Oh, you're both here," she said. She waited a moment, then added, "I spoke to Papa."

"At high volume," commented Randolph. His attempt at a joke fell flat.

Talking quickly, Georgina told them what had been said. "So everything is back as it was," she finished. "It was all a tempest in a teapot."

If only that was true, Sebastian thought. If only he could roll back the last few days and erase the gloomy thoughts they'd provoked. "Oh…good," he said.

Georgina looked distinctly disappointed. Sebastian tried to muster a more satisfying reaction, but before he could find the words, she repeated, "Good," in a strangled voice and rushed out. Sebastian silently cursed his inarticulate tongue. He took out his frustration on a nearby ottoman, giving it a kick.

"I should have left you alone," Randolph said. "I'm sorry. I was so taken by the story, I didn't think."

Sebastian kicked the ottoman again. The thing scarcely budged. It might have been stuffed with rocks.

"I'll go and call her back," Randolph said. "You two will want…"

"It doesn't matter," interrupted Sebastian. He thought of how, so recently, he'd longed, desperately prayed, for a few minutes alone with his fiancée. Now, he couldn't hold her, couldn't kiss her, without wondering if he was obliged to spoil everything.

"So, all's well again," said Randolph.

"Unh."

"It sounds like quite the epic scene. It seems you're getting a strong-minded wife."

"What?" Sebastian looked up. Randolph was examining him curiously. Had he given himself away somehow?

"Do you mind?"

"Mind what?" As he often did, he'd missed something. He had no idea what his brother was talking about.

"That Georgina is, um, such a spirited debater."

"Of course not." Sebastian was surprised at the question. "Why should I?"

"Well, I suppose because she's likely to turn her skills on you at some point. And a woman who can outtalk a Stane is…well, rather formidable."

The word *skills* made Sebastian think of something quite different. An intensely tactile memory flashed through him, of Georgina's legs wrapped around his ribs as they kissed. He turned away from his brother to hide a flush. "If she does, I expect I'll have deserved it. She's far cleverer than I."

Randolph blinked. "You…ah…you noticed?" He coughed. "That is, do you think so?"

Sebastian snorted. "I wager everyone thinks so."

"Yes, but… I mean, no."

"Did you think I was too stupid to realize it?" he asked bitterly.

"I do *not* think you stupid."

But Sebastian had no patience, in this moment, for kindly meant lies. "Why shouldn't Georgina speak her mind?" he asked, returning to his brother's original question. "Imagine what Mama would have done if someone had forbidden her marriage."

"That's rather difficult to picture. Papa is a duke, after all."

"Something else she wanted then."

Randolph considered this for several moments. "Ah. I see what you mean. A different style, of course, but equally forceful."

"Exactly." In fact, Sebastian admired Georgina's strength of mind immensely. He'd said so, hadn't he?

Silence fell. Sebastian didn't really notice. He was pondering the unfairness of life. He should be happy right now. As far as anyone else knew, all the unexpected obstacles had been cleared from his path. But, oh no, he'd had to create more of his own. He kicked the ottoman again.

"What's the matter then?" Randolph said.

"Nothing. You should go along and…do something else."

"I want to help you, to mend matters."

"So your job's done then."

"But the thing is, Sebastian, you don't seem to think so."

Evading his brother's steady gaze, Sebastian tried for a light tone, and thought he achieved a remarkable result under the circumstances. "Nobody's eloped. Georgina's father's turned up sweet. The wedding's back on. I'm tip-top, Randolph."

"Good."

And still his brother didn't go. "There's no need to hang about watching me as if I was a raree-show."

"No, I wasn't. I'm very glad all's well. And I also wanted... That is—" Randolph stopped.

"What?" Sebastian peered at his brother, curiosity overcoming his self-absorption. There was something odd about Randolph recently. He hadn't reeled off any verses of poetry in days, or amused himself with wordplay that flashed over Sebastian's head.

Randolph shuffled his feet. "I wondered if you could do me a favor."

Sebastian was startled. "Oh. Is that it? What do you need?" It was an unusual but not unprecedented request.

"Would you...would you write and ask Nathaniel to procure a lute?"

Sebastian felt his mouth fall a little open.

"One probably has to look in London, you see. I imagine they're not particularly easy to find."

"What the devil are you... What sort of loot do you imagine Nathaniel can get his hands on? He's a viscount, not a dashed buccaneer."

"Not *loot*," replied Randolph. "*Lute*. L-u-t-e. It's a musical instrument."

"Instrument?"

"It's stringed, something like a guitar." Looking embarrassed, Randolph mimed holding a guitar and strumming.

"You don't play the guitar. Do you? I thought you said you hadn't much time for music any longer." Randolph nodded. For the life of him, Sebastian couldn't interpret his brother's expression.

"Would you just do it and not press me?" Randolph asked. "As a brotherly gesture of goodwill."

When he put it like that, Sebastian could hardly refuse. "But why not ask Nathaniel yourself?" It would certainly be far easier for Randolph to dash off a letter, though he didn't mention that part.

"I'd rather not," his brother replied.

"Is there something off about these…lutes?"

"Of course not." But his brother looked embarrassed.

"Then why get me to ask?" Sebastian eyed him suspiciously. "Is it a prank of some kind? I request this lute thing, and everyone gets a good laugh out of it?"

"No, it's nothing like that!"

"Why then?"

"Well…it is a rather odd request."

Sebastian waited for more. Then, finally, he got it. "And the family already thinks I've run mad."

"No they don't!" But Randolph looked away.

"Daft Sebastian, raving on about packs of pugs and mysterious Hindus, eloping with his own fiancée."

"It isn't like that!" Randolph exclaimed. "But… you did ask for an ointment to repel the dogs."

He'd known almost from the moment that particular letter was posted that he'd gone too far there, Sebastian thought. Sykes had been right; they should have left it out. But at the time, he'd been desperate. Sebastian touched his pocket. It held the ragged cloth animal he now carried with him everywhere. Like a dashed talisman. Perhaps he *had* lost his mind. Maybe that was his real problem. "I suppose you've already written to someone about my previous existence as a tattooed Welsh savage?"

Randolph did not meet his eyes.

"Of course you have. No Gresham could resist a story that good." How agreeable it was to have a family that shared all their news, Sebastian thought bitterly. Letters—which he produced with such difficulty—flew back and forth among them as if they were a damned flock of carrier pigeons. The situation definitely had a lot of that thing Robert was always nattering about. Irony, that was the word.

"Mama was asking how things were going," Randolph muttered.

He looked positively hangdog. Sebastian couldn't bear it. He gave in. "Oh, very well," he said.

"Thank you!" For a moment he thought Randolph was going to shake his hand. Instead, he added, "I really appreciate it."

"Enough to tell me why you want the thing?"

Randolph shook his head, looking away again. "Not quite that much. Until I see, you know, how it comes out."

It was probably some expression or remark he'd missed along the way, Sebastian decided. Sort of thing that happened to him all the time. No need to emphasize his ignorance by persisting. "All right."

With a grateful nod, Randolph departed. Sebastian returned to his earlier brooding. He got nowhere, and after a while, he gave it up as a bad job and went upstairs to ring for Sykes. Might as well get the letter done. He wasn't accomplishing anything useful loitering in an empty parlor, acting like a mooncalf.

Sykes answered the bell with his customary speed and took up the pen without comment. Sebastian noticed that this instrument did pause over the page at the mention of a lute. "That's l u-t-e," he spelled out helpfully.

Sykes blinked at him. "The medieval musical instrument?" Here was Sykes the playwright, rather than the impassive valet. The former had been appearing more and more often at Stane Castle, and more strongly under the onslaught of strange events. It was as if the barrier between the two roles was weakening. This Sykes looked frankly curious and astonished.

"Is it medieval?" Randolph hadn't said anything about that. But then, he'd been dashed mysterious.

"Well, I know it was much used by the troubadours." Sykes considered. "Would that make it Renaissance?"

Sebastian hoped Sykes was asking himself, because he had no idea. "What's a troubadour?"

"A minstrel, a singer. Centuries ago, they composed songs and sang at the great chateaus and royal courts. Mostly French, weren't they? The name Eleanor of Aquitaine occurs to me. I'm not entirely sure why."

Sebastian watched him, marveling. The other man's thin face and brown eyes were alight with interest. He could just about see Sykes's mind racing. "You're never at a loss, are you, Sykes? How do you know so much?"

"Books, mostly." Sykes gestured toward the lower floors. "There's an extraordinary library here. I store up facts for later use. Never know what might be just the thing I need for creating a fresh character."

His brain must be stuffed full as a Christmas goose, Sebastian thought. It sounded deuced uncomfortable. "Right. Well, that's it. A lute."

Sykes gazed at him, his expression intensely inquisitive. "I suppose your brother will wonder why you want it."

Sebastian started to tell him that the instrument was for Randolph, and then wondered if he'd been told this in confidence. His brother hadn't said so outright, but he felt somehow that he had. "Ah, er, it's just a whim of mine."

"A…whim." Sykes spoke the word as if it was incomprehensible.

Meeting his skeptical look, direct and with no trace of deference, Sebastian realized that the time had nearly come, whether Sykes was aware of it or not. His valet wouldn't be with him much longer. Sykes the playwright would take over for good and all. That certainty roused a tremor of anxiety. An unwelcome, unacceptable loneliness put an edge on his reply. "That's it. A lute."

There was a fraught silence, as if something trembled in the air between them. Then Sykes set pen to paper again and said, "Indeed, my lord." He was the consummate valet once again.

Sebastian was glad to see it. There were no unsettling complications with this Sykes. "Oh, and tell Nathaniel all's well," he added. "Randolph wrote Mama about the…the barbarian thing. Say that's all over with and the wedding's going on as scheduled."

"I'm very pleased to hear that, my lord."

Sebastian nodded. The family would probably conclude that Randolph had saved his bacon. He found he resented that. "Tell him Lady Georgina fixed it up," he said, giving credit where it was due.

"Her ladyship is very resourceful."

Fleetingly, Sebastian imagined that his valet's tone was regretful. But that couldn't be right. "She is, isn't she?" He lost himself in thoughts of his betrothed's many beguiling qualities.

"Will there by anything else, my lord?"

"What?"

Sykes indicated the letter.

"Oh. No. Just the usual closing."

Nodding, Sykes completed the missive, folded it, and added a warmed wax seal. He passed it over, and Sebastian applied his signet ring. Retrieving the completed letter, Sykes rose. "I'll leave this for his lordship's messenger," he said.

"Yes." Sebastian stood and stretched. Somehow a letter always seemed a heavy task, even the way he did it. And how would he do it without Sykes? "Huh" escaped him.

His valet paused by the door. "Was there something else, my lord?"

Sykes stood poised, alert, the picture of a man ready to grapple with any problem. Sebastian was struck anew by how much Sykes had helped him over the years. He would be a great loss. "Thank you."

Sykes bowed. "Of course, my lord."

Sebastian wanted to say more, but he didn't know what. It just seemed he should take advantage of whatever time he had left with his clever aide.

With his customary acuity, Sykes sensed it. He waited.

"Marriage is a big step," Sebastian said, rather surprising himself.

The valet acknowledged this with a gesture that was half a nod, half a bow.

"It lasts for the rest of your life. Could be forty years. Decades anyway." Sebastian heard how ridiculous this sounded. If only he could force words to convey what he meant. Assuming that he knew what he meant. Which, in this case, he didn't.

"Are you all right?" said Sykes.

People kept asking him this. He must look as bewildered and worried as he felt, which made it worse. "The thing is…I've been thinking."

Sykes gazed at him, more the canny, intelligent friend than the valet once again.

Sebastian felt another impulse of gratitude. His brothers might well have made a joke of that remark: Hold hard, everybody; *Sebastian* is thinking! "Wondering, you know, what…what do you owe the…the person you're marrying?"

"Owe?"

He'd snagged the right word this time, Sebastian thought. *Owe* put it in a nutshell. But he wasn't sure how to explain further. "As you're getting acquainted, before the wedding. Many fellows don't, of course. Meet during the season, dance a few waltzes, too many glasses of champagne one night, and they find themselves on one knee making an offer." This wasn't going well. He blundered onward. "Next thing they know, hey presto, married, when they hardly know each other. Can't blame them for leaving out a few details. But if you have the time?"

"I'm not certain I understand you. My lord." It was as if both sides of Sykes answered, in turn.

"No. Who would?" That speech had been a sterling example of garbled nonsense.

"Is there something I can do for you, my lord?"

Sebastian looked at the other man, alert and immaculate by the chamber doorway. Sykes had stepped in when he was an angry, discouraged youth, and he'd watched over Sebastian—in a way, in the part of life where he continually struggled—since then. Now, Georgina had taken up the reins and smoothed his path. Not in precisely the same way, but she'd summoned the words to sway her father, as Sebastian never could have. He felt an obscure sense of being handed off from one minder to another. It was not a pleasant thought. "No," he said. "You can't."

"My lord?"

It was the wrong way round, Sebastian thought. He wanted to take care of Georgina, not be her charge. But could he? In one miserable instant, Sebastian's view narrowed so that all he could perceive was his one glaring flaw. His prowess on the battlefield and host of admiring friends were forgotten. His expertise in the outdoors and many acts of kindness seemed as nothing. What right did he have to such a wonderful woman? Wouldn't she, quite soon, begin to find him a burden? That notion hurt so much that he almost thought he'd rather lose her than face it. Only he wanted to marry her so very much.

Sykes put a hand on his arm. Unnoticed, he'd moved from the doorway. He looked genuinely alarmed. "Are you ill?"

"No." Sykes couldn't help him with this. "Perfectly well."

"Are you certain? My lord?"

"Of course." Sebastian regained control of his

expression. He hated feeling so transparent. "Go ahead and get that letter off, Sykes."

His valet hesitated, then bowed and left the room.

Alone, Sebastian sighed and rubbed his forehead. He hadn't felt so despondent in…well, in years. His gaze was irresistibly drawn to a shelf of books between the two windows of his bedchamber. He walked over and picked one out. Holding it, he realized that some part of him continually hoped that this time the thing would be different. Blessedly, miraculously, mended. He opened the volume. As ever, the letters on the page were crammed together in solid, tangled lines. No effort he could make would force them to realign into meaning.

He clapped the book closed. He wanted to throw it across the room, but he carefully replaced it instead.

And with that simple movement, he was elsewhere, fallen into a memory more than twenty years old.

He'd been in the great library at Langford, alone with his father. Even now, Sebastian couldn't imagine how that had happened, because the library was not his favorite room by any means. And with five brothers, he most often saw his parents in a crowd, rather than singly. Yet they were there, in his inner eye—his younger self and his deeply revered father.

Papa had been holding a book, and he'd read out a passage and invited Sebastian to comment. Or, really, to admire the sentiment; Sebastian had understood that much, even though the text had been a bit over his head. His father was offering to share a cherished idea with him. Naturally, he'd responded with great enthusiasm, delighted to be recognized in this way.

But then, his father had held out the book and suggested that he read the whole, which they could then discuss. Sebastian remembered that instant with agonizing clarity. Papa, the busy, sometimes distant duke, had looked so bright and eager. He'd offered the book like a precious gift, like the beginning of a bond. And Sebastian had had to refuse, because he'd known he couldn't do it and couldn't make other people understand why.

Sebastian's hands closed into fists. He was swept by a longing to hit something.

Of course he'd tried. He'd said straight out that he didn't read very well, no matter how hard he worked at it. But his father had heard his painful admission as a rebuff, an active youngster's lack of interest in learning. In an effort to be kind—Sebastian knew it had been kindness and self-effacement and love—Papa had brushed his attempted explanations aside. He'd smiled, passed it off with a light rejoinder, and turned the conversation to Sebastian's new hunter.

It had been partly a relief; Sebastian acknowledged that. His failure hadn't been exposed. He'd gotten misunderstanding rather than contempt. They'd had a lively, comradely discussion of the horse's good points. But it had put a limit on their relationship. Papa had never made such an offer again. Later, he'd found the intellectual kinship he'd been looking for with Randolph, and then to some extent with Alan, though their interests were different. Sebastian was shut out of those connections, and everyone thought it was by his own choice.

With a terrible sinking feeling, he wondered if it

would be the same with Georgina. Would they come up against places where they could go no further, get no closer? That wasn't what he wanted. He wanted… more…everything…a totality he didn't know how to label.

Sebastian snorted, turning away from the rows of books. How his brothers would gape if they could see him now. He was bluff, hearty Sebastian. Not a thinker. Not deep like Randolph, or witty like Robert. Certainly not brilliant like Alan. Right at the opposite end of the brotherly spectrum from Alan, in fact. Spectrum—he only knew that word because of Alan and whatever it was he did with light. None of them understood that, Sebastian reminded himself. He shook his head. Even Nathaniel, ever kind and protective, would smile at the notion that he, the thickheaded soldier, was wrestling with such convoluted ideas.

"Devil take it," Sebastian said aloud.

He would go riding. A good, hard gallop always swept the cobwebs from his brain. Indeed, he got his best ideas when he was on the move. His mind seemed to flow better then. And every member of the Gresham family acknowledged that he had no peer in the saddle. He could be proud of that. It was just the place to forget his troubles, for a little while at least.

Fifteen

WHAT HAD GONE WRONG? GEORGINA WONDERED AS she sat with her mother in the latter's workroom. She'd faced down her father. She was still rather amazed about that. Papa was treating her with more respect as a result. The situation at Stane Castle had returned to its... Well, *normal* might not be the right word, but to its former state. Sebastian, however, had not. As the days passed and their wedding approached, the ease and freedom that had been developing between them had disappeared.

He'd...reverted. He was once again the handsome, urbane nobleman—the duke's son—she'd first met in London. Admittedly, she'd been drawn to that man. He was attractive and assured; he could be dazzling. But she'd come to love the Sebastian who'd taken charge with calm authority while covered with mud in the ravine, who'd made her sisters laugh when they played lottery tickets, who kissed her with such searing passion that the mere memory made her dizzy.

The absence of that man had Georgina very worried. She'd tried to discover the reason, but he refused to admit that anything was wrong. Her questions seemed to simply slip off him, like rain running down a windowpane. Nothing could penetrate his polished manner. Which left Georgina imagining explanations that were far worse—had to be far worse—than reality. Her brain cycled back through early fears.

Had his visit given him a lasting distaste for her family? Was he was thinking derogatory thoughts about them behind his courteous facade? Or was it even more dire? What if he'd found, on closer acquaintance, that he didn't really care for her? She'd learned about the man behind his society poses. What if he, having done the same with her, had been put off? She didn't know what she'd do it if that turned out to be the answer. In fact, it couldn't be. It wasn't. She wouldn't believe it.

"I think we should hold a dance when the Greshams arrive," her mother said. "I shan't call it a ball. We can't muster enough couples in this neighborhood to merit the name. But we could manage something, don't you think?"

"Um?"

"Are you listening, Georgina? You complained that I was not paying any heed to your wedding, and now when I do, you are off in the clouds somewhere."

"Sorry, Mama."

"Surely you haven't changed your mind about marrying him, after all the trouble we've gone to?"

"No! Of course not." The *we* was rather good, she thought. Mama's part in making things right had been small.

"Well, what is it then?"

Georgina suppressed a sigh. It never failed. Her mother, usually oblivious to others' feelings, grew acutely aware just when you didn't want her to.

"Georgina?"

One of the dogs—because naturally they were surrounded by sleeping, scratching, panting pugs—came over and put a paw on Georgina's foot, gazing up at her with dark, liquid eyes.

"You're upsetting Nuala," her mother said. "She's very sensitive just now."

"I'm sorry, Mama." She reached down and patted the pug reassuringly. "You were saying?"

"That we should hold a dance when the Greshams arrive."

"Sebastian loves to dance. He's very good at it." Their waltzes were among her favorite memories of their time in London.

"Good." Her mother made a note on the page before her. "We just have to find enough young ladies for all those brothers."

"Two are bringing their wives," Georgina pointed out.

"Yes, dear, but they'll need other partners as well. I suppose we'll have to allow Hilda to dance."

"Really?"

"I see no harm in it. Certainly nothing like what she might do if we forbid her to attend."

The two women exchanged a speaking glance.

"It's an informal family party," the older woman added. "There's no need for her or Emma to be officially out."

"She'll love it," Georgina said. "They both will."

This time they smiled at each other, in harmony at

the thought of offering such a treat. "There's not much other entertainment to offer such august visitors," her mother went on then. "The shooting is very poor hereabouts, and Alfred keeps no coveys. But they're only staying for a week. And there is the wedding. That's a sort of entertainment in itself. And the reason they're coming, of course. No doubt your father will insist on taking them to see his pet earthworks."

Georgina imagined the duke and duchess on an expedition to view Offa's Dyke. Who knew? Perhaps it would interest them. As long as the ride didn't continue into the kind of session that had nearly ruined everything and sent Randolph running from the room.

"What does Sebastian say?"

"I beg your pardon, Mama?"

"Have you drifted off again? What's the matter with you? I asked if you had spoken with Sebastian about what sorts of things his family likes to do."

"Oh. No."

Her mother sighed as if she'd been busily planning this occasion for months and Georgina was the laggard. "Perhaps that might be a good idea?"

All at once, Georgina had to find Sebastian. Something trembled inside her, and she couldn't wait even a moment. She jumped up. "I'll do that right now."

"Georgina, I have a list of things yet to discuss."

"We'll do it later." She hurried out of the room before Mama could reply.

Rain sheeted down outside, showing no signs of stopping. It had come in on a cold wind that was a taste of the approaching autumn. Yet even knowing that

Sebastian must be indoors in such weather, Georgina had some difficulty finding him. At last, after inquiring among the servants, she traced him to the castle's billiard room, a generally unused chamber in the most modern wing of the old pile. Her father didn't care for the game, so he'd put the room to other uses.

Sebastian and Randolph were bent over the table, engaged in a game. They both straightened when she came in. "Didn't realize you had a billiard room," Sebastian commented.

She'd nearly forgotten about it herself, Georgina thought. They needed to consider such things before the Gresham party arrived. She'd gotten distracted from the duties of hospitality.

"Your butler mentioned it when we were talking of what to do in this filthy weather," Randolph chimed in. "We cleared off some documents, but we placed them in the same order." He gestured toward a sideboard stacked with papers. "I hope there'll be no objection."

"Papa never comes in here," Georgina replied. "I daresay he's forgotten all about those. He becomes fascinated by a topic and collects every scrap he can find on the subject; then he loses interest and moves on to another."

"Ah." Randolph nodded with the air of a tidy man who could not conceive of such disorganization.

Georgina sent silent signals in his direction, urging him to leave them alone.

They missed their mark. "He could hire a secretary to catalog all this," Randolph said. "Some fresh university graduate who would be glad of the work, and very likely impressed by the materials as well."

"I don't think he cares to," she replied in a discouraging tone. She tried to convey her ardent desire for him to go with a steady gaze, but Randolph wasn't looking at her. He'd gone over to the sideboard and was glancing through the stacks of paper.

"Ah, care for a game?" Sebastian asked in the silence that followed.

"My word," said Randolph. "Did you know that badgers eat several hundred earthworms every night?"

"I believe Papa has mentioned it," Georgina answered in her least enthusiastic voice. This too failed to reach Randolph. She sighed. "Mama was wondering about entertaining your family," she said to Sebastian. "What sorts of things they like to do."

He shrugged. "They're all fond of country pursuits."

"Robert isn't," said Randolph, coming back to the billiard table. "He's a creature of society drawing rooms. And James cares for nothing but ships."

"Robert likes to ride and shoot," replied Sebastian. "There's no need to take any particular trouble."

Georgina wondered whether she had the same idea of *particular trouble* as a duchess. She suspected not. At last, she caught Randolph's eye and gave him a look that could have ignited the kindling in the hearthside woodbox.

"Oh!" he said, rather as if he'd been stuck with a hatpin.

"What is it?" Sebastian asked, eyeing his brother in surprise.

"Ah, I…" Randolph backed toward the door. "Some important letters to write. Must go begin at once."

"But you said you had nothing to do this morning," replied Sebastian.

"Forgot," declared Randolph, and hurried out.

Sebastian watched him disappear through the doorway with a wry regret. For perhaps the first time in his life, he'd been glad of a chaperone. Randolph's presence had kept him from having to think about his dilemma. Now he was back in the thick of it. He wanted to be open and honest with Georgina. He took pride in being that sort of man. And with an equally strong resolve, he didn't want to expose his failings to her. Mostly, he wanted to forget he'd ever thought of the necessity.

She came closer. He caught a hint of the sweet scent of her perfume, which did intoxicating things to his senses. "Robert enjoys a game of billiards," he said. "So does my father, come to that. They had a tally going, years ago, as to who'd won more often."

Georgina looked at him as if she was gathering courage to charge a line of artillery. "Sebastian, you must tell me what's wrong," she said.

She'd asked before, and he'd fobbed her off. It made for short and stilted conversations, he thought sadly. "Randolph was beating me soundly," he tried. "A rout, really." He smiled, hoping to distract her.

It nearly worked. She paused and blinked. Her lips parted. She looked delectably kissable, and Sebastian was about to move in and do so when she said, "Really wrong. I know there's something. I'm…rather well acquainted with you now. After everything."

Memories of that *everything* tantalized and tormented him. How could forbidden actions—like making passionate love to a young lady on a bed of bracken—be so easy, while an unexceptional conversation— containing one damning admission, yes—could loom like a court martial? No one had ever told him this could be the case.

As the silence lengthened, Georgina stood straighter. "If you don't wish to marry me any longer, you must tell me. I simply… I couldn't bear it if I found out later that you'd gone through with the wedding because you're too honorable to cry off." Her voice broke on the final phrase.

"No!" exclaimed Sebastian, horrified. "How could you imagine…? I want desperately to marry you. I love you more than anything in the world." The profound truth of the words struck as he spoke them. He'd loved others in his life—his family, some close friends—but never like this.

Georgina was gazing up at him, wide-eyed. It seemed to Sebastian that hope and doubt contended in those green depths. He hated to see the second. He had to quell it. "At first, when we met, it was just that you are so beautiful," he explained.

"And rich," she suggested.

Sebastian writhed a bit at her dry tone. This *could not* be one of the times when he said the wrong thing, or searched unsuccessfully for words and botched a conversation. "There were other heiresses," he said. "I mean, they pop up now and then. Every season. But not like you."

"How not?" she asked.

"The things you said, when I asked questions, were so wise and clever." Sebastian suddenly realized that here was a confession he could make. "Ariel suggested it, you know."

"Ariel…your brother's wife? She suggested you offer for me?"

"No, no. That was my idea entirely. But when I was trying to find a way to catch your attention, in that dashed crowd of fellows always jostling around you, she told me to ask questions."

"Questions," repeated Georgina, as if the word was new to her.

"About your opinions and…and aspirations," he added, remembering one of Ariel's expressions. Best to make a clean breast of this part, he decided, now that he'd begun. "She gave me some questions to start with," he admitted. "But then she said I had to think up my own."

Georgina looked surprised. Beyond that, he couldn't tell. She didn't seem angry.

"It was hard going, I can tell you. I started hanging about the brainy fellows at my club." And hadn't they been astonished? They'd finally assumed it was for some joke or wager.

Georgina laughed.

Encouraged, Sebastian said, "But as I kept on, one thing built on another, and it started to feel like…" He nearly panicked. Words threatened to desert him in their usual, frustrating way. Then he had it. "Like moving from a trot to a canter. Natural. And I wanted to hear what else you'd say. It was…a wonder, the way your mind worked."

"You exaggerate," she said, her cheeks a bit flushed.

"No, I don't. Everyone knows you're the clever one. I've no pretensions to intellect."

"Nonsense."

It was an opening. He could go on and tell her the rest. But she was looking at him with such tenderness. He *couldn't* risk losing that.

"I didn't start to fall in love with you because you asked questions," said Georgina then.

Had she said "fall in love"?

"That began when I noticed that you really listened to what I said in reply."

She had said it, hadn't she?

"Most men simply endure a woman's remarks, you know, waiting for us to stop talking so that they can enjoy the sound of their own voices once again."

"Did you say 'fall in love'?" Sebastian finally managed.

Looking suddenly less certain, Georgina nodded.

"You can love a slowtop like me?"

"You constantly underestimate yourself, Sebastian. You must stop it. Of course I can. And do."

This was breathtaking, astonishing. By some magic, he'd won not just her hand but her love as well. He swept her into his arms. Or perhaps she threw herself into them. The movement was so mutual that it wasn't clear. The kiss that followed burned with passion, ached with tenderness, and dizzied with a new element that was far more than both.

Kiss followed kiss. Hands roamed, and bodies arched and strained. And then Georgina was sitting on the edge of the billiard table, and he was standing between her knees, pushing up her skirts. "Wait," Sebastian said, panting. "We must stop this." He started to step back.

"No, we must not!" Georgina commanded, pulling him closer.

"Someone could come in," he said.

"No one ever comes here."

"Randolph and I did," he pointed out.

"No one else."

"He knows I'm in here."

"He won't return, not after the look I gave him."
She smiled and tugged Sebastian nearer.

He was torn between raging desire and the need
to protect her. "What if your father wanted those
papers? Or Hilda? She seems to pop up just when
she's least wanted."

"Drat Hilda." But Georgina frowned. "Oh,
Sebastian, I want you so," she whispered.

"Wait." Sebastian strode over to the double
doors. They had locks, but no keys. He looked
around, found two small gilt chairs in a corner, and
jammed one under each knob. They wouldn't hold
under a determined assault, but they'd certainly
give warning if anyone tried to enter. "You should
have a silken bower," he said when he returned to
his love.

She put her arms around his neck and kissed him.
"I prefer a bed of bracken. Or this. It's…thrilling."

And then she wrapped her legs around him as well,
and every vestige of hesitation, or control, dissolved.
Sebastian was washed by a white heat that drove all
else before it. He slid his hands along the soft skin
of her inner thighs, pushing her skirts away until he
could make her gasp with pleasure. She kissed him
more deeply and busied her fingers with the fasten-
ings of his breeches. In moments, they were free to
meet in ecstasy. Sebastian had never experienced

such a combination of arousal and emotion. When she cried out his name, he felt like a man who'd won a hundred medals.

He continued to hold her as their breathing gradually slowed. She was lithe and soft and infinitely precious in his arms.

"I love you so," she murmured in his ear.

"I love you," he replied.

Georgina raised her head from his shoulder and smiled at him. "And I'll never look at this billiard table in the same way again," she added.

Sebastian laughed with pure joy.

"It will be our secret," she said with a provocative smile.

Sebastian drew back slightly at the word. But wasn't love enough? Many things could be overcome by love.

After a while, Georgina slipped off the table. They helped each other straighten disordered clothing and smooth tousled hair. "I shall be doing this for years and years," she said as she adjusted his neckcloth, "making sure you are ready for public view." She ended her ministrations with a tender kiss.

Feeling the broad smile on his face, Sebastian went to remove the chairs. He opened one door and found the corridor outside empty. Holding out a hand, he led his love from the never-to-be-the-same billiard room. Could he actually play a game with his father there after this?

They saw no one as they returned to the main part of the castle. It was a miracle, Georgina thought, that her mother hadn't sent someone to find her. Finally, just outside the entry hall, they heard voices.

"I cannot believe you would have been so unobliging," said Hilda.

"It was not a matter of being obliging," answered Randolph.

"And to save your own brother, too. Could you have been so selfish? I could not, if I had been able to help my sister in any way whatsoever."

Georgina started forward to the rescue, but Sebastian put a restraining hand on her arm. When she looked up, surprised, she saw that his eyes were twinkling.

"As I have explained to you, more than once," Randolph said, "I could not ignore legalities just because my own family was involved."

"Oh, legalities," interrupted Hilda, her low opinion of such things clear in her voice. "I'm sure you could have cajoled it out of them."

"I…cajole…the Archbishop of Canterbury?"

"If you had wished to," Hilda said.

"I most certainly could not, not after the way that he and I… And in any case, I did *not* wish to, and… and none of this matters any more. The difficulties about the wedding have been resolved."

"You're enjoying this," Georgina whispered.

"I've never seen anyone out-argue Randolph," Sebastian murmured. "But if anyone can, it's Hilda."

"What if I'd threatened to write the archbishop and tell him that you've been participating in bizarre pagan rites?" said Hilda.

The hidden pair exchanged an astonished look as Randolph sputtered, "What? What are you… What bizarre pagan rites?"

"Papa's Hindu ceremony."

"It wasn't. That wasn't a rite. Mr. Mitra said very clearly that it was of his own devising. It was rather a fascinating…experiment. Scientific, like Alan's work. And I am not required to explain my conduct to *you*."

"No, just to the archbishop." There was the hint of a laugh in Hilda's tone. "I think I must tell him."

"Is she storing up ammunition for future blackmail?" Sebastian whispered.

The idea seemed all too plausible. Georgina suppressed a groan.

"Perhaps I will inform him that you would benefit from an exorcism," said Randolph.

"What are those like?" asked Hilda. "Are there robes?"

"What sort of young lady asks…?"

"Well, none, of course," she said, cutting him off once again. "I'm heartily sick of being a 'young lady.' The proprieties get one nowhere, as far as I can see."

"Which is not very far at all," said Randolph.

"We must help him," whispered Georgina.

Sebastian nodded and stepped forward. They found his brother and Georgina's sister squared off near the front door of the castle. Randolph was glaring, Hilda smug. "Oh, hullo," said Sebastian, showing no sign that they'd overheard. "Not thinking of going out, are you? Still pelting with rain out there."

Georgina choked on a laugh.

"I was coming to speak to you," snapped Randolph, "when I encountered *Lady* Hilda."

He sounded far younger than his years, Georgina thought. Her sister had reduced him to her own level, as she could so easily do. For once, she was grateful. Hilda had saved them from an embarrassing interruption. Cheeks warming at the memory of that delicious interlude, she said, "Shouldn't you be in your bedchamber, Hilda?"

"I've been released from imprisonment. I assured Mama of my sincere repentance."

Randolph muttered something very like "Hah!"

"She sent me to find you," Hilda added.

Georgina and Sebastian exchanged a fleeting, congratulatory look. "Here I am," they said at the same moment, then laughed in unison.

This was how it would be when they were married, Georgina thought. They'd manage all sorts of matters together, in harmony. A lifetime of understanding glances lay ahead of her. Her spirits soared as she saw how love made it all easy. "Come along then," she said to her sister. She was ready to immerse herself in wedding details now, right after she had a serious conversation with Hilda.

Sixteen

As the family sat at dinner the following evening, Georgina looked around the table with warm contentment. It all looked so...normal. Mentally comparing it to the first night of Sebastian's visit, she felt a glow of achievement. The feeling was entirely different, and she'd accomplished most of the change herself. Hilda, taxed with Georgina's knowledge of her blackmail attempt, had recanted and even apologized to Randolph. Now, she looked almost demure on the other side of the board. Sebastian said that his brother had laughed about the incident, in the end.

Papa had been all amiable courtesy since their "discussion," and her mother had taken the bit between her teeth to manage the coming festivities. Emma was on her best behavior. Mr. Mitra remained a dignified, interesting guest. Georgina had begun to anticipate the Greshams' arrival, not only because it meant her wedding, but as a source of enjoyment, too.

It was true that Joanna Byngham remained deeply affected by her experience during Mr. Mitra's meditation. She'd sewn loose, flowing sleeves onto all her gowns, so long that they trailed along the floor as she moved, and had begun dressing her hair in a tall, braided crown. She talked more like a character from a gothic novel now than the sensible governess Georgina had known for fifteen years. She thought that even Papa was beginning to find it a little wearisome, though he clearly savored many of her pronouncements. They gave him opportunities to gaze at his Indian visitor with raised eyebrows, as if to say, "You see that I was correct." Mr. Mitra exhibited a particularly elegant version of pained endurance on these occasions.

Perhaps Joanna could be sent on a research mission, Georgina thought. She traveled to special library collections on occasion to gather information for Papa. Georgina knew the governess loved those trips. She would speak to her father about it.

As she ran her eyes down the length of the table, Georgina met Sebastian's admiring blue gaze and returned his smile. She loved him. He loved her. She'd never been so happy.

At that very moment, as if she'd somehow sensed Georgina's contentment, Joanna rose from her chair and spread her arms out at her sides, looking rather like an oversized bat. "It is imperative that I speak," she said.

All the others gazed at her. Papa sat back as if a play was about to begin. Hilda grinned. Mr. Mitra bowed his head and murmured something. Georgina rather hoped it was an incantation to impose silence.

"A spirit has come to me in dreams," Joanna intoned. "Long had it searched for one who could hear its tale. As the centuries passed, it nearly despaired, and then my senses were opened." She waved her arms so that her long sleeves fluttered. "To the talents and duties of my ancient heritage. A ritual must be held, as soon as may be, or doom will fall upon this family, even unto a thousand years."

"Oh, Joanna," said Georgina. She had a sudden urge to rest her forehead on the tabletop.

"I've had enough of this nonsense—" began her mother.

"Come, come, let us listen to what she has to say," Georgina's father insisted. He looked more than ever like a man ready to be entertained.

Hilda giggled.

"You propose to add a new family member." Joanna swiveled to point at Sebastian.

Georgina's beloved rocked back as if Joanna had actually poked him with her extended finger. On the other side of the table, Randolph stared like a man who couldn't tear his eyes away from a riveting spectacle.

"He must be woven into the threads of your regal bloodline," Joanna continued. She swiveled to point at Georgina's father. "By you, my lord."

Georgina could see that Papa liked that. His penchant for drama had been thwarted by her intervention, and this proposal played right into his current obsession.

"If he is not, all will fail. The marriage will sour, the castle will fall, the…"

"Joanna!" Georgina cried. "Stop this at once. How dare you say that about my marriage?"

Her old governess crossed her arms over her chest and assumed a regretful expression. "It pains me to do so, Lady Georgina. But the sacred charge of a priestess outweighs all other considerations."

"You are not a priestess!"

"I was," the other woman chanted. "And am. And shall ever be. It was shown to me in the temporal travels our guest guided." She turned to Mitra and bent her head as if acknowledging a peer.

Mr. Mitra rose with fierce grace. "Begging your pardons, one and all, but I must protest. This is not correct. Miss Byngham has allowed her imagination to…overwhelm her understanding. I see no connection here to my studies or methods. I-I repudiate it." Putting his palms together, he bowed briefly and walked out.

Joanna looked momentarily disconcerted. Then she shrugged and shook it off, murmuring, "The student can surpass the master."

"What sort of ritual would it be?" Georgina's father asked.

"Alfred!" said her mother.

Sebastian watched the marquess wave his wife's indignation aside. His host was very taken with the idea of an ancestral ritual, he saw, and he wasn't going to be deprived of the treat. It seemed a dashed silly idea to Sebastian, and he strongly resented the dire predictions about his marriage. But it didn't look as if the thing could be avoided. Ah, well. He'd stood on parade in the baking sun wearing thirty pounds of gear. He could face his future father-in-law and let him make a few passes with a magic wand or whatever the governess had in mind. Though it hardly seemed right to call her a governess now. And indeed, judging from the glare Georgina's mother was sending Miss Byngham's way, she wouldn't be one much longer. Not at Stane Castle at any rate.

"It is not complex," said Miss Byngham. "And yet every detail must be exactly right. All the family must attend, garbed in red."

"Garbed," Georgina's mother snorted.

"I shall officiate, of course," Miss Byngham continued, ignoring her employer with what Sebastian thought was dangerous insouciance. "We must have candles for fire, a bowl of water, and earth from Offa's Dyke."

The marquess smiled at that, obviously pleased at the inclusion of the latter.

"You will read a solemn welcome, my lord, with affirmations from your family."

"I think not," muttered Georgina's mother.

"And then Lord Sebastian will read his response. I have been gifted with the precise wording, you understand. It must be absolutely correct. You are well aware of the power of incantation."

She, and the marquess exchanged a complacent glance as Sebastian's world fell about his ears. He'd heard the phrase *my heart sank* before, but he'd never really known what it meant.

"I could say a blessing if you like," offered Randolph.

It had been years since Sebastian had really wanted to punch one of his brothers. Until now.

"I don't think this is really your province, Lord Randolph," Miss Byngham answered.

Hilda giggled again. Georgina glared at her.

"Your participation isn't necessary," added the

governess airily. "You are not a Stane, nor to be joined to them."

Randolph frowned at her.

Georgina's father rubbed his hands together, clearly entranced with this plan. "You know, I think the most difficult requirement will be the red clothing. We'll have a look in the attics. We've trunks full of old clothes up there."

"Alfred, you cannot mean to go through with this!" said his wife.

"Why not? It will be amusing, something to do while we kick up our heels waiting for the wedding." He noticed Miss Byngham's frown. "And important, of course. Say, perhaps we should wait until the Greshams arrive. The more family the merrier, eh?"

"No!" Georgina shouted.

Shouted was the only word for it, Sebastian thought. Her refusal echoed off the dining room walls.

The volume didn't faze her father. "Well, well, they're not needed, eh, Joanna? Though they'd be a welcome addition, I'd think."

The entire group seemed to hold its breath, waiting for her judgment. She was reveling in her new, self-manufactured importance, Sebastian thought.

"No," she said finally, with a touch of regret. "As I said, it is the Stanes welcoming a new member."

A number of her listeners relaxed.

"Though it goes the other way as well, doesn't it?" she added, galvanizing them again. "If Lord Sebastian's parents are interested, I daresay I could organize…"

"No!" exclaimed Georgina, almost as loudly as before.

"We'll keep it amongst ourselves," said the marquess

under the combined glares of his wife and two elder daughters. "Get it done before they come. What about tomorrow, eh? I daresay we can cobble together some suitable garments by then."

"Alfred," said the marchioness.

"Come, come, my dear, you look so very fetching in red." He gave his wife a tender glance.

To Sebastian's surprise and sharp disappointment, she flushed and smiled. "Oh, very well, but I'm far too busy to be rooting about in the attics."

"And you shan't be bothered. Joanna and I will find something."

"I'll help, Papa," said Hilda. "I know just the trunks to look in."

"Splendid. We'll organize some lanterns and go up after dinner."

Sebastian stood. The meal had become like a doomed rearguard action, where your unit was forced into a more and more untenable position, until there was no way out but slashing sabers. "No," he said, his voice choked. "Can't do it."

"Sebastian?" said his brother, rising as well.

Sebastian hurried from the room before anyone could question him. He heard Randolph calling his name again, but he ignored him. He had to get away, get outside, and try to think of some way out of this ridiculous snare.

Georgina sat frozen in her chair, her half-eaten dinner growing cold before her. She'd been so happy just a few minutes ago. She'd dared to think that she'd handled every difficulty, that all was well. Why had she tempted fate in such a foolish way? Was it her fault that the tranquil scene had collapsed like a riverbank undercut by spring floods?

Her jaw tightened. No, it was not. She looked at Joanna, still presiding over the table like a petty despot, visibly enjoying the powers that she'd made real by concocting this silly plan. Her old governess looked so…happy and…*fulfilled* was the word that occurred to Georgina. And gave her pause. There was certainly no malice in Joanna's expression. She wasn't *trying* to complicate Georgina's life. Perhaps she only wanted the years of research she'd done, as Papa lurched from one arcane subject to another, to mean something. Georgina could imagine wishing for that.

"We could tie red bows on the dogs," said Hilda. "And line them up like a little honor guard." She'd scarcely stopped grinning since this farce began.

Seeing the irritated look Joanna gave her, Georgina wondered if her youngest sister had been the last straw. Surely teaching Hilda must have been vastly frustrating. Hilda was more than uninterested in her studies; she actively subverted any effort to make her attend. Recalling the recent prank that had stranded her in a muddy ravine, Georgina sympathized.

"They dislike regimentation," said her mother, a vast understatement.

However understandable Joanna's feelings might be, Georgina couldn't let this go on. Not after seeing Sebastian's disgust at the plan. "Mama, really, we can't do this," she said.

Her mother was bent over Drustan, patting his head and saying, "No, you don't, do you?"

"We have too much else to manage," Georgina

added, appealing to her mother's perpetual claims of busyness. "With so many guests arriving."

But her mother waved this aside. "Your father says he will make all the arrangements."

"Indeed I will," he chimed in.

So Mama wasn't going to help. In desperation, Georgina turned to Emma. "You must agree with me. It's just too much."

Emma shrank back with a shrug, unwilling to state an opinion.

"Don't be a wet goose, Georgina," said Hilda. "It will be great fun. Like the tableaus we did that one Christmas, when Emma tripped over the candlestick and nearly set the draperies on fire."

This lighthearted comparison earned her another sour glance from Joanna.

"You pushed me," said Emma.

"Didn't."

"Yes, you *did*."

Georgina's sisters made faces at each other. Her mother cooed over the pugs. Her father conferred with Joanna. Sebastian had deserted her, and Randolph... Well, she didn't really feel comfortable asking him for help. She was defeated. It seemed they'd just have to go through with this "ritual"—before any more Greshams joined their party. "I'll go and ask Fergus for lanterns," she said.

"Good girl," replied her father.

The lanterns were found. Her father, Joanna, and Hilda headed off to rifle the attics for red garments. Georgina went to find Sebastian and tell him that it seemed they must go through the motions of Joanna's scheme. He'd looked quite revolted by the idea when he stalked out of the dining room. And she freely admitted that it was ridiculous. But he'd had time to adjust by now, and she was confident she could persuade him. He loved her. She felt a glow as she remembered the way he'd said it. A bit of playacting was a small thing to do for love.

Sebastian strode down the road along the outer wall of the castle. The rain was back, and darkness had fallen, but he'd been wet and cold before. He wouldn't take Whitefoot out into this weather; the poor horse had no anxiety to relieve and didn't deserve it. But he was almost glad to have a hardship he could easily endure. And so he walked, ignoring the rapid destruction of his evening shoes.

Sebastian had often imagined scenes in which his stupidity was exposed in excruciating detail. An important document had to be read out in order to save a member of his family—mother, father, brother—from…any number of dire fates. Only he could do it, and he…couldn't. An innocent would be saved an unjust accusation, if only he could make out the written evidence. A gang of his best friends dragged him into a game where the hated written word couldn't be avoided.

Being forced to take part in a fabricated ritual for no critical purpose had not figured in these imaginings. This seemed pure mockery by the fates. It wouldn't save anybody. It wasn't necessary. The person behind it wasn't even a friend. And there was the problem. Because the ritual was a silly nothing, a momentary role that another man might even enjoy enacting, he couldn't think of one good reason to evade it.

Sebastian took shelter in a thick clump of evergreens, finding a place near the trunks where the carpet of needles was nearly dry. Finding some solace in this bit of outdoor expertise, he pulled his coat closer around his chest and settled down to wait. He would stay out here until the denizens of the castle were abed. He knew this repeated ploy of his was childish, but he couldn't resist putting off the wreck of his hopes for a few more hours.

The rain eased to a slow drip. Now and then, a drop slithered through the branches and found its way to Sebastian, adding to his dampness. Still he waited until he judged enough time had passed. Then he pushed his way out of the soaking needles and started back. Under a cloudy sky, the way was dark. He placed his feet carefully, and yet was still surprised by a deep puddle that went right across the road. He slipped and fell, cursing, landing on his back in cold water. And mud. Mud seemed to be his fate in Herefordshire. He rose covered in it. "Devil take it," he muttered.

His trudge grew easier when the castle wall loomed up at his side. The slope kept the surface drier. He passed through the great gates, which he'd never seen closed, and under the stone arch into the stable yard. Here, he was startled to find two men with lanterns standing beside a horse.

"She came up lame miles from here," said one, sounding younger than his inches suggested. "I had to walk her. That's why I'm so damned late."

The other leaned down, shining his light on the

horse's near foreleg. He was one of the castle grooms, Sebastian saw. "I can't see nothing, my lord. We'll get her in a stall and take a closer look."

"Right, thanks."

No one had mentioned visitors, but it was none of Sebastian's affair. He edged along the wall toward the house as the groom led the animal away.

"Who's there?" asked the newcomer. He held up his lantern and peered across the yard.

Sebastian was revealed in all his muddy glory. He sighed and started to respond.

"Here, fellow, you can't just walk in off the road," said the other man. "I know it's a filthy night, but this isn't an inn. Everyone's abed."

He must look even worse than he'd feared, Sebastian thought. "I didn't..."

"I suppose you can sleep in the hayloft," the man interrupted in a more sympathetic tone. "I'll tell them. Mind you wash at the pump first. In the morning, go around that way." He pointed to a low entrance on the other side of the stable yard. Sebastian hadn't noticed it before. "They'll feed you in the kitchen before you go on your way."

The last was said firmly, rather the way Sebastian would have spoken to a homeless rambler who showed up at Langford. Who was this? He appeared to be only a few years beyond boyhood, but he spoke with easy authority. There was something familiar about him, but Sebastian couldn't put a finger on what it was. How he wished he could simply slip by him and escape to his bedchamber. "I'm Gresham," he said instead.

"What?" The man raised his lantern higher and stared.

"Sebastian Gresham."

There was a pause. "The fellow who's engaged to Georgina?" the other said incredulously then. "The duke's son?"

"That's the one."

"What are you doing out here at this time of night? Covered in mud?"

"I went for a walk." Sebastian was well aware that this sounded idiotic.

"A walk?" He stared. Sebastian waited for more questions. Instead the younger man said, "Has my father overwhelmed you?"

"Uh, er." Who was his father? What the deuce was going on?

"I'm Georgina's brother, you know." The new-comer came over and held out a hand. "Edgar Stane. Came up from university for the wedding."

Now Sebastian got it. The young man resembled his mother. He had the same round face, glossy brown hair, and slightly prominent blue eyes. He was above middle height, however, and burly like his father. Sebastian showed him his mud-caked palm.

"Ah." Stane's hand dropped. "Come, let's go in. I'm soaked, and you're… Whatever have you been doing?"

"Slipped and fell," said Sebastian. They walked in side by side. Sebastian tried to keep the bits of mud falling from his coattails to a minimum.

"So, ah, is all well here?" asked his companion. He sounded like a man who wasn't sure he wanted to know, but felt duty bound to inquire.

"It was," answered Sebastian bitterly. "Until Miss Byngham convinced them to hold this blasted ritual."

He was too tired to dissemble. Or to explain very clearly, he realized.

Edgar Stane stopped just inside the castle entry. "Ritual? What sort of…? Does this have something to do with my father's latest studies?"

"It's not Hindu. Mitra says definitely not."

"Mitra is the scholar from India? Papa wrote me about him. But what does Joanna Byngham have to do with it?"

"You may well ask," replied Sebastian gloomily. He was suddenly tired and very cold. He just wanted to get upstairs and out of his muddy evening clothes.

The younger man eyed him. "It seems a good deal has been happening."

"You have no idea."

"Right. Well, best I get one, eh?" He seemed remarkably unworried.

Sebastian headed for the stairs.

"I'm going to raid the kitchen larder," Edgar Stane added. "Strictly forbidden. But it's always easier to ask forgiveness than permission, isn't it? Care to come along?" His grin was engaging.

Sebastian liked his attitude. He wondered if he had found a possible ally. "There might be some hot water in the kitchen," he ventured.

"Reservoir beside the stove, if I remember correctly."

It would keep the mud out of his bedroom. Sebastian gave a nod and followed the heir of Stane into the back premises. He'd let Sykes explain his master's filthy garments in a pile on the kitchen hearth, he decided. His valet was endlessly inventive.

Seventeen

WHEN HE CAME DOWNSTAIRS TO BREAKFAST THE following morning, Sebastian discovered that no one was going to ask him if he intended to play his part in the ritual. Everyone simply assumed that he was. Indeed, all questions and objections had apparently been overborne by the manic energy of the event's proponents. Or forgotten in the excitement surrounding the arrival of Edgar Stane.

Unusually, the whole family lingered around the breakfast table. Emma hovered over her brother, plying him with food. Hilda pelted him with questions about his recent walking tour and his university activities, interspersed with more practical inquiries from their mother. Georgina listened to the answers with a fond smile. It was almost as if the king, or some equally august personage, had arrived, Sebastian thought. It seemed it was a grand thing to be the single son with several sisters, rather than just one of a crowd of boys.

It was obvious that the marquess was also delighted to see his son home again. He said little, but beamed on the scene like a benevolent blond bear. Miss

Byngham, on the other hand, sat at the far end of the board and visibly brooded over her displacement from center stage. There was no sign of Mr. Mitra.

Edgar received all the attention with patent enjoyment, responding to each question with kind enthusiasm and devouring every tidbit offered. He'd already heard the ritual plan by the time Sebastian joined them, and he looked more boyish than ever as Hilda gave him more the details, seeming both amused and intrigued. Clearly, he wasn't going to raise any objections.

Sebastian had had a good talk with him last night in the kitchens. Stripping down to your drawers before a man and washing off a coat of mud created a certain automatic intimacy, he'd found. While Edgar stuffed down stolen food like a starving schoolboy, Sebastian had dropped all the hints he could think of about the inappropriateness of this ritual idea. Without, of course, saying anything really negative about the Stane family. But here was Edgar apparently on board with it this morning. So there was going to be no help from that direction. Sebastian ate dourly, wondering what the deuce he was going to do.

After breakfast, Georgina's father bustled about like a troop commander on the eve of a royal review. There was no question that he was enjoying himself hugely. Joanna and Hilda were his zealous junior officers, chivvying a group of servants about the place. The only good news from this unlikely trio was that they'd decided they needed more time to prepare, as well as incorporate a part for Edgar. So the thing was now set for Friday, only two days before the Gresham family was due.

Sebastian discovered that Georgina had given in on every other point, insisting only that it be over and done well before their guests arrived. Otherwise, she ignored the upheaval and worked with her mother to perfect the arrangements for the wedding party. Edgar, on the other hand, was gradually drawn into the planning. Sebastian watched him grow more interested, even as he remained amused. He soon headed off to the attics to root about for some bit of paraphernalia.

Sebastian found no opportunity to speak to Georgina until he came into the dining parlor in the afternoon and found her facing Randolph over the cold collation spread for luncheon.

"I thought they didn't wish me to have anything to do with it," Randolph was saying.

"Joanna isn't keen," Georgina replied. "It's just that Papa has decided you should be there as a representative of Sebastian's family."

"Well, I should rather like to see it." Randolph had noticed his brother's entry. "I'll guard your flank, Sebastian," he added.

He meant it as no more than a brother's teasing; Sebastian knew that. But he couldn't suppress a wince as Georgina turned and smiled at him. "He doesn't need guarding," she said. "He'll be splendid, because he always is."

Sebastian allowed himself a moment's basking in her loving gaze. It made the world seem brighter. But he'd never been a coward. He was going to have to find a way to tell her.

Georgina looked past him and nodded. "Mr. Mitra."

The Indian gentleman bowed in his customary way

and went over to examine a selection of fresh fruit. "I have decided that it is best I return home," he said as he helped himself. "I have enjoyed your family's hospitality for quite a time." He acknowledged Georgina with a nod and smile. "I am most grateful. But the knowledge I attempted to impart in return…has not taken root." He made a graceful gesture with his free hand. "I am a poor teacher, it seems. I shall go back home to become a student again."

"I'm sorry if Joanna's…imaginative interpretation of your ideas is driving you away," Georgina replied.

Mitra sighed. "Please do not associate these two things, my Lady Georgina. Miss Byngham's…philosophy is wholly her own, as I have tried so often to explain. I only hope this is not the impression I leave behind in your country."

"But you will stay for my wedding?"

Mitra looked surprised.

"You've been here through so much of the…prelude. It just seems as if you should be there."

He bowed again. "I'm honored that you ask it of me, Lady Georgina. Of course I agree. As long as it is clear that I can have nothing to do with the…" Mitra appeared to search for a word to describe Miss Byngham's ritual. And fail.

Emma came into the room as Georgina nodded her understanding of his position. "Mama wants you," Emma said to her sister. She began collecting food on a tray she'd brought with her, including a very large pile of cold meat. "And some luncheon." She handed Georgina the now laden tray.

"We'll never eat all this beef," Georgina began. "Oh."

Sebastian steeled himself and stepped forward. "There's something we must discuss."

"For the dogs," Emma and Georgina said in unison.

"It's rather important," Sebastian said.

"Mama is ranting about sugared grapes," said Emma in a carefully dispassionate voice. "She seems to have gotten the notion that they are positively…obligatory for a duchess."

Georgina gave Sebastian a heartbreakingly lovely smile, but moved toward the door with the tray. "I'll see you later," she said. "As soon as may be." And then she was gone. Emma followed her out.

"You may as well give it up," commented Randolph from the dining table. He was applying mustard to a generous portion of sliced ham. "I have observed quite a few weddings by this time, and I can assure you that the groom's opinion is the last thing anyone wants."

"It's not about that," Sebastian muttered.

"Indeed, weddings are the province of women," said Mitra. He joined Randolph with his plate of fruit and bread. "Until you are taken to your bride's home on horseback and presented to her like a flower-wreathed gift."

The Gresham brothers stared at him. He was savoring a slice of peach and didn't notice. "These are exquisite," he said. "I recommend them to you."

Sebastian shook his head morosely.

"Have a bit of this ham then," Randolph said to Sebastian. "It's dashed good."

"I'm not hungry."

Randolph's fork paused in midair. "You're always hungry."

In fact, the remaining cold roast beef looked very appetizing. And there was a fine-looking wedge of cheese as well. Edgar came in just then to pile a plate. Setting aside his worries for the moment, Sebastian went to help himself.

Afterward, he drifted about the castle at loose ends. Georgina remained with her mother, and he was too distracted to do anything but wait for her. Finally, he retreated to his bedchamber and found Sykes there, looking over a pile of red cloth. "What's that?" Sebastian began, then realized he knew. "Oh."

"Yes, my lord. They've found you a doublet and a pair of hose. Very Shakespearean. No ruff, though." Sykes sounded a bit disappointed.

"I'm not wearing hose!" declared Sebastian.

"No, my lord, so I have already informed Lady Hilda. After a bit of…negotiation, she and Miss Byngham agreed that the doublet is sufficient. With black breeches." He shook out a garment and held it up. The red material was richly embroidered.

Sebastian looked it over. It was like a costume for a masquerade.

"Your evening slippers are beyond help," the valet added with a severe look. "It will have to be Hessians, which will look rather odd."

"Odd!" Sebastian snorted.

His valet nodded. "A point, my lord."

Sebastian paced the room. "The thing is, Sykes. This ritual."

A brief, intense conversation took place in silence, then Sykes cleared his throat and spoke in a very dry tone. "I have made some inquiries, my lord.

Expressing an interest in the communications from the beyond, you might say. You are not to be given the pages you are to read until just before the ceremony." His manner gradually shifted as he spoke, from correct servant to curious playwright. "According to Miss Byngham, the words must not be spoken until that moment, 'lest they be worn out with mundane use.' An interesting thought, eh? Acknowledging the power of an apt phrase. She has everything to do with the ritual locked in her bedchamber. No one is allowed entry, not even the maids to clean."

Sebastian nodded.

"I don't see how I could get in there," Sykes added. "And if I were to be caught…"

"Of course. I wouldn't ask you to try." He hadn't really expected to escape exposure. "I'd already decided to talk to Lady Georgina about…it."

Sykes nodded. "I think that's best. My lord."

Did he sound relieved? Sebastian almost thought he did. It was unmistakable. Sykes was on his way out of Sebastian's life. He was ready to let Sebastian find his own solutions. Which was all very well, Sebastian thought, but Sykes wasn't the one who had to tell the woman he loved that he was a dolt.

"I wondered," the other man went on. "Do you think you could manage a few notes? I'd be fascinated to hear what Miss Byngham has put together. I don't suppose I could observe? No, no that's not possible." His voice held the regret of a craftsman denied a potential treasure trove of knowledge.

"I'll do my best," replied Sebastian dryly. "I'm unlikely to have much attention to spare from my utter humiliation." There was no sense skirting the issue any longer. It would be all over soon.

"I'm sure you'll manage. My lord."

Yes, Sykes was cutting him loose. Sebastian was aware of a forlorn feeling, which could only get worse as this day unfolded. Still, there was no way out. If you had to charge the guns, it was best to set the spurs and get it over. He decided to wrest Georgina from her mother's clutches, no refusals accepted.

In the end, it wasn't as difficult as that. When he appeared in the marchioness's workroom and declared that Georgina needed some air, his hostess waved them off with hardly a protest. Georgina took his arm with another meltingly sweet smile, and they walked out into the garden.

The rain had passed, leaving bright-blue skies and warmer breezes behind. Flowers gleamed like jewels among the greenery, and sheltered nooks beckoned. Georgina moved to nestle within the curve of his arm. The scene might have been all he desired if not for the looming conversation. But he couldn't put it off any longer. That was almost harder. "I have to speak to you about this…ritual," Sebastian said.

"It's ridiculous, I know." She gazed ruefully up at him. "I am sorry. But at least it will be over before your family arrives."

"I can't do it," Sebastian said. His pulse accelerated as if he'd been running a race.

"What?"

"I won't be able to do it," he said.

Georgina gazed up at him, a hint of concern becoming visible in her green eyes. "Sebastian, of course it's silly. Papa gets these notions, and now Joanna has become even worse." She shook her head. "Sometimes I can't believe she's the same person. And she's egging him on. But it's not serious, you know. You can think of it as a bit of acting." She smiled encouragingly. "We can pretend we're onstage together in some dreadful melodrama."

"You don't understand. I can't."

She withdrew from him a little. "Papa will be utterly impossible if you refuse. You haven't seen him really... He'll throw the whole household into an uproar, right before the wedding! Most likely he'll try to call it off again."

Sebastian hated upsetting her. He would have given anything to simply agree. But he had to shake his head.

Georgina blinked as if she couldn't believe it and frowned. "It's such a small thing to ask, Sebastian. If you love me... You said you did."

"I do! More than anything. More than life."

"Then why can't you just do this?"

She sounded mystified, and hurt, and irritated. Which was bad. Not as bad as it was going to be when she knew the truth, Sebastian thought. But there was no drawing back now. He pulled a small book from his pocket. He'd brought it from a shelf in his bedchamber to help explain. And although his heart quailed, he marched forward. "There's something wrong with me," he began. "I've always been stupid about..."

"You are *not* stupid. I wish you wouldn't say it." She sounded almost petulant now.

"But I *am*, Georgina. I-I can't read." There, he'd

said it—starkly, without circumlocution or excuses, out loud—as he never had before in his life. He waited for her to take it in and despise him.

"What?"

"I can't read," he repeated. It was no easier to admit the second time. He opened the book and held it out before them. "When you look at this page, you see lines of words that make up sentences and tell you…whatever the writer wished to set down. I don't. I never have. I see a mass of tangled lines, with all the letters shoved together. I can't make head nor tail of them."

Georgina looked at the page, then back up at him.

"There's something wrong with me," he said again. He closed the book, shoved it back in his pocket, and waited for her reaction. It was a bit like hearing artillery shots whistling overhead and wondering whether the next would do for you.

"You look at printed words, and you can't see them as they are?" Georgina asked.

He nodded heavily. "And so I can't play my part in the deuced ritual. I won't be able to read it."

Georgina stared up at him for so long that Sebastian thought he'd burst. "And this is what was wrong?" she said then. "This is what had made you so distant?"

It wasn't quite the reaction he'd expected. "Worried about what to do," he muttered.

Georgina threw her arms around him and clung as if she would never let go. Startled, and confused, Sebastian embraced her gingerly. "I'm so relieved," she said against his chest. "I was imagining terrible things."

Wasn't this terrible enough? Sebastian wondered.

Had she understood him? Holding her was so wonderful that he couldn't bring himself to ask.

After a while, though, she drew back. She looked
much happier. "But how could this happen, that you
can't…decipher words?"

So she just hadn't really taken it in. The blow was
still to come. Sebastian let his arms fall to his sides
again. "There's something wrong with my brain," he
repeated bitterly.

"But Sebastian, there isn't. You know all sorts of
clever things. You carry on intelligent conversations."

"I wonder if your father would say so."

"Papa is not a good example," said Georgina
severely. "You're a fine commander of men. I heard
your colonel tell you so at an evening party. And look
at the way you can make a fire out of nothing and help
a shy young lady feel at ease at a London ball."

"You're being kind." Of course she would be,
Sebastian thought. She was that sort of person. She
wouldn't show him her contempt.

"Well, of course I am. I love you. But that's not all."

"You still love me?" He couldn't believe he'd heard
correctly. "After this?"

"Why wouldn't I?"

"But how can you?"

Georgina waved the question aside as if it was
ridiculous. "Have you spoken to anyone about this…
oddity? I don't suppose a doctor would be of any help."

"I've tried, but no one understood." He hadn't
been willing to say it outright to his father or his
tutors. The thought of appearing a dullard in their
eyes had been intolerable. He'd only been able to tell

Georgina because otherwise she'd think he didn't love her. "I can't always say exactly what I mean."

"Well, we all have that problem," replied Georgina wryly. She gazed into the distance as if deep in thought.

Amazed at the way she was taking the news, Sebastian felt hope reawaken in his breast.

"Is it something like being deaf?" she mused. "Or no, not quite that. Wait! Did you know that some people can't see colors properly? Mostly men, I think. When they look at red, it seems gray to them. They have no way of knowing the real color."

Sebastian stared at her.

"A scientist published a paper about it. Papa— you've seen how he loves odd bits of knowledge—he told us one night at dinner. I didn't really listen, I'm afraid." She shrugged guiltily. "He's always going on about something."

"Colors," wondered Sebastian. "Like light?" Alan might know about it; he followed all kinds of scientific developments.

"I expect so. But I do remember this much. Such people look at the colors we all see, and they simply cannot perceive them. It's just the way they're born. And certainly has nothing to do with their intelligence."

"You think it's that way with me?" He'd thought of his problem as stupidity for so long that he couldn't quite take it in.

"Yes, I do. And..." She paused to grip the lapels of his coat, demanding his full attention. "I don't care if you never read a word, Sebastian. I love you."

"Still?"

"Always."

There could be only one response to this, and the
two of them spent several intensely agreeable minutes
in one of the shrubbery nooks demonstrating the
strength of their attachment. When they had to step
apart, or else go too far, Sebastian said, "Sykes writes
my letters." He wanted to make a clean breast of the
whole matter.

"Does he?" replied his beloved, a bit breathlessly.
She put a hand to her tousled hair.

"He has a particular handwriting just for them. A
very bad one."

Georgina laughed. "How clever of the two of you.
Though I think, in that case, we will dispense with the
exchange of passionate love letters when we are apart.
Which I hope we shall not often be."

Sebastian gazed down at her, amazed and touched.
"You're perfect, aren't you?"

"Why, yes, I am," she said with another laugh.
"Oh, I am so glad that this was all. It's such a relief."

"Except for this blasted ritual," said Sebastian. "And
Miss Byngham insisting I read her…whatever it is."

"Ah." Georgina frowned. "Yes. I don't think we
want anyone else to know why you cannot. People
can be so spiteful."

How had he gotten so very lucky? Sebastian wondered. He felt as if a great weight, which he'd been
lugging around all his life, had fallen off his back.

"We need a plan," she continued. "I don't suppose
you could memorize her…composition? If I read it
out to you a few times."

"Oh yes," said Sebastian. "I'm a whiz at getting
passages by rote. Had to be."

"Well, then." She spread her hands as if the problem was solved.

"But Miss Byngham's got it locked in her room. Sykes told me no one's allowed inside."

"Does she indeed?"

A smile spread over Georgina's lovely face. It wasn't quite like any expression Sebastian had seen there before. She looked rather like a cat who'd spotted an unguarded cream pot.

"I expect I can get around that," she said. "Though I'll need your help."

He nearly snapped to attention. "Anything. Of course."

"At the proper time, you'll have to keep Joanna occupied for, oh, say an hour. Just to be certain."

"Mount a diversionary action?"

"What a fine way of putting it. Precisely."

"Just tell me when," Sebastian answered, thinking yet again what a delight it was going to be, having such an exceedingly clever wife.

Eighteen

IF ONLY THEY HAD A BIT MORE TIME, GEORGINA thought as she made her way to her mother's work-room very late that night, after everyone else was abed. But by tomorrow at this time, Joanna's ritual would be over, for better or worse. She had to act quickly, and every step had to go as planned. Sebastian had been gloomy about that last part. He'd said that a plan never survived first contact with the enemy. "It's not a matter of enemies," Georgina murmured as she stepped into the room.

The first necessity was to placate the pugs. A certain level of sleepy yapping in the wee hours was an accepted part of life at Stane Castle, but if the dogs went wild, it would draw unwanted attention. They knew her, however, and made no great fuss as Georgina crossed the room. She spoke to them softly, patting heads and responding to wriggling greetings on the way.

Sitting at her mother's desk, Georgina opened the bottom drawer and took out a great iron ring of keys. It held duplicates for all the modern rooms of the castle, and the older ones if they weren't lost, in case a key went missing. Papa called it a chatelaine, and he'd suggested, years ago, that Mama wear it at her belt, like the lady of an ancient manor. Mama had snorted at the idea that she would go about with a clanking bunch of metal weighing her down. She'd put it in the drawer and never looked at it unless asked to help open a door. She wouldn't notice its absence unless Georgina was very unlucky. If she was, she'd find some excuse.

Georgina wrapped the ring in a shawl she'd brought to keep it from making a noise and slipped out of the room and back along the corridors to her own chamber. She now had a key to Joanna's bedchamber. The trouble was, she had a great many other keys as well. No matter how long Sebastian kept Joanna occupied, she couldn't stand in the hallway outside her former governess's room trying a whole ring of keys. Someone was bound to catch her. Georgina carried the chair from her dressing table over to her own door, sat down, and began to experiment. The key for Joanna's room was likely to be similar to the one that opened her own. Surely she could narrow down the choices. She picked out a key and tried it. It wouldn't turn. She chose another.

An hour later, drooping a little in the chair and fighting repeated yawns, Georgina had done her best. She'd found the key that fit in her lock and compared it to all the others on the ring. She'd singled out ten to try and was *almost* certain one of them would work. As she got into bed at last, she began to manufacture reasons she might be hanging about in the corridor near Joanna's room. None of them seemed very convincing, but that was a problem for another day.

Sebastian entered the breakfast room far too early the next morning, while the servants were still setting out the food. He knew it was too soon, but with a mission before him, he hadn't been able to lie about in bed. He hadn't even summoned Sykes, but had dressed himself and come down. Now here he was with a good deal of time to kill. The thing was, he hadn't been certain when Joanna Byngham would appear.

He piled a plate and ate. He requested a pot of tea that he didn't want. He talked to Georgina's father and then to Randolph when he appeared. He endured his brother's speculations on the nature of the coming ritual and refused his invitation to take a brisk walk. He almost had to push Randolph from the room in the end.

Deciding that his lurking was beginning to look peculiar, and realizing that he didn't wish to meet Emma and Hilda, Sebastian went out into the corridor. A nonchalant scout of the surrounding area yielded an empty parlor. With the door open a crack, he could observe the entry to the breakfast room and be ready to pounce, while also avoiding irrelevant personnel.

Upstairs, Georgina lingered in the schoolroom, which was just down the hall from Joanna's bedchamber. As far as she could see, it had fallen completely out of use since Joanna's revelations. There were no signs of lessons being done or projects under way. Hilda must be delighted. Still, the abandonment was fortunate for Georgina. She could keep watch from here, spotting Joanna as soon as she rose.

When a housemaid came in to dust and asked if she needed anything, Georgina said that she was looking for a particular book. She had to stand at the shelves pretending to search, straining her ears for sounds from the corridor, until the girl was finished. This earned her a few curious glances.

Returning to her post, Georgina watched the corridor. It appeared that Joanna was sleeping later than usual, perhaps recruiting her strength for tonight. Or perhaps she was busily composing more ritual behind her closed door. Mama was going to have to speak to her eventually, Georgina thought. Everyone would probably be happier if Mama made other arrangements for Hilda's education. Joanna could… What would she do? She was so changed. She seemed totally unlike the woman Georgina had admired as a young girl. She couldn't expect to stay on as a…resident priestess. They would have to find her some congenial place. Georgina tried to think of one that might suit her, and failed.

At last, the door down the hall opened and Joanna emerged, her trailing sleeves brushing the floor as she walked. Georgina craned her neck, but she couldn't see the key Joanna used to lock up. She waited a few minutes to be sure Joanna wasn't coming right back and then hurried out to begin trying her keys.

Sebastian spotted Miss Byngham as she came down the corridor toward the breakfast room. Thinking strategically, he didn't accost her then. She'd be occupied with her meal for a while, and waiting until she finished would stretch out the time. Hilda was in there; no telling how long they might talk. He checked his pocket watch to begin tracking Georgina's hour. He hoped to give her more than that.

Georgina tried three keys without success. A maid came along carrying a pile of laundry—thankfully, not the same one who'd been dusting—and she had to pretend she was going into the schoolroom. Once the coast was clear, she managed three more attempts before she had to duck in there again. Her pulse had started to speed up. None of the keys had shown any sign of working. If she had to try more than ten, she might run out of time.

❧

Miss Byngham came out of the breakfast room a mere twenty minutes after she'd entered—a quick eater, seemingly. Sebastian stepped out of the parlor and into her path. "Good morning," he said heartily. "I wondered if I might speak to you."

She looked surprised. They hadn't really conversed beyond polite nothings.

"It's just that I have a few questions about the, er, ritual this evening." He and Georgina had agreed that this approach would make sense to Miss Byngham and flatter her as well.

"Of course," she replied graciously. "How may I aid you?"

Sebastian retreated into the parlor, drawing Miss Byngham along with him. He didn't want to be caught by Hilda, or anyone else, in the middle of his delaying action. He made a production of ushering her to a seat. "Is that comfortable?" he asked. When she blinked at him, he realized he was laying it on too thick in his efforts to draw things out. He sat opposite her and said, "I'm not sure what I'm meant to be doing tonight."

She gave him a benign smile. "As I've mentioned, the purpose of our ritual is to weave you into the Stane family."

"Not sure what that means," replied Sebastian, quite sincerely. "I'm a bit slow, I suppose."

"Not at all. It is an area almost universally neglected in our place and time. Think of it: all over England people are marrying. Through the ceremonies, they acquire a host of new relatives with little more than a handshake or a curtsy to introduce them. And then they are expected to look upon these strangers as part of their families."

She actually had a point, Sebastian thought. Which didn't mean that her approach to the issue was sensible. "But how does it work?" he said. "Your... weaving?" He tried a joke. "Sounds like Stane and I will be twisted in knots together."

Miss Byngham did not appear to appreciate the humor. "Not at all. There will be no...twisting involved."

"I beg your pardon," said Sebastian. "I'm a bit nervous about my part."

"You needn't worry about anything," she replied. "The words you speak, within the context of the ritual, will create the bond." She gathered her skirts to rise. "I should go. There are still many preparations to make."

They'd only been in the parlor ten minutes, Sebastian saw. "But…" he said desperately.

Miss Byngham looked at him, brows raised.

What could he say? "I thought…that is, shouldn't I…er, get into the right frame of mind beforehand?"

"No special preparation is required, Lord Sebastian. Simply clear your mind." Her tone suggested that she didn't believe there would be many thoughts to move out of the way. She rose and turned toward the door.

❧

The lock clicked, and Georgina let out a sigh of relief. Of course it was the very last of the keys she'd chosen that finally did the trick. She slipped into Joanna's room, shutting the door behind her. After a moment's debate, she relocked it, leaving the key in the hole. The heavy ring made it droop a bit.

Georgina looked around the room. She remembered her governess's quarters as a model of spare tidiness. What surrounded her now was the opposite. Colorful fabric scraps left over from Joanna's new sleeves adorned every surface, including the floor. Stacks of books from the castle library sat here and there, interspersed with discarded boots and gloves and empty teacups. Several millinery projects, along the lines of the headdress Joanna had shown her days ago, added to the chaos. How was she going to find anything in this clutter?

Georgina stood in the center of the chamber and turned slowly, scanning each pile. The materials for the ritual had to be somewhat organized. It was tonight after all. Joanna must have everything ready.

She went over to the small writing desk under one

of the windows. Papers littered the top and lay in drifts around it. Georgina riffled through them, reading a few words on each one before letting it fall. They all seemed to be notes rather than a finished piece.

❦

He had to think of something else to say, Sebastian thought. "Wait!"

Miss Byngham turned back, staring at the urgency of his tone.

"The thing is…" he said. What came next? "I'm…I'm rather…afraid I'll botch it." That was the ticket. Besides being perfectly true, the threat to her production was bound to worry her. "I'm not much for public speaking. Soldier, you know." He didn't have to feign concern. Despite Georgina's help, he was apprehensive. It seemed all too likely that he'd make a fool of himself tonight, if not worse.

"You won't be speaking, Lord Sebastian," the governess replied soothingly. "Merely reading a short passage. There is no possibility of making a mistake."

Here was another case of what his brother Robert called irony, Sebastian thought. There was no "merely reading" for him. "Yes, but everybody will be looking at me," he said.

"All of us will be in an exalted state," she answered. "The opening of the ritual will assure that. There will be no problems. Now I really must go." She moved toward the half-open door.

What the devil was an "exalted state"? Sebastian wondered. But she was escaping him. And the hour hadn't passed, not nearly.

All the pages around the desk held only fragments or gibberish. Georgina nearly despaired as she reached the bottom of the last pile. Perhaps some of them were parts of the ritual, but she'd seen nothing that seemed complete. Feeling uncomfortable, she peeked into Joanna's wardrobe. Only clothes. Once again, she turned in a circle in the center of the room. Where could it be? She'd been in here more than twenty minutes. And she had to copy the passage once she found it. If she found it. No, she had to. She would not fail Sebastian.

"Exalted," repeated Sebastian. It wasn't a word he was accustomed to hearing in the course of a conversation. "Just so." Miss Byngham was going. He had to stop her. "But...but...however did you get this idea in the first place?"

A spark of enthusiasm lit his companion's eyes. She stepped closer to him. "It is amazing, is it not? Until that memorable occasion under the guidance of Mr. Mitra, I had never before experienced pure inspiration. Did you not feel it yourself? The mystic connection to the past?"

"Not as you did." Which was not as Mitra meant them to, Sebastian remembered. He'd certainly felt something odd, though.

Miss Byngham waved a hand. "Well, there are many different degrees of sensitivity, I imagine. And of course, I have years of research behind me."

"Right."

She looked expectant. He floundered for a reply.

Just when Georgina was about to despair, she noticed a small wooden chest sitting on a shelf in the corner. Richly inlaid, it looked familiar, something she'd seen about the house. It was certainly a new addition here. Striding over she took it down and set it on the desk. There was a keyhole. If the thing was locked... But it wasn't. It opened under her hands. No doubt the key had been lost long ago.

Inside, she found a sheaf of papers tied together with a red ribbon. A moment's reading told her that she'd discovered her quarry at last. This was the ritual. Paging through it, she found the section she wanted. It was longer than she'd hoped. Praying that she would have enough time, Georgina cleared a space on the desk and sat down to write. She'd left nothing to chance, but had brought pen, ink, and paper with her in a small cloth bag.

"But...never anything like this before, in your research?" Sebastian managed.

Miss Byngham drifted further back toward him. "No. Although I have yearned. Perhaps you've come across Mr. Wordsworth's 'Ode: Intimations of Immortality'?"

"Uh, no." Sebastian didn't much care for this talk of yearning. Or intimations. Whatever they might be.

She didn't seem surprised at his ignorance. "It is quite a recent publication. A work of genius, I may add. When I discovered it, I was...ravished."

She waved her arms in a wide arc. Sebastian edged away. Ravishment was even worse than yearning.

"I've always felt that there would be more to my life than teaching," Miss Byngham continued. "A greater destiny. One can foresee these things, don't you think?"

"Er… I…" He was losing control of the conversation, Sebastian thought. If he'd ever had it.

"You yourself might have imagined finding a link to an ancient past? Coming from such an illustrious family?"

"No," he answered with complete sincerity.

"Ah, well." She bowed her head as if sorry for him and made a little motion with one hand. He couldn't tell if it was meant as a blessing or a dismissal. "I beg your pardon, Lord Sebastian, but I really must go." This time she didn't wait for a reply, but hurried from the room.

Practically sweating with the effort he'd made, Sebastian checked his watch. He'd managed the hour, but only just. He hoped it would be enough. He thought of following Miss Byngham, but what would he say if she noticed? He'd run out of ideas. He couldn't tackle her in an upstairs corridor to rescue Georgina. Still, perhaps he ought to try. He stepped out into the hall.

"You missed a very pleasant walk," said Randolph at his back.

Sebastian jumped like a startled hare and whirled on his brother.

Randolph took a step back. "Sebastian, tell me what's wrong."

"Nothing. You took me by surprise, that's all."

"You look like you've been harried to death."

"No, I don't."

Randolph examined him, then shrugged. "The thought of this…event tonight seems to be making everyone a bit skittish."

"I am not skittish," said Sebastian. A door slammed

in the upper regions, and he started again. Was it a sign that Georgina had been caught? Should he rush to help her?

"Obviously," replied his brother dryly.

There was no further sound, no uproar floating down the staircase.

Randolph put a comradely hand on his arm. "Sebastian, tell me again. You're not sorry to be marrying into this family, are you? Because you know I would help you disengage…"

"No!"

"All right. There's no need to shout at me."

"I must…I need something from my room," declared Sebastian. He'd patrol the corridors, make certain nothing had gone wrong. Leaving Randolph staring, he strode off.

"What are you up to?"

Georgina jumped. She whirled to find her brother observing her from the end of the corridor. Had he seen her relock Joanna's room? She tried to judge from his expression. "Nothing," she replied.

"Oh, come," He strolled toward her. "I've seen that look before. You're plotting something. Is it to do with this silly ritual tonight? I wouldn't mind helping you."

"No, I'm not. I was…just going to get something from the schoolroom." She should have used another excuse. If Edgar and the maids ever compared notes— which was thankfully unlikely—her behavior was going to be judged very odd.

"Really? What?" Edgar demanded.

"Just a book."

"I don't believe you."

Georgina summoned all the dignity of an older sister who had wiped his sticky face after an indulgence in sweets and helped him down when he got stuck in a tree. "Whyever not?"

"What's in the bag?" Edgar demanded.

Georgina clutched it to her side. It clanked.

Joanna came around the corner, stopping in surprise when she found the two of them practically at her bedchamber door.

Georgina jumped in before either of the others could speak. "Oh, Joanna, there you are. Edgar was looking for you. He has some suggestions for the ritual."

"Suggestions?" Joanna bridled and frowned at Edgar. "What sort of suggestions?"

Edgar glared at Georgina. He silently mouthed, *I will get you for this.*

"You'll have to ask him," Georgina said. Suppressing a spurt of laughter—more relief than amusement—she fled. Moments later, she stood with her back to her bedchamber door, heart pounding. It was over; she'd done it. She leaned there for the space of a few deep breaths.

When she'd calmed down a bit, she took the page she'd scrawled in Joanna's room over to her own writing desk. She needed to reinscribe the passage while it was fresh in her mind. She'd been writing so fast that some of it was barely legible. Then she'd go and find Sebastian. Dropping into the chair, she laughed again as she reached for her pen.

"You're really good at this," Georgina said to Sebastian some hours later. Afternoon light poured through one of the slitted windows in the old stone tower. They'd carried two cane chairs up to the second level, where they were unlikely to be disturbed, and settled to go over the words Georgina had copied. Above their heads, Mr. Mitra sat with a book, wrapped in several shawls against the chill, and ignoring them and all preparations for the evening's event.

"I've had to be," Sebastian replied.

Georgina looked at him with tender curiosity. "What did you do about written examinations at school?"

Sebastian grimaced at the memory. "Nothing I could do. I did try to explain to one of the masters, but he just thought I was a shirker." He shrugged. "I was one of the best on the playing fields, which counts for a lot at school. But everyone soon saw that I was stupid otherwise. *Nobly born numbskull* was the phrase, I believe." He hid the hurt and humiliation the label could still rouse.

Georgina put a hand on his arm. "You are *not* stupid, Sebastian. I forbid you to say that ever again."

He put his hand over hers, still scarcely believing his luck. "Sometimes I got a younger boy to read bits aloud to me. Told them it was good practice."

"For what?"

He shrugged again. "Pulpit, parliament, classroom. Didn't matter. And then I'd go and spout it back to a teacher, show him I knew a bit about his subject."

"That was very clever of you."

"I don't know. It seemed to annoy most of 'em. I expect they would have thrown me out if I hadn't been a duke's son and had so many brothers coming along behind me to pay their fees." Despite the pain of these memories, Sebastian felt an amazing freedom and lightness at saying such things out loud. It was as if Georgina had brought light to a place inside him that had always been shrouded in darkness.

She picked up the page and held it before her. "Try it again."

Sebastian recited the words she'd read him.

"That's perfect." She shook her head, gesturing at the writing. "I could never learn all this so quickly. Indeed, I'm not sure I could do it at all."

"Of course you could."

"I don't know, Sebastian. Joanna used to give me poems to get by heart." She made a face. "When she was still a governess. I never could manage it. I'm terrible at memorizing."

"Well, you didn't need to." He looked down at the sheet in her hand. "I suppose you'll be reading to me all our lives." He couldn't quite believe that she didn't despise him for this, despite all she'd said. "Are you sure you don't mind?"

"I shall enjoy it," Georgina replied.

"You will?"

"Yes. It will be one of our secrets. Husbands and wives should have things only they share." She gave him an enticing look from under her lashes. "Beyond the bedchamber, I mean."

He'd been aware of her beside him—her arm occasionally brushing his, the bright beauty of her face, the outline of her body under the folds of her gown. He always was. But at this remark, those sensations intensified. Memories flooded him. He ached to hold her as he had on that bed of bracken, to feel the eagerness of her response to his touch.

"Sebastian?"

His voice thick with desire, he said, "Yes?"

"Tonight, after all this nonsense is over…"

He waited as she seemed to gather courage.

"Will you come to my room?" Georgina murmured.

His pulse leaped. The request was unexpected and wildly enflaming.

"I miss you," she whispered. "I want you. We're practically married already."

"I consider you my wife. I don't need words from a parson."

"Then you will come?"

"I've never wanted anything more in my life. But if we were caught?" He wouldn't expose her to embarrassment or censure.

"It will be late. If you're found out of your room, you can say you were upset by the ritual."

"Perhaps I shall be."

"Then I can soothe you."

The images this evoked nearly drove him mad. "If you're sure."

"Perfectly."

He leaned forward and sealed their pact with a kiss. Georgina threw her arms around him, and in an instant were standing, pressed together, clinging to each other. The kiss went on and on. Sebastian didn't see how he could wait for the night. Every inch of him burned with need. How would he get through the hours until he could slake it?

He didn't hear the footsteps on the stairs until Mr. Mitra was upon them. The Indian gentleman's feet appeared at the top curve of the stone stair. Then his legs and the hem of his tunic. Nearly groaning aloud, Sebastian stepped back. Gently but incxorably, he pushed Georgina down into her chair.

Mitra's hands and chest and head emerged. He paused to give them a smile and nod. "Pardon the interruption. I must go inside for a few moments." He started down the next turn of the stair, his feet and legs disappearing once again.

The sound of yapping floated through the narrow windows.

Mitra hesitated, listening.

The sound grew louder. The dogs were clearly approaching.

Mitra sighed, head bowed, shoulders slumped. "I am most sorry to ask it, but would you consider walking with me, Lord Sebastian?"

"I'll go," said Georgina, rising. "Mama will be wondering where I am."

Her cheeks were flushed, her green eyes bright. Looking at her, Sebastian didn't care about the ritual any longer, or indeed about anything else. Let the evening be as strange as anyone could imagine. Let it be humiliating. Let the rest of them think him an oaf. Georgina didn't, and that was all that mattered.

She loved him, he thought. She believed in him and respected him. Somehow that eased the years of worry about being discovered, the shame about his limitations. It was a revelation. He hadn't understood until now how much could be changed by one extraordinary woman's belief in him. "We'll all go," he said, elation bubbling in his tone. "The pugs shan't trouble you today, Mr. Mitra."

The older man accepted this buoyant assurance with raised brows. He said nothing, however, merely giving them one of his characteristic bows. And the three of them descended together into the late-afternoon sunshine.

As she returned the key ring to her mother's desk on the way down to dinner a bit later, Georgina felt, without knowing it, precisely the same as her beloved. Whatever awkwardness the ritual might bring, it didn't matter. She could anticipate what came after. And then after that. Her life lay before her, a delightful prospect. The only difficulty was impatience for it to begin.

Nineteen

IT WAS AN ODD–LOOKING GROUP THAT CONVENED IN the room where this had all begun under the influence of Mr. Mitra's drumming, Georgina thought. They'd looked even stranger around the dining table in the selection of red garments salvaged from the attic trunks. Her father wore knee breeches and a brocade coat with wide skirts, both a rich scarlet. Lace foamed around his neck and wrists, and he kept fidgeting with it in delight.

Joanna had improvised a flowing robe from what Georgina suspected had once been draperies. She looked like nothing ever seen before within the castle walls. Hilda's deep-red gown had a tight bodice that came to a point at the waist and sweeping skirts that dragged on the floor all around her.

The Gresham brothers couldn't be less than handsome, but they looked uncomfortable—Sebastian in a crimson tunic over dark trousers and Randolph in a ruby velvet cloak. They'd made Randolph wear the bulky thing through dinner. And then Hilda had said he looked a bit like a Roman cardinal in it. Randolph had been eyeing his reflection in one of the mirrors ever since, seemingly torn between fascination and concern. Edgar, the last-minute addition, had been allowed to get away with just a red waistcoat.

Georgina had been given what Hilda insisted was a red silk gown. It was markedly flimsy, however, and Georgina suspected it was a nightdress of another era. When her protests had gone unheeded, she'd put on two petticoats under it.

And there the resources of the castle had run out. Emma and Mama both wore gowns of their own. Emma's was more pink than red, her mother's a garnet shade that was deemed acceptable.

A vase of red roses graced the low table in the middle of the room, and branches of candles all around them once again lit the scene. Joanna had stationed the Greshams on one side of the center and Georgina's family on the other, planting herself between. "We look like we're standing at a church altar, as we will be in just a few days," said Hilda.

"Not exactly," said Randolph.

"Silence," declared Joanna. "It is time to begin." She raised her arms. There was a rustling noise as various people retrieved the pages Joanna had given them as they entered. She glared until it quieted. "We are here to mark the entrance of a new member into the Stane family," she intoned then. "Though few recognize it in these modern days, this is a solemn occasion. A change to be noted and revered."

She nodded to Georgina's father. He stood very straight, looking vastly pleased with the scene as he referred to his sheet of paper.

"'A bloodline is an ancient thing,'" he read. "'It stretches back through centuries, and more. Further than we can know. It links us to a host of ancestors. A few we remember; many more we do not. But their legacy runs in our veins.'"

He was truly in his element, Georgina thought. The setting and the phrases had him almost wriggling with joy.

"'Others have lived in this castle before me,'" he continued. "'And will after. I am a link between past and future, a conduit for a valued heritage, one man passing along whatever wisdom I can muster to my children. And they to theirs. And so on down the years.'"

Georgina found that she was moved by the sentiments, and she could see that Edgar was as well. Whatever had happened to Joanna, her words exhibited surprising depths. Her former governess—former in more than one sense now, Georgina thought—turned to signal her mother.

"'I came here a stranger,'" Mama began, with less relish than Papa, and yet a definite solemnity. "'As many women had done before me. And I made this place my home, as others will do when I am gone. It should be acknowledged that this is no easy task. Not for the sake of bemoaning the difficulties, but to recognize the achievement.'"

Georgina watched her mother's face change as she read the passage she was seeing for the first time. She too seemed startled and impressed by what Joanna had produced.

Joanna moved both her arms, like the conductor of a small eccentric orchestra.

Georgina's parents read together, though not exactly in unison. "'Our eldest is leaving us now to found her own household elsewhere. Though she changes her name, she will always be a Stane, and thus we do not let her go but rather welcome another into our line.'"

Joanna allowed a dramatic pause, then pointed at Sebastian.

He held the page just as the others had, as if he was reading from it. He spoke loudly and clearly. "'I do not become a Stane. But from this day, I count them as my kin, extending the range of my relations. Families spread out over the land like a bright net, bonded and woven together.'"

Every word was familiar as he went on, but Georgina could never have repeated them as perfectly as he did. Watching him pretend to read, she felt proud and full of admiration and so very sad for the boy who'd had to struggle. Before he was done, she had to blink back tears.

As Sebastian came to the end of his part, a candle next to Randolph began to behave very oddly. The flame fluttered and started to hiss. In the next instant it shot up much taller than the others, burning a striking blue. With a wordless exclamation, Randolph backed away from it. Hilda moved closer, eyes bright with curiosity.

"It is a sign," declared Joanna, making passes with her hands.

They all watched, fascinated, as the candle rapidly burned down under this much-stronger flame. Wax curled and slumped into fantastic shapes, almost seeming to writhe at one point.

"The powers acknowledge our efforts," Joanna added.

"Astonishing," Randolph muttered. He'd moved a bit behind Georgina; she wasn't sure whether the others could hear him. "Imperfections in the wax?" he said. "Some sort of chemical contamination?" He moved further away from the group. "I must make a note," he murmured. "So much in the world is still a mystery to us."

"Come," said Joanna. She beckoned. Georgina and Sebastian obediently stepped forward. Joanna took their hands and pressed them together. Briefly, it seemed she might hold them over the last vestiges of the hissing candle. Georgina braced herself to rebel and felt a similar tension in Sebastian's fingers. In the end, however, Joanna merely extended them in that direction. "It is done," she said with a complacent smile.

Georgina's father broke into applause, which clearly did not please their mistress of ceremonies. Hilda joined in, then Edgar, then Emma. The peculiar candle flared up one last time and went out.

Randolph strode out of the room without looking back. Georgina's mother lingered briefly, but soon followed him. Her father went over to shake Joanna's hand. "That was splendid!" he exclaimed. "Better than a play, I swear."

"It was not an entertainment," she replied, pulling her hand away.

No, she would not be remaining here as a governess, Georgina thought, as Joanna began to pace the perimeter of the room, making more mysterious passes with her hands. It seemed unlikely that she would even want to stay to aid Papa's studies. She was going to require greater scope for her newfound talents.

The rest of them moved out of the room and along the corridor. Hilda and Emma chattered to Edgar about the amazing behavior of the candle.

Georgina and Sebastian shared one lingering glance, hot with the promise of what was to follow later tonight, and then avoided each other's eyes.

"Shall we have a brandy to celebrate?" suggested Papa.

He must be wrapped up in the ritual still, Georgina thought. This was hardly a company for brandies. "I'm quite fatigued," she said. "I shall say good night."

"I, too," said Sebastian.

"What, so early?" the older man asked.

"This evening gave me much to, er, contemplate," Sebastian said, earning Georgina's wholehearted admiration for the quick-witted charm of his answer. How could he ever have imagined he was stupid?

"Oh." Her father looked nonplussed, as if this should have occurred to him.

"I'll join you, Papa," said Edgar.

"*I* should like a brandy, too," said Hilda. "As would Emma."

"Oh…I…no," stammered their middle sister.

Emma needed a bit of time away from Hilda, Georgina decided. She'd have to see about that when she was married. Warm anticipation ran through her. Only a few days to wait now, and tonight… She dared a glance at Sebastian. He was looking at her with a tender hunger that was unbearably exciting. Georgina caught her breath. "Good night," she murmured, and headed for the stairs.

Behind her, her father was saying, "Not *that* special an occasion, Hilda. You may have some sherry, however."

"Can't have you befuddled with drink," Edgar added.

Their sister's giggle followed Georgina into the hall.

◈

Sebastian paced his bedchamber, wondering how much longer he had to wait. Could bear to wait. He'd sent Sykes away, after satisfying the man's curiosity about the evening's events, saying that he wished to sit up for a while. His valet no doubt suspected that something was afoot—the man was too clever to miss such things—but he would say nothing.

They should have set a specific time, Sebastian thought, checking his pocket watch yet again. But how long would Hilda, for example, be allowed to stay up carousing? How long would her father and brother linger over their brandy? Would Miss Byngham wander the corridors reveling in her triumph? Would the pugs be restless, reflecting their mistress's mood?

He could manage if he encountered one of them as he made his way through the castle. It wasn't that. He could simply claim to be restless after his…investiture? He was just…eager. And what a poor little stump of a word *that* was to express all he felt, Sebastian thought. If he could say everything that swelled inside him right now, he'd be like one of those fellows in a play, striding about the stage waving their arms and declaiming for ten minutes at a pop.

The hands of his watch crawled around the face. More than once, he was certain it had stopped. Finally, he judged it was late enough. At least, he could wait no longer.

Sebastian stepped silently into the corridor outside his room. He listened. Silence. Moving with a hunter's care, swiftly but silently, he walked along it, turned into another, and carefully counted doorways in a third. This one was Georgina's.

Despite the risk of being seen, he stood still for a moment. What if she'd changed her mind? She might be regretting her invitation, with no way to tell him. Well, if she was, of course he'd go. No question. But he truly hoped she wasn't. He took a deep breath and knocked softly.

The door opened at once. Georgina grasped his coat sleeve and pulled him inside, closing the door behind him. "I thought you'd never come," she said, throwing her arms around him.

Sebastian pulled her close. She was wearing a thin, lacy nightdress, and he could feel the warmth of her skin under his hands. The heady scent of her perfume made his head spin. It would be all too easy to lose himself in wanting her. But he was still worried. "What if someone comes looking for you?"

"Why would they?"

"I don't know. Bad luck. The perversity of fate."

"If they do, you can hide in the wardrobe," she whispered, a laugh in her voice.

"Not sure I could fit in there," he replied, smiling down at her.

"You'd have to crouch down among my gowns."

"Like the hero in a bad farce?"

"Exactly."

They laughed together. Then he kissed her, and jokes were forgotten as their hands and lips communicated more passionate sentiments.

When she strained against him, Sebastian thought he could feel the desire rising in her as strongly as it did in him. The idea filled him with a novel sort of pride. This extraordinary woman—as wise and beautiful as any he'd ever met—loved him. How had he managed that? Wasn't it more than he deserved? But she'd said not.

All thought evaporated as she pushed his coat over his shoulders and down his arms to pool on the floor. Her hands came back up under his shirttails, caressing his back, slipping round to his chest and making him shiver with desire. Sebastian went into a flurry of pulling off boots and stockings and breeches. He reached the end of his clothing just as Georgina let her filmy gown fall to the carpet.

They stood facing each other, utterly revealed. Well matched, Sebastian thought, and then wondered at himself. She was perfect, and he was…desperately in love with her. Perhaps that was enough. He held out his hands. She took them. Their eyes held as he led her to the bed.

With a soft laugh, she let go and jumped onto the mattress. Lying on the snowy linen, she held out her arms. He went to them.

Their lovemaking was the most exciting and tender and satisfying he'd ever known. Every touch seemed to deepen the bond they were creating, like an echo back and forth, only stronger each time rather than weaker. He reveled in the soft sounds he drew from her and the way she clutched him as she reached the pinnacle. He couldn't imagine anything finer than to be with her, in this way and all others, for the rest of his life.

Afterward, they lay side by side, hands clasped, letting their pulses slow. What he finally recognized as joy bubbled up in Sebastian. "I never knew how it would be," he murmured. "I never even imagined it."

"What?"

"To be with someone who knew everything about me and still loved me." He turned his head to kiss her shoulder.

"Everything about you is wonderful," she replied.

"No, it isn't. I'm not like you, perfect in every way."

Georgina got up on one elbow to gaze down at him. "I'm not, you know, Sebastian."

"As far as I'm concerned, you are."

"You're setting me up to disappoint you. And I'll hate that."

"After the last two days?" Sebastian was incredulous. Did she still not understand what she'd done for him? "You never could, if we lived together a hundred years."

With a tremulous smile, she snuggled up against him, her head on his shoulder. Sebastian tightened his arm around her. This was happiness, he realized. It filled him like a fine champagne, fizzing in his veins, making him pleasantly dizzy, though not the least fuzzed. Somehow, against the odds, he'd found his way to it. He only had to make certain he never let it get away.

Twenty

THE GRESHAM FAMILY ARRIVED AT STANE CASTLE IN A cavalcade late the following afternoon. From their various locations, they had met in Cheltenham and traveled the rest of the way into Herefordshire together.

Sebastian and Randolph stood in the drive to greet them. They'd had some warning from a servant who spotted the line of carriage and riders from the outer gateway. "The whole troop," said Randolph. He'd been restless since Miss Byngham's ritual.

The leading traveling carriage pulled up before them, with another just behind. Alan, Nathaniel, and Robert, riding beside the vehicles, dismounted. Three other carriages, laden with luggage and attendants, were directed to a side entrance by one of the grooms.

The door of the first carriage opened. The Duke of Langford emerged, then turned to offer a hand to his duchess. She took it with a smile and stepped lightly to the ground. As his father surveyed the castle with his customary urbane assurance, Sebastian wondered yet again whether he'd ever achieve such confidence. He'd often despaired. But suddenly, now, he almost thought he might, someday, with Georgina at his side.

Their mother embraced them one by one. "How are you, my dears?" she said.

"Very well, Mama," replied Sebastian. "Never been better!"

The buoyancy of his tone earned him an interested smile.

"Great heavens, what's happened to Violet?" said Randolph.

Sebastian turned to find that his brothers' wives had stepped down from the second carriage. And while Alan's mate Ariel was charmingly familiar—a small, curvy figure with silky brown hair and skin like ripe peaches—Nathaniel's new viscountess bore almost no resemblance to the dowdy young woman Sebastian had last seen at their wedding a few months ago. She was sleek and fashionable and…he groped for a word. Regal? The last time they'd spoken, he and his brothers had just left her future husband stranded naked with a wolf skin, Sebastian remembered. Abruptly, he wondered what tricks his brothers might be planning to play on him.

"She has come into her own," answered the duchess, "and brought Nathaniel along with her."

It was one of Mama's typical remarks. Sebastian had no idea what she meant. "Where's James?" he asked as three brothers and two wives joined them in front of the castle entry.

"Sailed away to the ends of the earth," replied Robert.

"He sent his apologies and best wishes," added Nathaniel.

"The navy gave him a new command?"

Robert shook his head. "No, he's quit the navy. He married a beauty from a tropical island, with piles of treasure and her own ship. They've gone off to be rovers."

"Rovers?" said Randolph. "You sound like a boy's adventure tale."

"Don't I, though?" replied Robert cordially. "It was the young lady who tried to shoot him."

"That was an accident," said Ariel. "Mostly."

The newcomers all seemed to understand this. He and Randolph had apparently missed a good deal. Sebastian looked forward to catching up. And it was very pleasant to be amid a jostling of brothers once again. But he was conscious of the Stanes waiting inside the great hall.

"Sebastian will be wanting to present his new family," said Violet, as if reading his mind.

"Will he?" murmured Randolph, giving Sebastian a sidelong glance.

Sebastian hoped no one else had heard him. And knew that hope forlorn. His mother, in particular, had ears like a bat. "Yes, come inside," he said heartily, turning to open the door.

The yapping began as the duchess crossed the threshold.

"Good God, you weren't joking about the dogs," murmured Nathaniel in Sebastian's ear. "Where's the Hindu gentleman? I hope he hasn't gone."

"You'll meet him at dinner," replied Sebastian out of the side of his mouth.

Georgina came forward, and Sebastian thought he might burst with pride as she greeted his family and then presented her own with graceful ease. Wanting it all to go well, Sebastian tried to catch every word in the babble of talk that arose then.

"Welcome to Stane, Duchess," said Georgina's mother. "Drustan, stop that at once!"

"Please call me Adele. We are to be family, are we not?"

"And I am Charlotte," answered the marchioness. "Drustan! He is such a little rogue."

"That would seem to describe him," said Sebastian's mother.

He knew that tone, Sebastian thought. Mama was amused and appalled and kindly determined to be polite. He kept his eyes off the floor. He did not wish to know what Drustan was doing. He was sure he wouldn't like it. Fingering the tattered cloth in his pocket, Sebastian edged closer to his mother.

"Of course, the Normans didn't have an easy time of it in this part of the country," the marquess was saying to the duke.

"My Norman ancestor married a Saxon lady," Sebastian's father replied.

You could not catch Papa out, Sebastian thought admiringly. It was simply an impossibility, like a thrown pebble falling up.

"Is that so?"

"She'd lost her husband at the Battle of Hastings. She had a large manor at Langford, which…riveted his interest."

"I knew the boy couldn't be a damned Welshman."

Or perhaps you could, Sebastian amended, as his father said, "I beg your pardon?" But then Georgina's father had special talents.

"I shall take you out to see Offa's Dyke once we get this knot tied for the children," the latter said.

As the duke professed himself pleased, Sebastian saw that Hilda and Emma had cornered Robert.

"Are you truly a pink of the *ton*?" Hilda was asking him.

Robert received the question with less than his usual savoir faire. He simply shrugged, then nodded.

"But why do they call you pink?" she added. "I've never understood that expression."

"I don't know!" Robert snapped, turning away and walking over to stand with Randolph.

Sebastian blinked. It was unlike Robert to be rude.

"Yes, our first grandchild," his mother said to Georgina's.

Sebastian turned and followed her gaze to Alan, who stood beside Ariel, holding her hand, at the edge of the group. His youngest brother never cared much for chatter. But Sebastian had never seen him look so contented, and Ariel was radiant.

What a thing it would be, Sebastian thought, to be a father. He looked around, glimpsing what seemed to be a similar thought on Nathaniel's face. One day they all would be, probably, and there would be a mob of children at gatherings like this. Numbers sprang into his head. If they each had two, that would be a round dozen young Greshams. Three each would be—good God—eighteen undoubtedly lively offspring! That might be worse than the pugs. But no, of course it wouldn't.

"And I'm sure you hope Violet will follow along soon," said Georgina's mother.

"Oh, there's plenty of time for that," said the duchess. "No hurry at all."

Sebastian thought that Violet was listening closely, while pretending not to be.

"I'll never forget how your mother watched me after we were married, like a hawk ready to swoop down on a pigeon," said his mother to his father.

The duke laughed. "She did rather."

"Rather? She bribed my maid to… Never mind." The duchess made one of her subtle moves, a mere gesture toward the stairs. And somehow the dynamics of the group shifted. Sebastian had seen her stop budding ballroom quarrels in their tracks and herd a crowd of partygoers more efficiently than a sheepdog. It was a kind of magic.

"Let me show you your room," said Georgina's mother in response. "You'll want to rest after your long drive."

"I heard you speak at Oxford," Edgar Stane said to Alan as the group moved. "It was astonishing."

Sebastian enjoyed Alan's smile. He had sometimes wondered how his youngest brother felt about the family's general inability to understand his work.

⤠

Everything was going more smoothly than she'd hoped, Georgina thought at dinner that evening. It seemed her fears had been groundless. Of course, the duke and duchess practically defined politeness. But His Grace actually seemed to be enjoying a discussion of dog breeding, though she was certain he had no interest in pugs. And the duchess was obviously charming her father.

Violet was talking with Mr. Mitra about India. From what Georgina could hear, she was balancing questions and travelers' tales in graceful proportion. The exchange seemed quite cordial, and it struck Georgina that Violet might rival the current duchess someday. She had blossomed amazingly in the months since her marriage. Georgina felt a little glow at the idea of such possibilities.

Across the table, however, things were not going quite so well. Perhaps they shouldn't have seated Robert next to Hilda. It had been a treat for her, and Georgina hadn't thought Robert would mind. He was looking surprisingly sullen, however, under the onslaught of her chatter. Quite unlike the darling of the *ton* that Georgina knew. In fact, she suddenly glimpsed a resemblance to Randolph that she wouldn't have predicted in this Gresham brother.

The latter was deep in conversation with Ariel. Georgina hadn't been aware that they were acquainted, and she wondered what they were finding to engross them so. Further down the table, Nathaniel was being kind to Emma. It was gratifying to see her sister beam under his gentle inquiries. The viscount was also managing Joanna Byngham on his other side with impressive dexterity. Georgina had caught him giving the governess perfectly blank looks once or twice, but he'd responded to her with grave courtesy. Nathaniel was, as she'd heard Sebastian say, a complete hand.

Scanning the rest of the dinner table, Georgina met

Sebastian's blue gaze. It was like coming to rest after some exhausting task, or bubbling with laughter at a shared jest. For a while, she lost herself in beatific visions of the future.

The meal wound down without any noticeable disruptions. At the marchioness's signal, the ladies rose to retire. Joanna excused herself in the corridor outside the dining room and headed toward her own chamber. The rest of them started upstairs. But on the upper landing, Georgina's mother was met by a servant, who bent to murmur to her. "I must check on Nuala," she said in response. "Do go on without me. I shan't be long." She hurried off toward her workroom.

"Nuala?" asked the duchess.

"One of the dogs," Georgina replied. She did not add that Nuala was on heat, or try to picture the scene her mother would face. She was just glad it wasn't taking place in a public room.

"Ah, yes."

They entered the drawing room. Hilda and Emma went to sort out some sheets of music for later. Violet and Ariel sat together by the fire. Georgina had started over to join them when the duchess said, "May I speak to you?"

"Of course."

"Let us sit over here."

The older woman drew her into a far corner of the large room, well out of the others' earshot. A quiver of apprehension went through Georgina. She hadn't done anything wrong. Had she? No, of course she hadn't. She glanced sidelong at the duchess, always the epitome of cool elegance. She could find no clue about what was to come. The thing was: one didn't expect her to simply chat.

"I don't mean to be abrupt, but the wedding is tomorrow."

Georgina nodded. They sat in facing armchairs, turned a little away from the other women.

"And I wanted to speak to you privately."

The duchess seemed uneasy, which was ominous. "Of course." What could this be about?

"I didn't have much opportunity to talk with you after your engagement was announced," the duchess said. "The season was nearly over. We were packing up to leave London. And I wasn't sure…"

Georgina began to be really alarmed. Any matter that could unsettle the Duchess of Langford must be dire indeed. Did she not want the marriage to go forward? Did she have some criticisms of the Stane family after all? A fire of rebellion rose in Georgina. She'd fight even this formidable woman for Sebastian!

"I couldn't make up my mind what was right," the duchess said. She frowned at the carpet. Georgina watched her. You could see traces of Sebastian, of all the Gresham brothers, in her burnished hair and chiseled features. "I felt I must say something." The duchess paused again, then seemed to make up her mind. "There are people who think Sebastian is dull-witted, but he isn't."

Relief flooded Georgina. If this was all. "I know," she said.

Sebastian's mother leaned forward, her blue gaze intense. "He lets his friends rally him about it. And his brothers. Playing the big, slow cavalryman. It's…

charming of him, I suppose. Although sometimes I could just shake him."

"I know," said Georgina. If Sebastian said he was stupid one more time, she might consider doing that herself.

"But in truth, he's as quick as any of my sons. In his own way. You mustn't be deceived by the…the act he puts on. I do wish, sometimes, that he would stop it."

"I *know*," said Georgina a third time. She leaned forward and put a hand on the duchess's knee to get her full attention. "I know."

"You…you do?"

The uncertainty and worry in the older woman's expression were a kind of revelation. If the Duchess of Langford had such doubtful moments, then everyone must, now and then. It gave Georgina an odd sort of hope for the future. "He told me everything," she said.

"And what is everything, exactly?"

"You don't know?" Georgina blinked at her in surprise.

The duchess sighed and sat back in her chair. "I know that Sebastian is all too ready to accept harsh judgments of his intellect. Without putting up much argument. I have observed, all his life, that he is…less adept with words than Robert, say. Or any of the others, really. But it is not everything—to be glib."

The last sounded like a cry from the heart, and Georgina agreed wholeheartedly.

"He finds the words eventually," the duchess continued. "If he doesn't give up trying. And I did not mean to criticize Robert, who is a marvel of wit."

Georgina nodded, remembering times when Sebastian had seemed positively eloquent.

"I know that Sebastian hates reading," the duchess continued. "I do not believe that he simply isn't interested, as my husband thinks. Sebastian won't speak about it. Or, no, he turns every attempt to mention the matter into a joke. In his bluff, I-am-only-a-simple-soldier role. I do get *so* weary of that pretense." The older woman fell silent, gazing at Georgina.

Now, *she* hesitated. They'd agreed that Sebastian's admission was their secret. She couldn't reveal it, not even to his mother. She longed to reassure the duchess—which was an amazing position to be in, she marveled. But what could she actually say?

"I would never ask you to betray a confidence," the duchess said, her tone full of reluctant understanding.

"Sebastian told me why he often feels dull-witted," Georgina replied carefully. "We…discussed the fact that it is not a good reason."

The duchess's face was tight with curiosity and concern. She started to speak, then pressed her lips together.

"I also told him that he must never call himself stupid again. If he does, I *shall* shake him. You may count on that."

Tears suddenly pooled in the older woman's eyes, just the blue of Sebastian's. "It is not necessary that I know the whole," she replied, her voice a little choked. "I'm just very happy that he told you."

Georgina struggled with tears herself. She saw Violet and Ariel glance in their direction and politely look away. They seemed interested, but not worried, which said a lot about the Gresham family.

Hilda started over from the pianoforte. Violet intercepted her with a question.

"That's the secret of a long and happy marriage, you know," the duchess said. She sat straighter, rapidly regaining control. "Speaking to each other. Not holding things back and letting them grow all out of proportion."

Georgina nodded her respect for the advice. It occurred to her that her parents did that, in their own slightly peculiar way.

Sebastian's mother took her hand. "You are so welcome in our family," she said.

A laugh escaped Georgina.

"What is it?"

"We welcomed Sebastian into ours, officially, last night."

"Officially? I'm intrigued."

"I can tell you all about that," Georgina replied. Her worries about shocking the Greshams had somehow evaporated. She proceeded to describe the ritual, in detail. "Randolph was frightened by the candle," she finished. "I don't blame him, you understand. It was rather…unnerving."

"And Sebastian read out a long passage," the duchess said.

Meeting her speculative gaze, Georgina recognized that here was an extremely sharp, observant woman. She'd seized on that crucial detail like the aforementioned snake striking. It would be a dreadful mistake to get on the duchess's bad side, or try to deceive her. Not that Georgina intended to, ever. Why would she want to? "I hope Randolph has enjoyed his visit," she answered, warmly evasive. "It's been somewhat unusual for a clergyman."

The older woman smiled, at the same time acknowledging the change of topic and allowing it. "He is a rather unusual clergyman."

Their joint laughter rang through the room.

"There's one of the prettiest sights I've ever seen," said Sebastian, glimpsing them.

Georgina turned. The men had come into the drawing room. It was a picture to take one's breath away—six tall, handsome Greshams grouped together. Poor Papa was quite overshadowed. From his peevish expression, he was well aware of it, too. On the other hand, Edgar, planted next to Alan like an acolyte, seemed oblivious.

"Why are you blocking the way?" demanded a lighter voice. Georgina's mother pushed through the masculine crowd, a small, plump figure among giants. "All's well with Nuala," she informed her uninterested house party as she strode over to the hearth. "Are you going to play something, Emma?"

The two women Sebastian loved most in the world gazed up at him. Telling himself there was no reason to worry if Mama chose to have a little chat with Georgina, he walked over to their chairs.

"I'm so proud of you," said his mother.

"So am I," said his beloved almost wife.

He didn't have the first idea why they should say so, at this particular moment, but he smiled down at them anyway. It didn't matter a whit whether he understood. If he needed to, he had perfect confidence that his wife would explain it to him in due course. The point was: he'd never been so happy in his life.

Twenty-one

LATER THAT NIGHT, WHEN THE YOUNG LADIES AND A weary Edgar and the older Stanes had gone to bed, the Greshams gathered in the library, catching up on the details of their lives. The brothers planned to sit up for some hours as a send-off for Sebastian on the eve of his wedding. "We should go up and leave the boys to their roistering," said the duchess to her husband after a while.

"That's a terribly old-fashioned expression, Mama," said Robert.

"Well, I am an ancient, about to be a grandmamma," she answered.

"A young and beautiful grandmamma," put in the duke.

They exchanged the kind of look that made a man squirm when it was his parents, Sebastian thought. And yet he liked seeing it, too, because it was such a good omen for his own future. They said their good nights and went out.

"Now we can pour liquor down your throat and befuddle you," said Nathaniel as the door closed behind them. "Any wolf skins about the castle? Robert?"

"No, there are not," said Sebastian. He didn't think there were. He'd been here for weeks and hadn't seen any. "Or any other sorts either. We'll have no pranks tonight."

"You didn't hesitate to pull one on me," Nathaniel pointed out.

"I'm sorry," said Sebastian.

"You are now, when it's your turn."

"That's it," he agreed.

"We'd need a fresh idea anyway," said Robert, looking about the room as if for inspiration. "Mustn't repeat ourselves."

"What did you do to James?" Sebastian asked, half interested and half worried. He pushed his large glass of brandy aside.

"We had no chance at him," Robert said. He sipped from his own drink. "He eloped," he added with an evil grin.

Sebastian winced as all of them gazed at him. The mistake about his supposed elopement had been explained, several times, but that didn't mean they'd let him forget it. Ever.

"More or less eloped," Robert amended. "They were in Southampton, and the ship was there, and they wanted to be off over the sea."

"James always wanted to be master of a ship," said Alan. "And now he's the owner as well." He sipped. "This is quite good stuff."

"And you're to be a father," Sebastian said. "The youngest of us first."

Alan smiled like a man who had everything he could want.

"And Nathaniel… Well, Violet's become a real stunner."

Nathaniel grinned in quite a similar way.

"It seems marriage is treating the Gresham brothers well." Sebastian fully expected to be as happy as his two brothers. Well, he already was. There was the small matter of Hilda becoming a member of his new household. That was worrisome. But they'd handle it. Georgina would, and he'd help. She was up to anything.

"Four of us," said Robert. He raised his second large glass of brandy to Sebastian to show he was included in this number. "The odds are against the remainder."

"Hey," said Randolph.

"Well, they are. How many happy marriages do you know of, amongst our set?"

Randolph looked uneasy as he thought this over. "It's not a case of odds," he muttered. "It's a matter of judgment and character."

"Why do you care?" Nathaniel asked Robert. "Haven't you always said you have no intention of contemplating matrimony until you're forty or so?"

"That's right," said Sebastian. "How did you put it? When you've dwindled into a deadly dull country squire, as good as dead, then you'll find some girl and marry."

"Go boil your head," replied Robert cordially.

This was odd, Sebastian thought. Of them all, Robert was usually the most lighthearted and carefree. "What's wrong with you?"

"Nothing is wrong with me."

"Not unrequited love?" murmured Alan.

"Nothing of the kind!" Robert exploded. "Why would you even imagine something so ridiculous?"

"Ariel says…"

Robert cut him off with a savage gesture. "She's your wife and very charming and lovely, but she doesn't know everything!"

Awkwardness descended over the room, which didn't happen often with the Gresham brothers. Sebastian examined Robert. Whatever could have happened to him?

"Ah, I nearly forgot," said Nathaniel, taking the lead to smooth things over, as he so often did. He rose and went over to a vacant sofa, taking a cloth bag from behind it. "I brought this along. There was no time to send it." He handed the bag to Sebastian.

"Wedding present?" Alan asked.

"Special commission," answered Nathaniel.

Sebastian untied the drawstring and let the bag fall open. A wooden stringed instrument, something like a guitar, but not precisely, was revealed. "What the deuce?"

"Your lute," Nathaniel said.

Robert and Alan gaped at him, and then at Sebastian, as he remembered, too late, his letter containing Randolph's request. "Oh," he said. "Right. The lute."

Randolph leaned to one side as if to dissociate himself from the conversation. Then, realizing that he was quite close to a branch of lighted candles, he jerked back in the other direction.

Sebastian couldn't hold back a laugh. He converted it quickly into a cough. "Lute," he repeated. "Thanks very much." He strummed the strings a bit for form's sake. The result was dissonant.

"What the devil do you want with a lute?" Robert asked.

"Just a notion I had." Sebastian strummed a bit more. He shouldn't enjoy the chagrin on Randolph's face, but he couldn't help it.

"How did you even hear of such an instrument?" Alan said. He wasn't quite as incredulous as Robert, but he looked deeply curious.

"The chansons de geste? *The Song of Roland*?" murmured Robert satirically.

Sebastian had no idea what these were, as his brother very well knew.

"You've never been musical," commented Nathaniel.

"Oh, well, now that I'm to be married…"

"You intend to entertain your new wife with a lute?" Robert shook his head. "Even for you, that is an idiotic plan."

Seeing Randolph cringe, Sebastian cheerfully agreed. There were times when being thought thick-headed could be helpful. He didn't mind being his brother's shield, dull as a block of wood. Especially now, when he knew it wasn't true.

❦

The wedding of Lord Sebastian Gresham to Lady Georgina Stane took place the following morning in the church near Stane Castle where the banns had been called. Nathaniel stood up with Sebastian, as the latter had with him. Emma and Hilda, demure in pink, supported their sister at the altar. Or perhaps it would be more accurate to describe Hilda as smug, Georgina thought.

Her youngest sister had exacted a promise that she could join them for the next season in London, when Georgina was to bring Emma out. Georgina had no doubt that Hilda had big plans for that visit. She didn't even want to contemplate what they might be. For now, however, Hilda was all compliance.

Georgina didn't feel the least bit nervous as she spoke her vows. Nor did Sebastian, as far as she could tell. She saw only a joy that mirrored her own on his face. And when they walked out after the ceremony, arm in arm, trailed by their families, they shared smiles wide with delight.

The group returned to the castle for a lavish wedding breakfast. Guests would be arriving for a celebratory dancing party this evening, some of them staying on to make up a more entertaining house party. But it was just Greshams and Stanes for now—along with Mr. Mitra—spread out around the grand blue reception room with plates of food from a buffet and glasses of champagne.

"It's difficult to sit still," Sebastian told his—at long last—wife. "I want to jump up and down and race about like an infant terror."

Georgina laughed. "I know. I feel the same. I think it's the relief of finally getting to this day. There were times when I feared we never would. When we were down in that ravine…"

"Or convincing your father that I'm not a Welsh barbarian…"

"Or scheming how to get through the ritual…"

Their smiles this time were tender. On the sofa cushions between them, their fingers laced together. "I don't suppose we could slip upstairs?" Sebastian said.

Georgina considered this very enticing idea and regretfully shook her head. "Mama would probably come pounding at the bedroom door. She feels she has made quite heroic efforts, planning this day."

He nodded. "We must march as ordered then. Until we leave tomorrow." He squeezed her hand.

Georgina felt a thrill at the thought of their wedding journey. The duke was lending them a small manor house in the Peak District. There would be riding for Sebastian and country walks and three weeks *alone*—no interruptions or obligations or alarms. It sounded like heaven. "We could walk about the room at least," she suggested, "and nod cordially at our wedding guests."

Sebastian sprang up and offered his arm. Georgina rose and took it, and they began a stately circuit of the large chamber.

Their mothers were nearest, sitting in a pair of armchairs. "I'm pretty confident I'll have a fine litter of puppies in a couple of months," the marchioness said. "So I could send you one for Christmas." She spoke as one offering a rare gift. "I'd pick out the most promising, of course."

"I fear a pug wouldn't get along with the Langford dogs," the duchess replied, warmly polite. "They're quite large, you know, and can be so boisterous."

"That's nonsense," Sebastian whispered into Georgina's ear. "My father has them perfectly trained."

She leaned closer as his breath stirred her hair.

Moved by the same impulse, they lingered by a window to listen, their backs to the room.

Georgina's mother laughed. "Oh, my pugs can hold their own. Indeed, one of Edgar's school friends brought a Great Dane along on a visit last year, and Drustan absolutely terrorized the poor thing. I wish you could have seen him leaping for its nose. And the huge creature backing into a corner, whimpering."

"Admirable," answered the duchess. "But I am so busy when we are in the country, always running about. Sadly, I wouldn't be able to give a pug much attention. They seem to require a great deal of company."

"Can you hear how much she dislikes the pugs?" whispered Sebastian. When Georgina shook her head, he added, "Well, I can."

"Oh, they can go with you anywhere," the marchioness countered. "Lady Drayton rigged up such a cunning little sling to carry hers about. I'll send you the design along with the puppy. Do you prefer a dog or a bitch?"

"You are so kind, but I really have to refuse. You must have so many people waiting eagerly for one of your puppies."

"Let 'em wait. They're not family."

"Irresistible force meets immoveable object," murmured Georgina.

"Care to make a wager on who wins out?" he whispered back.

"I have no idea how to choose."

"I'd back Mama against anyone."

"My mother told the queen that she was overfeeding her dog, at her court presentation," Georgina informed him. She nodded in response to Sebastian's surprised look. "We'd better move on, or she will pull us into the argument," she murmured.

Their fathers were seated together a little further down the room. "Offa had vision," the marquess was saying. "Kind of fellow who'd be building railways and canals today. Able to organize large projects and carry them out, you see. Change the very landscape."

"I do see," replied the duke. "That is an interesting perspective on the matter."

Georgina's father beamed. "I'll take you out to the Dyke tomorrow. Show you what I mean."

"I shall look forward to it."

"They seem to be getting along," whispered Georgina as they moved on. "I must admit I'm surprised."

"My father is interested in all kind of topics."

"They have that in common then."

The Gresham brothers had congregated around a low table where they'd assembled a large selection of food and a couple of bottles of champagne. Bent over their booty, they didn't see Sebastian and Georgina stroll close. "All right, Robert," Nathaniel was saying. "Enough. What the deuce is wrong with you?"

"Leave me alone," growled Robert.

"Well, I won't. You've been touchy as a bear with a thorn in its paw since we met up in Cheltenham."

"Drinking deep, too," said Alan.

"Robert was?" said Randolph. "That's not like you, Robert."

"What do any of you know about me?" Robert snapped.

Sebastian and Georgina exchanged a puzzled glance as Nathaniel said, "A good deal. After observing you for all of your twenty-eight years."

"Don't come all elder brother on me." Robert snatched up one of the bottles and left the group to sit by himself, filling his glass with a defiant flourish.

"Ariel says he's in love with Flora Jennings," Alan remarked. "Robert says she's dead wrong."

"I suppose Robert would know better about a thing like that," Randolph said.

"I wouldn't count on it," replied the youngest Gresham brother dryly.

"Well, and what if he is in love?" asked Nathaniel. "Why should that make him so touchy? You can't even speak to him these days."

"Miss Jennings doesn't like him."

Nathaniel blinked in surprise. "Everyone likes Robert," he replied. "He practically defines the word *likable*."

"Liking isn't love," Alan said.

"Well…no. It isn't, is it?" Nathaniel gazed at his wife for a long moment.

"Wait," put in Sebastian. "Flora Jennings. Isn't she Aunt Agatha's daughter? Met her once, last spring in London."

Alan nodded, his blue eyes glinting with humor.

"Aunt Agatha's daughter?" exclaimed Randolph. "Is she six feel tall and terrifying, like her mother?"

"Not at all," said Alan. "She's quite engaging and pretty. Very well educated, too." He obviously approved of the latter. "And Agatha Jennings isn't six feet tall, by the way. Quite a pleasant lady, really."

"A bluestocking? *Robert* in love with a bluestocking?" Randolph turned to look at Alan.

"To tell you the truth, I'm not sure what he is," Alan replied. "But I do know he's been unlike himself for weeks."

The rest of them contemplated this in silence.

"Anyone know where he's headed from here?" Nathaniel asked.

"House parties, I imagine," said Randolph. "That's what he does in the winter, isn't it?" His tone was a bit envious.

Sebastian pressed Georgina's arm lightly, and they moved on. She saw that Hilda, Edgar, and Emma were sitting with Mr. Mitra, which was gratifyingly kind and polite of them. As they moved closer, Edgar rose and edged toward the Gresham brothers' group. She was happy to see them welcome him. He sat next to Alan.

"People may believe what they like," they heard Mitra say as they passed the three remaining. "What they feel as truth in their hearts. But I feel that they must take some care about what they call it. An individual has no right to imply that a practice is... Hindu, for example, when they have..." He paused as if searching for words. They did not appear to come easy. "Made it up," he finished finally.

"Like Joanna did," said Hilda.

Mitra nodded. "Your Miss Byngham is a most enthusiastic and sincere person. I admire that in her. I wish her well. But her rituals are her own. You understand me?"

Hilda nodded. "I'll tell anyone who asks about it."

"Thank you" was the grave response.

Mr. Mitra treated her youngest sister with such courtesy, Georgina thought. It was funny and rather sweet. As for Emma, she looked as if she was longing to escape, but didn't quite dare join Violet and Ariel on a nearby sofa.

Georgina and Sebastian strolled on.

"I hope I shall have similar good news soon," Violet said as they passed. "Indeed I might…but it is too early to tell. Are you feeling well?"

"Pretty well," replied Ariel. "I've been sick. Not too bad."

Violet nodded sympathetically. "Even so, I can't wait. I want lots of children."

"Six sons?" asked Ariel with a smile.

The two young women looked around the room. "Not that many," Violet replied. "Though they do make a handsome group, don't they?"

"Breathtaking," answered Ariel with a laugh.

Georgina saw that they were both gazing at their own husbands as they made this judgment. She looked up at Sebastian. Handsome, certainly. But also so much more. A thrill went through her at her unbelievable good luck.

She tugged at his arm. They walked on, stopping by another long window to observe their chatting families. It seemed a mostly happy group. Their mothers did look a bit like duelists readying the next shot.

Robert, the only one on his own, noticed them. He rose, a little unsteadily, and raised his champagne glass. "To the happy couple," he cried.

The others broke off their conversations. One by

one, they stood and held up their drinks. "The happy couple," they all declared. Smiling, they sipped.

Sebastian grinned at them. Then he pulled Georgina into his arms and indulged in the kind of kiss he'd been dreaming of for hours. It was every bit as searing and sweet as he remembered. When he finally, reluctantly, drew back, they received a round of laughing applause from their families. Even the marquess joined in. Sebastian glanced down at Georgina, still grasping her hand. She read the message in his eyes as if they'd been wed for decades. Together, they faced the room and, in perfect unison, bowed and curtsied in acknowledgment.

*Keep reading for a sneak peek of the next book
in the Duke's Sons series*

Nothing Like a Duke

One

THE FRONT AXLE OF THE POST CHAISE SNAPPED AS ONE
wheel slammed into a deep rut, throwing Lord Robert
Gresham against the side window hard enough to
bruise. The loud crack, sudden sideways lurch, and
bumping drag that followed spooked the team pulling
the coach. The vehicle lurched and bounced as the
postilions struggled to get the four horses back under
control. Robert braced his legs and clung to a strap
until they'd slowed enough for him to push his way
out and help. He leapt to the head of the offside leader
and held on to wet leather. Mud from churning hooves
filled the air, spattering his top boots, pantaloons, and
greatcoat. A spray of the sticky stuff slapped his face
as the horse tried to rear. "Be still. It's all right," he
said, using the easy combination of reassurance and
command he'd learned from his brother Sebastian.

It was a number of minutes before the horses were
calm and the men could verify that the post chaise was
irretrievably damaged.

"We didn't see that dratted hole, milord, what with all the mud," said the elder postilion.

As if on cue, the rain started up again, a slow but penetrating drizzle. A chilly drop slipped under Robert's coat collar and trickled down his back. "A bad stretch of—" He looked up and down the narrow, rutted track. "I suppose one must call it a road." He noticed that one of the horses had pulled up lame. The coach tilted forlornly in the middle of the lane, which curved around a small stand of trees just ahead. "We need to move the chaise." If another vehicle came barreling around that turn, the results would be disastrous. Not that traffic appeared likely.

"We'll drag her off to the side," the man replied. "And Davy'll ride back to that farm we passed and see about help."

He didn't sound optimistic, and Robert imagined he was right. The replacement would be whatever old thing the farmer kept in his barn. And it would take a couple of hours to procure. He looked around. There were no houses in sight, no buildings of any kind, actually, although they were no more than ten miles, he estimated, from his ultimate destination.

Robert sighed. It had been a long, hard journey into the North. If he hadn't promised friends that he'd visit... but he had. Turning up his collar, he made his way over to the trees. The foliage, still thick in early October, kept off most of the rain. And it felt better to be out in the fresh air. He watched the postilions coax the team into dragging the coach off to the side. The younger one then mounted one of the horses and rode back the way they'd come. The other unhitched the remaining animals and led them over to a patch of grass, running his hands over their legs and checking for other injuries. Robert pulled out his handkerchief and wiped his face. The handkerchief came away muddy, and he suspected it hadn't removed all traces of dirt. He leaned against an oak and resigned himself to a stretch of boredom. So much for his early start today.

The rain dripped from the leaves overhead. A light wind rustled through them. The horses sampled the grass. The postilion settled himself under another tree. Robert thanked providence it wasn't colder. Time ticked past.

Gradually, Robert became aware of a sound beneath the murmur of water. It was a soft whining, as of some creature in distress, and intermittent. Just when he would decide he'd imagined it, it would start up again.

The next time this happened, Robert searched for the source. He had to wait through another period of silence before he found his way to a low bush. Raising one of its branches, he discovered a huddled bit of dark fur. When he bent to look closer, a small head lifted, and dark eyes met his.

It was a dog, quite young, he thought, soaking wet and shivering. As he eyed it, the whimpering began again. The sound seemed involuntary, because the tiny creature stared at him without demand, or hope. Even as he gazed, its head sank down again, too tired, or dejected, to resist whatever fate was about to descend. The brown eyes closed.

Robert straightened. He strode over to the chaise and pulled out one of the blankets provided to cover travelers' legs. Bringing it back, he draped it over the puppy and picked it up, wrapping the small shivering form in warm wool. Cradling the bundle in one arm, he retraced his steps.

"What's that there?" the postilion asked as he passed. "A rat?"

"No, a dog. A puppy, really."

"What sort of dog?"

"A mixed sort, I believe." It hadn't looked like any breed Robert knew.

"What's it doing out here, then?"

"Lost, or abandoned. Perhaps something happened to its mother."

"You ain't going to put it in the chaise?" said the other man.

"I am," said Robert. And suiting action to word, he climbed into the leaning vehicle and set the bundled blanket on the slanting seat beside him.

The puppy stirred and looked up at him. It was still trembling.

Robert reached out. The little dog cowered away, and Robert felt a flash of anger. What blackguard had taught this young animal to expect a blow? Moving slowly and unthreateningly, Robert rubbed the water out of its fur. Overall, it was black, a trifle shaggy, with odd stripes of brown along its sides, like tiny lightning bolts. Its ears were rather large for its size. They were pointed, but flopped over at the tips.

The puppy's shivering abated when it was dry. It nestled into the blanket until only its nose and eyes were visible.

Robert reached into the pocket on the inside of the

chaise's door and retrieved the remains of a sandwich packed for him at their last stop. The puppy flinched at the sudden movement, and trembled at the crackle of paper as Robert unwrapped it. "It's all right," he said. "Or, it may be, unless you need milk. God knows where I'd find that." He pulled a shred of beef from between the slices of bread and held it out. The puppy sniffed, but didn't move to take it.

Robert placed the meat on the blanket. The little animal hesitated as if it couldn't quite believe its luck, then lurched forward and snatched the beef. Teeth snapped and chewed. Perhaps the dog wasn't as young as he'd feared, Robert thought. Perhaps it was simply small.

They continued in this fashion until all the beef was gone and most of the bread as well. The dog gained enough confidence to take the last bits from his hand. Robert completed the ruin of his handkerchief by using it to wipe off the mustard. "Better?" he said when the animal would take no more.

The dog tried to stand, as if concluding that it was time to move on now that it had eaten. All four legs shook under its tiny weight, and it fell back to the blanket, which had shifted enough for Robert to see that the little creature was a male. "No need to stir," he said. "It's a foul afternoon."

Indeed, the rain was beating harder on the roof of the chaise. Robert cracked the door and asked the postilion if he wanted to join him in the carriage.

"I'll stay with the horses," the man replied from his refuge under the trees. "I'm used to being out in all weathers."

"If you're sure?"

"Certain sure, milord. Could you be sure that animal don't befoul the coach?"

"I'll watch him." Robert cupped a hand in the rain, wetting his sleeve, and offered the dog a bit of water. He lapped it up, and Robert tried twice more before closing the door and sitting back, feet braced against the sideways sag of the seat.

The rain pattered above. Otherwise all was silence. Waiting was tedious. Robert hadn't had anyone to talk to for hours, days. "What are you doing so far from a farm or village?" he asked the dog.

Wary brown eyes watched him.

"I expect it's a sad story, and you'd rather not think about it," Robert went on. "I don't suppose you know Salbridge Great Hall? I'm on my way to a house party there."

One of the dog's ears twitched.

"No, I hadn't heard of it either. But I understand that it's the showplace of its district."

The dog shifted in the blanket.

"Well, that's what Salbridge said. It's true we are speaking of Northumberland. The standards may be lower." Robert gazed out at the sodden landscape. "I've never been so far north. I begin to see Randolph's point."

His companion made an odd sound, something like a gargle.

"Randolph is my brother. One of my brothers. He lives up here. I thought that an added inducement when the Salbridges urged me to come. I can't think why just now."

A gust of wind rocked the carriage on its springs. The dog nestled deeper into the blanket.

"Precisely," said Robert. "But when friends beg for support one must rally 'round. I'm to lend luster to their gathering."

The small dog cocked his head.

Robert smiled down at him. "I assure you that luster is one of my gifts. Hostesses count themselves lucky to have me. They, er, vie for my favor. Unlike…but I'm not thinking of her. I've given up thinking of her. I'm going back where I belong."

The small dog's gaze had become unnervingly steady. It held no threat that Robert could see. He would have said, rather, that it was speculative, philosophical. Would have, if the idea hadn't been ridiculous.

"I like helping people enjoy themselves," he added in the face of that unwavering regard. "I'm good at it." And if he didn't feel quite as convivial as usual, Robert thought, well, he would soon recover his high spirits.

The dog curled up and went to sleep. Robert made himself as comfortable as he could on the tilted seat. And together, they waited.

Just under two hours from the time of the accident, a vehicle came trundling up the road. Robert's dire predictions were fulfilled when he saw the second postilion at the reins of a rough farm cart, with two thick wheels digging into the mud and a tattered canvas cover over the back.

"I thought you'd rather get on, even in this heap, than wait for a new chaise to be fetched, milord," the man said when he pulled up. "Don't rightly know how long that would take."

Standing in the muddy road, Robert eyed the rustic equipage and the two large farm horses pulling it. No doubt the ride would rattle their bones.

The men moved his trunk from the chaise to the cart. He was going to have to perch upon it, Robert saw. There was no room for anyone but the driver on the seat. At least the rain had eased. Gathering blanket and puppy, he climbed up.

"You taking the animal?" asked the older postilion.

"You expect me to leave him here?"

"Well, I dunno. He ain't a toff's sort of dog, is he?"

"Would you like him?"

"Me? I got no use for a dog."

It was just as well he refused, because Robert realized that he had no intention of handing the animal over. There was something curiously engaging about the small creature.

Lord Robert Gresham's subsequent arrival at the Salbridges' estate was quite uncharacteristic for a gentleman recognized as a pink of the *ton*. He was wet and muddy, his fine clothes horridly creased. He was worn out from the jolting of his disreputable vehicle. He had no hat—it had blown off during the last part of his journey and gone tumbling down an escarpment—and he carried a mongrel dog under one arm. Indeed, the grooms in the Salbridge stables very nearly turned him away. Thankfully, one who'd seen him in London came forward to confirm his identity.

"Broken axle," said Robert.

"Ah." There were general nods at this piece of information.

"Can some of you help me with these lads?" the postilion asked, climbing down from the cart and going to the massive horses' heads. "They've done well, and I promised to have them back tomorrow."

The grooms moved forward to help, and to retrieve Robert's trunk. He followed the latter two as they carried his luggage through the stableyard to a back door. He didn't intend to knock at the front in his current state and track mud across an immaculate front hall and staircase. He'd use the back stairs to find his assigned bedchamber and clean up before he greeted his hosts.

His luck was out, however. The Countess of Salbridge was in the kitchen, conferring with the cook, and so she was among the group that turned at his entry, blinked, and stared.

There was nothing for it. Robert smiled, swept off an imaginary hat, and gave her a jaunty bow. "Hullo, Anne."

"Robert?" she said, incredulous. "What are you... Whatever has happened?"

"Long story. Started with a broken axle on my post chaise. And, er, went on from there."

The dog chose this moment to pop his head out of the blanket and stare about the room, shifting slowly from one person to the next, and the next. A kitchen maid gestured. Robert thought it was a sign against the evil eye. The countess bit her lower lip.

"Go ahead and laugh," Robert told her. "I live to amuse."

She did. "Oh, Robert," she said after several moments of mirth. "Only you could carry off such a… memorable entrance."

He gave his audience another elegant bow.

❧

Several hours later, bathed and changed and feeling renewed, Robert sat in a luxurious bedchamber reading a letter from his mother, the Duchess of Langford. The missive had followed him from Herefordshire, where his family had most lately gathered for his brother Sebastian's wedding, to his rooms in London, and now here to Northumberland. Aware that he hadn't behaved quite like himself at the wedding, Robert wondered how he would answer his mother's inquiries about his well-being. The answer that came to him was—later.

Setting the page aside, he stared out at the sweep of gardens outside the window. Salbridge Great Hall might be at the ends of the earth from a Londoner's point of view, but it was a fine old stone pile. Parts of it looked to date from Tudor times, others from subsequent centuries. The interior had been refurbished with modern comforts.

The rain had lifted. Rays of afternoon sun illuminated turning leaves and late blooms, a manicured autumn vista. From this height he could see the River Tyne in the distance. "I am very well indeed," he tried, aloud.

From a cushion by the hearth, his newly acquired dog turned a steady gaze upon him. The pup's small stomach was rounded from the large bowl of scraps he'd ingested. Any other young dog would be dead asleep after such a feast, Robert thought, but this one was keeping a careful eye on his surroundings.

Meeting those brown eyes, and for some reason unable to look away, Robert had the oddest thought. He felt like a man who had always lived in a fine house, pleasing in every detail, and then one day discovered that a great cavern lay beneath it. In all his years, he'd never suspected the cave existed. When he explored this new subterranean realm, he found it a marvelous place, full of things he'd never dreamed of. The expansion excited and challenged him. But then, after a time, he'd encountered difficulties, bitter disappointments. And he began to wonder if the cavern was undermining the foundations of the house above, threatening general ruin.

Robert shifted uneasily in his chair. What the devil? That was not the sort of thought he would have had a year ago. It wasn't the sort of thought *anybody* had. "It's a relief to be back in my own, er, natural habitat among the *haut ton*," Robert told the dog. "I should never have ventured out into circles where my gifts aren't valued."

The dog stared. Not in a belligerent way, but as if he could see right through Robert, to the very back of his head.

"I'm not thinking about her," Robert said. "That was simply a…glancing reference. To the past. I told you, I've given up thinking about her."

One of the little dog's ears moved, just slightly, as if he'd heard something off.

"This visit will be like relaxing in one's own

comfortable rooms after a long journey," Robert added. "I am all anticipation."

The pup offered a soft response. Not a bark, or a whine, or a growl. Actually, it sounded uncannily like some ancient curmudgeon at the club clearing his throat. Robert waited, almost believing that some sort of crabbed pronouncement would follow. Of course it did not. He gazed at his new companion, who returned the favor with a solemn, unwavering regard. "I shall call you Plato," Robert said. "You seem to deserve the name."

He put the letter aside and rose.

"I trust you will behave yourself," he added, indicating the box of sand he'd shown the dog earlier. He had no idea whether the pup—Plato—would use it, should the need arise, but he hadn't wanted to leave him in the stables. Who knew how the pack there would receive him? Heading for the door, Robert wondered whether he could enlist his valet in Plato's care. Bailey would arrive tomorrow with some things Robert had wanted from London. Doubtful. Unlike his brother Sebastian, Robert had a strictly professional relationship with his personal servant. Better tip one of the footmen to check on Plato now and then.

Robert left his bedchamber, strolling toward the beautifully curved stairway that led to the lower floor, catching a glimpse of himself in a mirror as he descended. He did not, of course, stop to ogle himself in the glass. He was well aware that his new coat fit him to perfection. Weston was an artist with the shears. Robert knew he had the shoulders to fill it out, too, even if he wasn't as tall as some of his brothers.

He showed a fine leg in his buff pantaloons, and the careful tousle of his auburn hair flattered his handsome face. The folds of his neckcloth would excite the envy of the young men—and many of the older ones—here. He looked, in fact, exactly like what he was, a pink of the *ton*. And he did not care a whit why people called it pink or what that might mean. He'd given up thinking of such stuff.

There was a momentary hitch in Robert's step as he once again forced his mind away from the subject of a certain young lady. If she was incapable of appreciating his gifts, then she could just…go hang. He'd had much more fun back when he didn't think of her. Hadn't he? Yes, of course he had. And he was here to have it again.

Robert reached the bottom of the sweeping stair and walked along a lower corridor toward the buzz of conversation in the great drawing room. The tone was bright and excited, full of expectation. Gerald and Anne were known for their lavish hospitality, and for providing a perfect balance of planned activities and freedom at their house parties. Not here. They hadn't lived in this house before the old earl's death last year. But their established reputation as artists of diversion had lured guests all this way from town. Robert assumed there would be hunting, though he didn't know the country, as well as walks and riding and indoor games and music and more. Or, guests could choose to lounge about with a novel in front of the fire on a crisp October day, or write letters, or whatever they liked. It was a familiar, beguiling prospect.

Robert entered the drawing room, a large chamber that ran along the back of the house, with a row of tall glass doors that gave onto a terrace above spreading lawns. Beautifully decorated in buff and blue, it was dotted with comfortable groupings of sofas and chairs that encouraged conversation. Just now, however, at midafternoon, most of its denizens were clumped together discussing plans for the latter part of the day.

It was a promising gathering, Robert thought as he paused near the door. There were several young couples he counted as good friends and others closer in age to their hosts.

The largest group, though, was clustered around Lady Victoria, the daughter of the house. She hadn't received a proposal during her first season, and so her parents had invited a number of eligible young men, along with some of her female friends to balance the numbers. Robert ran an appreciative eye over the latter, noticing several very pretty faces that he'd seen about town. He thought he'd danced with one or two of these ladies. In a minute he'd recall their names.

Robert's closest friend among the Salbridges, the eldest son and heir, was not present. Laurence was off at his intended bride's house for the hunting, Robert remembered. Some suspected he'd offered for the Allingham chit chiefly because her family had a huge estate in Leicestershire, but Robert knew that to be only secondarily true. Laurence had been quite taken with Marie as well. He'd told Robert so. Of course, her enthusiasm for sport was probably part of the attraction. Robert smiled at the thought.

Lady Victoria gave him a brilliant smile in return. He couldn't have asked for a warmer welcome. Robert started forward to join the group.

He'd hardly taken two steps when the sounds of an arrival behind him made him turn back to the door. Then, for a moment, he thought he was delirious. It couldn't be. But the figure standing in the opening was solid flesh, not a phantom. "What are you doing here?" he said.

"I've come for the house party," answered Flora Jennings.

She was as beautiful as ever. In a simple pale gown, her figure was a marvel of subtle curves. Her black hair was dressed in curls, wisps falling about the pale skin of her face, clear-cut as an antique cameo. It was a serene picture, until you noticed the fire in those cornflower-blue eyes.

"I was invited," she added with a touch of familiar asperity.

"You can't have been." He hadn't expected to see her again, unless he sought her out. They moved in completely different circles of society. The sight of her here was like running into his mother at a bare-knuckles boxing bout.

"Do you imagine I would push in without an invitation?" she said.

The snap of challenge in her voice brought back countless verbal jousts. She was inarguably, unmistakably, here. "I don't think you could," he replied. "I'm only surprised to see you among people you profess to despise. Don't you have cuneiform tablets to translate in London? Or something?"

She frowned at him. He was quite familiar with the expression.

A sturdy woman in her midforties emerged from

behind Flora. She had sandy hair, regular features, and a gown that proclaimed fashionable good taste. "Hello, Lord Robert," she said.

Here was the explanation for Flora's presence. Harriet Runyon was related to a great swath of the nobility, and was received everywhere despite a marriage once thought beneath her. No doubt she'd wrangled the invitation. "Mrs. Runyon."

With her customary air of sharp intelligence, and of brooking no nonsense, she said, "How pleasant to see you."

Robert's refined social instincts signaled a whiff of danger, like the rustle in the undergrowth just before something formidable bursts out to surprise you. Which was odd. "And you, ma'am," he said. He offered them an impeccable bow. "Welcome to Salbridge."

Robert resumed his walk over to the group of young ladies. Lady Victoria greeted him warmly, as an old friend she'd known since her early teens. He set himself to entertain them, and soon elicited a chorus of silvery laughs. It wouldn't hurt a bit to let Flora Jennings see how charming most females found him.

Two

"Do smile," said Harriet Runyon.

Flora exposed her teeth. That would have to do for this crowd of lavishly dressed people who had all turned to stare at her when she came in, and then turned away again with cool disinterest. That was what they did, Mama would say. They turned their backs. Flora could almost hear her mother's voice, retelling the story of her ejection from society after she defied her aristocratic family and married a poor scholar, a tale of fears becoming real and pain masked with truculence. All her life, her mother had assured her that they could expect nothing but disregard or snubs from the *haut ton*. That history had made walking into this room rather like stepping into the lions' den. But she'd been braced for it. She knew how to put up a brave front.

And she didn't care what they thought. She hadn't come to make a splash in society. She'd come…her thoughts tripped up here and came to a stop over the fact that Lord Robert had not been glad to see her. Through all the months of their close acquaintance this year, he'd greeted her so warmly whenever they met, with a smile that was nearly irresistible. She'd grown accustomed to the welcome in his intense blue eyes, begun to take it for granted. She hadn't known that until a moment ago, when she'd found it gone.

On the other side of the opulent room, he was surrounded by a circle of pretty girls, in gowns that cost more than any three of hers. He looked utterly at ease. He was making them laugh; clearly they found him charming. He didn't spare her a glance. Anger, and apprehension, flooded Flora. Now that they were in his exalted social circle rather than her much more humble one, he meant to snub her, just as Mama had foretold. She'd thought she was mistaken about him, but what if she wasn't? She'd had years of rigorous mental training; she was not prone to mistakes of judgment.

And who would believe, after all, that a darling of London society, and the son of a duke, was truly interested in the unfashionable daughter of a scholar? Of course, she'd thought that his claim to be fascinated by her intellectual pursuits was some sort of jest. According to everything she'd been taught, men like Lord Robert Gresham were nothing *but* shallow posturing, through and through.

And here came the sardonic inner voice that Flora both dreaded and appreciated. It pointed out that Lord Robert had actually buckled down and studied her father's writings on Akkadian. He'd hung about her home in the dowdy precincts of Russell Square for weeks. He'd followed her from London to Oxford. He'd given her that melting smile whenever she encountered him. Until today. Until a minute ago.

Flora felt an unfamiliar sinking sensation. She looked longingly back at the hallway, wondering if she could still escape.

"Stop scowling," murmured Harriet at her side. "Really, Flora. You must do better than this. We should go and say hello to our hosts. Come and meet the Salbridges."

"I don't think so."

"Flora, this isn't like you. Compose yourself." Harriet moved so as to partly shield Flora from the other guests. "What *is* the matter?"

"I shouldn't have come," Flora murmured.

"Are we going to rehash all that again? Now? This is not really an appropriate time and place, my dear." When Flora said nothing, the older woman sighed and quietly began to tick off points with the air of a woman who had cited them before. Which she had. "You enjoyed your brief taste of society in Oxford."

"Parts of it," said Flora. It had seemed so pleasant, then, to wear prettier dresses and attend evening parties and…fritter away her time, Papa would have said. She'd met Lord Robert's mother and discovered that a duchess could be both sensible and cordial, not the least high-nosed. But she saw now that a few outings in a university town were nothing compared to a true conclave of the *haut ton*.

Harriet looked exasperated. "You decided, you wished to increase your social experience."

She had wanted more from life than she'd accepted previously, Flora admitted silently. But for some reason, she hadn't pictured a host of strangers from the upper reaches of society giving her sidelong glances, wondering who in the world she could be. There seemed to be so many of them. Well, who did they think *they* were, these…natterers?

"And you were quite forlorn when Lord Robert left town with no plans to return," Harriet added.

"I was not!" She spoke far too loudly. Heads turned. Conversations faltered.

Harriet gave the crowd an impenetrable smile. They subsided.

"I was *not* 'forlorn,'" Flora hissed. What a limp, pathetic word! She'd never been forlorn in her life. It was the opposite of all she'd been trained to be— acute, observant, active, and intelligent. "I may have missed his…conversation. I took Lord Robert at his word, you see, that he wished to be…a friend. And now I arrive here and find that he is quite displeased to see me." Flora kept her voice rigidly steady. "He was not glad. At all."

"He probably wasn't," Harriet replied.

"What?" She'd expected a denial, or at least some sort of excuse.

"When one is running away from something," her older friend said, "one often doesn't like to be chased. At first."

"I am *not* chasing him!" Flora spoke more softly this time, but with utter revulsion.

"I didn't say he was running from you," Harriet pointed out.

Flora felt her cheeks redden. But curiosity overcame embarrassment. "What did you mean?"

"We really haven't time for a philosophical discussion." Harriet gave the gathering another bright, general smile. "So, are we to do this or not? It would cause a minor scandal to simply turn and leave. And I must say that you won't get another invitation as brilliant as this one, Flora."

What did she want? Across the room, one of the girls around Lord Robert gave a musical trill of laughter. He looked achingly handsome, and charming, and…inordinately pleased with himself. What was that slang phrase—a care-for-nobody? That seemed to apply. As far as she could see, that is, as he pointedly did *not* look in her direction. All the other times they'd been in a room together, he'd concentrated on her. It had been a heady, tantalizing experience. But the *ton* hadn't been watching then, she thought. The idea hurt, but Flora faced up to it. If she'd been wrong to change her mind about him, it was best that she find out, once and for all. Then she'd know what to do.

Flora put her shoulders back, her chin up. In any case, everything didn't have to be about, was *not* about, one maddening man. She gave Harriet a nod.

"Good girl. Come along. And, my dear?"

Flora looked at her chaperone.

"A smile is not a concession," Harriet added with a lift of her sandy eyebrows. "It is a…a tool, shall we say. A rather versatile one. It can pry things out or smooth things over. Substitute for things one doesn't wish to confide. Very useful."

The thought made Flora smile.

"Much better." Harriet led her over to a couple near the center of the large room and introduced her to Gerald and Anne Moreton, Earl and Countess of Salbridge. They were both about Harriet's age, and Flora knew they'd been friends for years. That connection had made her invitation possible. The countess was also a distant relation of Flora's mother. She strongly suspected that Harriet had reminded her of this when her hostess asked, "How is Agatha? I haven't seen her in an age."

"She's well," Flora replied, not quite truthfully. Back home in London, her mother was fretting, as agitated as Flora had ever seen her. She'd admitted that it could be helpful for Flora to extend her social horizons, while being terribly worried about what might happen to her when she did.

"You're also a cousin of Robert Gresham's, are you not?"

Flora suppressed a start. She doubted that Harriet had provided this information. It seemed the countess had made her own inquiries. "Very distant," she said, proud of the unconcern in her voice. "Third or fourth, perhaps. We used to try to work it out when I visited at Langford as a child." There, let her noble hosts chew on the fact that she'd stayed at a duke's home. They needn't know that *all* the visits had been years ago. Flora felt her resolve returning. She'd decided to come here, and she'd been taught to trust her own thought processes, even when she didn't quite fathom them. She would not draw back, and she did *not* feel Lord Robert's presence at her back like a constant pulse of heat. That was irrational.

"You must meet our daughter," the countess said. At her signal, one of the young ladies left the circle clustered around Lord Robert and joined them. "Victoria, this is Miss Flora Jennings."

It was actually Lady Victoria, Flora thought, as they exchanged bobbing curtsies. The room was full of titled people, some of whom would certainly despise the daughter of an obscure scholar. Who'd been worth a dozen of any of these fribbles, she thought automatically. Flora caught herself. One did not draw conclusions before an experiment had really begun. She didn't have proof of their witlessness. However certain she might be, she mustn't overgeneralize. Papa had taught her more intellectual rigor than that.

"How do you do?" said Lady Victoria Moreton in a soft voice.

Everything about this daughter of the house seemed soft. She was a creature of rounded contours and wide brown eyes, several inches shorter than Flora, garbed in a white muslin gown. Her brown hair was sculpted in gentle waves about her pretty face. There was something old-fashioned about her, Flora thought, though her dress was certainly the latest thing. She looked as if she'd never had anything denied her in all her years.

"You must present Miss Jennings to the young people," the countess said. "I think we've gathered quite a lively group, Miss Jennings, even so far from town." And then, her duty done, the hostess turned to talk to Harriet.

Flora followed Lady Victoria back to the knot of guests that included Lord Robert. As they joined them, Flora was irresistibly reminded of a herd of horses, jostling and sidling when a new animal was introduced into their ranks. The idea made her smile. A medium-sized gentleman across the group smiled back.

Lady Victoria introduced her and recited a list of names, moving around the circle. Flora memorized them with the automatic precision of a trained mind. The task offered no difficulty to one who'd been drilled on cuneiform symbols from the age of seven. She was received with politeness as a minor novelty. She wasn't someone they knew, and people like this expected to know everyone important, Flora thought. There was a stir of silent speculation when Lord Robert mentioned that they were already acquainted. "Cousin of mine," he added.

With three words he'd slotted her into a recognized category, Flora saw—a visitor from the far edges of a great family. Possibly a poor relation, considering her gown. She couldn't dispute such a verdict. It was perfectly true. And Lord Robert Gresham was perfectly free to point it out to his grand friends, if that was what he wished to do. Never mind his claims, this spring and summer, to value other measures of worth—intellect and education and industry. It was a very good thing she'd come here, Flora thought. If she hadn't, she might have kept on believing him.

Everyone returned to their previous conversations. It was actually a relief not to be the center of attention any longer. At first, Flora thought they were playing some kind of geography game, naming prominent places in London. Then she realized they were establishing where they'd last met, weeks ago, during the season, with bits of reminiscence about certain balls or evening parties. As she had attended none of them, she had nothing to contribute. Members of the *haut ton* were rather like butterflies, she thought. They

hovered, vividly colorful, above the lower reaches
of society. They flitted from one gorgeous locale
to another, oblivious to the misfortunes that befell
others not so very far away. They were stunningly
decorative. After a few minutes, she caught Harriet's
admonitory eye and remembered to smile.

Flora stood and listened. She was accustomed to
being the center of lively discussions at home, but
she didn't really mind being left out of this one.
The topic was dull, and anyway she would be better
occupied observing and analyzing the people who
were to be her companions for the next month.
Now that she had their names, she could put faces to
the descriptions Harriet had provided on their long
journey up to Northumberland.

The room was dotted with attractive young men.
Well born, well heeled, well bred, Flora thought.
Well behaved, well set up. No, she was stretching
now. But they were all those things. Harriet had told
her that they were here for Lady Victoria. Or perhaps
vice versa. Good matches, in any case, lured in by the
hunting and hospitality toward a possible settlement of
the girl's future. It was a common thing, Flora knew,
and she couldn't summon quite the level of derision
she might have expressed in earlier years. People had
to meet, after all.

Her gaze lit on Lord Robert and skipped away before
he could catch her looking. He was the handsomest of
them all, in her opinion. Harriet had said he wasn't
considered a likely suitor, though he'd be welcome
if he decided to show interest in Lady Victoria, ten
years his junior. Only three years separated the two of

them, thought Flora. Harriet had warned her to avoid mentioning her age, as some would consider twenty-five to be nearly on the shelf. Lord Robert turned to smile at a young lady with copper-colored hair. He looked delighted with her. Lady Victoria joined them. Flora felt a pang in the region of her heart. With fierce discipline, she dismissed it.

The young female guests were Lady Victoria's age, her particular friends, Harriet had said. Flora noted that they hadn't been chosen to make the daughter of the house shine in comparison. Several had to be judged much prettier than Lady Victoria; she must be generous or confident, or perhaps both. Flora banished a sneaking wish that she'd been less magnanimous. All the girls looked so assured and graceful in their pale muslin dresses.

Flora realized that Lord Robert was coming toward her. Her pulse sped up as he stopped by her side.

"I've come to beg your pardon," he said. "I was rude. Please accept my apologies."

Flora could only nod. He hadn't spoken to her so curtly even when they'd been mired in one of their running debates last summer. He seemed different in other ways as well. His clothes looked more—she groped for a word—complicated than they had in Russell Square and Oxford. His neckcloth was more intricate, his waistcoat more opulent. More than that, though, he had a larger *presence*. If she'd thought of it at all she would have predicted that he'd be less impressive surrounded by the cream of the *haut ton*. Outshone or overshadowed with other noblemen all around him. In fact, it was the opposite. He stood out—polished, assured, every inch a duke's son. And just, perhaps, the tiniest bit intimidating?

"I was startled to see you," he went on when she didn't speak. "Knowing how you hate the fashionable set."

"Hate is a strong word."

"We can dispute my word choice, but you cannot deny that you've expressed contempt for the *ton*. Emphatically and often."

"Contempt is—"

"Another strong word. Indeed." He smiled at her.

Abruptly, treacherously, Flora was ambushed by a memory. It had been late, at her home in Russell Square. A group of her father's old friends were making their farewells to her mother. She and Lord Robert had lingered in a dim corner of the drawing room. She couldn't recall how that had come about, but it was one of the rare moments when they *hadn't* been arguing. Indeed, they'd been in charity with one another, for once. And he'd looked down at her with admiration, and tenderness, and longing. She couldn't mistake it. His gaze had sent shivers through her body. She'd wanted to step into his arms and lose herself in a wild kiss and let passion take them where it would.

Flora blinked and swallowed. She'd shoved that simmering desire away, out of sight, almost out of mind. She'd been so sure that he'd walk out of her life as easily as he'd walked in, that he would make a fool of her. Then, recently, she'd wondered if she was mistaken. Now she faced a new version of this unfathomable man.

About the Author

Jane Ashford discovered Georgette Heyer in junior high school and was captivated by the glittering world and witty language of Regency England. That delight was part of what led her to study English literature and travel widely in Britain and Europe. She has written historical and contemporary romances, and her books have been published in Sweden, Italy, England, Denmark, France, Russia, Latvia, the Czech Republic, Slovakia, and Spain, as well as the United States. Jane has been nominated for a Career Achievement Award by *RT Book Reviews*. Born in Ohio, she is now somewhat nomadic. Find her on the web at www.janeashford.com and on Facebook.